A JANUARY TO REMEMBER

A NOVEL

L. B. JOYCE

ALSO BY L. B. JOYCE

This book is the sixth in the series,
Twelve Months, Twelve Love Stories ~
A Million Decembers
For the Love of July
February's Angel
Promise Me November
An Unexpected June
A January to Remember
September's Moonlight Serenade
Goodbye Heartbreak, Hello May

Holidays in White Oaks Valley -
A Grand Slam Kind of Christmas

Well, here we are, halfway through the series. Can you believe it? I know I certainly can't. Now that there are so many characters to keep up with, I've added in a little update for a few of the characters, present and past, near the end of this book. I hope this will help refresh your mind as to who is who.

That is, all except for Anna and Nicholas. Somehow, we need to get them back, as they were the start of this whole line of love stories.
I guess we shall see.... Enjoy!

One day I will marry my friend.
The one I laugh with, live for, dream with...
the one I love.
~ Anonymous

CHAPTER 1

There are three things I want...
I want to see you. I want to hug you.
And most of all, I want to kiss you.
So, hurry home to me.
~Anonymously Yours

One more block...only one more block... come on, you've got this. Then it's all downhill from there.

This is what Hannah Michaels was mumbling under her breath as her feet hit the pavement, one very small step after the other. Yes, she'd admit, she wasn't moving very fast. But she was still pretty proud of what she'd accomplished. Since her first attempt a week ago, her running skills had improved quite a bit. That she wasn't gasping for breath, convinced she was going to die before she made it up the last hill, was a miracle in itself.

In fact, this is where she was now, at the top of the hill. If she squinted, she could almost see her condo.

Thank God...

Now, don't start imagining Hannah as one of these fitness fanatics, all about running marathons and gym memberships. Because this was *so* far from the truth. Extreme physical fitness wasn't her style, not by a long shot. And something she'd given up a long time ago. She found it too stressful. And she certainly wasn't one to waste her money on trips to a gym.

No, if it came between coffee and the gym, coffee would win by a landslide.

She needed her coffee.

The bottom line? She wasn't really into any form of exercise, with running coming in at last place. Especially on this overcast and windy January day in Cleveland.

It had been the latest forecast from the weather channel that had her decide to get in one last run. Supposedly, they were in for a drastic change. A cold front was moving in from Canada, projected to hit sometime later this evening. With snow, lots and lots of snow.

So, she considered this as her one last and desperate attempt at self-improvement.

It was just that, well... she wanted to look her best. More like she *needed* to look good... really good. She'd go as far as to say she wanted to look hot. Or, at least know she'd made the effort.

Even though hot might be pushing it a bit.

Yeah, but don't worry. She knew she wasn't going to work any miracles. But mentally, she would feel a lot better knowing she'd given her best shot.

And why was she suddenly so crazy, gung-ho about this?

Sean Young...

After almost seven months of only being able to visualize him in her mind, the sound of his voice sometimes lost in the long distance calls between them, he was finally returning to Cleveland. At this very moment, he was in flight from Australia.

And, believe it or not, he was on his way to see her.

This would be the same Sean Young who was a pitcher for Cleveland's baseball team. The same team her sister Sophie's husband Chester played for.

And for some reason, one that she still was finding so hard to believe, Sean had taken a liking to her. So much so, he had actually sought her out.

Three times this had happened.

Well, you can't really count the first time, Sophie and Chester's wedding. The two of you never talked or were even introduced to each other. But he'd asked about you, wanted to know who you were. So, this has to count for something, right?

Thinking about this, she smiled, something very rare to come by while she was running. It was also a reminder she needed to stop daydreaming about him, pay more attention to where she was going. She'd already almost wiped out on a patch of ice.

Again, it was January.

But back to Sean. She couldn't believe she was finally going to see him again. In less than twenty-four hours she would be able to get lost in his smile, feel his arms around her and melt into one of his kisses. For almost seven months, she had been waiting for this.

She'd almost forgotten what he looked like.

Oh, come on... get serious. Who are you trying to kid?

How could any woman not remember a man like Sean?

Over ten thousand miles had separated them these past seven months. And even with the dozens of phone calls, and an even higher number of text messages, she was worried.

A man like Sean, with his amazing good looks and sexy demeanor? Why, he could be snatched up in less time than it took for him to flash one of those devastating smiles of his.

As her Aunt Louise would say, Sean was a keeper. He wouldn't have to lift a finger to have a woman fall in love with him. One look, and her fate would be sealed.

Hannah should know... since this was exactly what happened to her. Catching her completely by surprise, she had fallen for him before she even knew what hit her.

She liked everything about him.

Starting with his sexy Australian drawl. Rough, yet at the same time, so divinely husky. When he said her name, it was like a caress, sending a warmth through her, everywhere.

She would never be able to get enough of his smiles. Or the way the corner of his eyes crinkled in agreement whenever he sent one her way. It was enough to make her forget her name, who she was, or even what day it was.

A very dangerous situation, since smiling was something he did almost all the time.

Then there was his cowboy hat... how he wore it as though it was the most natural thing in the world. Tipping it with a casual flick of his wrist when he greeted her, he had her believing what they shared was special, known only to them... maybe even a secret they shared.

And how about the way he called her darlin'? This was enough to melt her heart, even more so when he threw in this endearment with the tip of his hat.

Or those long eyelashes of his? But you don't want to even get started on those.

She could go on... and on... and on.

It felt like forever since they were last together. This had been an evening last June, at Sophie and Chester's first annual summer barbecue. A night, for Hannah, that had been nothing short of magical.

She could still remember every... single... detail....

How, when he first saw her, he took her into his arms and gave her a kiss that set the tone for the rest of the night.

Halfway into the evening, he'd grabbed the bottle of wine and their glasses from their table. Taking her hand, he'd started to run. Across the lawn and down to the Lake Erie beach bordering Sophie and Chester's backyard, they ran. Breathless and laughing, they'd wandered along the water's edge until they found a sheltered area to sit.

They'd talked about everything.

He told her how it had always been his dream to play professional baseball in the states. She'd shared her dream of becoming an author of children's books. She enjoyed illustrating books, but she wanted to write, too.

They had discussed their favorite colors, favorite songs, and the movies they last saw. They compared living in Cleveland to his hometown in Australia, and where they'd like to live. And they shared stories about their families and friends.

Not once had they ran out of things to say. Any silence between them had been a companionable one. Along with the perfect opportunity to share a kiss or two. If she had known the next morning, he would be on a plane to Australia, she would have tried to fit in even a few more.

It was only when Sean checked his phone to see it was almost dawn, they'd made their way back to Sophie and Chester's house.

Besides the soft glow coming from the upstairs windows of Hudson and Trevor's room, the house was dark and silent. The deck and yard had been cleared, their cars the only vehicles still parked on the lawn.

Sean had insisted on following her home, where they lingered over their goodbyes, reluctant to part. Scheduled to leave in only a few hours for an eight-days of away games in Minnesota, Boston and Detroit, he'd promised to call the first chance he got.

He'd promised her, when he got back, they would go on date. It would be their real first date. He wanted to take her out to dinner, her choice of restaurant. They would celebrate, make a night of it.

The next day, she waited, checking her phone for what had to be a hundred times, to see if he'd called. But it wasn't until early evening his name finally flashed on her phone.

As soon as he spoke, the unsteadiness in his voice told her something was wrong. His voice shaky, he told her his grandfather had called to tell him his father had blacked out while on his usual morning inspection of their property. One of the ranch hands had found him on the ground and unconscious, his horse standing guard. Now in the hospital, the doctors couldn't predict how long his recovery would be.Or, if he would recover at all.

So, Sean was on his way to the airport. How long he would be in Australia, he couldn't tell her. But the promise he'd made to his father to be there for his mother if something like this happened, was one he would never break.

For almost a week, Hannah heard nothing more from him. No call, no text, no email. When he finally did call, the news wasn't good. His father had suffered a stroke and his recovery would be a long one.

So, with permission from the team's management, Sean gave up his place on the team roster for the remainder of the season. His tentative plan was to return sometime after the first of the year.

And now, almost seven months later, January had finally arrived, Sean's father had made great strides in his recovery, and Sean was scheduled to fly into Cleveland in only a few hours.

So... Hannah was excited. And she was happy. But, she was also very nervous. What if, for Sean, things had changed? Chatting on the phone and texting was nice, but it wasn't the same as spending time together in person. Sean could take one look at her and wonder what he had ever seen in her.

This is what had brought on her sudden need to exercise. Along with the salads she had suffered through for almost every meal over the past week. What she wouldn't give for a cup of Café Latte's signature blend coffee and one of their homemade banana muffins.

She'd also considered changing things up a bit, starting with her appearance. Maybe a new hairstyle, if only to update her look. But when she casually mentioned this to Sean, he had reacted so strongly against this, she promised to only get her usual trim.

And the dress Sophie had talked her into for the dinner date Sean had promised? It was by far the most revealing and sexiest dress she'd ever owned.

There was also a box from Sweet Abby's in her refrigerator, filled with a half dozen of Abby's salted caramel brownies. Abby had made up a new batch only yesterday for her. This was because Sean had raved about them at Sophie and Chester's barbecue, even going as far to bring them up during one of the phone calls they shared.

So, she was ready.

More than ready.

A big gust of wind came right at her, almost stealing the last bit of energy she had.

The temperature was also starting to drop, a misty rain beginning to fall.

Now even more eager to get back to the warmth of her condo, she was relieved to see she was almost to the bottom of the hill.

And this was when she made the biggest mistake of her life.

She decided to take a shortcut. Her plan was to cut in between the cars parked along the curb and make a quick dash across the street to her condo. This way, she wouldn't have to run another half-block to cross at the intersection.

She should have been more careful.

She knew better.

Seriously? What had she been thinking?

And everyone—at least everyone who was halfway intelligent—knows you should always look both ways before crossing a busy street. And if you didn't? There was a really good chance this could only lead to a complete disaster.

Yep, this was definitely a no-brainer.

But evidently your brain wasn't working properly that day, was it?

When she darted out into the street, the last thing she heard was the horrified yell from a guy on his motorcycle as he slammed on the brakes. Then, almost as if this was happening in slow motion, she watched as he tried to swerve out of her way.

But, before she could react, the back of the bike spun around and right into her, sending her flying head first into one of the parked cars.

There was a flash of light, followed by an agonizing pain.

After that?

Nothing...

CHAPTER 2

Sophie Mazzori wound up the toy car to send it sailing across the nursery floor and right between twins Hudson and Trevor. Now seventeen months old, this always managed to send them both into a fit of giggles.

She laughed, quickly crawling over to grab the car from Hudson. Lately, anything he could get his hands on, he would fling it across the room.

Or right at Trevor.

Chester claimed this showed he had the making a future baseball player. But Sophie disagreed. It was clear Hudson was testing them, she told him. They shouldn't be encouraging this kind of behavior.

After she wound up the car, again sending it rolling across the floor, her phone rang.

She picked it up to see the call was from Hannah.

She groaned.

What could Hannah possibly be worried about now? Ever since Sean let her know he was finally returning to Cleveland, she had been a bundle of nerves.

Sophie would be willing to bet Hannah had sent her more calls and texts about Sean in the last few days than she had during the whole time he had been away. She wondered if Hannah was calling from the boutique. She hoped so. This would mean she finally tried on the dress Sophie had picked out for her to wear on her dinner date with Sean.

She sighed.

But this was no guarantee Hannah would be wearing the dress. There was a good chance she'd already decided it was too short, too form fitting and definitely too low cut.

Yes, Sophie would admit the dress was almost, if not quite, all of these things. But not to the point it was risqué. No, the fitted style was just sexy enough to make Sean see what he had been missing while he was gone.

After all, Hannah did ask you to pick out a dress. She told you she wanted a dress that would make her look her best, and this dress fit the bill.

She answered the phone, starting right in with her greeting. "Hey, it's about time you called. Please tell me you're at the boutique with Aunt Louise, you tried on the dress, and you love it to pieces."

This was greeted with silence.

As Sophie was about to add more, a woman's voice came at her, one she didn't recognize. The tone was very clipped and professional. "Hello, I am calling for Sophie Mazzori. Your number was listed in Hannah Michael's phone contacts as her sister. Is this who I'm speaking with?"

A warning flashing through Sophie's mind, she stilled. Her hand going to her mouth, she felt her heartbeat accelerate, her stomach muscles clenching in response.

This wasn't good. No, this wasn't good at all.

"Yes, this is Sophie. Who is this? And where is Hannah? Did something happen to her?"

"My name is Erin. I am a RN at University Hospital. There was an accident and Hannah was transported here just a short time ago. As a close family relative to Hannah, we thought you should know."

Sophie hadn't realized she had come to her feet. Trevor and Hudson, sensing the sudden change in her mood, grabbed on to her legs, clamoring to be picked up.

She swallowed, her response shaky. "What happened? Is it bad?" Clutching the phone tightly to her ear, she closed her eyes. "Please... tell me she'll be okay?"

"I'm sorry, I'm not authorized to give out any information over the phone other than she is here. I can only tell you Hannah is receiving the best care possible. When you arrive at the hospital, there will be someone who will be able to answer your questions."

In a panic, Sophie glanced down at the boys. They were both clinging to her legs and had now started to cry.

You need to call Chester. You need to call him right away. Hang up the phone and do this. Now.

Chester had gone to the ballpark to work out in the gym. He would know what to do, because right now, she couldn't think at all.

"I'll be there as soon as I can." She sank back to the floor, and holding the twins, she ended the call and hit Chester's number.

Within ten minutes, he was home. His team mate and close friend Kevin, who had also been at the gym, was with him. He smiled reassuringly at Sophie. "I've come to take care of your two little guys."

At Sophie's skeptical look, he grinned. "I told Chester, since Abby was told she could go into labor any day now, and we'll soon be the parents of one of our own, we can use the practice. But, don't worry, Abby is on her way over as we speak." He picked up Trevor, who had begun to cry. And with Hudson hanging on to his leg, he waved Chester and Sophie towards the door. "Go... and don't worry. Abby and I can handle this."

Before Chester drove the SUV out on the main road, he glanced over to see Sophie was sitting rigid in the passenger seat, wringing her hands. He reached over to nudge her chin with his finger until she faced him. "It's going to be okay, angel."

She searched his face, trying to take comfort in his words. *"Oh Chester...* I hope so. I wish they could have told me something. *Anything...* The fact they didn't, makes me worry even more."

For the remainder of their drive, with Chester occasionally reaching over to squeeze her hand, they were silent. There was nothing more to say.

All they could do was pray.

Across the country, Sean Young jammed his suitcase in the overhead compartment of the plane. After he was settled in his seat, he pulled his phone out of his pocket. Agitatedly tapping the screen with his fingers, he watched the rest of the passengers file onto the plane.

It appeared everyone was in a good mood.

Except for him, that is. He was tired. He was worried. And he was having a hard time trying to understand.

Why wasn't Hannah answering her phone? You've called her at least a half-dozen times in the past hour.

He wanted to let her know it looked as though, believe it or not, he was going to arrive in Cleveland earlier than scheduled. At this layover in Houston, he'd miraculously managed to snag an earlier flight.

Closing his eyes, he rested his head back against the seat.

Ever since he'd scheduled his flight three long, *long* days ago, all he had been able to think about, all he wanted, was Hannah.

He couldn't wait to take her into his arms and gaze into her beautiful eyes. Then his plan was to kiss her until she melted right into him. Like she always did. He couldn't even begin to explain what this did to him.

He had already decided this would be only the start of making up all the time they'd lost. Not only while he was in Australia, but also those long months between the time he first talked to her—the day Chester and Sophie welcomed their twins into the world—to when they finally met up again in the coffee shop.

The entire time he was in Australia, he'd missed her so damn much. Some nights, to the point he couldn't even sleep. Tossing and turning, he'd let his imagination take over, thinking about what it would be like to have her with him.

Not the best thing to do when you have to get up at the crack of dawn to work another long and grueling day on the ranch.

He knew his mum and dad had hoped this trip home might turn

into something more permanent. But the understanding parents they were, they never came out and told him this.

They had probably noticed how eagerly he was looking forward to returning to the states, thinking he wanted to get back to playing ball. But since he wasn't ready to share his feelings for Hannah with anyone, even them, he was fine with this.

No, he wanted to keep this to himself. It was all too special, so new.

A wry smile on his face, he shook his head. All the games his parents had sat through, traveling from one field to the next, one tournament after another. He owed his parents so much. This was why he hadn't even hesitated to return home when his grandpa called.

But now it was time for him to get his own life in order. And he knew he wanted this to happen with Hannah. From the very first moment he saw her at Sophie and Chester's wedding, he had known she was the one.

She still was. And always would be... of this, you're certain.

If she ever answered her phone.

He hit her number. Again, there was no answer. After dropping the phone in his lap, he tipped his hat down over his face, welcoming the privacy.

The rustle of clothing sent a cloud of perfume drifting in his direction. This, along with the sound of heavy breathing, had him cautiously lifting his hat. Opening one eye, he was just in time to see a more than ample bottom wiggle into the seat next to him. This was accompanied by a loud and very dramatic sigh.

Before he could lower his hat, the owner of these labored moves turned and looked right at him.

Everything about the woman was loud and flashy. This included the laugh she gave as she reached over to give an enthusiastic pat to his knee. "I must say, you're what I'm going to miss most about the big ol' state of Texas. You men and your cowboy hats. I never knew such a simple article of clothing could be so darn sexy. If I could, I'd grab on to you and take you home with me."

Edging slightly away from her, he almost blurted out he wasn't from Texas. But he put a quick halt to that. She would be sure to comment on his accent, and then he'd be forced to tell her he was Australian. This would invariably be followed by all the curious questions people had about his homeland.

He shook his head. He couldn't understand most American's fascination with his country. Hell, he was the same as everyone else.

Well, maybe just a little tougher. And definitely a lot smarter.

And right now? He had no desire to carry on a conversation with this woman. It wasn't that he didn't want to be sociable. No, this wasn't the reason. There was only woman he wanted to be talking to right now, and this would be Hannah.

Call him childish, but this was just the way it was.

He gave the woman a slight nod and pulled the hat down over his face again. Surprisingly, she had no response to this. In fact, she remained silent throughout take off and until they were well into the air.

Just as he began to think the flight wasn't going to be that bad after all, she put in her earphones and started singing along with the songs she was listening to on her phone.

She sang loud.

Very loud.

And *very* off key.

It was a relieved and weary Sean who made his way to baggage claims to collect his luggage. As he watched the luggage bouncing by on the slow moving carousel, he took out his phone and once more tried Hannah's number.

Again, no answer.

He didn't know what to think at this point. Nothing was making sense. When they last talked, a little over twenty-four hours ago, give or take a few, he'd swear she was just as excited as he was about their reunion.

At least this was the impression she gave.

So, what the hell happened?

His luggage in hand, he hailed a taxi. As he gave the driver his address, he saw on the dashboard it was almost five, pushing nightfall here in the states. This meant it would soon be dark.

It had started to snow, a few flakes here and there. It didn't look too bad. But again, this was Cleveland, where a few random snowflakes could turn into a major blizzard in an instant.

Removing his hat and dragging his hand through his hair, he shoved the hat back on again. He dug his phone out of his pocket and hit Hannah's number again, almost angrily hitting end before the call went over to voice mail.

He gave a frustrated sigh,

But now he was more than worried.

Something wasn't right.

CHAPTER 3

Scared to the point she was terrified, Hannah was refusing to open her eyes.

She was also afraid to move. She had only tried this once, to find even the simple bend of her finger was enough to send a streak of pain shooting throughout her whole body.

She also wanted all the bedlam around her to stop... people running back and forth, speaking in a hurried and tense tone of voice. A voice one might use when they weren't exactly sure what they were doing. Or fearful about what was about to happen next.

She had this terrible feeling, whatever they were talking about, it had something to do with her.

And none of it was good.

But this wasn't the only reason she was scared. What was most frightening, her mind appeared to have gone almost completely blank. This was to the point if they did ask her something, even as simple as her name, she knew she wouldn't be able to give them an answer.

To put it simply, she wasn't quite sure who she was, where she was, or why she was even here.

She was desperately trying to recall what had brought her to this state. But, where there should be a memory of that time, again there was only a huge, empty space. And if anything did happen to pop into her mind, if only for a millisecond or two, it was all jumbled and didn't make sense.

She tensed, detecting the slight rustle of fabric as someone came to stand next to he, resting their hand lightly on her arm. "Hannah? Hannah Michaels… are you awake?"

So, this is good. At least now you know your name must be Hannah.

Hannah Michaels. This was a start.

She desperately rolled this bit of information around in her mind, hoping it would jog her memory.

But she got nothing.

Again, the voice came at her. "Hannah, can you open your eyes? Please? We're all waiting for you to do this. We're all worried about you."

They're worried about you? Why? What did you do?

The voice became stern, more of an order. "Come on, Hannah. We're here for you. Open your eyes."

No, she couldn't do this… open her eyes. Or maybe it was more like she didn't want to, as it would only bring more questions coming at her. And she knew with a certainty, she wasn't going to have the answers.

But it appeared this person with all the questions had no plan of giving up.

Gently brushing the hair from her face, their tone of voice softened. "Hannah, honey… *come on.* The faster you respond and open your eyes, the sooner you'll be able to go home. Your family is here to see you. They've come all this way to be with you and have been waiting for quite a while for you to wake up."

All this way? Where had they come from? And exactly how long have they been waiting?

Slowly, and very reluctantly, she finally opened her eyes, squinting against the brightness of the lights.

She was looking directly into the face leaning over her. It was a nice face. A woman's face with a smile that traveled up to settle in the corner creases of her eyes. As though she was truly happy to see her.

Her hand going to Hannah's forehead, her words came out in a long sigh. "*Ah…* this is good. You're coming back to us. Are you in any pain? You can just nod or shake your head if you don't want to speak."

Was she in any pain? She didn't think so. Not if she didn't move. If anything, she felt like she was floating, sort of how she felt when she had more than one glass of wine.

Is this what happened? Did you drink too much wine? For some reason, even with the little you know right now, it just doesn't seem like something you would do.

She tried to shake her head. A big mistake. Because now she would have to change her answer to a yes, she was in pain, a lot of pain. She grimaced as this traveled in a rolling wave throughout her body, leaving her almost unable to catch her breath.

Gently adjusting the blankets, the woman slowly shook her head. "Hmm… you're shaking your head no, but the expression on your face makes me think your answer is really a yes. In a little bit, we'll give you something stronger for the pain. But for now, try not to close your eyes 0r go back to sleep. This will come in time. Instead, try to relax and think good thoughts until the doctor stops by to check you out. No doubt, he'll want to ask you some questions. But it may be a while, since the ER is unusually busy today."

With one final comforting touch to her forehead and before Hannah could even gather up the strength to respond, the woman disappeared from view, leaving two words echoing in Hannah's mind.

Doctor?

ER?

Oh, God… what have you done?

CHAPTER 4

Hard things are put in our way, not to stop us,
but to call on our courage and strength.
~ Anonymous

Sean had literally dropped his luggage on the floor of his condo, grabbed his keys and gone sprinting out to his car. That it actually started, after sitting in his garage the whole time he was gone, had him closing his eyes in relief.

Hopefully you can take this as a good omen?

Evidently not.

Because twenty minutes later, here he was, back into the driver's seat and slamming the door shut.

Frustrated, he tossed his hat on the passenger seat.

That certainly hadn't turned out as you hoped, had it?

He'd rung Hannah's doorbell at least ten times before he'd finally accepted she wasn't in her condo. And now, after buckling his seatbelt and starting up the car, he had no idea where to go next.

Drumming his fingers on the steering wheel, he tried to think. Maybe he should drop by Chester and Sophie's house and casually inquire if they knew where Hannah might be?

Or are you making something out of nothing?

Good Lord, he didn't want them to think he was some kind of maniac... but at the same time, he couldn't get the nagging thought out of his mind something bad had happened. There was this unknown fear he couldn't silence, warning him Hannah was in some kind of trouble.

He watched the snowflakes flutter down onto the windshield before he glanced over at his phone on the passenger seat. Should he try calling her one more time? Maybe he'd get lucky and she'd answer. Then she'd give him a perfectly good reason why she hadn't answered before.

Hell, he didn't care what her excuse was... he'd be happy just to hear her voice.

A faint smile flickered across his face. He'd been waiting a long time for this day. Just knowing he was going to see her again was what had kept him going these past few months.

Sending up a silent prayer, he hit Hannah's number.

Again, nothing.

He leaned his head back, his eyes closed.

Think... you need to think...

Chester glanced around at the small groups of people seated in the rows of chairs filling the hospital emergency waiting room, all of them united in their hope for a sign of good news. Some, including him and Sophie, had now been waiting much longer than one should have to wait.

He gave a silent thank you the chairs were only half occupied. He didn't want to even think about how long they'd be waiting, if most of them had been filled.

He hated hospitals.

As far as he was concerned, nothing good ever came out of the time spent in one. But, wait... he'd have to take that back. There was the birth of Hunter and Trevor. They definitely made up for all the other times he'd been forced to step inside a hospital.

So, maybe he should change this to he hated emergency rooms. After all, the last time he'd been in one... this very same room, in fact... was when Livy lost her baby.

Leaning back in his chair and stretching out his legs, he gave a long, weary sigh.

He felt Sophie stir beside him, her inquiry barely audible. "What time is it?"

Chester glanced up at the oversized clock on the wall, momentarily stopping to wonder whose idea this had been. Because, come on... such a huge and blatant reminder of the time was the last thing someone wanted to see when they were in an emergency waiting room.

He turned to gaze down at Sophie. "It's about five minutes later than the last time you asked me."

At the hurt look she gave him, he reached over to massage her shoulder. "Sorry, angel, I didn't mean for it come out that way. I'm just a little frustrated, I guess. It seems like we've been waiting for a long time."

He peered more closely at her worried face. "When is the last time you had something to eat or drink? Let me go get you something from the cafeteria. The last time anyone came out to talk to us, they made it sound like we may be in for a long wait."

She shook her head. "No, I don't need anything to eat. I think it would only make me sick." A look of panic came over her face. "I don't want you to leave me."

Wrapping his arm around her, he pressed a kiss in her hair before he responded. "I'm not planning on going anywhere. But, you need to keep the faith, angel. Hold on to the belief everything is going to be all right and Hannah will be fine. I know it's hard, but..."

Irritation filling her, she abruptly pulled away from him. Running her hand through her hair, she could feel it shaking. "Chester, how can it be all right? They told us she got hit by a motorcycle. To then go flying head first into a car. How can anyone be okay after that?"

Her voice becoming choked, she gazed down at her hands in her lap. "When I talked to Hannah yesterday, I wasn't very nice. I almost cut her off because the boys were sleeping and I wanted to finish the book I was reading before they woke up. What if…"

When he saw her bottom lip starting to quiver, he pulled her against him, his words a whisper in her hair. "Oh, sweetheart… don't even start thinking like this."

"Sophie Mazzori?"

This summons, coming from a nurse peeking around the door opened to the waiting room, had Sophie nearly knocking Chester onto the floor as she shot out of her chair. He watched as she kept nodding as she listened to what the nurse had to say. After the nurse handed her something, she turned and began making her way back to him.

She was holding a phone. But what was even more important, she was smiling.

His shoulders slumping in relief, he smiled back at her. "Well?"

She sank down next to him and rested her head on his shoulder. He could feel her shaking against him.

After s short silence, she took a deep breath before she gazed up at him. "She said Hannah has opened her eyes and seems to be conscious of her surroundings. Now they're waiting for the doctor. Once he assesses her condition, he'll come out and talk to us. Since this might take a while, she told me this might be a good time for us to go get a coffee or something."

She looked down at the phone. "She gave me Hannah's phone. She said it kept vibrating, so we might want to check it out to see what's going on."

He hugged her against him, pressing a kiss in her hair. "Thank God for that. The fact she's conscious has to be a good sign, I would think."

Slowly coming to his feet and giving a long stretch, he held out his hand. "Come on, let's go get that coffee. It sounds like you're going to need it. I know I could certainly use some."

Still gazing down at the phone, Sophie didn't hear him. She looked up at him, a stricken look on her face. "*Oh no*… it's Sean calling. What do I do?"

He shrugged. "You need to answer it. If he is the one who's been calling, he's probably wondering what's going on."

So, very hesitantly, she hit answer. "Hello?"

Sean had decided to call Hannah one more time and if she didn't answer, he would drive over to Chester and Sophie's house.

"Hello?"

He almost went into shock. Finally, he was getting an answer. At the same time, he was a little confused. This wasn't the way Hannah always answered his calls. No, she would say, Hey, cowboy — with him answering — your one and only, darlin'.

Yeah, he knew this was silly and he couldn't even tell you how it got started, but he liked it. And he knew she liked it, too. This was because she always gave this soft little sigh after he answered her.

No, this definitely wasn't the Hannah he expected to hear.

"Hannah?"

After a short silence, Sophie spoke. "Sean, it's me, Sophie. Chester and I are at the hospital. Hannah... well, she was in an accident. We don't know much at this point, only that she has finally opened her eyes and was able to respond to a one of the ER nurses. Now we have to wait for the doctor to come out and tell us more."

He closed his eyes, his whole body becoming still. Except for his heart... this was beating in a panic, his throat tightening in response.

No... this can't be happening. You were right... something is terribly wrong.

He swallowed. "What happened?"

She told him what little she knew, this met by his silence.

Running his hand over his jaw, Sean vaguely noted the snow was coming down harder now, collecting on the windshield. He wondered if it was going to keep up, adding more inches to what was already on the ground. Was it going to turn into a full-blown snowstorm?

But why are you even thinking about this? This is the least of your worries right now.

He needed to go to Hannah. He needed to be there for her.

"Sean?"

He blinked at the sound of Sophie's voice, his mind snapping back to attention. "Where are you? What hospital? I need to see her." This all came out before he realized Sophie might be wondering why he was so insistent. After all, he and Hannah hadn't really been dating all that long. Hell, they hadn't even been on what you would call a real date. This was supposed to happen tomorrow night.

Dinner, remember? You'd promised her dinner. And maybe even dancing.

Dragging his hands through his hair, he groaned. "That's if this is okay with you, of course. It's only that I'm back in Cleveland now. We'd made plans to go out to dinner tomorrow night. Sort of like a celebration. So, it's only right… well, what I mean is…"

She swiftly interrupted him. "It's okay, Sean. I understand. Really, I do. I know Hannah was looking so forward to seeing you."

What she said should've made him happy, but it didn't. Nothing was going to sound right or feel right to him until he was able to see Hannah with his own eyes. He blinked, trying to swallow past the tightness still in his throat. "If you give me an idea of where you are, I'll try to get there as soon as I can."

After Sophie gave him directions to the hospital, reminding him more than once to, please, *please* be careful and drive safely, he was finally pulling out of the condo parking lot.

Because of the rapidly deteriorating road conditions, his progress was slow. Even with his windshield wipers on high, it was almost impossible to see. Cursing under his breath, he tried to tell himself this was probably for the best. At least he couldn't dwell on what had happened.

The confidence he'd started out with was now slowly beginning to fade.

He had a bad feeling about this.

A really bad feeling.

After what felt like hours, but in reality, was only a little over forty minutes later, Sean was trying to shake off as much snow as he could from his hat and leather jacket before he entered the hospital. It had taken him a while to find a parking space, finally snagging one a good distance away. With the way the snow was coming down, coating everything in sight, including him, he now felt like the abdominal snowman.

He shivered, trying not to think about the eighty-degree weather he'd left behind in Australia. It was going to take him some time to get used to this cold weather again.

Searching the waiting room, he saw Sophie and Chester talking to someone. With the white coat the man was wearing, he assumed it was a doctor and not even taking the time to think if it was all right, he made his way over to them. As soon as Sophie saw him, she turned to the doctor. "Doctor Sullivan, this is Sean Young. He's a very good friend of Hannah's. He just flew in from Australia a short time ago."

Dr. Sullivan smiled as he shook Sean's hand. "Ah… I bet you're wishing you stayed right where you were with the weather we have going on right now."

When Sean only responded with a quick nod, he cleared his throat, getting back down to business. "Well, then… I was just explaining Hannah's condition to Sophie and Chester. First, let me start out by saying she was a very lucky young woman to come out of this with only bumps and bruises. She is going to be sore for maybe a week or two, and probably all black and blue, but as far as we've seen, nothing was broken. What we are a little worried about, she seems to have some memory loss. Not about everything, just here and there. This is very common with head injuries. It can be temporary and it can also be permanent. Unfortunately, with most cases, we're unable to predict which of these will happen."

Faced with their worried expressions, he smiled. "You need to think positively. The brain is amazing in how it can repair itself and it's not going to give up easily. From what I've seen in the past with someone like Hannah, young and in good shape, I can safely predict there will be a positive ending to this. But you will need to be patient."

He glanced down at the clipboard he was holding. "After more observation, we'll be moving Hannah to a room. Which means you'll be able to see her in the next hour or two. Hopefully, your visit will spark her memory, because what happens in the next twenty-four hours will determine how long we'll be keeping her here."

He gave them an almost stern look. "But, once she does return home, we ask you make plans for someone to stay with her for the first few days. Or at least until her memory shows enough improvement and she can safely be on her own."

After he left them, Sophie glanced over at Sean. Hoping to ease the worried expression on his face, she put her hand on his arm. "Sean, Hannah was so excited you were coming back. She has been counting down the days… no, I should say the hours, since you called to tell her. She had a dress picked out for dinner and everything."

Sean's smile was shaky. "I was looking forward to seeing her, too." He hesitated. "I didn't know I was going to miss her so much. We texted and talked on the phone, but it's just not the same. Now, I can only hope I'm one of the things she remembers."

A short silence followed, both Chester and Sophie unsure of how to respond. Nervously shifting his hat between his hands, Sean was the first to speak. "If you guys are going to stay, I hope you won't mind if I wait with you. I need to be able to see her for myself."

Chester nodded. "Sure, of course. We got coffee a while ago, but decided to wait for you before we went down to the cafeteria for something to eat. With your long travel time, you're probably ready to drop. When's the last time you ate anything? Not counting airline food, of course."

Sophie actually started to laugh, while at the same time she was shaking her head. "Sean, you'll have to excuse him. His cure for everything is food."

She grinned at the long look Chester gave her. "But, it's okay. I'm glad we waited, because I'm hungry now that we've learned things aren't as bad as we feared."

She smiled over at Sean. "So, come join us. You can tell us how everything worked out at home. How is your father doing? I believe Hannah told us he's doing so much better now? You must be so relieved. Your mother must be so happy, too."

Encouraged by Chester and Sophie's sincere interest, Sean filled them in on the situation back in Australia as they headed for the cafeteria.

Again, he was filled with that comforting feeling that maybe this town really could become home to him.

As long as home was with Hannah.

He only had to believe everything was going to be okay.

Yeah... that's all.

CHAPTER 5

*H*annah hurt everywhere.

And this was even when she tried to stay completely still.

The nurse had left after giving her a lecture on dealing with pain, emphasizing this was not the time to be stoic. There was something they could give her to ease the pain and bring on a healing sleep.

But Hannah told her no. She was afraid to take any kind of drug, even aspirin, fearful it could take away what remained of the memory she had left.

Every so often something would flash through her mind, but then it would just as quickly disappear before she could grab on to it and hold on. From what she'd learned from the nurse, she'd been involved in a collision with a motorcycle, her name was Hannah Michaels and she had a sister Sophie. This was who was at the hospital now and would soon be coming to see her.

For some reason, she knew about Sophie, that she was her sister. But she couldn't bring up a picture of her in her mind. The nurse told her not to worry. Maybe when she saw Sophie in person, this would spark more memories.

Oh God... you hope so.

There was a rustling outside the door to her room, the sound of people talking softly. One voice catching her attention more than the others, her heart began to beat faster.

As soon as Sophie walked into the room, Hannah was caught up in a whirlwind of memories, almost as if a huge bin of information had suddenly dropped from the sky to fall right into her mind.

Overcome with emotion, she started to cry.

This, of course, had Sophie bursting into tears right along with her. So much so, she could hardly get out what she wanted to say. "Oh my gosh, Hannah… we were all so worried." Moving closer to her, but afraid to touch her, Sophie spoke very slowly. "You do know who I am, don't you? They told us some of your memory might have been lost."

She was quick to add. "Temporarily, we're hoping."

Bracing for the pain she knew would follow, Hannah nodded. After a long pause, she finally spoke for the first time since she'd opened her eyes, her voice coming out in a hoarse whisper. "Nothing seems right. And… so much pain."

Spent by just these few words, she closed her eyes.

She heard Sophie move the chair closer to the bed before she reached over to gently hold her hand. "I can imagine. Coming face to face with an oncoming motorcycle will do that to a person. But we are a tough bunch, you, me and Brian. We can overcome anything when we put our minds to it, right?"

Hannah gave a slight nod. She was busy processing this new information.

Brian…

This was another name she recognized. Brian was her twin brother. He had a demanding job, dealing with computers. Since this involved a lot of travel, this meant he couldn't be here.

But that she even remembered him was more than enough.

But Sophie was here. And this is what mattered, since she was her lifeline, the only connection she had to what her life was right now.

This sent a sudden rush of panic through her… she needed to make sure Sophie wouldn't be leaving. At least not for a while.

Opening her eyes, she gazed intently at her. "Don't leave... please stay..."

Sophie vehemently shook her head. "Of course, I'm not going to leave. Not until I know for sure you're going to be all right."

She grinned. "This will give Chester a chance to bond with the twins."

Chester...

Hannah knew who Chester was, too. He was Sophie's husband. He was a baseball player. A tiny sliver of satisfaction filled her that she was able to remember this.

But... the twins? The only twins she knew were her and Brian. So, who were these twins Sophie was talking about?

"The twins? Who are the twins?"

She watched as a look of concern flashed across Sophie's face at her question, to be quickly replaced with a bright smile. "Chester and I have two boys, your nephews... Trevor and Hudson. I'm sure you remember them. They're about seventeen months old. They love you and always get so excited when you come to visit. They call you nah-nah."

No, she didn't remember them. But she watching the anxiety beginning to fill Sophie's eyes and wanting this to go away, she nodded.

Sophie wasn't fooled, patting her hand. "It's okay if you don't remember them right now. I'm sure with such a mess of information whirling around in your mind right now, it must be impossible to get it all straight."

Hannah closed her eyes again. No, this was the problem. Right now her mind was only an empty space, leaving her with nothing to work with. She'd give anything to have a mess whirling around in her head right now. She'd welcome whatever she could get.

You'd welcome anything. Even the smallest little hint...

Sophie hesitated, unsure if she should say what she wanted to say next. But she felt she owed this to Sean. "Sean is here, too. As soon as his flight landed, he came to the hospital. He's very worried about you. Do you want to see him?"

Almost as if in response to what Sophie said, a sharp pain shot through Hannah's head, before barreling down through the rest of her body. This sending her into a panic, she gazed wildly at Sophie.

Sean? Who was Sean? Why did you have such a strong reaction at hearing his name? And why would he be so worried about you?

When Sophie saw how distressed Hannah had become, she decided to drop the subject of Sean, reassuringly stroking her hand. Within minutes, completely done in by just this simple conversation, Hannah fell into a restless sleep.

Sophie glanced over at the entrance to the room. She needed to tell Chester she'd promised Hannah she would stay with her. She was also faced with the terrible task of telling Sean that Hannah didn't remember him.

But after she'd slowly untangled her hand from Hannah's hold, she sat with her a little longer, feeling the need to watch over her. She was finding it hard to leave, horrified by the bruises and scratches that covered her face. The nurse had told them this probably made Hannah look much worse than she felt, but Sophie was skeptical. She had to be in a lot of pain.

She also couldn't clear the visual image that kept popping up in her mind of a motorcycle bearing down on Hannah. She felt sick when she thought about how much worse it could have been.

Finally, and very cautiously, she moved closer to Hannah. Reassured by her soft, even breathing, she quietly began to leave.

At the door, she paused. She seriously didn't know if she'd be able to handle the look of disappointment on Sean's face when she told him Hannah didn't remember him. She definitely wasn't going to tell him how agitated Hannah had become when she'd mentioned his name. No, she was going to tell him to hang in there and not give up hope.

Abruptly returning to Hannah and reaching into her pocket, she pulled out a roll of Lifesavers. These little candies had worked miracles with her and Chester, so why not give them a chance to work their magic on Hannah?

And Sean, too.

She set the roll on the bedside table. Then, throwing back her shoulders and taking in a deep breath, she left the room.

Since leaving the hospital, Sean's mind had gone on auto-drive. His movements almost robotic, he maneuvered his car along the slippery and snow-covered roads. In fact, he'd become so intent on following the car in front of him, he almost missed the entrance leading to his townhouse. After barely making the turn, he barreled his way through the unplowed driveway leading to his garage.

He shut off the ignition. Sitting in the eerie silence of his garage, he didn't move.

He didn't think he'd ever felt this depressed in his life. And now, exhaustion had set in to the point he didn't know if he had it in him to make the short walk to his condo.

He felt like he'd been caught up in some kind of bad dream. How else could one explain something like this happening?

And why the hell did it have to happen to you?

He groaned, closing his eyes. What was wrong with him? Hannah was in the hospital, in pain and now possibly robbed of part of her past. And here he was, feeling sorry for himself?

What kind of person acts like this?

With a long, weary sigh, he slid out of the car and was about to close the door when he saw his hat on the passenger seat. He went to put it on his head, then changed his mind and tossed it into the back seat before giving the car door an extra hard slam.

He wasn't going to wear the hat. Not until he had Hannah back.

When he finally did put it back on, it would be because he was her one and only cowboy again.

CHAPTER 6

*S*ean was up early.

If anything, he hadn't slept at all.

He had spent most of the night and into the early morning hours, reading as much information he could find on the internet about head injuries and amnesia.

His head now filled with all kinds of medical terms and conflicting theories, he was left feeling more confused than before.

The one thing he did learn? The brain was pretty well equipped to deal with trauma. If given the chance, along with time and a little help, it could repair itself.

Of course, if the damage that occurred was too severe, the chance of recovery was less likely to happen. But in cases such as Hannah's, every article he'd read, dwelled on the need for patience. This, along with physical and verbal reminders of the past from her family and friends, could eventually lead to a complete recovery.

Patience... you can do this. You've had plenty of practice at this when you're on the mound, pitching a game. Hadn't everyone on the team remarked about this?

So, he had come up with a plan.

He was going to spend every minute he possibly could with

Hannah. Since he didn't have to report for spring training until the middle of February, he had plenty of time to share.

This would be a good a time to let you know, Sean's best and most consistent trait was he never gave up.

Certainly not when it came to something like this.

Take baseball for example… the guys on the team knew they could always count on him when things began to fall apart in a game. If he was on the mound, he'd answer with a solid pitching performance to keep the opposing team in check.

And if he wasn't pitching? He was right there in the dugout, ready to cheer the team on.

So there was absolutely no way he was going to give up on Hannah.

He had showered, dressed, and was now standing in front of the open refrigerator, searching for a possible breakfast idea. But because of his long absence, there was nothing to be had.

This meant, if he wanted something to eat, he would have to go out and get it.

And he knew exactly where to go.

Forty-five minutes later, a longer drive than usual because of the snow-covered roads, and an impulsive stop at a local florist shop, Sean pulled into the half-filled parking lot of the little coffee shop, Café Latte.

He entered to find it was less crowded than on that June day when he had stopped in on a whim to get a coffee. That Hannah had been there, almost as if this encounter had been planned, still blew his mind.

This had to be fate… what other explanation could there be?

Even more of a reason for you to make this stop today.

He gazed around at the few occupied tables, the low buzz of quiet conversation just barely audible over the background music.

Now he understood why Hannah liked it better when it was less crowded. Today, it felt cozy, more relaxed. A place to sit back and forget about the cold and snowy conditions outside.

The aroma of fresh brewed coffee and just baked pastries a reminder of why he was here, he went up to the counter to order two large coffees and two banana muffins.

The woman who waited on him kept stealing quick glances at him. After she placed his order in front of him, she hesitated, as if there was something she wanted to say.

He wondered if she recognized him, or wanted an autograph. Not that this happened a lot… hell no. But when it did, he always tried to be accommodating. After all, besides being flattering, he felt he owed this to the fans.

He raised an eyebrow. "Yes?"

She immediately became flustered, her cheeks flushing. "You've been here before, haven't you?"

Recognition suddenly dawned in her eyes. "Wait… now I remember… it was with Hannah Michaels, wasn't it?"

Surprised, he nodded. "Yes, to both of those. And you are?"

She became even more flustered. "I'm sorry. I'm Ellie. Ellie Cook. Hannah and I went to school together. And she comes here a lot."

She frowned. "Not lately, though. The last time she was here was a couple weeks before Christmas. She seemed sort of lost. When I asked her about it, she just smiled and said something was missing. But she wouldn't tell me what it was. So, I've been hoping she'd stop by, so I'd know she's okay." She peered more closely at him. "Have you seen her lately?"

Sean didn't answer. He couldn't. He was having a hard time getting past what Hannah had told her.

He wondered… had she been referring to him when she said something was missing?

He stared down at the two cups of coffee Ellie had set in front of him, overwhelmed by a deep sadness.

God… is this some kind of test you're giving me? A way to show how good of a person I can be? If so, I want you to know I'm going to fix this… honest.

He exhaled a long breath. "Hannah was in an accident. She was out running and was hit by a motorcycle."

At the horrified expression on Ellie's face, he quickly added. "She's going to be fine. She has quite a few bruises and scratches, but nothing was broken. But she did have a bad blow to her head and is having a few memory problems."

His smile was wistful. "I thought maybe if I brought her one of your muffins and a coffee, it might bring back some of what she'd lost."

Ellie was shaking her head. "*Oh, no...* I'm so, so sorry. But I'm sure if she knows you're there for her, everything will work out. I remember when you were here that day, the two of you looked like you knew each other so well. You both looked so happy."

Sean took out his wallet and after throwing a twenty on the counter, he picked up the coffee and bag of muffins. "Unfortunately, one of the things she doesn't remember, is me." He shrugged. "This isn't easy to take, but I like to think it's going to be all right."

She gave him a bright smile, nodding vigorously. "Of course it will. I'm sure it will."

After he studied her for a moment, he abruptly turned and headed for the door. He could only hope she was right.

Ellie called out to him. "Let Hannah know I'm thinking of her and I hope she'll be stopping in soon."

He barely nodded. His mind was already on his next stop... the hospital. After what Ellie just told him, he was even more eager to see Hannah.

He was a man on a mission.

CHAPTER 7

Hannah was in a terrible mood.

She was mad at everyone.

This would include everyone here at the hospital and everyone she knew. Even if, right now, she couldn't remember them.

Most of all, she was mad at herself.

She hadn't slept very well last night. But this was her fault, because she'd refused to take any medication for the pain. Again, she didn't want to take the chance the medication might wipe away any memory she had.

Sophie had stayed with her until almost midnight, when Hannah practically ordered her to leave. She would be fine, she told her. After all, look at how often someone kept coming in to check on her?

It had to be at least every fifteen minutes or so.

And, yes, she was mad about this, too. Did she really need to have her blood pressure checked every fifteen minutes?

She didn't think so.

But do you want to know what she was most upset about? This would be the reason she'd landed in the hospital in the first place.

When Sophie first told her what happened, she'd denied doing such a thing. She found it hard to believe she'd be careless enough to run between two parked cars, to then dart out onto a busy street.

This just wasn't something she would do.

Did you even check to see if someone was coming? And where were you going that you were in such a hurry?

Stupid… it was just *so* stupid. What had she been thinking?

And now after spending the last twenty minutes with the doctor, she was not only mad, but totally depressed. After asking, what seemed like a million questions, writing everything down in such a slow and leisurely manner she wanted to scream, he'd given her this stern look, shaking his head. She wasn't ready to go home yet, he'd informed her. They couldn't fool around when it came to head injuries. So, it would be best if she stayed in the hospital for at least another day or two.

The only thing that registered with Hannah was the number two.

Two? Two more days? Was this really necessary? After she'd given him every reason she could possibly think of to convince him she was ready to go home?

But too weary to argue, she gave in. He'd won this round and she would stay one more day. But tomorrow, at this same time, she would be on her way home.

She stared down at her breakfast tray and what was supposed to be a soft-boiled egg and a piece of toast. Unfortunately the egg was nothing like any soft-boiled eggs she'd ever had. Not only was it tasteless, it was also the consistency of rubber. And the toast was as hard as a rock.

She shoved the tray away, instantly regretting this move when a sharp pain shot through her chest, almost taking her breath away. Slowly leaning back against the pillows, she closed her eyes and tried not to cry.

Who knew bruised ribs could cause such agony?

And this was another thing she wasn't too happy about. Out of nowhere, the tears would start to fall and she couldn't stop them for the life of her. The nurse told her this was in response to the trauma she'd experienced, comparing it to a short in an electrical wire. In Hannah's case, even a small change in her emotional state could set her off.

Great... just great. Now you're also beginning to act like a crazy person.

So, not only was she mad, starving and constantly on the verge of tears, she was also one step away from crazy. It was as though she'd lost complete control of her life.

And she didn't like this… not one bit.

She knew everyone was concerned about her. But she was more than capable of taking care of herself. She'd be willing to bet she'd recover much faster if she could sleep in her own bed.

Her eyes still closed, she became aware of a rustling noise, as if someone had come into the room.

She frowned.

She definitely didn't feel like talking to anyone. And she certainly didn't need to have her blood pressure checked again.

So she decided to pretend she was sleeping.

Whoever it was, had now come closer, bringing a breath of fresh air into the sterile room. There was also the hint of spices and leather thrown in. She found the combination so comforting, and for a brief millisecond or so, surprisingly familiar.

But again, before she could grab on from what memory this evolved, it was gone.

She could now sense this mystery person had settled in the chair next to her bed. Slowly turning her head, she cautiously opened her eyes, just a crack.

It was a man. But not just any man. He had to be the most attractive man she'd ever seen. Seriously, he looked like he could be a model. In fact, she'd be willing to bet this is what he did for a living.

His eyes alone were enough to make her want to follow him anywhere. A deep, warm brown, they were framed by these incredibly long eyelashes. They were eyes that, even though she knew nothing about him, let her know she could trust him with her life.

Whoa... what is happening here? Maybe you really are going crazy...

She swiftly closed her eyes again. Evidently, there was some kind of mistake. He couldn't possibly be here to see her. Unless he was a member of the hospital staff?

Oh, please... don't let him be a psychiatrist. Or a social worker, here to ask more questions.

She certainly didn't need this and not from someone like him, who, going by his appearance, was living the perfect life. No way would he ever even think of running out in front of a motorcycle.

She sensed he'd leaned in even closer. "Hannah?"

He knows your name? So, does this mean he knows you? But how?

This was when she remembered the condition of her face. Earlier this morning, she had asked the nurse for a mirror, but after she saw her reflection, made even worse by her horrified expression, she wished she hadn't. Both of her eyes were black and blue and there were scratches and even more bruises scattered over the rest of her face. She could easily pass as an actor in some kind of horror movie.

Or better yet, a roughed up and angry raccoon. Let's just say she wouldn't be winning any beauty contests right now. Certainly not the best way to impress this absolutely gorgeous man who was now sitting close enough to touch... if this is something she'd want.

And you do... so much... Which doesn't make sense. Because you don't even know him. Or if you do, you certainly don't remember him.

"Hannah, darlin'... it's me, Sean."

Darlin'? Sean?

Sean... this was the name Sophie had mentioned to her. So, evidently, she did know him? But this was impossible. Because, come on... how could someone, as perfect as he seemed, no longer be a part of her memory?

She opened her eyes again, this time, falling right into his. For a few breathless seconds, neither of them moved, her gaze searching, his determined. When she finally averted her gaze, a smile lifting the corner of his mouth, he reached over to gently tuck one of her curls behind her ear.

Sean couldn't believe he was finally touching her, the silkiness of her hair running through his fingers. After the first shock of seeing her bruised and scratched face, wishing the pain she had to be experiencing could be his, he no longer noticed anything else except that she was okay.

To him, she was the most beautiful woman in the world.

But there was one thing he was having a hard time with and this would be the confused look in her eyes. Even more so, that he was the reason for this. This was not what he remembered from when they were last together.

You're going to fix this. Somehow, you'll bring her back. No matter how long it takes.

"Hey…" He reached for her hand, linking his fingers with hers. He knew he was taking a chance by doing this, but now that he was with her, there wasn't any way he could not touch her. "How are you feeling? I imagine you're still pretty sore?"

She nodded, while at the same time she slowly pulled her hand from his. Even though, surprisingly, it felt so familiar.

But, before she let her guard down, she needed more information. She was still trying to get over how every nerve in her body had come to life when he tucked her hair behind her ear. Or how she'd been filled with a yearning to lean into his touch, if only to keep it there a little longer .

She gazed over at the entrance of the room. Where was Sophie?

You need her as a buffer. With the state you're in, you certainly can't handle this Sean on your own.

Sensing her uneasiness, Sean immediately switched gears. Hauling himself out of the chair, he smiled down at her. "I brought a few gifts to cheer you up."

He crossed the room to where he had set the flowers he'd picked up at the florist. Every color and variety filling the large vase, he held it out for her inspection. "I thought this might add some sunshine to your room."

When he set it on the bedside table, he noticed the roll of Lifesavers. He sent her a big smile. "Lifesavers… I haven't had one of these since I was a kid."

He was happy to see this brought a smile from her, along with her sudden flood of words. "Take one… take as many as you want. I'm pretty sure Sophie left them here. According to Chester's aunt, sharing them brings good luck to all involved."

She sighed. "Something it appears I need a lot of right now…"

"I'll finish off the whole roll, if this is what it takes to bring you back to the Hannah we all know and love." After giving her a wink, he handed her a stuffed teddy bear. "I know it can't replace Boo-Bear, but hey, think of this as Boo-Bear number two, sort of like a long lost relative, shall we say."

Holding the teddy bear, sporting a big pink bow, she gazed up at him, completely bewildered. "How did you know? I've never told anyone about Boo-Bear." She frowned. "At least not that I know of."

Relieved she finally seemed to be more comfortable with his presence, he sat next to her again, his gaze slowly traveling over her face. "The last time we were together, we'd shared a few childhood memories and somehow, you got it out of me I used to have a stuffed rabbit I named Fred."

At the slight smile touching her lips, he smiled, too. "I know… not very original, but it worked for me. I carried that rabbit around with me everywhere, probably longer than I should have. You told me you had a favorite teddy bear you named Boo-Bear, but whom you lost when you were about eight years old. You were on vacation and somehow, the bear was left behind on the beach. For the longest time, you believed Boo-Bear had been swept away in the waves, to drown. But I told you this probably hadn't happened. Do you remember what I told you?"

She slowly shook her head, mesmerized by the deep, husky tone of his voice, drinking it in, savoring every word.

He smiled. "I told you another little girl had probably rescued him and even to this day, Boo-Bear was living a happy life."

He reached out to tuck her hair behind her ear… again compelled by the need to touch her. When she briefly closed her eyes at this, he cleared his throat. "I also promised if I ever found another Boo-Bear, I'd get it for you. So, when I saw this bear, almost as you'd described, it was just too coincidental." He shrugged. "I had to get it for you."

He hadn't planned on buying the bear.

But when he stopped at the florist to buy the flowers, the bear was sitting on the counter, right in front of him. As though it had been waiting for him. After the clerk assured him she could add a pink bow, he saw this as a sign the bear was meant to go with him.

She slowly shook her head. "I don't remember. I remember Boo-Bear getting lost, but I don't remember telling you this. Or your promise."

Her bottom lip beginning to quiver, her voice was shaky. "I'm sorry. I don't remember a lot of things."

She closed her eyes, her voice dipping to a whisper. "I don't remember you. I'm sorry, but I don't. I wish I could, because you seem so nice, someone I'd like to know, but…"

He swiftly jumped in to reassure her, his smile also an attempt to hide his disappointment. "That's okay, we'll just take things as they come."

To say he was having a hard time with all of this would be putting it mildly. But the reminder of that one word, stressed again and again in the articles he'd read, kept hammering away in his head.

Patience, patience, patience.

He cleared his throat. "I have something else for you."

Her lashes fluttering open, he was pleased to see this brought on another smile. It was a tiny smile, but enough to make him feel hopeful.

"You do?" There was an eagerness in her voice.

Smiling, he nodded. "I do. I made a stop at Café Latte to get you a muffin and a coffee. I got the same for me. I thought if you hadn't had breakfast yet, we could have it together."

She reached over and lifted the lid off of the disastrous remains of her breakfast. After they both stared down at the unappealing remains, she glanced over at him. "This was breakfast."

One look at her scrunched up and distressed face, he was more than happy with his decision to stop at Café Latte.

He grinned. "Oh boy, it looks like I may have possibly saved the day… or should I say the morning, huh?"

He handed her the bag with the muffins and sitting back in the chair, he watched her open it.

She peered into the bag before she glanced over at him. "Banana, my favorite." Slowly letting go of the bag, she looked anxious. "Was this where we met? At Café Latte? Were we friends?"

He wondered what she would say if he told her what her reaction had been the first time they met, and he'd suggested they become friends. My God, she'd practically took off in a gallop to get away from him. It was when they met months later at Café Latte, she'd confessed she ran off because his choice of words had led her to believe he only wanted to be friends, but nothing more. Something he'd obviously been too dense to pick up on the first time.

Definitely another one of your less than stellar moments. But then, first impressions have never been one of your best traits.

Unfortunately, whenever he was around the opposite sex, what little intelligence he had stored away in his brain completely eluded him. This had any attempt at a smooth conversation coming out entirely different from what he'd planned. This invariably started out with him saying something stupid, to then follow with all kinds of excuses before he finished it all off with a bumbled apology for just about everything.

But right now? His plan was to take it slow, choose his words and actions carefully. If this meant they had to go back to being just friends, so be it. He was in no hurry.

Remember? Patience is the key.

So, a smile tugging at the corner of his mouth, he nodded. "Ah, yes… I guess you could say we were friends. More like good friends. Which I hope we still are."

He took the bag from her and taking out a muffin, he smiled at her. "So, do you want butter on this? I seem to remember this is what you did."

He suddenly remembered the coffee, handing her one of the cups. "Here, it should still be hot. I stopped by the nurse's station and had them warm it up in their microwave. Drink up while I butter this muffin for you."

Slowly bringing the cup to her lips, she watched as he meticulously went about buttering the muffin. He appeared to be completely happy as he did this, as though there was no other place he'd rather be.

When he glanced up to see she was watching him, his smile confirmed this.

And, even though she knew nothing about this Sean, or what kind of relationship they shared before her accident, she wondered… maybe this time they could possibly become more than friends?

Little did she know how happy Sean would've been to know what she was thinking.

"Hannah?"

Holding the buttered muffin, darn if he wasn't giving her another one of those sexy smiles of his.

"Here you go, darlin'… enjoy."

Sean slowly came to his feet, and extending his hands high over his head, he gave a long stretch.

He had spent a little over two hours with Hannah, much longer than he'd planned. And even though she still didn't remember him, she seemed to have enjoyed his company.

He didn't want to leave. If he was with her, he would know she was okay. Which was silly. After all, she was in the hospital, with around-the-clock care.

She would be fine.

So, after reaching into his pocket for his keys, he smiled. "You should get some sleep. This is what you need to heal." He winked. "One of the many things I learned in my late-night search concerning head injuries."

Then he nodded to what was left of the roll of lifesavers. "Since I finished off almost half of those, maybe I even managed to get some good luck going here."

He was debating if he should give her a kiss before he left, if only on her cheek, when there was a commotion out in the hallway.

They both glanced towards the entrance to the room at the sound of a child's loud wail. This was followed by a familiar voice. "Hudson, no, you can't eat that. It's been on the floor. Give it to me."

Another cry erupted, this becoming louder as Sophie came into the room, juggling a baby in each arm.

After Sean quickly moved to take one of the babies, Sophie mouthed him a silent thank you before she turned to Hannah. "Well, here they are… your nephews. As you can see, they're quite a handful. Don't believe what people tell you about twins, that they're easier to take care of because they keep each other occupied. From what I've learned, this isn't true."

She shook her head. "Believe me, together these two are double-trouble, twenty-four-seven."

She nodded at the baby in her arms. "This is Hudson. Sean is holding Trevor. Don't worry, they won't be here long, because Chester will be here shortly to pick them up. I thought it might be good for you to meet them."

She set a squirming Hudson down on the floor, where he immediately made a bee-line for the stuffed bear Sean had brought for Hannah. Holding it in his hands, he gave them all a big grin before flinging it right at Hannah.

Sean burst out laughing. "*Whoa…* he's got quite an arm on him. Maybe we can use him as a back-up on the team."

Sophie groaned. "You and Chester both. You only see this throwing phase he's going through as a sign he has a good arm. You tend to overlook that he aims right at someone or something, and eventually this is going to lead to trouble."

Sean came to stand next to the bed. He was still holding Trevor, who was squirming in his arms. He kept reaching for Hannah, chanting her name.

"Nah-nah, nah-nah…"

This should've made Hannah happy. But instead she wanted to cry. Because, honestly? She didn't remember him or Hudson. To her, they were just two little toddlers. Very cute little toddlers, yes. But that was all.

She didn't feel a connection to either of them.

Since Trevor was so determined to be with her, she reached for him. This brought Sophie to her side, shaking her head. "*Oh, Hannah…* don't feel like you have to hold him. I know how much you're hurting, and I don't want him to jolt or poke you. As little as he is, he can be pretty strong."

Evidently, Sean felt differently. Carefully settling Trevor next to Hannah on the bed, they watched as he curled up against her, put his thumb in his mouth and closed his eyes.

Her mouth falling open in surprise, Hannah gazed up at Sean. "I can't believe this. You'd think he'd be afraid of me because of how awful I look with all these bruises and everything."

Unable to resist, Sean again reached over to wrap one of her curls around his finger, letting it linger there a little longer than necessary. "You're beautiful, Hannah Michaels. Inside and out. It would take more than a few bumps and bruises to not see this."

He smiled down at Trevor, who already appeared to be drifting off to sleep. "Look, even Trevor agrees with me."

And his indecision as to whether or not he should kiss her? This was now a no brainer. Gently nudging her chin up with his thumb and pressing the softest of kisses to her mouth, the teasing glint in his eyes was a contradiction to the huskiness of his voice. "I hope it's okay my kiss landed on your mouth. But it's the only part of your face that wasn't bruised and I don't want to hurt you."

He grinned. "Lucky for me, I'd say."

Before she even had time to think about what he said, or more importantly, about the kiss he'd given her, he'd already headed for the door. There he turned, sending her a wink. "I'll stop by later to see how you're doing."

With a wave, he was gone.

CHAPTER 8

If only we could choose which memories to remember...
~ Anonymously Yours

Sophie turned to Hannah, a huge grin on her face. "*Wow...*what just happened here? And what went with both of you before I got here? From what I just witnessed, it sure looks like Sean has charmed his way right back into your memory."

Still reeling from Sean's kiss, even as short and simple it had been, Hannah slowly shook her head. "No, I don't remember him, not at all. And nothing really happened. He did most of the talking, filling me in on some of the time we'd spent together, time I've seem to have lost"

She nodded towards the teddy bear and flowers and on the bedside table. "He brought the teddy bear and flowers. He also brought coffee and muffins so we could have breakfast together."

She ran her hand through her hair, giving a frustrated sigh. "I feel so stupid, not knowing what is expected of me, or how I should be feeling. Especially with him."

Sophie was still grinning. "Well, he certainly appears to be very sure about his feelings for you. That you have no memory of him, doesn't seem to bother him one bit. So, maybe right now, this is enough for the both of you." Her gaze darting to the floor, she suddenly almost dove under the bed, reaching for a quickly disappearing Hudson. "No, Hudson… you shouldn't be under here."

After she settled him on her lap, she gave him a hug. "Why can't you be like your brother and take a nice nap. Look at him, sound asleep next to Nana."

This sent Hudson into a crying fit, giving Sophie no choice but to settle him on the other side of Hannah. Like Trevor, he popped his thumb in his mouth and closed his eyes.

Hannah eased back against the pillows, a long and exhausted sigh escaping her. "It looks like these two may be here for a while, so maybe you can tell me what you know about Sean. And what kind of relationship we had. I'm struggling here."

Sophie settled comfortably in the chair. She was already smiling, as there was nothing she liked better than watching a romance unfold.

Or better yet, helping it along.

Chester teased her about this all of the time, but he was becoming just as bad. Well, maybe not quite, but he was slowly coming over to her side. Look how he had such a big part in getting his sister Livy back together with Sam. And now they were getting married in about a week.

Now observing Hannah's confused expression, she took a moment to decide where to start. She smiled. "Well, let's see. I'm pretty sure you're in love with him, completely and there's-no-going-back-kind-of-in-love with him. This all started when you both showed up at the hospital at the same time when Hunter and Trevor were born."

She frowned. "If you had told me about that, or if Sean had told Chester he wanted to meet you, we could've set the two of you up together. But neither of you said anything. So, another several months went by until you met up again. In June, at Café Latte."

"Café Latte? *Ah…* so this is why he brought the muffins and coffee from there…"

Sophie grinned. "Yep… your favorite coffee hangout. You both just happened to show up at the same time again. Hmm… another coincidence? I don't think so. I'd have to say it was more like fate. You had dinner with him that night. Then you made plans to meet up at the barbecue Chester and I had for the team a couple days later. The two of you were inseparable that evening. You took off for a walk down the beach and didn't return until the early morning hours."

She shook her head. "I was worried and wanted to go look for you. Where Chester wasn't concerned, telling me he trusted Sean completely. When I quizzed you the next day about what happened, you claimed you talked the whole time. You also told me he was the one. You were crazy about him… you'd fallen completely in love with him."

Hannah's mouth dropped open. "I told you all that?" She groaned, closing her eyes. "How can I not remember something so important? It's bad enough I can't remember him as a person, but not to remember I was in love with him? How is this possible?"

Sophie laughed. "Yes, that's exactly what you told me. But the next day, Sean got a call from home. You know his home is in Australia, right?" At Hannah's nod, she continued. "His grandfather wanted him to come home because his father had a heart attack. And now, after being gone for the past six months, he has finally returned to Cleveland. I'm sure this was only because he wanted to see you. After all, spring training doesn't start until next month."

She sighed. "You'd made plans to go out to dinner with him… tonight. It was going to be your first actual date. We'd even picked out a dress for you to wear."

When Hannah didn't say anything, the confused expression still on her face, Sophie sighed. "Did he tell you the first time he saw you was at our wedding? That he asked who you were because he wanted to meet you?"

Hannah slowly shook her head.

Sophie nodded. "Yep, this is when it all really began. He'd just arrived in the states for spring training and nobody really knew anything about him. So, Chester decided to invite him to our wedding. But the two of you never talked that night."

Her eyes closed, Hannah shook her head as Sophie continued. "Yeah… before he left for Australia, things were going good and now that he was coming back, you were really looking forward to seeing him. But now, with the accident…"

After a long silence, she sent Hannah a questioning look. "I take it, he told you he's a pitcher… and a really good one, too. Everyone on the team really likes him."

She grinned. "He's also become very popular with the press, they follow him everywhere. I'm sure it's that sexy accent of his and he's just so darn cute."

A thoughtful look came over her face. "I'm surprised they haven't shown up at the hospital when they learned he was back in Cleveland."

A look of horror came over Hannah's face. "*Oh… my… God…* what if they find out he was here to see me? They won't try to come to my room, will they? Oh, Sophie… I can't let anyone see me like this."

Immediately realizing her mistake telling Hannah this, she shook he head. "Oh, I don't think you need to worry. I'm sure Sean will make sure this doesn't happen. He's not one to encourage the publicity. Like Chester, he's very protective of his personal life."

At the same time she made a mental note to tell both Chester and Sean they needed to be careful. And she needed to do this soon.

She changed the subject. "So, back to Sean, what else did he tell you?"

"He talked about his trip home, and how he's glad to be back, ready for spring training. But not a lot of details concerning us." Hannah shrugged. "Just a hint, here and there."

Sophie nodded. "*Hmm…* I can understand that. He doesn't want to throw everything at you and confuse you even more. Or have you thinking he's trying to push you into something you're not sure about. He wants you to remember everything on your own."

She gazed around the room before she grinned over at Hannah. "Flowers, teddy bear, breakfast… he hit every category, didn't he? Looks like he's planning on hanging around."

Hannah gazed down at Trevor and Hudson, now both asleep, before she glanced over at Sophie. "I'm finding this all so hard to comprehend. I look into his eyes and I completely lose my train of thought. To the extent I can't even think straight. I feel like I'm in high school again and have a crush on one of the popular guys or something."

Sophie laughed. "Well, in case you haven't noticed, he seems to be pretty taken by you, too."

They both looked over as Chester come striding into the room, a big smile on his face. "Hey, Hannah… how's it going? I see you haven't lost your winning ways when it comes to the boys."

As if by magic, both Trevor and Hudson's lashes flew open at the sound of Chester's voice. Scrambling to sit up, they cried out to him.

"Daddy, daddy…"

Chester quickly scooped them up, settling a toddler on each hip. "Hey, you two, you don't want to hurt nah-nah. I have a feeling she's still pretty sore." Shifting the boys more comfortably against him, he glanced from Hannah to Sophie. "So, any progress here? Any new memories popping up?"

When they both shook their heads, he shrugged. "I'm sure it will all come back in time. I ran into Sean on my way in. He told me he's going to stop by as often as he can. You couldn't ask for a better memory coach. He's a great guy."

He turned to Sophie. "I'll take these two off your hands, maybe take them over to see my Aunt Evelyn. I'll see you when you get home. No rush."

Trevor and Hudson squirming in his arms, he smiled over at Hannah. "You just hang in there. Maybe once you get home, everything will fall back into place. Again, if anyone can help you get through this, it would be Sean."

After a quick kiss to Sophie's cheek, he was gone as quickly as he'd arrived.

Sophie sent Hannah a quick glance. "I'll be right back." Running out of the room, she caught up to Chester, grabbing his arm.

He turned to her. "*Whoa…* what? Did I forget something?"

She spoke in an exaggerated whisper. "No, but you need to warn Sean about the press. If they find out about this, they'll be on it in a flash. You know how they're always looking for stories about him. Hannah would just about die if they managed to get a photo of her."

He shifted Trevor and Hudson more securely in his arms, while at the same time, he dodged Hudson's attempt to grab his ear. He chuckled. "I'm sure she won't 'just about die' if this does happen, but I'll warn Sean. He's pretty good at handling the press and from what he told me, I know he'll do whatever needs to be done to protect Hannah."

He leaned over to give her a kiss. "I'll see you whenever you get home. Love you, angel."

She watched as he went striding down the hall. Her curiosity taking over, she started running after him again. "Chester, wait… what did Sean tell you?"

Darn if he didn't start to laugh, not even turning around as he answered. "That's confidential, between me and Sean. Maybe I'll tell you later. Then again, maybe I won't. Still love you, angel."

"Love you, too." She could hear him responding to Trevor and Hudson's baby talk as he pushed the button for the elevator.

She was smiling as she hurried back to Hannah. Sometimes she still found it hard to believe he was her husband.

How did you get so lucky?

Once she was back in Hannah's room, Sophie began rummaging through her purse to finally pull out her phone. "I was going through my photos this morning and I found two of you and Sean. They were taken at our barbecue. I'm pretty sure I sent them to you, but it can't hurt to look at them again. I love the second one."

She handed Hannah the phone.

In the first photo, the camera had caught her and Sean in the middle of a conversation. She was gazing at him as though he was telling her the most interesting thing she'd ever heard. It was obvious there was something very special between them.

In the second photo, his hands framing her face, Sean was kissing her. Their eyes closed, they were completely caught up in the kiss.

Hannah had no idea of how to deal with this. A part of her was scared to death. While at the same time, she wanted to show Sean the photos the next time she saw him, to see what his reaction would be. Maybe even going as far to suggest they try out the same kind of kiss they were sharing in the photo?

Just to see if it might kindle a response in her? One that might spark her memory?

Now if this isn't proof you're going crazy, you don't know what is. Not only have you lost some of your memory, you've also lost a big part of your mind. The part controlling your ability to think logically.

"So?" This came from Sophie.

Hannah shook her head, something she'd been doing entirely too much over the past forty-eight hours. She suspected this was why her head had now begun to ache even more. "It's hard for me to even think anymore. I look at the photos and I don't feel like it's me that I see. While at the same time, there's something so familiar, something that I can't quite figure out."

She dragged her hand through her hair, sending Sophie a look of complete despair. "Oh gosh, Sophie… I don't know…"

Sophie came over to give her a hug. "I'm sure everything will start to fall into place with time."

Clinging to her, Hannah almost didn't want to let go.

"I hope you're right… I really do."

Once Sophie had settled back in the chair, she smiled over at Hannah.

"So, what else shall we talk about? How about Abby? I have a feeling, since you can't remember the twins or Sean, you also have no idea Abby is pregnant and due any day now. Everyone it betting it's a boy. But I think it's going to be a girl. Don't ask me why… it's just a feeling I have. Kevin is fit to be tied because Abby is still working long hours since she promised to make both the cake and cookie favors for Livy and Sam's wedding. I've been trying to help her, but with Aunt Louise not scheduled to return from Paris for another week, I have the boutique to run, too. Thank goodness it's off season for Chester right now. It amazes me how happy he is spending time with the boys. He never complains."

When she stopped to take a breath, she saw Hannah had closed her eyes. So she kept talking. "Aunt Louise was frantic when she heard about what happened. Uncle Paul, too. She kept asking me if they should come home early, but I think I finally assured them you should be okay. I know how much she loves the time she has in Paris with Uncle Paul. Livy and Sam also send their love and are keeping their fingers crossed you'll still be able to come to the wedding. Remember, you asked Sean to go with you. I can't wait. It should be a great wedding."

She smiled over at Hannah. "There are so many other people who are asking about you, wanting to know if you're up for a visit."

There was no response. This was when she realized Hannah had fallen asleep. After leaving a note to let her know she would stop by later, she tiptoed her way out of the room.

When she arrived at the main entrance, she passed by two men, one quickly averting his gaze. For some reason, he looked vaguely familiar. But when she turned around to get a second look, he had disappeared.

Oh well... maybe he was a fan of Chester's and recognized you. You should be used to this by now.

Without a second thought, she pulled on her hat and mittens and pushed open the door.

It was still snowing.

CHAPTER 9

Sean left the warmth and comfort of Hannah's hospital room to be greeted by a parking lot full of snow-covered cars. After he finally located his car and started it up, he began the tedious task of brushing the snow from the windshield.

He was almost finished when a white van came to a sliding stop behind him. This was followed by the sound of doors flying open and a loud shout. He whirled around to see two men, one carrying a camera, bearing down on him.

He recognized the man, without the camera, as a reporter for the local news. A big smile on his face, he greeted Sean like an old friend. "Hey, Sean... long time no see. Almost didn't recognize you without your hat. Can we talk a bit?"

Sean groaned.

Damn... the last thing you want to do right now, is an interview.

The reporter, who's name Sean now remembered was Joe, ignored this and got right down to business. "Everyone here in Cleveland is going to be thrilled when they find out you're back and ready for the new season. They've missed you... hell, we've all missed you. But there's also been a lot of speculation about why you came back so early, instead of waiting until February to report directly to spring training. Is it true what we're hearing? Someone you know, the rumor going around it's your girlfriend, was in an accident?"

Frowning, Sean dragged his hand through his hair. He had forgotten all about the damn press. Of course, they'd be curious as to why he was here. Most of the guys waited until February, reporting straight to Arizona.

A sudden smiled tugged at his lips.

Girlfriend?

They thought he was visiting his girlfriend? Well, yeah... he liked the sound of this. He would be more than happy to have everyone think Hannah was his.

Then it suddenly registered... this wasn't good.

Good Lord... Hannah. What if they try to get to Hannah? Whatever you do, you need to make sure this doesn't happen.

As if he hadn't a care in the world, he shook the snow from his hair and casually stuffed his hands in his pockets before he shot both men a big grin. "Yep, it looks like you caught me. I was visiting one of my fans who is in for a short stay. You know me, always trying to spread some Aussie cheer. I also have another friend's wedding coming up in about a week, along with a few other things I need to take care of before I report to Arizona. You know, just the usual stuff... check up on my place, pay some bills." He grinned. "It's not all fun and games playing ball, you know."

The disappointment on Joe's face was almost comical. It was obvious he had been expecting a big story.

After he answered the few questions Joe fired at him, the majority about his time in Australia and the team, Sean watched the two men get in their van and slowly drive away. But they didn't go far, pulling into another space about two rows away.

This concerned him.

What were they planning?

He got into his car and while he was waiting for the heat to kick in, he pulled out his phone and called Chester.

"Hey, what's up?"

At Chester's greeting, he started right in with the reason for his call. "Sorry to bother you, but I just got waylaid in the hospital parking lot by Joe, our friendly local reporter. He had his trusty camera guy with him. He informed me there are rumors going around that my girlfriend was in an accident and she's in the hospital. I think I handled it pretty well… told him I was only visiting a fan."

He took a deep breath. "The last thing I want is for someone to go into the hospital and start asking Hannah all these questions. Or worse yet, start taking photos. She doesn't need this right now. I don't even want to think about how upsetting this would be for her."

Chester's long sigh came through the line. "*Damn…* I got valet parking because of the boys, so I must have just missed them. I was only there for about five minutes. I just left Sophie and Hannah. Did they leave?"

Sean glanced over to see the van was still there. "Nope, still sitting in their van, probably watching me, watching them."

Chester groaned. "*Geeez…* this means they're probably waiting for you to leave before they go inside."

He began to chuckle. "If they run into Sophie, I wouldn't want to be in their shoes for all the money in the world. She's not a fan of the press and their so called 'up to date and honest' news. I have to remind her every time we go out, not get too carried away. Otherwise, she ends up saying something she shouldn't. Trust me, she already has."

He took a few moments to think. "You need to leave, or act like you're going to leave. Then go back into the hospital using another entrance and ask to speak with security. Tell them not to allow anyone near Hannah's room unless they're cleared by either me or you. In the meantime, I'll call over there to confirm this. Good luck."

Sean laughed. "Thanks. I'm on it."

After brushing the snow off his car a second time, Sean had finally left the hospital and was heading home.

He was smiling.

Besides the encounter with the press, he was feeling really good about how his visit had gone with Hannah. If he wasn't mistaken he had sensed a spark of some kind between them.

Yeah, it was a brief spark, but it was there. And he would be willing to bet she had felt it, too.

This was confirmed by the way she leaned into his kiss. He liked to think this was because, like him, she hadn't wanted it to end.

Yeah, you're going to stick with this.

For him, that kiss had been the highlight of his morning. He was also pretty damn proud of how he had pulled it off. Granted it wasn't what you'd call a 'wow' kind of kiss. And definitely nowhere what he would've liked to give her.

But it was a start.

A really good start...

By the time he pulled into his garage, he already had a plan of what he wanted to happen the next time he went to see her.

He was a determined man, now more eager than ever to get them back to where they were before the accident.

Yep, everything was going to be just fine.

He had nothing to worry about.

Right?

Joe had waited for about twenty minutes after Sean drove away before he nodded over at Evan. A rookie, Evan had only been working with him for about a week.

"Come on, let's go. It's show time."

After he stepped out of the hospital elevator onto the third floor, Joe scanned the busy hallway before he turned to Evan, giving him the signal to follow him.

"Hey, how's it going?" He smiled, his attention diverted by a petite blond nurse coming out of one of the rooms.

Man, she was hot.

He couldn't help it... he liked women, all women. Any shape and size, it didn't matter... he liked them all.

After one more appraising glance, he turned back in the direction he needed to go, almost running into a cart loaded with floral arrangements.

Sending a quick glance up and down the hall to make sure he didn't have an audience, he plucked a rose from the nearest vase. No one would miss it, and since he had no idea what was going to happen when he finally found room three-thirteen, it could very well come be the ice breaker he needed.

What woman didn't melt when presented with a flower?

Room three-thirteen was the room he was looking for. This was the room assigned to Hannah Michaels, the 'mystery girlfriend' of Sean Young.

Hopefully, this is where they would find her.

His voice going low, his next words were directed to Evan. "Try to act completely natural, like we're here visiting a friend. The room we're looking for should be coming up on the left. I want you to wait until we're just about to go in before you take out your camera. Then, as soon as you get a good angle, take the photo. Take as many as you can. Then we'll beat it out of here."

He gave a short laugh. "Hell, why am I telling you all of this? You know what to do."

He sent a nervous glance over his shoulder. "Thank God Chester Mazzori's wife didn't recognize us. What were the chances she'd be leaving the same time we came in? I sure as hell don't relish the possibility of dealing with her. She's not shy when it comes to telling the media what she thinks of them. And since this mysterious girlfriend of Young's is rumored be her sister, who knows what would've happened if we had walked into this Hannah's room and found her there, too."

When there was no response from Evan, Joe shot him a quick glance.

He didn't look happy.

He gave him a light punch in the arm. "Hey, come on… lighten up. We're not doing any harm, we're just trying to keep Young's fans informed on what's new in his life." He gave a short laugh. "After all, this is what you signed up for."

When this earned him only a shrug, he gave an exasperated sigh. Why the hell did this Evan take on the job? He obviously wasn't tough enough for this line of work.

Yeah, maybe this 'reality photography' wasn't for him.

Weddings or bar mitzvahs might be more his style.

When Joe and Evan entered Hannah's room, she was sound asleep. So that they were there, didn't even register.

Nor did she hear the rapid clicks of a camera.

When she later woke, opening her eyes, the first thing she saw was the rose on the bedside table.

She smiled.

Nope, she had no idea.

But maybe it was better this way.

At least for now, it was…

Then again, maybe Hannah had nothing to worry about.

Joe was in a bad mood. He couldn't believe, after the hour they spent hanging around at the hospital, along with the long drive back to the office, made even longer because of the miserable road conditions, their efforts had been a complete waste of time.

He threw his keys on the desk and turning to Evan, his anger was more than evident. "What the hell? What do you mean you lost the photos you took at the hospital?"

Refusing to meet his eyes, Evan shrugged. "I have no idea what went wrong. When I went to download them, they weren't there. These things happen."

He picked up his camera, examining it like he'd never seen it before. "It's not all that big of a deal. I'm sure you'll get plenty of other stories in the next few weeks with spring training right around the corner."

Evan was uncomfortable he had to lie to Joe. But, he couldn't let those photos get out. When he saw the poor girl asleep in the hospital bed, her face all banged up, he knew there was no way he was going to give the photos to Joe.

Nope, motorcycle accidents were a subject he wanted nothing to do with… never again. He'd lost the person he loved, more than anyone else in the world, because of a damn motorcycle.

And he still blamed himself, and probably always would, for what happened. Trying not to think about how different the outcome would've been, had he stood his ground.

He closed his eyes.

You don't want to go there. Not now. Not here. Not ever again.

Puzzled by his behavior, Joe studied him.

Why the hell does he have his eyes closed? Does he think this is a good time to take a nap? Or is he trying to shut you out?

This is when it hit him.

Be it personal or what, Evan had deleted the photos on purpose. There was a reason he didn't want them published.

Damn…

This was the third photographer he'd gone through in less than a year. What the hell was wrong with these guys? Hadn't any of them ever heard of the saying, a photo is worth a thousand words?

Evidently not.

You couldn't let your emotions get the best of you in a job like this. He should know. He had done this once, a mistake that had almost ended his career.

He threw himself down in his chair, nodding over at the only other chair in the room. "Sit."

After Evan sat, still refusing to meet his eyes, Joe studied him for a very long and uncomfortable moment.

Then he gave a long sigh. "You probably think you know what I'm going to say, don't you?"

Evan nodded.

"Well, you're wrong. I'm not going to let you go. For some stupid reason, I like you. And from the photos I've seen, I know you have the talent to become a great photographer. So, I'm going to give you another chance. But it won't be with me."

Evan shifted uncomfortably in his chair before he cleared his throat. "I appreciate the offer, but..."

Joe waved his hand to silence him. "Hear me out. They need a photographer in the Home, Arts and Travel department. I have already told them I was sending you to talk to them. I built you up as this big, upcoming star photographer. So, if you blow them off, it's going to make me look bad."

For what felt like an eternity, Evan said nothing. Then he nodded. "Okay, I'll go talk to them. But I can't promise you anything."

You can't promise anyone, anything. You tried that once and look what happened.

Joe watched him walk out of the room. He was almost in shock, something that usually never happened.

How was it this kid had turned everything around? As though he was doing him, yours truly, a favor? He couldn't promise anything? Then to top it off, he hadn't even thanked him for this new opportunity?

As if on cue, Evan, poked his head into the room. "By the way, thanks for the referral. I appreciate it. And I'm sorry it didn't work out. We have different goals, I guess."

He took a deep breath before his next words, his voice filled with emotion. "Six months ago, and two weeks before our wedding, my fiancée Kelsie was killed while riding on the back of a motorcycle. Her brother was driving and he was also killed. They were hit by a teenager who was texting and didn't see the stop sign."

He shrugged. "This is why I deleted the photos. I couldn't do that to the poor girl. I only hope she knows how lucky she is, so blessed. I don't even want to tell you what Kelsie and her brother looked like after the accident. I know I'll never forget."

He paused to collect himself before he glanced over at Joe, shaking his head. "It was supposed to be me on the back of that motorcycle. But I let Kelsie talk me into letting her go first. I can't tell you how many nights I've stayed awake, wishing it had been me."

With that, he left.

Slowly leaning back in his chair, for the longest time, Joe didn't move.

He finally picked up his phone and dialed human resources, bracing for the conversation he knew would follow. They weren't going to be happy to hear he needed another photographer.

After he ended the call, he hit another number. He wanted to talk to Beth. She always made him feel better. And right now he wasn't feeling all that great.

He should've told Evan, after he saw Hannah Michael's bruised face, he hadn't been able to stop thinking about how fragile life was.

Maybe this would've made him feel better?

He sighed, shaking his head. Probably not.

But if he takes the job with the Home Department, you're going to make a sincere effort to be his friend, something he needs badly right now. It's time you took the time to help someone else.

Maybe it was also time to finally take that next step with Beth, make their relationship permanent. Looking into a new line of work might also be a good idea. Because even though he was only in his early forties, it was obvious he was getting too old and sentimental for this job.

When Beth answered the phone, he could feel his whole body relax at the sound of her voice. He smiled, this coming through in his greeting. "Hey babe, I've been thinking... how about we go out to dinner tonight? Someplace nice... maybe Jake's Place. I know you've been wanting to go there."

He took a deep breath. "There's something we need to talk about."

CHAPTER 10

*H*annah would give just about anything to be able to go home.

Seriously, anything...

She had now been in the hospital for two days and as far as she was concerned, this was two days too many. She was fine and she was ready to go home.

Yes, she was still sore... everywhere. She'd admit to this.

She still couldn't take a deep breath without a sharp pain shooting through her chest, bringing her to feel lightheaded. Walking from the bed to the bathroom was enough to leave her spent and out of breath. She was also still crying for no reason. And with all of the bruises and scratches on her face, now even more colorful and pronounced, she knew she looked like she'd been in a fight... big time.

And you'd lost.

She also couldn't stay awake more than a few hours at a time, almost too exhausted to even think. How this was possible, she had no clue. After all, it wasn't like she was doing anything.

But despite all of these things?

She still wanted to go home. Desperately, she wanted this.

Propping the pillows up behind her, frustrated by how long it took her to accomplish this, she gazed out the window. Now almost early evening, it was still snowing. She was pretty sure it hadn't stopped all day. Becoming almost hypnotized by the dancing and swirling flakes, her eyelids began to grow heavy.

Wasn't the nurse always reminding her sleep was the best medicine? And if this resulted in her going home, then she was going to sleep as much as possible.

She closed her eyes, her intention to do just that.

A gentle, but insistent knocking woke Hannah.

Groggily opening her eyes, she gazed over at the entrance to the room.

There was a man standing there, almost hidden behind the huge vase of flowers he was holding. When he saw her open her eyes, he sent her a tentative smile before he cautiously made his way over to the bed.

She peered more closely at him.

Do you know him?

She didn't think she did. And by the hesitant way he approached her, it was as though he wasn't quite sure if he knew her either.

Or if he was even in the right place.

If she had to guess, she'd say he was her age, give or take a year or two. His dark blonde hair was down to his shoulders and he had that, not quite, but almost bearded look going on. He was dressed very casually in a dark red knit shirt, jeans and a black leather jacket.

But what caught her attention, were his eyes. They were a deep, piercing blue... intense. They were the kind of eyes that could change in an instant, letting you know exactly what he was thinking.

After this close inspection, she was still pretty sure she didn't know him. But, in the state she was in, this wasn't a guarantee she didn't.

He cleared his throat, a hesitant smile on his face. "Hi, my name is Michael... or Mike, whatever you want to call me. Stewart is my last name... er...Mike... Michael Stewart."

He shrugged. "I'm the guy who ran into you with my motorcycle."

Abruptly shifting the vase to his one hand, he wiped his other hand down his jeans.

He couldn't believe how damn nervous he was. *Good God,* look at how he was sweating. But at his first sight of the bruises on her face, the knowledge he was the one responsible for this, he seriously felt almost physically ill.

He must have called the hospital more than a dozen times over the past two days to check on her condition. But even after they finally told him she was out of intensive care and now listed in satisfactory condition, he knew he wouldn't be able to rest until he could see this for himself.

You shouldn't even have been riding the damn bike. It's winter, for God's sake.

But it had been one of those rare warm days for January and his one and only shot at getting the bike over to the shop for some detail work he wanted done. This was made even more urgent by a winter storm predicted to hit later that day.

And look what happened...

Ever since the accident, he hadn't been able to erase the memory of those few harrowing seconds as he tried to avoid hitting her, to then watch her go sailing into the parked car.

He'd been so sure, when she had crumpled to the ground, to then remain completely motionless, he'd killed her.

Even now, thinking about this, he had to close his eyes and take a deep breath at the uneasy churning in his gut.

He opened them to find Hannah was struggling to sit up, the expression on her face a sign of how painful this was. He inched closer. "No, no... please don't feel like you have to move. I don't want you to undo any progress you've made."

He anxiously searched her face. "You're going to be okay, aren't you? I can't tell you how many times I called the hospital to see how you're doing." He frowned at the memory. "But they don't tell a person much. It was only when they told me you were out of danger, I was finally able to relax."

He studied her even more intently. "You are, aren't you? Better, that is?"

She nodded, to then promptly burst into tears.

You can imagine how this went over.

He sent a quick glance over at the door, nervously wondering if he should summon one of the nurses.

Fortunately, there was no need for this. Swiping at the tears with her fingers, Hannah took a deep breath "I'm so sorry. This is something that seems to have become the norm. I start crying and don't know why."

She gestured towards the chair. "Please, sit down. I can't tell you how glad I am you're here. I need to apologize for running out in front of you. I don't know what I was thinking and I can't even imagine what it must have been like for you."

She slowly sank back into the pillows, shaking her head. "Unfortunately, I have no recollection of what happened. I've also lost some of my memory. I've been told it could eventually come back, but there's no promise of when or if this will happen. So, I can't even tell you what made me do something so stupid."

Relieved to actually see her in person, and to know she was okay, he was more than ready to forget she had been the cause of what happened. He shook his head. "It doesn't matter who was at fault. The important thing is that you're going to be okay."

An awkward silence coming between them, he thrust the vase of flowers at her, to then become embarrassed when he saw what a struggle it was for her to hold it. He swiftly took it from her and set it on the table.

This was when he noticed all of the other flowers about the room. "Geeez... I guess you don't really need any more flowers, do you? It's obvious you have a lot of people that care about you."

He shook his head. "Darn... I should have thought of something else to bring, but since I didn't know quite what to expect..."

As his voice died out, Hannah swiftly spoke. "No, no... I love them all. And you didn't have to bring me anything. Coming to see me is more than enough. Truly, it is."

He relaxed at this, slowly sinking into the chair before he gave her, what was finally a genuine smile. "Good, now I know your name is Hannah. But what more can you tell me about yourself?"

He stayed, chatting with her, for almost an hour. During this time, she learned he was in business for himself as an accountant and on the weekends, he enjoyed taking off on his motorcycle with no real destination in mind. Originally from Minnesota, he had moved to Cleveland a little over a year ago and he was still trying to find his way around. But he'd recently bought a condo, which made him feel like everything was finally starting to fall into place.

The more they talked and as he watched Hannah laugh at something he said, he realized how he'd really like to have her as a friend.

Maybe even more than a friend.

This came as a complete surprise to him, because this was not at all what he'd planned. No, his intention had only been to stop in, make sure she was okay and then leave. He had certainly never thought he'd want to get to know her better.

Come on... you can't seriously think she'd be the type who'd want to go riding across the country with you on the back of your bike.

Not after she'd gone through the experience of being mowed down by one.

He almost laughed out loud at the craziness of this. Then he was frowning. Maybe this was a sign it was time for him to get rid of the bike?

Yeah, maybe you need to grow up and start driving a vehicle like everyone else. A pick-up. Yeah, a red one... with all the extras. You could go for one of those.

As soon as these thoughts popped into his head, he knew it was time for him to leave.

Sell his motorcycle?

Where the hell had that come from? And wasn't it a little too soon to be thinking about any kind of relationship with Hannah?

What about that cute girl you've had your eye on? The girl who works at Café Latte? Admit it... lately your trips there for coffee have been more of an excuse to see her. Because there's something about her...

Confused, he looked down at his watch before he abruptly stood, sending her a smile. "I should leave. You need to rest and I have a meeting I need to be at in about twenty minutes. But why don't we exchange phone numbers and I'll give you a call in a couple of days to see how you're doing? I want to keep in touch." Suddenly anxious they do this, he picked up her phone from the table. "Is this your phone?"

Hannah watched as he added his number to her phone. Then, after another promise he would be calling, he left.

For a few moments, she stared at the empty doorway. Was he only trying to be nice? Or did he really want to get to know her better?

Come on... seriously? Look at you... all bruised and banged up.

How was it, with the condition she was in, she was suddenly a woman of interest? Not only one, but two very attractive and available men? If someone had ever told her this was going to happen, she would've told them they were crazy.

She glanced around the room. It was like a garden, almost every available space taken up by the many flower arrangements and gifts she'd received.

She smiled. Mike, or Michael, was right, there were a lot of people who cared about her. And now, finally realizing this, she felt totally overwhelmed by the outpouring of love and concern.

Suddenly her aches and pains didn't seem all that bad. Yes, she wasn't too happy about this memory loss thing, but she would get through it. Like Sophie said, they were a family of fighters, ready to weather every storm.

As she watched the snow falling outside her window, she realized there was only one more thing she needed to make everything feel right.

This would be Sean.

Little did Hannah know, he was on his way to her room at this very moment.

In fact, he passed by Michael Stewart as he got off the elevator, where they greeted each other with a smile and a nod.

Whistling as he made his way down the hall, he was carrying two cups of coffee from Café Latte, along with a bag holding two of the banana muffins Hannah liked so much.

His hope was she was feeling better, maybe even enough to go home tomorrow.

When Hannah heard Sean greeting one of the nurses outside in the hall, she couldn't have stopped the smile that spread across her face even if she'd tried.

It became even bigger when he walked into the room.

At this unexpected greeting, Sean paused for a moment to study her, comforted by the feeling that always came over him when he was with her. That everything was as it should be.

It appeared things were looking up.

So, the smile he gave her was just a bright.

CHAPTER 11

You're my one last chance. The one I thought I'd never have.
~ Anonymously Yours

Sam Bridges was suddenly wide awake.

Confused, because he was pretty sure he hadn't been asleep for all that long, he turned and reached for Livy.

She wasn't there.

Ah... you should've known this is why you woke out of a sound sleep. You're so attuned to her, you sense the instant she's gone. Even now, it seems, when you're asleep.

Scratching his head and giving a big yawn, he sat on the bed for a few minutes before he made his way out of the bedroom and slowly ambled down the hall.

He had a pretty good idea where she was.

Sure enough, he walked into his office to find her sitting at his desk. Her attention completely focused on her computer screen, she didn't even notice he was there.Crossing his arms over his chest, he cleared his throat.

Startled, she jerked her head in his direction, her eyes going wide. This was followed by a very hesitant, if not suspiciously guilty, smile.

"Hi…"

Slowly shaking his head, he walked around the desk and moving behind her, he began massaging her shoulders. "Baby, what are you doing? Please don't tell me you're checking on wedding things again."

She leaned back into his hands and closing her eyes, a long, almost purring-like sigh came from her. "*Oh my,* that feels so good."

She was stalling, because she really didn't want to answer him. Checking 'wedding things' was exactly what she was doing.

So, it was best if she ignored his question. "Seriously, you could do this forever."

"Don't even think about it, because I'm not." He was trying not to smile. He knew exactly what she was doing, he always did. She was trying to change the subject. So, he made every attempt to sound stern. "Because, right now, you're going to shut off the computer and come back to bed."

But he was still massaging her shoulders. Because, let's face it, he really couldn't deny her anything, no matter what it was. If it were possible, he'd give her the world and everything in it.

Twice.

He gave a long and very drawn out sigh. "I woke up because I sensed you weren't in bed with me and when this happens, it appears I can't sleep."

He deepened the massage. "I need my sleep, baby. I've got a big day tomorrow, jam-packed with meetings. This was something I set up so I could get everything finished before the wedding and our honeymoon."

His hands had now moved down to gently massage her arms. "You should be sleeping, too. You're going to drive yourself crazy with this wedding. Remember? It's supposed to be the happiest day of our lives and no matter what happens, everything is going to be perfect, I promise you this."

He lowered his head, his lips pressing a slow kiss to her shoulder. Moving in a slow trail up her neck, his mouth finally came to hover over hers, the warmth of his breath brushing against her lips. "You want to be awake for all of that, don't you?"

When she gave a slow nod, her head falling back to give him better access to her mouth, he gave her a lingering kiss, following this with a smile.

"I thought so. I want that, too. I also know what I don't want, and this is you on the verge of passing out from exhaustion. Not when you'll finally be my wife."

Her lashes fluttering open, her eyes met his and suddenly she didn't care about the fact there was only a little over a week until their wedding and they still hadn't settled on the final menu. Or received a call back from the florist. Or even that the seating arrangements for the reception weren't yet to her liking.

He was right… she was worrying too much, when all that really mattered, was the two of them… and that they were getting married.

And right at this moment? What mattered was him. And how it would be really nice if he would kiss her again.

This is what he always does to you. That expression about being putty in someone's hands? When he comes at you the way he did just now, this definitely applies to you.

As though he could sense what she was thinking, he reached over to put his hand on hers, pressing them down and together to close the computer. "And no… I am not going to kiss you again, not until we're back in our bed."

He proceeded to pull her out of the chair, his voice becoming even deeper. "But I promise, now that I'm awake, when I do kiss you, it will be more than enough to make you to forget all about whatever you were looking up on your computer."

Livy was smiling as she let him lead her down the hall and into their bedroom.

Putty?

Seriously… this fit her to a tee.

After a long and leisurely stretch, Livy gave a contented sigh.

She pressed a quick kiss to the corner of Sam's mouth.

He smiled, his hand drifting down over the silky smoothness of her skin to pull her closer. He never tired of having her next to him like this after they made love. Everything about her was intoxicating, this intimacy they shared even more so.

His voice was deep, most decidedly sexy, she'd have to say. "I take back what I said. I don't need sleep. Not when I have you."

Pressing a kiss to the top of her head, the tone of his voice became serious. "But you need to stop with the wedding stuff, okay?"

She burrowed her face in his chest. "I know. I'm sorry. I never thought I'd turn into one of these crazy and over-the-top brides, but look at me…" She gazed up at him. "But, to give me credit, when you came into the office, I was trying to rearrange the seating for the reception."

She hesitated, a worried expression on her face. "I'm worried about Hannah and Sean. Sophie told me Hannah might be going home tomorrow, but she still hasn't regained all of her memory. So, I want to make sure to seat them at a table she'll feel comfortable."

She sighed. "Poor Hannah… when she came to the bridal shower, she was so excited about Sean coming back to Cleveland. Then this accident happened…"

Sam was trying really hard to listen to what she was talking about. And yes, he also felt bad for Hannah. But right now, it was a struggle to even keep his eyes open. He had told Livy this was because she made him feel so relaxed when they were wrapped up in each other's arms like this. She had him cruising on a whole different level, not a care in the world. Loving everything and everyone he knew.

Starting with her… always with her.

He didn't even try to hide his huge yawn. "Sean will be there and I'm sure he'll take good care of her. And if they can get through this, well… they'll be able to tackle anything that shows up in their future. Look at what we went through and we're still together, stronger than ever." He leaned in to give her a kiss. "Only eight and a half more days, baby."

She sighed against him. "I know… I can't wait. Love you."

Already almost asleep, his response was barely a mumble. "Love you, too…"

Closing her eyes, Livy was smiling as she drifted off to sleep.
Like him, she slept so much better when he was with her.
Seriously, it all came back down to that theory.
You know… the one about putty.

CHAPTER 12

Soulmates...
Two halves of the same soul.
Joined together in life's journey.
~ Anonymous

*H*annah was going home.

Yes, after a three day stay in the hospital, she was more than ready. But if she were honest, she'd admit she was also a bit apprehensive, wondering if she was really up for this.

What if once she was in her condo, nothing looked familiar? She knew she was an artist, that she illustrated books. Thank goodness, this she remembered. But for the life of her, she couldn't remember what it was she was working on right now.

Or if she was working on anything at all.

Maybe once you're home, everything will make sense? Yeah, you just need to wait and see.

Now sitting on her hospital bed, this was just one of the many worries occupying her mind. When she should instead be listening to the list of instructions the doctor was checking off as he read them from his clip board.

She was trying to give him her full attention, she really was. She had heard him say she wasn't to take any trips alone, to the grocery store or any other place she frequented, even if she thought it was familiar to her.

There was also the subject of driving... this definitely not an option. She shouldn't even think of driving a car for at least a week, or more.

And, finally, the doctor couldn't seem to stress this enough... it was imperative she had someone stay with her until she felt comfortable being alone.

But as much as Hannah knew all of this was very important, she now had even more of a reason for her lack of concentration. Sean had come to stand by the door to her room. After he sent her a smile, followed with a wink, he remained where he was, listening to the doctor.

You can imagine the effect this had on Hannah. He was suddenly all she was aware of, all she could think about. Everything and anything else had flown right out the window.

It certainly didn't help every time she chanced a glance in his direction, she was caught right up in his gaze. This invariably having him to send her another one of those smiles he was so good at.

His smile is going to be the death of you. I'll bet this is what attracted you to him in the first place.

There was also the intoxicating scent of leather and the outdoors that always announced his presence. She'd swear it had traveled all the way across the room, sending her an invitation to draw in a long, deep breath to take it all in.

She closed her eyes and proceeded to do just that.

"Hannah... are you still with me here? Or, are you having trouble concentrating?"

Her lashes flying open, she sent the doctor a guilty smile. "I'm sorry... I guess...well, I guess I still find this all so overwhelming But I'm sure I'll be fine."

By the skeptical glance he sent her, it was obvious the doctor wasn't as confident as she was.

He frowned, peering at her over the rim of his glasses. "I hope you've arranged for someone to drive you home? You do realize we can't release you if you don't have a designated driver. You'll also need someone to stay with you once you're settled in. I can't emphasize this enough. Right now, you may feel you're up to the challenge, but you need someone to fall back on until you're comfortable on your own."

He slipped his pen in the breast pocket of his white coat and gave her a very serious look. "Memory loss can be tricky and isn't something to be taken lightly. Think of it as a puzzle, with you still searching for that last piece to finish it off."

Shaking his head, he chuckled after he said this, obviously pleased with his analogy.

Before she could even open her mouth to respond, you guessed it, Sean sauntered casually into the room to answer for her. "I can take Hannah home. I'd be more than happy to do this."

His gaze swiftly shifted over to her. "If she's okay with this, of course."

His relief apparent, the doctor turned to Hannah. "Well, it looks like this may be the solution we're all looking for, as this young man seems more than willing to take you on. If you're agreeable with this, we can get everything set up and you'll be out of here in no time."

Hannah gazed curiously over at Sean. "Are you sure you want to do this? You must have better things to do than watch over me."

Sean took a few moments to think this over before he shook his head. "No, I'd honestly have to say I don't. Not a darn thing. I've already stopped by the ballpark to make sure everything is in order as far as my status with the team. I even worked out at the gym while I was there. But besides that? Nope… I'm at your service, ma'am."

His hand going up to tip his hat, this was when he remembered his decision not to wear it until Hannah was his again.

The brief thought popped in his mind… maybe the hat could be instrumental in making this happen? A visual reminder of sorts. Tucking away this information for later, he slowly lowered his hand, his gesture now more of a salute.

Hannah wasn't sure about Sean's offer. He seemed hesitant.

"Maybe I should check with Sophie first. She might be disappointed if I didn't ask her to take me home."

You know darn well this is as far from the truth as you can get. If anything, she'll be thrilled with Sean's offer.

She sent him a smile. "Not that I don't appreciate the offer, but…"

A brief flash of disappointment crossing his face, he nodded. "Sure, I understand. But I'll wait here until you talk to Sophie. She's on her way as we speak."

Ready to move on to his next patient, the doctor cleared his throat. Once he had their attention, he began making his way to the door. "It sounds like you have options. As soon as you decide what to do, let the head nurse know your plans."

He smiled over at Hannah. "I must say, Hannah, it looks like you had a guardian angel watching over you. Or you were the recipient of a miracle with the way things turned out. Remember, if you have any unusual headaches or dizziness, go to the emergency room as soon as you can."

He nodded over at Sean. "Take good care of her, okay?"

Whipping his phone out of his pocket, he was out the door before she or Sean could even respond.

Sean sat next to the bed. Slowly stretching out his legs and casually crossing his ankles, he proceeded to study her. He didn't say a single word.

After what felt like an unusually long time, too long in fact, Hannah sent him a nervous smile.

He smiled in return, the tenderness in his voice enough to majorly alter the beat of her heart. "You're looking much better. Not that you looked bad… I don't think that could be possible. But with your bruises starting to fade and the color coming back in your face, you're looking like the Hannah I remember. Scrapes and all."

He gave her that devastating grin of his, the corner of his eyes crinkling in agreement. "You, Hannah Michaels, look like a prize fighter that won the final match. With flying colors."

Her fingers slowly creeping up to her cheeks, for a few moments, they didn't move, their eyes locked. Then, even though up until now she'd been able to keep her emotions from getting the best of her, this is exactly what happened.

She burst into tears. And these were no ordinary tears. No, it was as though the floodgates had been flung open. She seriously wanted to lay her head down on the bed until she had exhausted every single tear she was holding inside.

A look of panic on his face, Sean hitched his chair closer to the bed. He was also confused.

What brought this on? Was it what you said? She had to know you were kidding, didn't she?

This was the last thing he'd wanted to happen. He never wanted to see her cry, least of all, because the tears had been brought on by him.

He reached for her hand. "Oh, no, no… I didn't mean what I said in a bad way. I was only teasing, Darlin'. Honest."

She lifted her head, her expression one of such sadness. "Darlin'?"

He was filled with the sudden urge to tip her face up to his and kiss every single one of her cuts and bruises. And her mouth… definitely, he would kiss her mouth. If only to give her the proof she needed to know how beautiful she was.

He wanted that rush that hit him when they'd shared a kiss in the past, the feeling that everything was right in his world.

In their world…

Yeah, he'd even go as far to say they were, what the hell was it they called it?

Soulmates?

Yep… this is what they were… *soulmates.*

Proof of this went all the way back to the phone calls they shared while he was gone. He'd swear he actually felt the vibes traveling through the lines between them.

Yeah, he knew this sounded darn-right-crazy. But he liked it.

He smiled, reaching over to wipe away her tears with a quick swipe of his thumb. "Yeah… about darlin'… this was something that happened right after we met. I don't know how I came up with this, or why. It was a spur of the moment kind of thing that just seemed so right. If you'd rather I didn't call you this, I understand."

She shook her head, a stray tear slipping down her cheek "No, don't stop. Maybe… just maybe, it will register somehow in my mind… help me remember."

She sighed in frustration. "I feel so bad that you've been so nice, bringing gifts, the coffee and muffins from Café Latte and even taking time to stay and keep me company. And I still can't remember you. Yet at the same time, there's something I can feel, but can't seem to get within my grasp." Searching his face, hers was desperate. "If I could, maybe everything would fall back into place. At least with you…"

He was silent. Then, reaching out to gently cup her chin in his hand, he tipped her face to his. He was smiling as he brushed his mouth over hers, his words a whisper. "I have an idea. Let's try this."

His tongue gently parting her lips, his kiss was gentle, searching.

For Hannah, this brought on a kaleidoscope of feelings. Some were new, while at the same time, there was something so familiar about the way his mouth felt on hers, suggesting this was not the first time they'd shared a kiss like this. Suddenly desperate for more, she leaned in closer to keep the kiss going.

When he finally drew back, it was to see her eyes were still closed, her lips parted. He cleared his throat. "So… did that help?"

At the deep huskiness of his voice, her lashes slowly fluttered open to find she was looking right into his eyes. A tiny smile curved her lips. "I'm not quite sure… maybe we could try it…"

The words weren't even out of her mouth before his mouth descended on hers once again. And this time, his kiss went deeper, with just a hint of passion… just enough to send a shudder through her. Her hands drifting up his arms, she sighed against his mouth.

"Hannah? Sean?"

Abruptly pulling apart, they glanced over at the entrance of the room to see Sophie standing there, her arms crossed and an amused expression on her face. Flashing a big grin, she casually sauntered over to them. "Well, hi there... I can't tell you how relieved I am to see the two of you seem to be getting along. "

She turned to Hannah. "Does this mean you're getting that feeling back? Finding a connection? Or, better yet, is your memory starting to kick in?"

The heat rising in her cheeks, Hannah shrugged, nonchalantly combing invisible tangles from her hair with her fingers.

But Sophie wasn't fooled by this.

And Sean?

Slowly coming to his feet, there was a huge grin on his face. "Hey, Sophie... good morning. And in answer to your question, I believe Hannah and I are doing just fine."

Sophie nodded. "This is good to hear. I just talked to the doctor and he told me you offered to take Hannah home and even stay with her for a while?"

His gaze going to Hannah, he reached over to tuck a stray strand of hair behind her ear before he turned to smile at Sophie. "Yeah, I'm pretty sure I almost have her convinced this would be a good idea."

Sophie sighed... it was a huge sigh. "You can't even imagine how relieved I am to hear this. Because as we speak, Chester is outside waiting in the SUV. He has two whiny and sad little guys with him. Trevor and Hudson woke up this morning with fevers and judging by the way they've been acting, they're feeling quite miserable."

She gave them a stricken look. "I hope they didn't pass it on to you. They were fine when I brought them the other day."

She made a face. "This is what I was talking about before. This is the real story when it comes to twins... they share everything. Even more so when it comes to what you don't want them to share. Like getting sick."

Sean shook his head. "It's settled then. You need to be with your two little guys. I know how it is with kids. My brother Ryan's little girl Carly, who just turned three, will only settle for her mum and dad when she's not feeling well. So, I'll be more than happy to take Hannah home."

He waved his hand towards the door. "Go... we'll be perfectly fine.

And if something comes up and we need your help, we know how to reach you."

It was more than obvious Sophie was eager to get back to her family as, thanking them over and over again, she began inching her way towards the door. Ignoring the desperate expression on Hannah's face, she sent a quick wave before she slipped out of the room.

Sean glanced over at Hannah. From what he could see, she wasn't too happy about this latest development. "Hey, are you okay with this? I don't want you to feel pressured. But you do need someone to take you home and right now, I seem to be the best choice." He grinned. "If not the only choice."

She sighed. "I really don't have much of a say, do I?" Immediately realizing how ungrateful this sounded, she sent him a quick glance. "What I mean, it's obvious I need help. And you're here... so..." She shrugged.

Well, this certainly hadn't come out any better, had it?

She nervously began smoothing the blanket across her knees. "I guess I should be thanking you..."

Or maybe it would be better if you just closed your mouth and said nothing at all?

After a few moments of silence, she sneaked a glance over at him. He was studying her, a bemused smile on his face.

How surprised she would've been, if not completely flabbergasted, had she known what he was thinking.

And what exactly was going on in Sean's mind right now?

He had definitely gone off on a whole different train of thought. Truth be told, he was in the midst of a revelation.

Yeah, he'd admit, somewhere in the back of his mind, he'd been slowly gearing up for this to happen. But at the same time, he hadn't been quite ready to put himself out there

But now? The same Sean Young who had so recently vowed he was done with women altogether, had now joined that select group who were lucky enough to find the woman of their dreams. The woman they planned to share the love of a lifetime.

Yep, he was definitely in love... a no fooling around, no holds barred kind of love. If he could, he'd yell it from the rooftops for everyone to hear.

Ah... but there was a slight problem. Hannah didn't seem to be on the same page. At least not the Hannah who was with him now.

That time will come. Again, you only need to be patient.

Buoyed by these thoughts, he came to his feet. His hands shoved in his pockets, he cleared his throat. "Whatever you want, I'm here for you. You just name it, and it's yours, okay? But if you'd rather I leave, I'll take off."

He'd take off?

Of course, Hannah didn't want this. Because, even though she tried to convince herself this was only because he was her ticket out of the hospital, she knew she was in denial.

If he's not here, you can't stop thinking about him. It feels right when he's with you and wrong when he's not. And none of this was making sense.

But then she was beginning to think nothing in her life was ever going to be normal again.

She sighed. "Okay. Hopefully, I'll be able to pay you back in some way."

His lips twitched in a smile at the hopeless tone of her voice. "There's no need for that, darlin'. After all, we did agree to be friends. And this is what friends do."

He reached over, gently nudging her jaw with his knuckles "Chin up, okay? Soon, this will all be behind you."

"Hello there... I heard the good news. So, I'm here to help you get ready to go home."

This cheerful greeting came from Ruby, Hannah's favorite nurse on the floor. After she and Sean shared a few words, he turned to leave. "I'll leave you to do your thing while I camp out in the visitors lounge. Let me know when Hannah is ready to leave."

He reached up to tip his hat to Hannah. And just as quickly, he dropped his hand to his side when he remembered he wasn't wearing it.

Confusion flitted across Hannah's face. There was something so familiar about his gesture, but before she could get it to pop up in her mind, as with every time before, it disappeared.

Ruby watched Sean send one last glance over at Hannah before he left. She laughed, shaking her head. "Girl, you have hit the mega jackpot with that one. I don't think he could be any more obvious about how he feels about you. He's a man in love. As my mama would say, he's wearing his heart on his sleeve for everyone to see."

Hannah stared at her in disbelief. "In love? You think he's in love with me? Oh no, I don't think so. He's just being nice."

Ruby nodded, slowly. "*Hmm...* you think he's just being nice? *Noooo way...* I'm sorry, but I'm thinking you getting all banged up like you did, you're still not thinking clearly. If a man ever looked at me the way your man looks at you, I'd marry him in an instant. Before someone else came along and grabbed him up. He's a keeper, that's for sure."

She studied Hannah before she grinned, shaking her head. "Why is it, we can never see what's right in front of our nose?"

Hannah didn't have an answer to this.

Her man? In love?

Ruby was imaging things.

CHAPTER 13

It was mid-afternoon before Hannah was finally released from the hospital.

Now unlocking her front door and walking into her condo, she wanted to get down on her knees and kiss the floor in relief. This would be the same laminated floor she'd hated ever since she purchased the condo two years ago.

But now? To her, they looked absolutely beautiful.

This was how happy she was to be home.

She was so thankful everything looked familiar. She couldn't even begin to explain how she worried she was it would be like walking into a home that belonged to someone else.

She wandered into the kitchen and stopping to finger the drawing supplies spread out over the table, she gave a sigh of relief. She recognized one of the drawings, a character illustration in a series she'd been illustrating for an author for the past four years.

Finally, some of the tension in her shoulders begin to fade.

Standing back, Sean watched all of this, not quite sure what he should be doing. His hands stuffed in his jean pockets, his expression remained cautious as she'd picked up one of the drawings. It was only when she placed it back on the table, he moved closer.

He cleared his throat. "So… what's the verdict?"

She spun around… well, let it be noted this was more of a slow twist. Any fast move of any kind was still enough to make her feel like she might pass out from the pain.

She sent him a hesitant smile. "These drawings look familiar, at least I can relate to them. I know I'm the person who did the artwork and I recognize the characters in the drawings."

She then went on to search his face. Intently studying his features, her smile slowly faded. "But I still can't place you. What I mean… I see you only as the person I just met for the first time in the hospital." She gazed around the room. "I feel like you've never been here. And you would think I'd remember something like this, wouldn't you?"

Her eyes began to tear up. "I thought maybe… well, that you—"

He swiftly interrupted her. "I don't think you should start worrying about that just yet. You don't want to put too much pressure on yourself. Let everything come back on its own."

Even though he smiled when he said this, he was having a hard time hiding his disappointment. Like her, he'd hoped once she was in the familiar surroundings of her condo, more of her memories would pop up.

When he saw her bottom lip had begun to quiver, he gave her a big grin. "Come on, you're home. If nothing else, this is a reason to celebrate, no?"

When her only response was a brief nod, he made his way into the kitchen, where he began rummaging through the cupboards. "First things first… I'm going to make some coffee. Then we'll figure out what to do about dinner. I don't know about you, but I'm starting to get hungry."

Grateful for the distraction, Hannah began clearing away the drawings and markers. Picking up one of the finished illustrations, she studied it. This is when the reality of what she was up against began to sink in.

What's going to happen if you can't do this anymore? This is all you know.

She shakily began gathering up the markers, only to throw them back down on the table. Abruptly wrapping her arms tightly around herself, the look on her face was desperate.

For a few moments, she didn't say anything. Then, dragging her hands through her hair, she gave a frustrated sigh. "I'm going to take a shower. And wash my hair. Maybe then I'll feel better."

He nodded. "I'll tell you what… while you do that, I'll go pick up some groceries. Your refrigerator is pretty empty."

He hesitated, to then send her a teasing grin. "About the only thing I found of interest is a box of Sweet Abby's salted caramel brownies. Which I must say, are my favorite." He shook his head. "But like banana muffins, you can't live on brownies alone."

He didn't tell her about the card tucked under the string tied around the box. With a message from Abby.

Special Order for Hannah's Sean
One half-dozen Salted Caramel Brownies

Almost holding his breath, he waited for Hannah's reaction, hoping…

But, after sending him a puzzled glance, she shrugged. "Sophie must have left them there when she stopped by to pick up something for me to wear home from the hospital. They're your favorite? Well, you're more than welcome to have some."

And now it was Sean who was frustrated. Almost angrily, with the promise he wouldn't be gone long, he left. Resisting the urge to slam the door behind him.

Leaving her staring after him, wondering if she had said something wrong.

During his drive to the grocery store, Sean did a lot of thinking.

Along with throwing out a lot of silent, and sometimes not so silent, advice to himself. He'd liken this to his version of a pep talk. At the same time, he tried to remind himself he should be more than happy with how everything had progressed so far.

Patience… patience… patience…

Yeah, you keep telling yourself that. Everything is going to be okay. After all, it's been only three days since her accident.

He was strolling aimlessly up and down the aisles of the grocery store, tossing whatever caught his eye into his cart, when he was approached by two extremely excited and giggling teenagers. They immediately began telling him all about how they played softball for the local high school.

After smiling for way too many group selfies with them, waiting patiently until they finally found one they agreed on, he meandered over to the checkout counter.

There he observed the elderly couple ahead of him in line. Arguing good-naturedly about the man's precise arrangement of items on the counter, they reminded him of his grandparents.

He wondered… would he and Hannah be lucky enough to grow old together like this couple?

He shook his head, a wry smile on his face.

Umm… first things first… you're getting way ahead of yourself here.

Hannah had to remember who he was before there was even a chance of this happening.

Sean was greeted with the sound of music when he walked into Hannah's condo. His arms loaded with bags, along with the largest bouquet of flowers he could find, he smiled when he recognized the song playing was an instrumental version of a song from a Disney movie.

He paused to listen.

> *So, this is love… and now I know,*
> *the key to heaven is all mine…*

Yep, he knew this one. He was pretty sure it was from Cinderella. And heaven? Yeah, he could agree with that…

Not that he was what you would call a Disney fan. No, he was more into country music. But since his niece Carly had come along, he'd listened to his share of Disney songs, Cinderella one of her favorites.

Humming along with the music, he put the groceries away before searching the cupboards for a vase. Since Hannah had left all of the arrangements she'd received in the hospital with the nurses and other patients, he'd decided she deserved a new bouquet, just for her.

The flowers arranged to the best of his ability, he saw she'd left BooBear on the counter. A smile coming over his face, he picked up the bear and silently made his way down the hall to peek into her bedroom.

Hannah was curled up on the bed and fast asleep. He covered her with the quilt he found at the foot of the bed and after tucking the stuffed bear next to her, he headed for the door.

"Sean?"

He turned to see her eyes were open. Making his way back to the bed, he smiled down at her. "Yes, ma'am?"

She smiled at this. "Thank you." Briefly closing her eyes, she gave a long sigh. "I'm so sorry. I've ruined everything, haven't I? Your homecoming… everything. I still can't believe I did something so incredibly stupid."

Carefully sitting on the edge of the bed, he reached over to tuck a strand of her still damp hair behind her ear. The tenderness in his gaze was enough to make her close her eyes.

He sighed. "Darlin' open your eyes… I want you to look at me."

After she did as he asked, he cleared his throat. "You didn't mess up anything. Like I told you before, this will all eventually become only a memory. Just think of it as a minor setback in our… uh, your life."

A smile lit up his face. "Think of it as a January to remember. Why, it's as if you've been given a second chance. With me right here by your side, hopefully making it all worthwhile."

Comforted by what he said, she watched as he slowly gazed around the room, pausing to linger on a dress that was hanging on her closet door.

This reminded Sean of the dinner he'd promised her, celebrating his return to Cleveland. He wondered if this was the dress she'd told him about in one of the many phone conversations they'd shared.

The dress she'd chosen to wear for this dinner.

His hand moving to cover hers, he nodded over at the dress. "I'm thinking that dress is hanging there for a reason? Could it be the dress you'd planned to wear for the dinner I'd promised you?"

She sighed. "I don't know. I don't remember it. Nor do I know why it's hanging there."

She looked so sad, he gently squeezed her hand. "Well, I have a feeling it is. You told me it was blue and this dress is definitely blue, so it all adds up."

He gave a deep sigh. "I was so looking forward to taking you out on an honest-to-goodness date. A *real* date."

She was puzzled. "A real date?"

He didn't respond right away. It always took him a few seconds to clear his head of the fact she couldn't remember what was still so clear in his mind.

Again, patience....

He smiled. "Yeah... we never really had, what I guess you'd call, an official date."

Slowly shaking his head, he chuckled. "No, we did things the hard way, it seems. All of these chance meetings, only to lose track of each other, all over again. So, the last time we were together, the night of Chester and Sophie's barbecue, I told you I wanted to take you out to dinner, wherever you wanted to go. Unfortunately, it was the next day I found myself on a plane back to Australia."

He was silent for a few moments, his thoughts going back to that time. "Yeah... not only was I was worried about my father, I was also upset I was leaving you. This made the flight feel a hell of a lot longer than usual. But it was in one of our phone calls, I told you our dinner plans would still stand when I returned. So, as soon as I reserved my return flight, we picked a date. This would've been last night."

He glanced once more at the dress. "It would be such a shame if you didn't get to wear the dress, because I can already imagine how beautiful you'll look."

He tilted his head, searching her face. "Now there's no reason we can't pick a new date for dinner. It might even be a good way for us to get to know each other again, shake up some of your memory."

It was the wistful expression on his face that had her nodding. "I guess we could give it a try." Realizing how awful this sounded, she quickly added, "I mean, yes. We could do that."

She suddenly smiled. "Like you said, it would be a shame not to wear the dress."

He chuckled and after pressing a quick kiss to her cheek, he stood. "A terrible thing, indeed. But now, I'm going to let you get some sleep. I'll just hang around, watch some TV, check my emails, whatever. If you need anything, just call me. I'm not planning on going anywhere."

At the door, he turned to her. For one long moment, their eyes held, an uncertainty hovering between them.

She wanted so badly to ask him to stay, even if only until she fell asleep. But she couldn't get up the nerve to do this. The words wouldn't come.

While he was wondering what she would say if he offered to stay, at least until she fell asleep.

He hesitated, waiting….

But a smile was all she gave him.

So, he left.

It was when Hannah adjusted the quilt, she found Boo-Bear.

Keep on believing,
and the dream you wish will come true.

When she finally fell asleep, there was a smile on her lips.

After finally finding a comfortable position on the sofa, Sean turned on the TV. But his heart wasn't in it. He turned down the volume, staring at the silent screen.

He sent a quick glance over at Hannah's bedroom door. Maybe he should check on her, just to make sure she was okay?

What if she needed something? Like a glass of water or something.

For heaven's sake... what's wrong with you? You left her only about ten minutes ago. She's fine. She's not a child.

He rested his head back against the cushions and stared up at the ceiling. It was only right to be concerned. Need he have to remind you she was hit by a motorcycle?

He knew damn well it wasn't his imagination she seemed so lost, looking to him for help. And the kind and compassionate person he was, of course he wanted to be there for her. If only to make the confusion disappear from her eyes.

Yeah, he'd simply hold her in his arms until she fell asleep. That's all, nothing more.

Hmm... you're getting ahead of yourself again, buddy...

But when he had started to leave the room, he'd swear she was about to ask him to stay. He'd even hesitated for a second or two, hoping this would happen.

But, no such luck...

After one more glance back at her bedroom and giving a long, frustrated sigh, he began flipping through the channels again, finally settling on a basketball game.

Only a few minutes later, he dozed off.

It had been a long day.

It was the loud rumbling of the snowplow that woke Hannah.

She opened her eyes, and for a few seconds, she thought she was still in the hospital. Relieved to find she was in her own bed, she glanced over at the clock on the nightstand to see it was six-fifteen.

She closed her eyes and burrowed back under the quilt. It was early, she didn't have to get up yet.

Her lashes flying open, she was suddenly wide awake.

Wait a minute... six-fifteen in the morning... or six-fifteen in the evening?

She slipped out of bed and pulled aside the window shade. Even though everything was still shrouded in darkness because of the heavy cloud cover, she could see the sky was beginning to lighten in the horizon, signaling the arrival of a new day.

From the deep layer of snow now covering everything in sight, it had obviously been snowing all through the night.

She watched the snowplow make another sweep over the parking lot before she glanced back at the clock. How was it possible she'd slept for over twelve hours?

This was when she remembered Sean.

Oh, no... Sean... Was he even still here?

Refusing to look in the mirror, because she certainly didn't need to be reminded about the sad condition of her face, she pulled a brush through her hair.

She glanced down at her flannel pajamas… should she change into something else?

You're crazy. He's not going to care. And what exactly would you wear? The dress hanging on your closet door?

After a quick spray of perfume and a feeble attempt to smooth the wrinkles out of her tee shirt, she cautiously made her way into the living room. There she found the TV tuned into a sports channel, the volume barely audible.

And, just as he'd promised, Sean was still there. Stretched out on the sofa, he appeared to be sound asleep. His arm was flung across his forehead, the remote clutched in his hand.

Silently making her way over to the sofa, she carefully eased the remote from his hand and turned off the TV. After she set the remote on the coffee table, she turned to see his eyes were open and he was watching her.

Sean had felt Hannah's presence almost immediately, the familiar scent of her perfume nudging his senses.

For him, it had been a long night, broken up only by a visit from Chester shortly after Hannah had fallen asleep.

Sean had opened the door to find him standing on the front steps, holding a huge box. He had come bearing food from his Aunt

Evelyn… a hell of a lot of food. Sean would swear there was enough to feed a dozen people, or more.

After Chester left, the remainder of the night had been pretty uneventful.

After all, a man can only watch so much TV.

So now, when Hannah turned back to him and before she even had a clue of what he was planning, he gently pulled her down onto the sofa.

After he carefully tucked her against him, he gave a long, contented sigh. "Well, Hannah Michaels, this is a pleasant surprise. I can't even begin to tell you how glad I am to see you've finally decided to wake up. I swear, I must have checked on you a dozen times and each time, I found you dead to the world."

He nuzzled his face in her hair, taking in a deep breath of the fragrant herbal scent of her shampoo. "But this is good. Sleep is the best possible thing for you. I'm sure you're feeling much better."

Hannah wasn't talking, completely overcome by this sudden closeness between them. And even more so, by him. The deep huskiness of his voice, the hard length of his body fitting so perfectly against hers. The sound of their beating hearts, so close she'd swear she could feel each beat of his. And his scent, that intoxicating combination of leather and spice.

All of this together, and coming at her all at once? Why, no wonder she was speechless.

Slowly exhaling a long, steadying breath, she relaxed against him. Unsure of where to put her hand, she tentatively rested it on his chest.

He responded by reaching over to link her fingers with his.

This was all she needed.

Yep, this did it…she was lost.

Completely.

Cautiously curling in even closer to him and closing her eyes, she was ready to stay right where she was. Heck, she'd stay for as long as he'd let her.

Her move made Sean extremely happy. This was the Hannah he remembered. The Hannah who'd never hesitated to let him how she felt about him. His fingers sifting through her curls, his voice was a low rumble in her ear. "You must be hungry, no?"

She rested her head back against his shoulder to gaze up at him. "I'm starving. I think the only edible food I had while I was in the hospital, were the banana muffins you brought."

He chuckled. "Well, it's nice to know I was appreciated. Proof you need to keep me around, if only to keep you from starving. But you need more than muffins if you want to heal."

He tucked her hair behind her ears, his fingers lingering longer than necessary. There was just something about the silkiness of each curl slipping through his fingers that soothed him.

He cleared his throat. "It appears you're one lucky woman. Very much loved, too. While you were sleeping, Chester stopped by with a ton of food, enough to fee an army. Compliments of his Aunt Evelyn, he said. Pizza… lasagna… homemade bread and some kind of chocolate cake. I think there was even a huge salad in one of the containers."

He grinned. "I had some of the pizza. It was fantastic."

She crinkled up her nose, shaking her head at the mention of salad. For some reason, the last thing she wanted was a salad. If he ate pizza, then she would have the same. She knew it was morning and one didn't normally eat pizza for breakfast, but she didn't care.

"I think I'll have pizza." She gazed up at him to see he was smiling. When he didn't respond, only continued to smile, her features scrunched up in concern.

He chuckled. "You always make me smile when you scrunch your face up like a little kid. It's so easy to tell what's going on in that beautiful mind of yours. But I've told you this before."

Beautiful mind? Hmm... you like the sound of that.

But at the same time, she frowned. Granted, it was nice to know she made him smile. But that he was able to know what she was thinking? This was a little concerning. Especially, since lately, all of her thoughts seemed to be wrapped up with him.

Not quite sure where the frown was coming from, he quickly went on to reassure her. "It's all good, trust me. So, you want pizza? Pizza it will be. You stay right here while I fix a plate for you."

He pulled himself up into a sitting position, removing his arm out from under her. Unfortunately, this sent her sliding right off the sofa. She came down hard on the floor, the impact sending a sharp pain shooting from her bruised ribs and barreling through her like an out of control bus. Or, considering the recent events, an out of control motorcycle might be a better choice of vehicle.

At least this is what it felt like to her.

Only after the worst of the pain had subsided and she was finally able to catch her breath, she glanced up at him.

Sean had dropped to the floor next to her, afraid to even touch her. He was horrified. *"Damn... I'm so sorry. Are you okay?"*

Her smile was wobbly. "I'm okay. I'll be fine."

But this didn't turn out to be entirely true. Because, for some reason, even though this was the last thing she intended, she burst into tears.

"Oh, sweetheart..." He groaned, moving closer. "These tears are telling me you're not okay. Here, let's get you back on the sofa." Mumbling to himself the whole time, mostly about what a klutz he was, he gently lifted her onto the sofa.

He looked so upset, she tried to give him a weak smile. "I'm okay, and I don't know why I'm crying... it just happened. I don't seem to have control over a lot of what I do now... I'm such a mess."

Gently stroking her cheek, he shook his head. "Well, getting dumped on the floor certainly isn't going to help matters."

He stood. "Now, let me go and get that pizza before I do something else to you."

Hannah set her empty plate on the coffee table and leaning back against the sofa cushions, she gave a long, contented sigh.

She smiled at Sean. "That was perfect. I can truly say, it was by far the best breakfast I've ever had."

And this was mostly because of him. Something you should tell him.

"Thank you for sharing with me."

He set his empty plate on top of hers. After all, there was no reason he couldn't have another piece of pizza… or two. As he'd told Hannah earlier, it seemed like he was always hungry.

He smiled over at her. "You'll need to thank Chester's Aunt Evelyn. I'm just the middle man here."

He shrugged. "It's always nice to have someone to share a meal. And I can't think of a single person I'd rather to do this with, than you."

Their eyes meeting, her heart shifted into that ridiculously galloping beat he always seemed to bring on when he made comments like this. And again, caught up in the uncertainty hovering between them, unsure of what was to come next, they were both silent.

He finally gave a slight shake of his head. Abruptly coming to his feet, he took their plates and loaded them in the dishwasher, he came to stand next to her.

Even though this wasn't what he wanted, he needed to leave. She was probably tired of him hanging around. And he was becoming too comfortable being with her. After spending time on the sofa together, holding her in his arms, his thoughts on what he wanted to do and what he should do, had become blurred.

Yep, you need to leave.

He picked up his jacket, glancing over at the window. He cleared his throat. "It looks like the snow has let up a little, so if it's okay with you, I'm going to take off. You'd probably like to have some time to yourself and I have a few things to do."

You're not being truthful here, are you? She only had to say the word and you'd stay. Yeah, you'd be more than willing to do this.

He waited, but she said nothing. So, he decided to give her another chance.

He gave a casual shrug. "I don't want to overstay my welcome."

Unfortunately, these little hints Sean was sending?

Hannah missed them completely.

She was too busy thinking how she had so quickly let herself become so dependent on him and now, the prospect of being on her own seemed so overwhelming.

But she couldn't expect him to stay with her forever. And what could possibly go wrong? It wasn't like she was going to go gallivanting off on her own. With the condition she was in, she couldn't even imagine taking such a risk. For all she knew, she might not be able to find her way back home.

She gave a frustrated sigh.

It's almost like you're a prisoner in your own mind.

"Hannah?"

She gave him a bright smile. "I'll be fine. If I need anything, I know I can always call Sophie. I already feel guilty, having taken so much of your time."

He was next to her in a flash, reaching over to run his fingertips down the side of her face. "Darlin'… I don't mind in the least. You can call me anytime. I'm here for you, even if it's in the middle of the night and you just need to talk. Or you're scared. This is a promise."

He grinned. "Even if it's ten minutes after I leave."

Impulsively, she reached over to give him a hug. He responded with a sharp intake of breath, his hands hovering over her as though he was hesitant to touch her.

It was when he slowly lowered them to his sides, she pulled back, embarrassed. "I'm sorry… I didn't mean…"

He felt like a jerk.

But, give him a break… he was trying so hard to maintain some kind of control. For a brief moment, it felt like everything was back to where it should be… she was the Hannah he remembered. He was so tempted to pull her deeper into his arms and do what he had been wanting to do ever since his plane touched ground in the states.

And this would be to kiss the living daylights out of her. Hell, he'd been dreaming about this since he last kissed her back in June.

But no… right now it would be better if he were to leave.

He sighed, running his hand through his hair. "No worries. You call me anytime, about anything. And I mean this, cross my heart and hope to die."

He started for the door, but when he turned to say one last goodbye, he saw she was smiling at what he'd said.

So, what the hell… he was going to risk it and take things one step further. "Hey, one more thing, about that dinner I promised you. Why don't we plan on Saturday night? This is three days from now and by then, you might welcome a night out. If not, no big deal… we'll just change it to another night."

He smiled. "So, what do you think?"

She didn't even take the time to think about this before she nodded.

And if he wasn't mistaken, her smile became even brighter. But then again, he could be grasping at even the smallest of signs she was coming around.

But hey, for now? He was more than satisfied she'd agreed to dinner.

"Okay, then… it's a date." He winked. "I can't wait to see you in the dress." Continuing on his way to the door, he paused, his intention to tip his hat.

Damn… again, you're not wearing it.

Nope, he was determined to wait for that sign from Hannah.

You know the one… to let him know she was his darlin'…

As he was her one and only cowboy.

After Sean left, Hannah began analyzing almost every single thing he'd said. She was searching for some kind of clue, hoping something would click, sending everything falling into place.

Unfortunately, she got nothing,

So, it looked like she'd have to wait until she saw him again, when they went out to dinner. But first? She needed to take a closer look at that dress.

Within a few minutes, she was holding it up against her, studying her reflection in the mirror.

She wondered… how long had it taken Sophie to convince her this was the dress? Because it certainly didn't seem like a style she'd normally wear. At least not the Hannah she thought she was.

The dress was short. Really short. There also wasn't very much of the rest of it, since it dipped low in the back.

She did a quick search through her closet. There she found every-thing was what she could imagine wearing.

She sent another glance back at the dress.

She didn't understand.

Seriously? What in the world had you been thinking?

At the same time, she couldn't stop thinking about what Sean had said... how he couldn't wait to see her in the dress... that he knew she'd look beautiful.

She sat on the bed, fingering the silky material of the dress.

She did like the color. A deep blue, it fell somewhere between a royal and navy blue. And blue was her second favorite color, right after red.

Her mouth slowly curved into a smile

Soooo... Sean thought she'd look beautiful?

Hmm... she had the dress.

And she definitely had the time.

So, it couldn't hurt to try it on.

CHAPTER 14

*I*t was the night of Hannah's dinner date with Sean. She would be the first to tell you, never in her life...*never*...had she spent so much time getting ready for a date.

Nope, never, ever, ever...

For the past couple of hours, or make that more like since she woke up this morning, she'd been running around in a frenzy.

And what had she accomplished during this time?

Evidently not enough, since you're still not ready.

She glanced over at the clock on her nightstand. Sean would be at her door in about fifteen minutes.

Her back to the mirror, she gazed over her shoulder at her reflection. Was it her imagination, or was the dress getting shorter each time she looked at it? She smoothed it down over her hips, pulling at the skirt of the dress in an attempt to make it longer.

But this only sent the neckline dipping even lower.

Definitely a no-win situation.

She turned, her distraught expression coming right at her.

There is no chance you'll be able to pull this off.

She sighed, extremely frustrated. The only reason she was even wearing the dress was because of Sophie. In fact, she was still smarting from the lecture Sophie had given her.

It was time for her to step out of her comfort zone and quit dressing like an old lady, Sophie had told her. For crying out loud, had she been living under a rock? If not, she would know this dress was conservative compared to what most women wore these days.

You told her you had no desire to step out of your comfort zone. You were perfectly happy with the way you dressed.

Sophie had ignored this, merely shaking her head. Instead she went on to remind her how good she looked in the dress. She looked fantastic, as a matter of fact. And finally, correct her if she was wrong, but hadn't Hannah told her Sean said he couldn't wait to see her in the dress?

So, what more did Hannah need to be convinced this dress was the right choice?

Hannah had no answer to this. And to be honest? She had grown tired of talking about it. From past experience, she knew the chance of winning an argument with Sophie was about one in a billion.

So, here she was… dress on, hair styled and makeup applied. She only had to slip into her shoes, and she would be ready.

Giving a long dramatic sigh, the way she looked at it, she'd given it her best shot.

This didn't stop her from making a mad dash for her closet for one last look. Maybe there was something she missed, a less revealing choice she could change into really fast.

But the sound of the doorbell nixed that possibility.

Darn... didn't that figure.

She gave one last critical look in the mirror. At least there was one positive note. With a little make-up, the bruises and scratches on her face were no longer that noticeable. She looked almost normal.

Whatever was considered normal anymore. Because according to Sophie, you wouldn't know, would you?

She slipped into her heels. After fluffing up her hair and pulling her dress down in one last desperate attempt to make it longer, she took a deep, calming breath.

This was it.

She was as ready as she'd ever be.

Sean had missed the entrance to the parking lot of Hannah's condo. Not once, but twice. This goes to show you the state he had managed to work himself into.

Yes, just what the hell is your problem? You'd think this was the first date you've ever been on.

Yep, he had managed to turn what was usually a fifteen-minute drive, into one more than double that time.

Thank God you'd decided to leave early.

He was nervous. Nervous as all get out.

He didn't know why. He had been perfectly fine all day. It wasn't until he was finally dressed and ready to leave, he'd began to self-doubt every single thing about himself.

Starting with what he was wearing.

He wasn't sure, was he dressed appropriately for the restaurant Hannah had decided on? The last thing he wanted, was to embarrass her with his lack of fashion sense.

Damn...

Back home, he'd never worried about how he dressed. Nope, where he came from, the style of dress was more relaxed. Your newest and cleanest jeans, paired with a nice sweater or shirt, would pass most dress codes of the restaurants he frequented.

When you went to the gym earlier to work out, you should have asked the guys for advice.

Nah... not a good idea. This would have turned into a free-for-all with the comments and razzing.

Again, he did have his pride.

After he had finished getting dressed, he'd studied the result in the mirror. He leaned in closer to get a better look. He turned his head and, running his hand through his hair, this was when he realized he should have sprung for a haircut. His hair was looking a little shaggy, curling over his collar.

Well, this was a hell of a time to start thinking about that, wasn't it?

Frowning into the mirror, he'd adjusted the collar of his sportscoat. After flicking some lint off the sleeve, he'd peered in even closer. Was it his imagination, or did the sleeves look a little too short?

Deciding it might be in his best interest to leave the bathroom before he found something else to criticize, he had gone to get his boots.

This is when some of his confidence made a comeback. He had spent so much time polishing them, he could almost see his reflection in the leather.

They looked good… really good. Made his whole outfit, he'd have to say. This putting him in a much better mood, he had been whistling when he went out to start up his truck.

And now, here he was, finally standing at Hannah's front door.

Combing his fingers through his hair, he adjusted his collar.

He suddenly groaned, slapping his hand to his forehead.

Flowers… when he went to the gym earlier, why hadn't he stopped to pick up a bouquet for Hannah? This would have been a nice touch.

He wanted everything about this night to be perfect, a time they would both look back on and always remember. A story to tell their grandchildren. Proof that true love can overcome anything.

Yeah… even if the one person suddenly doesn't remember who you are.

After he gave a vigorous shake of his head, if only to bring back some of that confidence he'd lost, he took a deep breath.

He had this.

He rang the doorbell.

When Hannah opened the door, Sean was gazing up at the star-studded sky. For a few moments, they both remained silent, taking in the peacefulness that always comes after a fresh snowfall.

Sean would swear there was a feeling of anticipation all around them, the promise of magic in the air.

His gaze scanning the sky, he finally spoke. "Look at all of the stars… millions of them. This reminds me so much of home. There is nothing more beautiful than riding horseback at night through a freshly fallen snow, with only the stars to guide you. Someday, I hope to be able to show you…"

He turned to her, his words fading into silence at the sight of her. His gaze was so intent, she felt like she was being pulled into him.

At the same time, she was gripped by a sudden sadness. What he wanted from her, she wouldn't be able to give him.

This was because nothing had changed… he still hadn't found a way back into her memory.

"Hi…" This came from her in barely a whisper.

He briefly closed his eyes, but not before Hannah saw the flash of disappointment there.

She immediately thought his reaction was because of the dress.

It was all wrong.

You are all wrong. Why didn't you go with your intuition and choose something else?

She glanced down at her dress. After she ran her hands down the skirt in another attempt to make it longer, she anxiously glanced up at him, her words running into each other because of her embarrassment. "The dress is all wrong, isn't it? It's too short and the neckline is too low. I don't know why I agreed to wear it in the first place. But Sophie was so insistent"

She shook her head. "Not that she forced me to wear the dress. No, of course not. And I do trust her judgement. But this was obviously not the best choice for me. So, I was about to change into something else. But then you rang the doorbell and I thought… well, what I mean is, I thought maybe it would turn out okay… I'd be able to carry it off. But, I guess I was wrong."

Her bottom lip beginning to quiver, her next words were barely audible. "If you don't mind waiting a few minutes, I'll go change. It shouldn't take long."

Backing away from him as she spoke, she was trying so hard not to cry.

The fact this hadn't already happened, was anything short of a miracle.

Sean wanted to kick himself.

Seriously... what the hell is wrong with you?

His reaction had nothing to do with the dress.

It was in response to her greeting.

He'd been hoping, just maybe, this date would trigger her memory and she'd slip back into the Hannah he knew. To then go on and greet him the same way she had with every phone call they shared while he was away.

Again, you know the one... where she'd say, "Hey, cowboy..." and he'd answer with, Your one and only, darlin'."

Yeah, he knew the possibility of this happening was probably a billion to one, but he wasn't ready to give up hope it would. This explained why, for about a half of a millisecond, he couldn't hide his disappointment.

And now look what he had done.

In one quick move he swept her into his arms, his groan muffled in her hair. "I am so, so damn sorry. It's not what you think. It's not about the dress. Honest, it's not. I had been hanging on to this crazy hope, when you saw me, everything would come back to you. Me, included."

He pressed a kiss in her hair. "But now it seems I've gone and ruined everything."

Hannah was wondering if a part of what he wanted might actually be happening. What other explanation could there be for how she felt in his arms, everything so right, so familiar.

As though she had been here before.

She relaxed against him and closing her eyes, she became lost in the sound of his husky drawl. "Believe me when I say you look absolutely beautiful. You're perfect… the dress is perfect. Everything about you, is perfect. But I'm not surprised. The moment I saw the dress hanging in your bedroom, I knew you'd rock it."

A slow smile curved her lips.

Rock it? He thinks you rock it? You like the sound of that.

He leaned back to gaze down at her. Even though her eyes were still closed, he was relieved to see the beginning of a smile on her lips. His voice dipping even lower, he gathered her back against him. "I'd be very disappointed if you changed into something else. Because, you… Hannah Michaels, take my breath away. I consider myself a very lucky man to be your date for the evening."

His hands drifted down her back. Because of the low cut of her dress, he came in contact with the smoothness of her skin. It was when a shiver ran through her, he realized they were still outside, standing on the steps.

And it was cold.

Very cold.

Proof of this was the way the snow was sparkling like glitter in the moonlight.

He quickly guided her inside. "What are we doing? You must be freezing. Let's get your coat on you so we can get an official start on this date."

Determined to make her forget their rocky start, he began talking about the evening ahead as he helped her with her coat. "I'm excited. And starving. I can't wait to try the restaurant you decided on."

She looked up at him, a laugh bubbling up in her throat. "You're always starving."

He impulsively pressed a kiss to her cheek. "Yep, this is true. But right now? I'd have to say, what I'm most hungry for, is you."

Their eyes met, for one brief moment he'd swear he saw a flicker of recognition in hers.

And then it was gone.

He leaned in to press another kiss to her cheek. He wasn't going to let this worry him, not yet.

Remember?

Patient…

Yep, he only needed to be patient.

In the parking lot, Sean brought them to a black pick-up truck with a temporary license plate.

It had that shiny, new vehicle look.

He pulled out his keys, setting the lights flashing, the doors unlocking.

He was trying so hard to be casual about this, but failed. After all, he'd wanted a truck like this for the longest time.

Hannah grinned up at him. "Did you just get this?"

He opened the passenger door. "Yep, I did." He gestured to the inside of the truck before offering her his hand. "Your ride awaits, beautiful."

She shook her head. "Sean, I'll never be able to get up there. Not with this dress. Maybe if I had jeans on. Or…"

Her protest was silenced as he scooped her up and dropped her gently on the seat, After he slid into the driver's seat, he grinned over at her. "See, together, there's no problem we can't solve."

As soon as he pulled out of the parking lot, he began talking non-stop. About the restaurant, the conditions of the roads, anything he could think of. Then he fell silent, absentmindedly tapping his fingers on the steering wheel.

She glanced over to see a scowl on his face. This was concerning. Was he was beginning to think this night was a mistake? Something they really weren't ready for?

Umm… maybe you should say something?

She placed her hand on his arm. "Is something wrong?"

The tapping coming to an abrupt halt, at first he didn't answer. Then he shrugged, a wry smile on his face. "I guess I wanted tonight to be perfect. But, I screwed it up right from the start, didn't I?"

He let out a deep sigh. "I wish we could start over again."

She waited until they were stopped at the next light before she held out her hand. "Hi… I don't believe we've met? My name is Hannah Michaels and I illustrate children's books."Her head tilted, she smiled. "I'm curious… are you from around here? Because, by your accent, I suspect you're not."

A smile slowly spreading over his face in response, he took her hand. "I'm so pleased to meet you Hannah Michaels. My name is Sean Young, and just to warn you, I've a tendency to say the wrong things, at the wrong time, on just about every occasion. But if you bear with me, you'll see I always mean well."

He lifted her hand to his mouth, pressing a kiss to her fingers. "And no… I'm not from around here. I came to the states to play baseball for as long as they let me. But I'm thinking I could very easily be persuaded to stay here for even longer. Suddenly this town is beginning to look like a place I'd like to settle down."

Settle down? Is he telling you this for a reason? Or again, are you reading too much into his words?

Her gaze caught up in his, she wondered what he would do if she leaned over to kiss him. Of course, this would only be a simple hello-I'm-so-happy-to-meet-you kind of kiss. Wasn't it an accepted gesture to share a kiss with someone you just met? On the cheek, or wherever?

This opportunity lost when the light turned green, she leaned her head back against the headrest, studying him as he drove.

She didn't get it … how could she not remember him? It just didn't seem fair. There had to be so many other things she could've forgotten, memories she'd be more than happy to no longer have.

She sighed. This turned out to be at the exact same moment he turned to look at her.

He smiled. "Hey… talk to me. About anything. You… me… us. You can ask me anything."

What attracted you to me, or to the Hannah you knew before the accident? And what would you like to happen next?

Of course, she didn't ask him either of those. Give her *some* credit. Instead she went for something safe. "What made you decide to buy a truck? Is this what you're used to driving?"

After he made a turn at the next light, he chuckled. "Hmm… out of all the things you could ask me, this is really something you'd like to know? I was hoping for something more personal. Like… how happy am I am we're finally having our first 'real' date?"

He shot her a smile. "And my answer to that would be I'm very happy. But in reply to what you asked… yes, I do have a truck back home, but it's nothing like this one. It's old and has reached the last of its' days. So, I thought it was about time I treat myself to a new one."

He ran his hands over the steering wheel, a big smile lighting up his face. "This is a great truck… it's got everything a man could want. It will be nice to have in case I need to haul things."

She started to laugh. "Haul things? And what would you be hauling?"

He shook his head, attempting to be serious. "You never know. I believe in being prepared. You may thank me someday when you have something you want hauled across town."

Like when you move in with me. So I can have you with me all the time.

He blinked.

Where had that come from?

Pushing this enticing thought to the back of his mind, he glanced over at her.

She was grinning. "Ah… I see. This is good to know. Even though right now, I have no intentions of hauling anything, anywhere. I like my condo."

He nodded. "You never know what's in store for you. I have a feeling there's a whole new chapter ahead of you, a wonderful adventure just waiting to happen."

"What kind of adventure?" Hannah knew she was taking a chance in asking him this, but she was intrigued. It was almost as though he knew something she didn't.

Highly possible, since right now, he knows a heck of a lot more about you than you do.

He took time to think about this before he answered. "I have a feeling the only person who has the answer to that, is the Hannah you were before the accident. So, I guess you'll have to wait and see."

She was silent. Then with a slight shake of her head, she gave him a bright smile. "I guess you're right."

She ran her hand over the console, smiling over at him. "And I do like this. You can see everything when you're up so high."

He was smiling again, the sound of her laugh, music to his ears. It made him happy. But, then again, everything about her made him happy.

His hand coming down on hers, he linked their fingers together. She didn't say anything. Better yet, she didn't pull away.

Instead he heard her give a soft little sigh.

For now? This was enough.

They drove down Main Street, right into the town of Chagrin Falls.

Hannah glanced over at Sean. "So, what do you think? Is this small town enough for you? I've always thought it would be the perfect setting for one of those TV Christmas movies."

He nodded. "It's perfect. We'll have to come back during the Christmas season when everything is open. You can show me around."

Christmas? This was almost a year away. She wasn't going to let herself get carried away, imagining this. Since anything could happen between then and now. In fact, if she was smart, she'd think of this night only as a dinner shared between friends.

Yeah... good friends.

How ironic was this? Because, according to Sophie, this is exactly what had made her run away the first time she met him. When she thought he only wanted to be friends.

Her gaze going to the window, she gave a frustrated sigh.

"Hannah? Are you okay?"

Sean was watching her, a concerned look on his face.

No, she wasn't. Not by a long shot.

"Yes, I'm fine." Following this with a big smile, she pointed over to a building on their left. "The restaurant is right over there. And there's an empty parking space right in front. How lucky are we?"

Lucky? Yeah...

CHAPTER 15

Across town, Abby Kardell set her pastry bag down on the table. She needed to take another break. It seemed like the longer she was pregnant, the more breaks she took. Because of this, everything took so much longer to finish.

Like these cookies setting on the counter in front of her. She was decorating them for Livy and Sam's wedding, something that should've been done yesterday.

She leaned back in her chair, massaging her aching back with her hands. At the same time, she smiled. This happened every time she looked up at the mural Kevin had hired a local artist to paint. On the wall behind the counter, it featured her company name in bold print.

Sweet Abby's

She loved everything about it… the bright colors, the whimsical designs of baked goods swirling around the name and the way it all popped out at you. It made her happy.

But most of all, she loved that Kevin had taken the time to surprise her with this. It was an early present for their wedding anniversary coming up next month, he'd told her. The last needed touch to prove her dream of having her own cookie business had finally become a reality.

Still smiling, she picked up her pastry bag of icing. She only had to add the final details to the cookies on this tray and she would be done.

Then she could relax.

Finally.

She was exhausted. With the pregnancy and about everything else in general.

It would be a big help if everyone stopped calling her. She realized this was because they were concerned. And excited about the baby. But she was tired of answering all of their questions.

She had thought of turning off her phone, but Kevin had gone almost ballistic when she had casually mentioned this. So, if only to calm him down, she said she'd try her best to answer the calls. But she wasn't going to make any promises.

She smiled, thinking of the conversation she had with Sophie only about an hour ago. It had been an easy call for her, since Sophie had talked non-stop the entire time. Most of her conversation had centered on Hannah's dinner date with Sean tonight. She declared this as close to a miracle you could get, considering the condition Hannah had been in only about a week ago.

Sophie also told her Hannah still couldn't remember Sean… or the twins. And even though she remembered Abby and Kevin, she had been surprised to hear Abby was pregnant.

Fingering the pastry bag, Abby shook her head. The fact that Hannah had come to her baby shower only two weeks ago, but was now surprised to know she was pregnant, was mind boggling to her. She couldn't even imagine how frustrating this had to be for Hannah… or Sean.

Her thoughts drifted to Sean. He was such a cutie with that husky Australian drawl of his. And the way he wore a cowboy hat as though it was so completely natural, even here.

She frowned. Come to think of it, the last time she saw him, he hadn't been wearing the hat. She hoped this didn't mean he was giving it up.

Sean was what she envisioned a real honest-to-goodness cowboy would be and she didn't want him to change.

But the hat didn't really matter. Even without it, he and Hannah would still be perfect together. And if anyone could help Hannah get through this, it would be him.

You might even be supplying a cake for them in the near future. With maybe a cowboy themed groom's cake?

Her mind now drifting off to cake designs, she let out a big sigh, running her hand through her hair. She needed to stop daydreaming so she could finish and go home.

Setting the next cookie in front of her, she went to work, the comforting hum of the huge restaurant style refrigerator the only sound in the room.

Abby had finally finished. Setting the pastry bag on the counter, she raised her hands over her head and arching her back, she gave a long stretch. The baby responded with what definitely felt like a somersault. Massaging her baby bump, she smiled.

She glanced over at the clock hanging over the ovens. It was almost nine. This probably explained why she was so tired. For some reason, she had a much harder time waking up this morning. Almost to the point she'd wanted to crawl back in bed and go back to sleep.

She couldn't wait until the baby was born. She also couldn't wait to have Kevin back to the way he was before she became pregnant.

She sighed.

She loved Kevin. She loved him with all her heart. But, over these past nine months, he'd driven her over-the-top-crazy. Hoping to have some relief from his constant hovering, she'd even suggested he go out of town with the guys for a long weekend. Just for a break... have some fun. Anywhere, even Vegas. She didn't care. Just somewhere away...

His response? He'd been horrified she'd even thought he'd consider something like this. He could never leave her alone in the state she was in, he'd told her. No way.

So, she'd tried to be more patient.

If only he'd stop worrying, something he did all of the time.

He worried about how many orders she took on, if she ate enough, got enough sleep, worked too hard, didn't put her feet up... the list went on and on. He had spent countless hours online, checking out reviews for everything baby related, from formula to furniture. He wanted to pad every visible corner in their condo. This was even after she'd gently reminded him the baby wouldn't be moving around all that much for the first few months. So, the possibility of falling into sharp corners wasn't going to be happening all that soon.

He'd also baby proofed every single cabinet and drawer in the whole condo. This meant it was a constant fight to open them when she needed something.

Seriously, she could only take so much.

And now, with the baby due to arrive at any moment, his concerns had suddenly taken on a whole new direction. Did Abby think he was ready to be a father? Because he was now worried he wasn't.

What if he wasn't good at it? What if the baby didn't like him? Or, one of his biggest fears... what if he dropped the baby?

Again, the list was long. She'd done her best to reassure him, but this hadn't been enough to erase the worry lurking in his eyes.

She glanced over at the clock again. It was now nine-fifteen. Slowly easing herself up out of the chair, she walked, or more like waddled, over to the pantry to get the cellophane bags for the cookies. Once the cookies were packed up and ready to go, there was only one more thing to do and this would be to assemble the cake. But she still had a couple of days before she needed to do this.

The cake layers were in the freezer, along with a huge tub of frosting. The fondant decorations were all finished and carefully layered in a sealed container, ready to be applied to the cake as the final step.

She was very proud of how organized she was.

Waddling back over to the table, she got to work on bagging the cookies. Once she finished and the cookies were carefully packed in a huge bakery box, she added the box to the other boxes of finished cookies stored in the pantry.

It was now almost ten.

Time to finally go home.

Raising her hands over her head, she gave another long stretch.

And, this is when it happened…

Her water broke.

She froze, feeling completely helpless as a gush of warm liquid seeped through the fabric of her leggings.

Oh, no… this must be it.

Her hands started shaking so hard, it took her about five minutes to finally calm down enough to push the right buttons on her phone to call Kevin.

One ring… two rings… three rings…

Where was he?

On the fourth ring, he finally answered.

"Sugar?"

She opened her mouth. But nothing came out.

"Abby? Are you there? Are you all right? Answer me…"

The panic coming through in his voice was what finally got through to her. A huge gulping sound coming from her, she managed to choke out his name.

"Kevin…"

And darn if that was all she could manage.

But amazingly, Kevin understood what was going on. He took a deep breath, the tone of his voice reassuring. "Sugar, are you still at the bakery? Is it time?"

Her words finally came pouring out. And they came fast. "Oh my God, Kevin… my water just broke and I suddenly can't remember what I'm supposed to do next. Can you come here? Or maybe I should drive home and you can meet me there…I finished the cookies and I was just about to clean up, so once I do that, I'll…"

"No!" This coming out in a shout, he briefly closed his eyes. With the state she was in, he needed to step it up and be the calm one for once. "You stay right where you are. I'm pulling on my sweats as I speak."

This was exactly what he was attempting, hopping around on one foot like a crazy man. While trying to pull his sweats up over his other leg at the same time.

He suddenly chuckled. "I hope our little bundle of joy isn't going to be offended if her daddy smells like sweat and old gym socks."

This had Abby smiling. "Her? You think it's going to be a girl?"

He chuckled again. A sudden calmness had fallen over him. This was the moment they had been preparing for all these long months, what they were so excited about. And now, he couldn't wait.

He was ready. *So ready*

This was also the time for him to take over, be the strong presence Abby needed. He wanted her to know he would be with her, every step of the way, to make sure everything went right.

"Yeah, for some reason I have this feeling we'll be welcoming a little bundle of everything pink into our family. A little miniature Abby. It doesn't really matter though, girl or boy. I don't care. I just want the two of you to be all right."

This was met with silence.

"Abby? Sugar, are you still there?"

"I… I think… but I… I think I'm starting to have contractions." This came out in a long wail.

So, of course, he panicked.

His phone, pressed between his shoulder and his chin, went flying when he went to grab his sweatshirt. Hitting the slick concrete floor, it went sliding under the bench. Diving down after it, he went head first into the corner of the bench.

Hard.

Really hard...

The pain raced through him like a bolt of lightning, to the point he saw stars.

"Damn..." This coming out in a long groan, he reached up to see if he had a welt from the contact. His fingers came away, covered in blood.

"Kevin? Are you all right? What happened?"

Jesus... you can't let her know what happened. She'll freak out.

He slowly pulled himself on to the bench. Closing his eyes at the sudden dizziness that engulfed him, he managed to keep his voice calm.

"Sugar, I'm fine. I'll leave here as soon as I can. You stay put and I'll be with you before you know it. Unless you want me to stay on the phone with you?"

Oh, God... please, help me out here. Please, please have her say no.

Evidently, God was listening.

Abby vigorously shook her head. When she realized he couldn't see this, she started to giggle, her emotions taking over and all at once. Fearing this could turn into tears, she took a few deep breaths before she answered. "No, I'll be fine. I'm afraid you'll get distracted if you have me on the phone. You might hit something. Or someone. Be careful, okay? I want you here in one piece."

Encouraged by her giggle, he reached for his towel and, holding it against his head, closed his eyes.

If she only knew...

He took in a deep, shaky breath. "Okay, sugar. I love you."

"I love you, too."

The towel still pressed to his head, he stared down at the silent phone, trying to get his bearings. He wasn't feeling so hot.

Damn... what are you going to do?

"Hey... what's going on here? Are you hungover or something?" At the sound of Chester's voice, Kevin brought the towel down from his forehead.

There was a loud intake of breath followed by the hesitant touch of fingers to his forehead.

"What the hell did you do? Get in a fight with your locker? It looks pretty serious, buddy. I think you're going to need stitches."

This made him feel even more queasy. This should have been enough of a warning to stop him from trying to stand.

But it wasn't. This sent the blood draining from his face and he began to sway.

"Whoa..."

The next thing he knew, he was back on the bench, head down on his knees and staring down at the floor.

It was Chester's voice, sounding like it was coming through a tunnel, that finally filtered into his consciousness. "Hey Kev, come back to me. We need to get you to the hospital. You know as well as I do, you can't fool around with head injuries."

Kevin went to shake his head… another bad move. He rasped out his next words. "Can't. Gotta go to Abby… at the bakery… water just broke."

"Damn…"

This was followed by a long silence before Kevin felt Chester sit down next to him. "Okay… this is what we're going to do. I'm going to call Sophie, ask her to pick up Abby and take her to the hospital. In the meantime, somehow, without you passing out again, we're going to get you into my SUV and to the hospital."

At Kevin's start of a muffled protest, Chester put his hand on his shoulder. "Kev, listen to me. You don't have a choice here. Think of it this way, in the end, we'll wind up in the same place… at the same hospital. We'll get the doctors to fix you up and I wouldn't be surprised if you're with Abby before she even gets assigned to her room. Are you with me on this?"

At Kevin's slow nod, Chester gave a huge sigh of relief. "Okay, let me call Sophie. You stay right where you are. Keep that towel pressed to your head."

He suddenly chuckled. "You're going to have one hell of a story to tell this baby when he or she gets older."

It was only after he saw the hint of a smile on Kevin's face, he pulled out his phone and called Sophie.

CHAPTER 16

Doubt can obscure the true vision of the heart in an instant.
~ Anonymous

Both the hostess and the bartender recognized Sean the moment he and Hannah walked into the restaurant.

Needless to say, the service from that point on was over the top, fit for a celebrity.

This included a special visit to their table from the head chef. Exclusively for them, he would be preparing his specialty dessert. This would be his signature Chocolate Extravaganza Torte. It was the dessert that had won him top honors in The Most Decadent Chocolate Dessert Contest, sponsored by the Manhattan restaurant, Dine & Dessert.

This, of course, would be on the house.

Even though they were interrupted as least a half dozen times during dinner, Hannah was amazed at how pleasant and friendly Sean had been with each request. Be it a photo or an autograph, he treated each and every person as though they were the best of friends.

Sean had just signed an autograph for one of the other restaurant guests when their server arrived with the promised dessert.

A chocolate lover's dream, it consisted of four layers of chocolate cake, filled and frosted with a rich chocolate butter cream frosting. Coated with a mirror smooth, dark chocolate ganache and garnished with chocolate curls, it was a culinary work of art.

The server set the plate on the table. Wringing her hands, her forehead was creased with concern. "We're so sorry about how often your dinner has been interrupted. We hope this dessert will more than persuade you to come back and dine with us again."

Sean's smile was warm. "Hey, don't worry about it. The service, the food, the drinks… everything was great. I have a feeling this will become one of our favorite places. And it's obvious the chef knows the way to a woman's heart." He gestured to the dessert. "I'd be willing to bet, if Hannah had to choose between me and this cake, I'd be the one to lose out. It looks amazing."

The server let out a big sigh. "That's good to hear. Also, the band should start playing in about ten minutes. They're really good. If you can, stay for a dance or two. Or just to enjoy the music."

After she had left, Sean reached over, covering Hannah's hand with his. "You're doing okay? Anytime you want to leave, just tell me."

Leave?

Of course, she didn't want to leave. If she were to suddenly be granted one wish, whatever she desired, it would be for this night to go on forever. She wanted to gather it all in, memorize every moment, so she could tuck it away forever in her mind.

Heaven knows you have plenty of space there right now.

Without any warning, as had been the norm since the accident, her emotions took over, her eyes filling with tears.

"No, I don't want to leave. Honestly, I don't." Unfortunately, this came out in what sounded like a sob. When she tried to mask this with a laugh, it erupted in a loud hiccup.

Pressing her hand to her mouth, she shook her head. "I'm sorry. This keeps happening. It comes on so fast and I can't shake it. No matter how hard I try."

He moved closer, reaching over to brush his knuckles over her cheek. "Darlin' it's okay. I understand."

He sent a glance around the room, a smile lurking at the corner of his mouth. "Even though it seems your tears may have everyone thinking we could be in the midst of lover's quarrel. I'm wondering if this calls for a kiss? If only to reassure everyone we're okay?"

He cleared his throat. "Yeah… I like the sound of that. But if not? Don't worry. You go ahead and cry your eyes out if this is what you need to do."

He sent another glance around the room. "I don't see any press lurking in the shadows, so no worries there. This is the kind of situation they like to build on, the kind of story they think the public wants to hear. The more drama, the better."

Lover's quarrel? Press lurking in the shadows?

Her tears forgotten, she cast a nervous glance around the restaurant to see they were still attracting quite a bit of attention. A few tables away, a woman was trying to catch her eye, waving like mad.

Hannah sent her a tentative smile before she glanced over at Sean. His eyes meeting hers, the message in his suspiciously came across as a dare.

Okay… it looks as though you need to make the next move here.

This wasn't something she'd normally do, either as the Hannah of the moment or the Hannah of before the accident. But she decided to be brave. Placing her hand on his arm, she leaned in and pressed a soft kiss to his mouth, her lips lingering at his slight intake of breath.

She began to pull away, but framing the side of her face in his hand, he held her captive. His mouth so close and extremely inviting, she could hear the hint of a smile in his voice. "Darlin'… you're killing me here. But I see what you're doing. And I like it… I like it a lot."

His voice dipped to a whisper. "But I think we can both do better. *Hmm…* how about we give this a try…"

His mouth settled on hers, his kiss traveling through her, everywhere… catching every nerve, turning her bones to water. She knew there wasn't a chance of this actually happening. But this was the only explanation that even came close to how his kiss made her feel.

And even though she knew this had probably garnered more attention than they'd planned, she didn't care.

She didn't care one bit.

This kiss was more than worth it.

Sean leaned back in his chair, a smile on his face.

He'd be willing to bet it was a carbon copy of the bemused smile he could see on Hannah's face.

This is good... this is really good.

He cleared his throat.

After she took a slow sip of wine, if only to give her rapidly beating heart a little time to settle down, Hannah sent him a breezy glance. At least this was the look she was going for.

Picking up her fork, she glanced down at the dessert, then up at him. "So, you're definitely planning on sharing this with me, aren't you? Because I happen to know you like sweet things. Like banana muffins, right?"

Scooping up a forkful of cake, she sent him a teasing look. "You know you want some."

His gaze intensified, his eyes turning a darker shade of brown. But it was the sudden seriousness of his expression that had Hannah waiting, the fork paused halfway to her mouth.

His eyes held hers. "You're absolutely right, Darlin'. I love all things sweet. Especially those with eyes so blue, they can make a man forget his name with only a single glance. Or with hair like silk, begging to be touched."

His gaze traveled over her face, to finally end at her mouth. Then he leaned in even closer, a huskiness taking over his voice . "Or with a mouth, beautiful and perfect in every way... definitely made for kissing."

He watched, smiling, as a slow blush began to fill her cheeks.

Whoa... you didn't even know you had it in you, did you? Hell, if anything, Hannah made it easy.

Yep, he was feeling pretty damn proud of what he said. It looked like this romancing thing wasn't going to be that difficult after all. And he wasn't even finished yet.

He raised his glass. "So yes, I like sweet things. Some, so much more than others."

Then he brought the glass to his lips and drank, his eyes never leaving hers as he slowly set the glass back on the table.

Hannah was staring at him, her lips parted in an invitation for one of those kisses he had just claimed her mouth was made for.

She didn't move.

"Hannah?"

She blinked, and looking down at the forkful of cake she was holding, she slowly set it down on her plate.

You need to say something. Something clever.

But she was having a hard time. His compliments had her flustered, leaving her completely tongue-tied.

Eyes so blue?

Hair like silk?

And the best of all…

A mouth made for kissing?

Tell him… tell him you'll be more than happy to be his sweet thing… in a heartbeat, you will.

She gazed right into his eyes. "I… thank you. I…" She nodded. "I… I like you, too. I really do."

A smile tweaked the corner of his mouth. "*Ah…* you like me. That's good to know." He nodded. "Really good, I'd have to say."

He nodded again, still smiling.

Her heartbeat thundering in her ears, Hannah wondered if he could hear this across the table. Even in the busy restaurant.

Or if he knew what she was thinking.

There was one thing she did know. Everything had changed with this kiss. This fragile relationship they shared, this uncertainty because of the part of her that was still missing? It had now risen to a whole new level.

They had completely crossed over the line separating friendship and love.

Big time…

While all of this was swirling around in Hannah's mind, Sean's thoughts weren't as complicated. He was wondering if she had any idea what she did to him.

And this was without even doing anything.

What was it they say? Bewitched? Yeah, that's it. She has you under her spell.

And he was okay with this.

More than okay.

It was their server who broke the silence between them.

Immediately zeroing in on the untouched cake, she smiled over at Hannah. "What? You haven't tried the dessert yet? The chef is waiting for your review. What am I supposed to tell him?"

Her glance sweeping the table, she groaned. "Oh no… now I understand. I never brought out your coffee I'm so sorry. I'll go get it right now. If I'm not mistaken, we just brewed a fresh pot."

Almost grateful for the interruption, Hannah went to respond. But the server had left, already half way to the kitchen.

Resting his arms on the table, Sean nodded towards her plate. "In order not to disappoint her, you better make a dent in that before she comes back." He grinned, his next words mimicking hers. "You know you want to."

She looked down at the cake before glancing over at him, her mouth curving into a smile. After she picked up her fork and scooped up a generous chunk, she held it out to him. "You first."

He chuckled, shaking his head. "That's okay, go for it. I'm willing to wait."

She tilted her head, slowly nodding. "Okay, but let it go on record, I did offer."

Her gaze never leaving his face, she slipped the forkful of cake in her mouth. Her eyes drifting shut, the expression on her face was one of complete bliss.

He leaned forward, watching in fascination as she set the fork down on the plate before she gave a soft moan.

"Oh my… this is so good."

Sean abruptly sat back in his chair, an unexpected heat flooding him. This simple and what should have been an ordinary act of eating a piece of cake had affected him more than it should.

God, yes... way more.

He wanted to get out of his chair, walk around the table and pull her up against him. Then he'd capture her mouth in a kiss that would make her forget all about dessert.

Or anything else, for that matter.

Yep, he would become the center of her attention, the one to bring this look of rapture to her face.

Instead, he slowly dragged his hand down over his jaw, hoping this would mask the tortured groan that escaped him.

Well, you started it. Blame it on the kiss.

It appeared what had started out as a dare had now set off a chain of events entirely out of their control. He hadn't planned on something like this happening.

Not tonight, he certainly hadn't. His plan was to take it slow, follow Hannah's lead.

The whole patience thing... remember?

But it was now a whole new ballgame. Be it the kiss or whatever, it was clear everything was going to be okay. The Hannah of now was still the Hannah of before. At least when it came to her feelings regarding him.

He smiled at her.

She returned the smile.

And this time, when she offered to share the cake, he didn't refuse.

He had to admit, it really was good.

Down to the last forkful of cake, Hannah offered it to Sean. "Here, this last bite is yours."

He shook his head. "I wouldn't dream of denying you the last bite. I have a feeling if I did, for the rest of our lives, you'd be quick to remind me of this."

A smile spread across his lips. "And never would I even consider doing this on our first *real* date."

She paused, the fork halfway to her mouth.

The rest of your lives?

Flustered at even the possibility of this, she shoved the cake in her mouth. In an attempt to avoid the knowing smile on his face, she made a big production of patting her mouth with her napkin before she placed it on the table.

She glanced over at Sean, her breath catching in her throat. Casually stretched out in his chair, his elbow was on the table, his chin in hand. If she didn't know better, she'd swear he looked as though he'd settled into a pose for a celebrity magazine photoshoot. Or maybe like what you'd expect to see featured on one of those erotic romance novel covers.

Not that she ever read these types of novels. This observation was coming from what she had seen online and in bookstores. But you know the type... the guy is sprawled out right in front of you, sexy and shirtless. And your imagination is sent soaring.

Of course, Sean wasn't shirtless. But her mind grabbing on to the possibility of this sent the heat soaring to her face. This, along with her suddenly racing heart, had her in a panic. Almost making a dive for her water glass, she nearly sending it flying across the table.

My gosh... get a hold of yourself. That you're even thinking like this is crazy.

This is when she realized Sean was watching her. Clasping her hands tightly together on her lap, she gave him a bright smile, nodding down at the empty plate. "Well, It looks like you've missed your chance."

His gaze traveling over her face, he gave her a slow smile. "I believe I have all I could possibly want right now. What is it they say, save the best for last?"

He nodded. "Yep, definitely applies here."

He stood, holding out his hand "Come... while you were ignoring me, gobbling up your dessert, I was more than patient, waiting for you to finish. And now that you're done, I want to dance with you."

She refused to take his hand, an expression of mock horror on her face. "That's not going to happen until you apologize for your comment. I did not *gobble* down that cake. I don't *gobble.*"

Laughing, he reached for her hand and gently helped her up out of her chair. It was not until they were on the dance floor and she was in his arms, he finally responded.

He was grinning. "Darlin'… now that I have you where I want you, I'll gladly apologize."

He suddenly peered down at her, a concerned look on his face. "I'm not hurting you, am I? By holding you too close? I keep forgetting you're still healing."

Hurting you? By holding you too close? How could this even be possible?

She shook her head. "As long as you don't try to show off, surprising me with your fancy dance moves, I'll be fine."

"Good." His breath brushing across her cheek, his words were a husky whisper in her ear. "Because this feels so right, you in my arms. I believe we fit together very well, Hannah Michaels, don't you?"

When she didn't respond, he pulled back to gaze down at her. The sadness in her features tugged at his heart. "What is it, baby? Tell me."

She rested her head against his shoulder, her response barely audible. "I wish I could go back to the Hannah you want me to be, the one you remember. The Hannah I'm supposed to be. But right now, I feel so confused, caught up in between." She lifted her face up to his. "But what if—?"

His reaction was instantaneous. His answer, the kiss he gave. It was the only way he could think of to let them forget, even for a little while, the nagging uncertainty always hovering in the back of their minds. The what-ifs and whys, refusing to leave.

She hid her face in his shoulder, a shaky laugh escaping her. "*Oh my...* what are you doing to me? This isn't me… I don't kiss men on the dance floor. And certainly not during dinner in a restaurant." She shook her head. "I'm beginning to think, what little common sense I had somehow got caught up with everything I lost."

His hands drifting down to her waist, he pulled her closer. "Well, you haven't lost me. And your impulsiveness is one of the things I love most about you. You aren't shy when it comes to sharing what you're thinking. This leads me to believe life with you is never going to be boring."

He pressed a kiss to her forehead before pulling her even closer. "Now, no more talking. Let's enjoy the rest of this dance, ok?"

She nodded. Then she did exactly what she told him she never did. Linking her fingers behind his neck, she reached up give him a sweet, lingering kiss.

Judging by the look on his face, her impulsiveness paid off.

The band was on break and Sean and Hannah were headed back to their table.

"Sean? Is that you?"

A warning sounding in his head, he tensed, momentarily coming to an abrupt stop.

The voice was all too familiar. With an almost irritating East Coast twang to it, it was also one he knew he would never be able to forget.

That it was now coming at him so unexpectedly brought on a deluge of memories. Unfortunately, they were memories he'd spent so much time trying to forget.

And now, if you could, you'd like to run right out of the restaurant.

Instead, he feigned ignorance, continuing to their table. And for one brief moment, he thought he was safe.

But, damn, if the voice didn't become even more insistent.

"Sean? It really is you, isn't it? What a coincidence, out of all places, we would both be here tonight."

He tightened his hold on Hannah's hand and with a feeling of dread, he turned to find he was face to face with Amanda.

The one woman you never wanted to see again.

Clutching the arm of the man she was with, she gave an annoying giggle.

Another one of her traits he'd found so annoying, this jarred his memory in an even more unpleasant way. For some odd reason, she thought her giggle was sexy. Or, as she put it, a sure-fire way to drive a man wild. She had made it a point to remind Sean of this many times. Until she finally drove him to make the mistake of telling her she was wrong.

It wasn't sexy at all.

Yeah, she never did let you forget that. This was when you first learned of how fierce her temper could be.

If he wasn't mistaken, shortly after this was when a change had come in their relationship. She was no longer the sweet, loving woman he remembered from when they first met. They began arguing about everything, finding fault with each other. Dreading the thought of spending time with her, he had made excuses to stay away. And he'd be willing to bet she had been relieved.

At the time, the complete fool that he was, he blamed their failure to get along on the elaborate wedding plans that had taken over their lives, monopolizing their time. It was no longer about them anymore. The wedding was the only thing that mattered.

Love was no longer in the picture. With him as the first thing to go.

But, to be truthful, were you ever really in love with her?

Maybe?

At least he had thought he was. But, he couldn't help think she had been more in love with the whole fanfare of getting married. With him cast as the part of the groom, the one necessary key in making her childhood dream of a fairy tale wedding come true. If he'd been paying attention, he probably would've picked up on this from the beginning.

But, hey… he's a guy. His brain doesn't work that way. He was more interested in the end result, not all of the hoopla that led up to the event.

The bottom line?

Together, for them nothing worked. And after what was supposed to be their wedding day, he never expected to see her again.

But the lucky guy that you are, here she is… standing right in front of you.

He glanced over at Hannah to see she was studying Amanda, a

wary expression on her face. His hand settling on her waist, he pulled her against him. Tight enough for her to glance up at him in surprise.

Hannah was curious. And a little confused. But this was to be expected. She was witnessing a side of Sean she had never seen before. What was it about this woman that made him so angry, so tense?

She watched as he cleared his throat, his greeting overly hearty. "Hey... Amanda, long time no see. Are you here for a visit? I thought you had gone back to Boston for good." He gestured to Hannah. "This is my date, Hannah Michaels."

He smiled down at Hannah, pulling her even closer. "Amanda and I, we used to... well, I guess you would say we knew each other a while back."

Sean was nervous.

Of course, he was. What man wouldn't be when he suddenly finds himself face to face with the woman who at one time had been his fiancé?

Now, just to be clear. His engagement to Amanda was one of the many things he had shared with Hannah the night of Sophie and Chester's barbecue. But unfortunately, Hannah wouldn't have any recollection of this.

So, completely clueless, Hannah gave Amanda a warm smile. When Amanda response was only a curt nod, this had Hannah falling right back into her high school days, reliving the helplessness of trying to measure up against one of the popular girls in her class.

There's no way you can compete with this woman. Nope, not a chance.

But any normal woman would feel threatened by Amanda. Everything about her was perfect. Her professionally cut and highlighted, long blond hair. Her expertly applied makeup. The impeccable fit of her dress, what little of it there was.

And then there were her shoes... Hannah had always wondered if women actually wore heels that high. Well, here was the proof they did.

A smug expression on her face, no doubt because of what she was about to share, Amanda's smile was overly bright. "What Sean is neglecting to tell you, I was also once his fiancée."

By the startled reaction of Amanda's date, it appeared Hannah wasn't the only one surprised by this news.

But before anyone had a chance to comment, Sean gave a short laugh. "Yes, this is true. But, I believe you were the one to put an end to that, weren't you?"

He grabbed Hannah's hand. "We need to be on our way. Enjoy your evening."

He gave Amanda and her date a quick nod and moved so quickly, it took all of Hannah's concentration to keep up with him. But this didn't stop her from stealing a glance back to see Amanda was staring in their direction, the calculating look on her face enough to make Hannah wonder if she should be worried.

Once they were seated, the only sound at their table was that of Sean's fingers, drumming on the table.

He abruptly glanced over at Hannah.

She sent him a nervous smile.

He groaned. What was he doing?

You're acting like an absolute jerk... this is what you're doing.

He scooted his chair next to hers. After reaching for her hand, he nervously cleared his throat. "Hannah, I'm so sorry. Running into her tonight was the last absolute last thing I expected. It has definitely thrown me for a loop."

She didn't know what to say. So, she just nodded.

This had him moving even closer. "I want you to know, my engagement to Amanda was one of the first things I told you when we met. I didn't want anything from my past to come back to haunt us."

A wry smile flashed across his face. "Not that I had a wild and sordid past. Trust me, I spent more time riding horses and herding cattle than I did socializing. Running a ranch is a big job. Our engagement and what followed was completely out of my comfort zone. It was also a huge mistake."

She didn't want to know, but she had to ask. "Did you end the engagement? Or, did she?"

He reached out to tuck her hair behind her ear. "She did."

Not even realizing she had been holding her breath, waiting for his answer, she slowly let it out.

This is not what you wanted to hear.

And now there was so much more she needed to know. Such as... since Amanda was the one who ended it, did this mean he still had feelings for her? Had he tried to get in touch with her after she cancelled the wedding, hoping to persuade her to change her mind? And after seeing her tonight, if she told him she had made a mistake, would he want to give their relationship another try?

Yes, she needed to know all of these things. Because it was obvious by his behavior, he still wasn't over what happened.

You think this? You really think this? After everything he's said and done for you?

She wasn't sure... she just wasn't sure.

So, yes... what it came down to, she needed answers.

Her gaze held his. "Tell me again what happened."

The need to make the worry in her eyes disappear, he dove right in. "Amanda and I met when she came to Australia to visit her college roommate, who lived in my hometown."

He shook his head. "I never met anyone like her. An only child and used to getting her way, before I knew it, I had been swept up in all of her plans, and we were engaged. She told me she liked the idea of being the wife of a professional baseball player. It was so romantic. But I think it was more about the attention it brought her, the press, social media, and so on. So when I got drafted by a team in the states, she pushed the wedding plans into high gear. She wanted the wedding to be in Boston, where she was from. Over five-hundred people were invited."

The look on his face was one of bewilderment. "How does one know that many people? I had no idea who most of them were. All so pretentious, I'm pretty sure they viewed me as this slow-witted-and-whiskey-drinking-cowboy kind of guy. Sadly, they probably thought their opinion of me was justified after they had the pleasure of witnessing my long and pathetic wait at the altar."

Her hand going to her mouth, Hannah shook her head. "Oh, no… she didn't…"

He nodded. "Unfortunately, she did. She skipped out on me, an experience I wouldn't wish on anyone, even if it might seem like the right thing to do at the time. Definitely not with everyone there to witness your shame. All five hundred of them."

After running his hand through his hair, he gave a long sigh. "I don't remember leaving the church. I only knew I wanted to get the hell out of there and in the privacy of my hotel room. I was in shock, I was embarrassed, and I had no wish to talk to anyone. And as far as I was concerned, there was nothing to discuss."

He gave a short laugh. "And Amanda? Believe it or not, this is the first time I've seen her since."

Hannah reached for his hand. "She never gave you any kind of explanation?"

Encouraged by her touch, he linked their fingers together. "No, she never did. No call, no text, and no email. Nothing."

Gently caressing her fingers with his, he held her gaze. "Hannah… Amanda and I were never intimate, let alone spent the night together. Hell, she hardly let me touch her. If we kissed, it was on the cheek or a quick peck on the mouth. She told me she wanted to wait until we got married. Then it would be special, she told me. She was very insistent about this."

He shook his head. "I often wonder if things would have been different had I known then what I know now."

The hustle and bustle of the restaurant swirled around them. While they both remained silent, unsure where to go from here.

Sean was the first to speak. "So, now you know about Amanda and what part she once played in my life. I've told you everything."

But for Hannah, this wasn't true. There was one thing he hadn't shared with her. And it was the one thing she needed to hear more than anything else.

"Do you still love her?"

His head jerked up, his look one of disbelief. "Love her? *My God,* sweetheart… I don't think so. I'm pretty sure any love between us got swallowed up in the grand scheme of things."

He brought her hand to his mouth, pressing his lips to her fingers "Now, you and me? We're a whole different story."

Abruptly coming to his feet, he pulled her up out of her chair. "Come on, the band is back from their break. I want to dance with you again. Everything seems so much better when I'm holding you in my arms."

As they slowly moved to the music, Sean holding her close, Hannah tried to tell herself everything was going to be fine. She was getting worked up about nothing. Amanda would be going back to Boston, where she'd find someone else to have the wedding of her childhood dreams.

And Sean would forget all about her.

But there was one little nagging detail Hannah wasn't able to shake. This had to do with Sean's response to her question. This would be if he still had feelings for Amanda.

> *"Love her? My God, sweetheart… I don't think so. I'm pretty sure any love between us got swallowed up in the grand scheme of things."*

Think… he didn't *think* there was any love between them?

Wouldn't this be something he should know for sure?

And just like that, a sliver of doubt began to settle in the corner of her mind.

Sean could feel the difference in Hannah by the way she responded to his touch. When they'd danced earlier, it was as though they were one, her body fitting against his like a glove.

And now?

She was tense. Even though they were touching, they weren't

touching at all. The only explanation he was able to come up with would be they no longer had that special connection between them. And unfortunately, he was the one responsible for this.

She doesn't trust you. Something you said made her think you weren't telling her the truth.

He rested his cheek in her hair, closing his eyes.

Damn...

Was he ever going to get this right?

CHAPTER 17

A bby was wide awake. More so than she had been at any time in the past nine months.

If you were to take in account everything that happened in the past six hours, you'd think she'd be exhausted.

But she wasn't.

Well, maybe this was stretching the truth a bit. Her body was bone tired. But her mind was so busy processing the miracle she and Kevin witnessed, she wasn't yet ready to let this moment be taken over by sleep.

The miracle they both now knew as Madeline Rose.

And yes, she had red hair. A full head of it, as a matter of fact.

She was the most beautiful baby they ever saw.

Unable to tear her gaze away from Kevin, who was sitting in the chair next to her bed, she smiled at how carefully he was cradling the little bundle of pink in his arms. He'd already checked out Madeline's little toes and fingers, before moving on to examine the rest of her.

He'd declared she definitely had Abby's mouth and nose. He also swore she gave him a smile when he whispered her name.

She was perfect, he claimed. Perfect in every way.

Abby smiled, remembering the hearty first cry she gave when she entered the world, letting everyone know she'd arrived. She wondered if this had Kevin re-thinking his comment he'd be more than happy if the baby turned out to be a little spitfire, just like her mom. Because it sure sounded like she already was.

Shifting slowly in the hospital bed, she saw Kevin was gazing over at her, the expression on his face one of pure awe.

He opened his mouth to speak, but wound up shaking his head instead.

She reached over the space that separated them, smiling when he linked his fingers with hers.

He smiled back at her. It was the smile that always made her melt. Slowly shaking his head, his voice was husky with emotion. "We did good, sugar. She's beautiful, isn't she? I can't believe she's finally here." He paused to give her a big grin. "I told you it was going to be a girl. And the red curly hair? That was a given."

He winked. "Paybacks, sugar… paybacks."

He gazed down at Madeline again before he rested his head on the back of his chair and giving a long sigh, he closed his eyes

Abby pulled herself to the side of the bed, trying to get closer to him. She was worried. She'd noticed earlier how he'd close his eyes for a few seconds, almost swaying on his feet before he'd quickly sit down. When she'd asked him if he was okay, he'd quickly assured her he was fine. She wasn't to worry.

He certainly didn't look fine.

Below the huge bandage on his forehead, the whole right side of his face had already turned all shades of purple and was beginning to swell.

So, she certainly couldn't but help worry.

When she and Sophie had arrived at the hospital, she had been whisked almost immediately to a room. There she had tried to block out the sound of Sophie's nervous chatter, while at the same time, she tried not to think about how her contractions were coming closer and closer together.

Looking over expectantly when anyone entered the room, to only be disappointed when it wasn't Kevin, she'd begun to fear the worst, thinking he was never going to show up. This was even after Chester had called with a message from Kevin... he was going to be fine, she shouldn't worry and he'd be joining her very soon.

Unfortunately, it was almost an hour before he'd burst into the room, a look of pure relief on his face when he saw her. And even though she was shocked at the seriousness of his injury, she was so thankful and relieved he was finally with her.

It's bad enough you always worry when he's out on the field. Especially after Chester got hit by that line drive during spring training. Never did you think he'd get hurt in the gym locker room.

"Kevin?"

At her whisper, Kevin jerked his head in her direction, unable to hide his grimace because of the pain.

He had such a God-awful headache. He was trying so damn hard to ignore it, but finding this impossible. He frowned. He didn't have time for this. He had to step it up, be the strong one for Abby and little Madeline.

Abby was waving her hand in front of his face. "Kevin, are you okay?"

This was when he saw her eyes had filled with tears, one slowly beginning to roll down her cheek. Was this one of those emotional-crying-for-some-unknown-reason onslaught of tears Chester had warned him about? Or was she crying because of him?

Oh, please don't let it be because of you. She doesn't need to be worried about you at a time like this. You should both be happy, taking the time to enjoy this new chapter of your lives.

He brought her hand to his mouth, pressing a slow kiss to her fingers. "Sugar, I'm fine. Yeah, my head is hurting a little, but I'll be okay. Please don't cry." He gazed down at the small bundle in his arms. "Look at her... sleeping so peacefully." He grinned over at her. "I think she likes me."

This brought a shaky giggle from Abby. "Of, course she does. Why wouldn't she? She knows she's got the best possible daddy ever."

He smiled over at her. "The same goes for her mommy." He chuckled as he adjusted the blankets more securely around Madeline. "I wouldn't be the least bit surprised if this wasn't all a set up. Probably as soon as we get her home, she'll start crying non-stop."

They were both contentedly watching Madeline sleep when a nurse came bustling into the room. She smiled. "Well, you two must be doing something right. This is the second time I've been back to check on you and both times, your precious little one has been sleeping."

She reached down to take Madeline from Kevin, smiling at the little squeak she gave at the move. "*Aw*, hear that? She doesn't want to leave you. But it's time for me to take her down to the nursery. We'll keep her there for this first night so you two can get some sleep."

She peered more closely at Kevin. "I'm also going to get you some medication for that bump on your head. I can see by your eyes, you have some pain. Am I right?"

Abby was the one who answered. "Yes, please. I'm so worried about him."

With the promise she'd be right back and pushing the rolling bassinet, the nurse left the room.

Kevin gazed longingly over at the bed.

Maybe if you get even a couple hours of sleep, you'll feel better.

Abby saw this, moving to the far side of the bed before she smiled over at him. "Here, there's more than enough room for both of us. And look at all of these pillows."

Moving very cautiously, he finally made it onto the bed. Once he was settled next to her, her put his arm around her.

Closing his eyes, he gave a long, exhausted sigh.

For the longest time, there was only silence. Kevin was the first to speak. "I'm sorry, sugar. I definitely screwed this up, didn't I. As usual, I overreacted."

She settled more comfortably against him. Sliding her fingers under where his were resting on his chest, she smiled when he linked them together. Her words came at him so softly. "Have I told you lately how much I love you? Because I do... so, so much. Every day that I wake up with you beside me, I know everything is the way it should be. And now we have Madeline. I can't believe how lucky we are."

This had him smiling, headache and all. "You can tell me you love me as often as you want. I'll never tire of hearing this. I love you, too. And, yeah, we are lucky. So, *so* lucky."

He suddenly groaned, closing her eyes. This brought her abruptly up into a sitting position. "What's wrong? Is your headache worse?"

"No, no, it's not that. It's just that I... well, I wanted to give you something special when the baby finally arrived, but it's at home. I completely forgot about it in all the craziness that went on with my head."

She was leaning on his chest, a big smile on her face as she searched his. "What is it? Tell me..."

He grinned. "But then it wouldn't be a surprise." At her disappointed look, he chuckled. "Okay, I'll give you a little clue. It goes around your neck. It sparkles... a lot. Maybe in a couple different places"

He was trying to act as though it was no big deal, but it was. The necklace was one he'd designed just for her. But this was the extent of what he was going to tell her. He wanted her to at least be a little surprised when he finally gave it to her.

"You got me a diamond necklace? Oh, Kevin..." And then she was kissing him. So, of course he had to kiss her back. It was the nurse, returning as promised, that had them springing apart.

An indulgent smile on her face, she handed Kevin a pill and a small cup of water.

"Here is your medicine. This will help you get a good night's sleep. And don't you worry about Madeline. We'll take great care of her."

They watched her leave before Abby moved to lay back by his side.

He reached out to stop her. "Stay right where you are, sugar. I like the feel of your heart beat against mine. It lets me know you're mine and helps me forget all about my headache."

So, this was how they both fell asleep.
Abby, dreaming about babies and diamonds.
Kevin, dreaming about Abby.
But then, all of his dreams were about her.

CHAPTER 18

*J*ake Martin gazed up at the night sky, made even darker because of the heavy cloud cover. He took in a long, deep breath, filling his lungs with the refreshing winter air.

After being cooped up in the hot and crowded restaurant kitchen for what felt like a million years, you need this... boy, do you need this.

He was exhausted.

The past six hours at his restaurant had been brutal. He'd turned out one dish after another in record time, barking out orders until he'd become hoarse. He hadn't even been able to take a break until about forty-five minutes ago, this made possible only because it had been time to close the kitchen for the night.

Ever since the Cleveland Now magazine came out a week ago, featuring an article about his new restaurant, Jake's Place, business had gone through the roof. Unable to accommodate all of the calls for reservations, they were booked up solid for the next six months.

Yep, hands down, tonight had to be one of the craziest nights you ever experienced as a chef. Even more than on the restaurant's opening day.

Deciding to open his own restaurant had turned out to be both a good, and bad thing.

Good because he was finally able to do things his way.

Bad, because he worked twenty-four-seven and had very little time for himself, if any at all.

He sighed, wearily massaging the back of his neck. Maybe it was because he was so tired, but tonight he'd caught himself feeling a small twinge of jealousy, noting all of the couples who came in to share a great meal and a glass of wine or two. To then linger over coffee and dessert while they listened to the jazz piano player he'd been so lucky to find.

You want this, too. But you're beginning to wonder if it's ever going to happen. Luck certainly hasn't been on your side in that department.

After pressing his face in his shoulder to muffle the huge yawn that had suddenly snuck up on him, he glanced around the almost empty parking lot.

It was starting to snow. As he tried to get a better grip on the heavy box he was holding as he waited for Amber to open the trunk of her car, he wondered why he was even surprised at this. It hadn't stopped snowing since Christmas. He glanced over at the main highway, hoping the snowplows had already started making their rounds. The last thing he felt like dealing with right now, was a drive home on snow covered and slippery roads.

It wasn't looking good, the few cars passing by much slower than usual.

Damn...

He wanted to go home and crash. Maybe have a glass of wine and check his phone for any messages before falling into bed.

Yeah... and to think, just recently, the Cleveland Now magazine also recognized you as one of the city's most eligible bachelors and this is as exciting as your life gets these days. How ironic is this...

He watched as two cars skidded their way into the parking lot. The conversation and laughter, coming from the two couples as they emerged from the cars, carried through the silence as they headed towards the entrance of the bar. Open for at least another four hours, he was glad this wasn't his responsibility.

Nope, his main area of concern was the kitchen.

You're fortunate to have Joel managing the bar and everything that goes along with it. One of the smartest things you ever did, was partner up with him.

He wearily shifted the box to his other arm. This was when he suddenly realized Amber had been chattering away, non-stop and he hadn't heard a word she'd said. She'd opened the trunk and now turning to him, she started to laugh.

"You've completely zoned out on me, haven't you? *Geeez...* I don't know what's going on with you, but you've been so preoccupied lately. If I had to guess, I'd say it has to do with a woman. So come on... spill. It's me, remember?"

She sent him what she hoped came across as a casual grin? "Am I right?"

He loaded the box in the trunk before he turned to grin back at her. If he had to choose his favorite out of all the people who worked with him at the restaurant, it would be Amber. An aspiring chef, not only was she very talented and a favorite with all of their customers, it was such a relief to know he could always count on her to take over when he needed to take a break. If even only for an hour or two.

Amber's husband had been killed in a vehicle accident five years ago, leaving her with two children to raise on her own, a daughter who was now ten and a son, who just turned seven. Since it had always been her life-long dream to become a chef, she opted to use part of the insurance money she received from the accident to pay for culinary school.

He could still remember how timid she'd been when she first started at the restaurant, ducking out of his way whenever she saw him. If he did try to talk to her, she was hardly able to stammer out her words.

And now they had become the best of friends.

Jake knew that everyone thought he and Amber should try to

make a go of it. He liked Amber, he really did. He also liked her kids, they were great kids. But Amber was not the woman he wanted.

He was pretty sure Amber knew this. Only because, one night after they closed down the restaurant and everyone had left, they'd sat at the bar and downed a record number of iced teas, along with a more than generous serving of the restaurant's signature nachos appetizer between them.

This was when he told her all about Gracie.

You mean you poured your heart out to her, giving her the very long and complicated details of the relationship you and Gracie share. If you remember, you didn't leave the bar until almost four in the morning.

"Jake?" Amber was peering up at him, a curious expression on her face. "Are you okay?"

He groaned. "*Damn,* I'm sorry Amber. I think I've about reached my limit after the night we had tonight. It doesn't help I haven't been sleeping all that great lately. A lot on my mind, I guess."

A wry smile flashed across his face. "And in answer to your question? No, there's no woman in my life right now. If that happens, I assure you, you'll be the first to know."

She studied him for a few moments. She knew this was his subtle, yet kind way of letting her know he would always think of her as only a friend and nothing more. But it wasn't like she hadn't expected this. She'd watched his face when he'd told her about the shaky, on and off again, relationship he and Gracie shared. She could hear in his voice how much she meant to him. There was no doubt he was in deep. It was also obvious, when something finally did click between them, be good or bad, Gracie would still be the only woman for him.

And this makes you mad. If you could find a way to meet up with this Gracie, you'd try to knock some sense into her. Jake deserves so much better than this.

Instead, she sighed, slowly shaking her head. "I don't know if I quite believe you. Just remember I'll always be here if you want to talk."

She gave him a bright smile. "Now, let's go in and get the rest of the boxes. Ben is going to be thrilled when he sees all this food you're giving him. By the way, he told me he's still waiting for you to stop in at the shelter so he can meet you in person. I'm pretty sure he's going to hit you up for your chicken parmesan recipe. He told me they fight over it when it's on the menu. This certainly doesn't surprise me. I don't know anyone who doesn't love that recipe."

Jake put his arm around her as they made their way back into the restaurant. He was smiling. "He's more than welcome to the recipe, even though I think we both know your version is better."

He laughed. "Yep… one of these days, there's a good chance I won't be able to boss you around anymore. I'll be working for you instead. So, I need to take advantage of the time I still have with you."

Amber shot him a quick glance.

Maybe she was wrong?

Hmm… maybe there was hope for them after all. Because as much as she was attracted to Joel, Jake's friend and co-owner of the restaurant, Joel certainly didn't seem to feel the same about her, always going out of his way to avoid her. One of these days, she was going to ask him why.

Yeah, right… like you could ever get up enough nerve to do this.

"Hey, earth to Amber… are you still with me?"

She looked over to see Jake had grabbed one of the two remaining boxes and was holding it out to her. "This one is for you. It's the lighter of the two. Let's go out the bar entrance this time. I need to tell Joel we're taking off."

When Jake and Amber walked into the bar, Joel called out from where he was behind the bar, mixing a drink. "Hey, Jake… you're just the man we're looking for. We need you to settle this discussion we're having about the Regency Party Center. The rumor going around is it's up for sale."

After he put his box down on the bar and set Amber's next to it, Jake gave him a surprised look. "The Regency is for sale? Wow… interesting. I know it's been under the same ownership for a long time, fifty years or maybe even longer. Whoever the buyer is, I hope their plan isn't to tear it down and build high end condos. I can see this happening, since it's a prime location, on the lake and all."

Joel was trying to pay attention to what Jake was saying, but he was more interested in watching Amber. He didn't even realize he was staring at her until she moved, catching his gaze.

She smiled.

It was a hesitant smile. As though she was waiting, or more like wondering, why he was looking at her. If maybe there was something he wanted to say.

And Joel's mind went completely blank. In a panic, he began grabbing glasses and washing them like they'd never been washed before.

Of course, you want to say something to her. Starting out by telling her how beautiful she is. But, in order to do this, you need to be able to get the words out of your mouth.

And, as had been the case in the past, this probably wasn't going to happen.

Whenever Amber came into the bar, he felt like he'd been hurtled back in time, when he was a shy and gawky teenager and completely clueless when it came to the opposite sex.

There was something about her that had him thinking it was about time he grew up, settled down and started acting his age. Maybe get married. Buy a house, with a big lawn... even a mower to cut the grass. Of course, there would also be kids. Three of four, maybe? He'd take them to the zoo. Play catch with them on the newly mowed grass. Hide filled Easter eggs for an egg hunt on Easter morning...

Yeah... this is all he wanted... a respectable life. All the things, up until now he'd been trying to avoid, comfortable with his single life.

Until he'd first laid eyes on Amber about a year ago.

Yep, this is how long you've known her and you still haven't carried on a conversation with her that wasn't about the weather. Or if the restaurant was going to be busy that night. Or even just a casual how are you doing, I'm fine and see ya later kind of exchange.

Up until now his excuse was he had nothing to offer her.

You're only a bartender, for God's sake.

But this no longer held true. After what seemed like way too many days and nights of juggling classes and bartending, sometimes feeling as if they had all blended into one long exhausting journey, he'd finally received the notification he'd passed the bar.

He, Joel Kennedy, was no longer just a bartender.

Nope, he could finally add the title of lawyer after his name.

That this happened, was something very few people knew. Except for Jake... he'd known for a couple years now. And even though he didn't understand Joel's reasoning, he'd promised to keep it to himself.

Now don't get him wrong. He had nothing against being a bartender. It had served him well. And he actually enjoyed the job and the people. It's only that he'd worked so damn hard to get where he was, and now he was ready to take on the world.

And maybe, even Amber... you know, ask her out on a date.

He sent her a quick glance to see she was still watching him. This had him almost dropping the glass he was holding.

Damn... why can't you at least maintain some of your dignity and play it cool?

His concentration now on rinsing off the glass he was holding in his hand, he didn't realize she'd moved closer.

"Hi, Joel... how's it going?"

At the sound of her voice right next to him, he did exactly what he'd been trying to avoid... he dropped the glass. Which resulted in that-makes-you-want-to-cringe-sound of glass shattering into what had to be a million pieces.

A sound impossible to ignore.

So, not only was Amber so close he could reach out and touch her, something he suddenly craved more than anything, everyone in the bar was staring at them, their conversations coming to a dead halt.

Damn... damn... damn...

He flashed a big grin around the room. "Don't fret, I got it under control. So, go back to what you were doing."

It was after he'd cleared away the broken glass, he realized he'd completely ignored Amber. He glanced over to see she had slipped onto one of the bar stools and her elbows resting on the bar, she was still watching him.

She smiled. "I'm sorry. Did I make you do that?"

Thinking how easy it would be to get lost in her smile, he found he was moving closer to smile back at her. "No, it's sort of a tradition around here. Whenever a pretty girl walks into the bar, we flip a glass." He cleared his throat, shaking his head. "But you? You deserve more than a flip. In fact, I'm pretty sure the glass shattered on its' own, overcome by your beauty."

What the hell? Where did you get that from? Talk about corny. She's going to think you're completely out of your mind.

Daring to shoot a quick glance over at her, he was surprised to see she was blushing. This prompted him to say more. "I know, it sounds a little unbelievable, right? About the glass shattering, that is. Not about you being beautiful. Because that, without question, it the honest truth. At least for me it is."

Okay, okay... you need to take it easy here. Next thing you know, you'll do something crazy like ask her to marry you and she'll go running right out of the bar, scared to death.

Yeah, if he wasn't careful, he was going to start rambling. This is what he always did when he got nervous. Especially when he was around women. He glanced down at the broom in his hand. Why couldn't their conversation be like the one he'd imagined before in his mind... how he'd planned it would go the next time he saw her?

Well, this was the next time. And as far as he was concerned, a do or die situation. He needed to make his move and it needed to be perfect.

Shoving the broom in the corner, he turned to see she was leaning in even closer, the scent of her perfume coming at him even through the kitchen smells that still lingered in her clothes and her hair. It was a floral scent, Jasmine maybe? With a touch of vanilla and musk?

He wasn't sure, since he didn't know much about perfume. He only knew he liked it. He liked it a lot. Yeah, he could get used to it... everywhere. Here, at home, even in his bed. Especially in his bed...

You need to stop. You're getting way ahead of yourself.

He vigorously began stacking the clean glasses, sending her what he hoped was a casual smile.

She smiled back at him. "Jake told me."

At his confused expression, she leaned in closer. "About passing the bar. Don't be mad at him, it just slipped out. He's so proud of you. So am I. I know how hard it is to realize your dream." She grinned. "You need to have a big party... celebrate with everyone you know. You deserve it."

He didn't respond, instead searching her face. This had her worried. Maybe she'd said too much? Yeah, Jake had told her not to say anything, but this new information about Joe explained why she'd always been so intrigued by him. She, of all people, knew how hard it was to juggle a job and go to school at the same time. There was also the fact he just didn't seem to fit the bartender role. He was too soft spoken, too reserved, his mind always appearing to be focused elsewhere.

She couldn't believe how relieved she was when a slow smile spread across his face, while at the same time he reached over to touch her hair. At her inquiring look, he shrugged. "It looks like you have a piece of parsley, or something, stuck in your hair."

Even though he was holding the offending bit of parsley in his fingers, he let them linger in her hair as he spoke. "A party, you say? That sounds like a great idea. But do you know what I'd rather do instead?"

She slowly shook her head, her heart suddenly skipping a beat at the intensity of his gaze.

"See? I got it." After holding out the piece of parsley for her inspection, he then went on to carefully tuck her hair behind her ear. "I'd rather celebrate with you. How about dinner? At the fanciest and most expensive restaurant around. Then we'll do the town, stay out until the wee hours. We can go dancing, watch the sunrise together. Or even take a long walk in the snow. Whatever strikes our fancy."

He watched the blush deepen in her cheeks. He had a feeling this was because of his remark about the sunrise. Again, he'd let the scent of her perfume take him away, a longing building within him. "It will be a celebration of what we've both accomplished, how far we've come. Because I do believe we're two of a kind, Amber Snow."

His head tilted, his smile was so sincere, the message in his eyes giving her every reason to trust him. Then he cleared his throat, his voice coming out husky and to her, so, *so* damn sexy. "Yeah, this is what I'd like more than anything."

Her lips parting, she tried, but couldn't seem to come up with her answer. Nope, not even a simple yes or no. She felt as if they were caught up in a magical slice of time, a moment where her answer could very well decide her future. A future that would include him.

That he even knew her last name was so surprising to her. But then everything about this whole encounter between them felt more like a dream than reality. How was it, what started out as only a casual conversation had evolved into an invitation of a dinner date?

My God, she was ready to climb right over the bar, grab him by the shoulders and kiss him until he kissed her back. If only to find out if they were on the same page.

Joel had no idea what was going on in Amber's head right now. He was only trying to be patient, waiting for her answer.

It wasn't that he was worried

No… because he could feel it… the connection was there.

And he knew she could feel it, too.

That vision, of a house with a big lawn, flashing through his mind?

He smiled.

Finally…

Jake shot another glance over to where Amber was seated at the bar, talking to Joel. It was obvious something was happening between them, so he was biding his time, waiting for the right moment to join them.

He wasn't blind.

He was well aware of how Joel watched Amber when he didn't think anyone noticed, a look of longing on his face.

He also observed the change in Amber's demeanor when she saw Joel come into the room, almost going out of her way to completely ignore him.

The one time he'd casually asked if she liked Joel, she had become so flustered, vehemently denying any such thing. They were only friends, she'd told him. What had even made him suggest such a thing? She hardly even talked to him. This all coming from her in such an angry sputter of words, he'd backed off, quickly changing the subject.

Well, from what he could see, things had now changed.

Only when Amber burst out laughing at something Joel said, he slowly sauntered over to them. When they finally glanced over at him, he smiled. "So, it looks like the two of you are finally hitting it off, no?"

His arms crossing over his chest, Joel proceeded to stare him down. "So, you had to go and spill the beans, huh? Can't I trust you with anything?"

Jake had the grace to look embarrassed. "Yeah, well it wasn't all me." He nodded towards Amber. "I don't know how, but she somehow managed to get it out of me. And hey, come on… this is something you should be shouting from the rooftops. I know I'm so damn proud of you."

He put his arm around Amber, giving her a hug. "I'm proud of the both of you and I know you'll both be a success at whatever you decide to do next."

He held up his hand. "But, don't even think of picking up and moving somewhere else. You're the kind of friends I need to have around."

Joel smiled over at Amber. "I'm not planning on going anywhere. Not now."

The blush spreading across Amber's face had Jake pulling his keys out of his pocket. He waved over at the boxes. "If you can excuse the company of this woman for a few minutes, we need to load these boxes in her car. I need to get home. I'm beat."

Making his way from behind the bar, Joel picked up one of the boxes. He turned to Amber. "*Hey…* this is heavy. You really shouldn't be carrying this." This was accompanied by a stern glance over at Jake.

Jake groaned. "*Oh geeez…* here we go. Trust me, she's probably stronger than the both of us. I'd be willing to swear on this. And now you're going to start spoiling her? She'll be impossible to work with."

When Amber made a half-hearted attempt to take the box from Joel, he moved it out of her reach and headed for the door.

Jake glanced over at her as he picked up the other box.

She shrugged, giving him a big grin.

His answer was a long, resigned sigh.

"And so it begins…"

CHAPTER 19

As soon as Jake opened the door to his condo, he knew something was different. This had to do with the scent that filled the room, a scent he would recognize anywhere. It was a combination of florals and spices with just the tiniest hint of musk.

It was the scent that was Gracie.

Very slowly, so slowly, he set his keys down on the hall table and removed his coat. It was almost as though he was afraid if he moved too fast, everything he was now hoping to believe, would disappear into thin air. Taking Gracie along with it and leaving his condo back to where it had been before.

He glanced down at the large take-out bag he was holding. He'd brought it home from the restaurant and now, for a brief moment, he wasn't quite sure what to do with it.

You need to walk into the kitchen and put the bag in the refrigerator. Now go... do it.

With a quick shake of his head, he did exactly that. After standing in front of the refrigerator, staring at nothing for a few seconds, he finally closed it.

Again, he was unsure of what he should do next.

But this was to be expected. This is what always happened when Gracie came back into his life. She filled his mind, she filled his senses, he couldn't think worth a damn.

He lost track of everything.

Everything, that is, except her.

He hadn't seen her since the last time she showed up, back in June. This was almost seven months ago when he'd found her sitting on the front steps of his condo and probably at the lowest she'd sunk in her life.

He only had her with him for two days. Then, with his help, she checked herself into a rehab facility recommended to her by another recovering friend.

When she left the facility five months later, she called to tell him she was going to take some time to herself before she saw him again. She needed to do this, she told him. She wanted to become completely in charge of her life and she had to do this alone. She felt very strongly about this and hoped he would support her decision.

But, she made it very clear she was not doing this for only her... this was for him, too.

For them, she told you.

This was when she asked him to be patient with her for just a little while longer.

Patient?

This had been the story of his life for as long as he'd known her. He couldn't even begin to count the number of times he'd watched her leave, to then muddle through the days that followed, waiting for her to come back into his life.

Patient... yeah, you're the king of patience. You've definitely become an expert at it.

These past two months hadn't been easy. After her call, he'd heard nothing from her, not even a short text to let him know she was okay.

So, hanging on to the tiniest sliver of hope he possessed, he could only pray she'd meant what she said. And maybe, just maybe, when she finally did come back to him, it would be for good.

And now? It looked like this last bout of patience may have finally paid off.

He knew she'd entered the room, he could sense her presence. He turned from the refrigerator to find she was standing by the door, where she remained, a hesitant smile on her face.

Briefly closing his eyes, he out a long, shaky breath.

The change in her was amazing.

This came through in the confident way she was standing, no longer slouching as had been her usual stance of the past, as though she was trying to hide within herself. This new image she gave off, was of a woman who was finally comfortable with who she was, ready to take on whatever life handed to her.

A small smile slowly spreading across his lips, he continued his inspection, taking his time to slowly drink in every inch of her.

She looked beautiful… everything about her. Her hair, which he'd always told her was the shade of a rich caramel, was still long and hanging free. Reflected in the kitchen light, it was shining with healthiness. Her complexion was glowing, her eyes clear and still as beautiful an ice blue as ever.

They were like pools of light… he'd swear he could drown in them.

But right now? He wasn't ready to do that. He wanted to get his fill of everything about her.

His gaze sweeping over the rest of her, he saw her body looked toned and no longer thin to the point she appeared anorexic. In fact, her new curves made her seem even more sensuous and desirable. Imagining how she would feel under his hands when he finally held her against him, it was a struggle for him to not make the move to do exactly that.

"Jake?"

He blinked. At her tentative smile, he realized how long he'd been staring. He knew he should say something, but for the life of him, he couldn't. The lump in his throat wouldn't let him.

His eyes welling with tears and every possible emotion coming at him all at once, he took one slow step after another until he was only a few feet away. It was when she matched his moves, the space reduced to only inches, he was finally able to speak, this coming out in a hoarse whisper.

"Gracie..."

Somehow, and he couldn't tell you who moved first, nor did it matter, she was in his arms and he was kissing her like a man possessed.

Finally... this is what he'd been dreaming of over the past months, what had enabled him to keep going, one day at a time.

He pulled her closer, his hands sliding under her sweater. The softness of her skin under his fingers was nothing short of intoxicating, the shiver he could feel course through her at his touch, sending a jolt of heat through him. Groaning her name, he pulled her even harder against him to deepen the kiss.

He'd swear, if he had his way, he'd never let her go. He'd keep this kiss, this moment, going forever. The fact she had wrapped her arms around his neck and was kissing him back just as passionately, told him she wanted the same.

But before they took this any further, there was something he needed to know, something he needed to ask her. And he wanted to be looking into her eyes, when she gave him her answer.

He buried his hands in her hair, his gaze slowly traveling over every inch of her face to finally end at her mouth... her beautiful mouth. God knows how many times in the past months he'd brought up this same vision from his memory.

And now she is here... and she is real...

"Please tell me you're here to stay."

This time, as hadn't happened in the past, she didn't look away. Her eyes holding his, they sent a message that up until now, he'd only been able to hope for. "If you want me to, yes. But..."

He put a halt to what she was going to say. "*Yes*...this is all I've ever wanted. For always, Gracie..."

Another groan coming from deep inside of him, again his mouth claimed hers. It was a kiss that left them both breathless.

Stroking the smooth softness of her skin with his thumbs, his voice was husky with longing. "Peaches, I've been so patient. I can't even begin to tell you how much I've been waiting for this moment. Tell me you'll let me love you so we can make a start at erasing the time we've been apart... all the time we've lost."

Yeah, don't worry. He was completely aware there was something she'd wanted to share with him, this part of the reason he cut her off with his kiss.

But, come on, any hesitation on his part was to be expected. Over the years, their relationship had always been haunted by uncertainty, with him always the one left behind, wondering what was going to happen next.

Or, the unthinkable... wondering if anything was going to happen at all.

So, this time, for at least a little while, he wanted everything between them to be perfect, no shadows in the background.

Wishful thinking... yeah, he knew this.

She briefly closed her eyes, resting her head against his chest before she spoke. "Jake, listen to me... I want what you want. I've wanted this for as long as I can remember." She gazed up at him. "It's me... peaches. Remember? The shy thirteen-year-old who tagged after you and Sam every chance I could get, idolizing your every move. And nothing has changed. But, first we need to talk, so I can tell you everything..."

Again, he cut her off. "No... no... you don't need to tell me anything. I don't need to know. Even though you drive me crazy sometimes, there is nothing that could be so bad it would turn me against you. What is it they say? For better or for worse? This will always hold true for me. You will always be the only one for me."

He suddenly grinned. "Unless, of course, you were to criticize my cooking."

Encouraged by her smile, he pressed a kiss to her forehead. "I mean it. You've spoiled me for anyone else and I'm afraid now you're stuck with me."

She was shaking her head as she pressed her hands against his chest and stepped back. She took his hand. "First, I want you to come with me. There's something you need to see."

He let her lead him down the hall to the spare bedroom. Even though he'd already made the decision whatever she wanted to show him, it wasn't going to make a damn bit of difference.

She was his and he was hers.

This was all that mattered.

She cautiously pushed open the door to the spare bedroom. He saw the lamp on the nightstand was lit.

She nodded towards the bed.

There was a small child curled up under the covers and fast asleep, a little girl with long, dark curly hair. A worn and stuffed toy rabbit tucked under her arm, he could see a trace of tears on her flushed cheeks.

He glanced over at Gracie, to see she was anxiously watching him. At his confused expression, she shook her head and holding her finger to her lips, she steered him out of the bedroom.

She carefully shut the door, leaving it open just a crack, before she spoke in barely a whisper. "You've just met Anastasia Louisa Belle."

At his raised eyebrow, she grinned. "Yeah, I know it's a lot of name for such a little girl. We've given her the nickname of Bella."

We? Who was it, you want to know, that made up this we?

Jake was having an inner battle with himself. He wanted to ask more, but what he didn't want to hear, was this child was Gracie's. The thought of her having a child with another man, well… right now this would be almost too much to take. He'd always thought of Gracie as his. Even after all she'd been through, he'd always hoped she'd remain true to him.

He cleared his throat. "Is she… well, what I mean, is Bella…"

Swiftly pressing her fingers to his mouth and shaking her head, she looked directly into his eyes. "No, no… she's not my child. She's the daughter of a friend."

She watched as, even though he tried, he was unable to hide his inner sigh of relief. In a way, she was disappointed he'd even asked her this. But she also understood. She'd certainly given him so many reasons to believe the worst of her, wondering what went on all of the time they were apart.

She glanced back at the bedroom door, the protective look in her eyes tinged with sadness.

He was hesitant to even ask. "A friend?"

She nodded. "Yes, my friend Angie. At least she used to be my friend. We kept in close touch over the years and there were times I couldn't have made it without her. So, I made a promise, if anything were to ever happen to her, I would make sure Bella had a good home." She shrugged. "So, here we are."

She gazed up at him, her eyes bright with unshed tears and pleading with him to understand. "I have the papers Angie had written up, giving me the right to adopt Bella. If I don't, I'm so afraid of what will happen, who she'll wind up with."

She shook her head. "None of it would be good, Jake. She needs to be with someone who loves her, who will take care of her and give her a good life."

Her bottom lip starting to tremble, her voice becoming choked. "She's only four and I'm all she has."

He pulled her into his arms, pressing a kiss to the top of her head. "This is one of the things… and there are many, may I remind you… that I love about you. No matter how bad things get for you, you never stop caring about everyone else. Granted, this doesn't always turn out that great, but your heart is always in the right place."

He nodded towards the bedroom. "You don't even have to ask. Bella will always have a home with us. If you love her, I'll love her just as much."

Framing the side of her face in his hand, his intention to give her another kiss, this was when he noticed she was wearing the necklace he'd given to her.

"The necklace I gave you… you're wearing it. You weren't the last time I saw you."

A sudden smile lit up her face. "It was Bella who found it when we were cleaning out the apartment, tucked between the sofa cushions. Since then, I've never taken it off. It's what kept me going."

The kiss he gave her was the kiss of a man who was finally sure of where he stood. "Come on, let's go to bed."

At her hesitant look, he smiled. "I only want to be close to you, hold you in my arms. Now that I know you're here for good, I can wait for the rest." He brushed the hair back from her face. "But maybe until then, we can sneak in a few kisses to make up for lost time?"

He gazed down at her as they began walking down the hall. For the life of him, he couldn't stop smiling. "I'm thinking you're right. Maybe it's about time you did tell me everything so we can make a fresh start. But, just to warn you, it's probably only going to make me love you even more."

She came to a halt, gazing up at him. And through the tears beginning to spill down her cheeks, he could finally see what he'd so patiently been waiting for.

She really was here to stay.

She leaned against him, burying her face in his shoulder. "Oh, Jake…"

And Jake? What was he thinking?

Believe it or not, as he held her in his arms, he was wondering if she was hungry. This was because, for him, food was the cure for everything. It was a celebration… and even more, an offering of his love.

He smiled down at her. "I can't even begin to tell you how glad I am that you're here. But, first things first, are you hungry? If you are, I brought home one of my newest creations from the restaurant and there's more than enough for two. I want to get your opinion on the flavors. What do you think?" There was a teasing gleam in his eyes. "I might even name the dish after you."

When she nodded, a big smile on her face, he pulled her back into his arms for another kiss.

Suddenly, not only was he wide awake, but he was starving, too.

He was hungry for everything.

CHAPTER 20

These three are what always remain ~
Faith, Hope and Love.
But always remember, the greatest of these is love.
~Anonymous

as that the doorbell?

Struggling out of a sound sleep, Hannah tunneled her way out from under the quilt as the sound once again echoed loudly through the silence of the night.

Yep, it was definitely the doorbell.

She squinted over at the clock on the nightstand. When she saw it read one-thirty-three, she pulled the quilt back over her head and closed her eyes.

As far as she was concerned, whoever it was, they could just go away.

It rang again… and then again. And now, it sounded even louder. She'd swear it was like a siren going off. After a long pause, fooling her into believing it had stopped for good, it rang again.

This was a definite sign, whoever it was?

They weren't planning on giving up.

She groaned, throwing off the quilt. Dragging her hands through her hair, she stumbled down the hall to the front door.

They better have a really good reason for such a late-night visit.

She peered through the peephole, her anger swiftly turning to confusion.

Sean?

Why is Sean standing on your front steps?

His head tucked down in his collar and his hands shoved in the pockets of his leather jacket, he was staring down at his boots. She watched as he lifted his head to gaze up at the snow flurries whirling around him.

He groaned, his words just barely audible through the door. "Come on, Hannah... open the door, darlin'... I need you."

Her hands flying to her face, she was now wide awake. His words sending her heart pounding erratically in her chest, she stepped back from the door.

He needs you? Well, what are you waiting for? The man just said he needs you. Open the door.

Adjusting her tee shirt, pulling up her flannel pajama pants and fluffing up her hair, she opened the door.

Their eyes locked and for a few moments, they didn't move. Intently searching her face, it was as though he was seeing her for the first time. While she remained silent, waiting for him to explain.

She didn't understand. Wasn't he supposed to be at Sam's bachelor party? She was pretty sure he'd told her it was going to be an all-night affair.

She moved closer.

Was he drunk?

She didn't smell alcohol on him. And he did tell her the most he planned on drinking was only a beer, or maybe two.

She'd been somewhat skeptical about this, because, come on... this was a bachelor party. With a bunch of guys who were conveniently staying the night at a hotel only a short walk away from the bar they had chosen for the event.

And if anyone did drink over their limit?

The walk from the bar to the hotel on this frigid January night would be more than enough to sober them up in a hurry.

It was only when an example of the weather they were dealing with came at them in a blast of whirling snow, the wind howling around the building for effect, she stepped aside so he could enter.

After she closed the door, she turned to find his gaze hadn't wavered.

He cleared his throat. "Hey, I..." Removing his hands from his pockets, he took a step closer.

She moved closer, putting her hand on his arm. "Are you okay? I thought you were hanging out with the guys tonight. Did the bachelor party break up early?"

He came at her so suddenly, she had no time to react. Pulling her into his arms and walking her backwards until she was sandwiched between him and the wall, he groaned her name right before his mouth came crashing down on hers.

He gave her no chance to question, no time to think. The passionate onslaught of his kiss made sure of this.

The coolness of his skin from the icy outdoors, along with the few snowflakes lingering on his face, was a complete contrast to the searing heat of his mouth. A faint moan escaping her, her heartbeat soared into high gear in a matter of seconds,

Aroused by her response, his hands moved down over her, tracing her curves before he pulled her even closer. His mouth became more demanding, his kiss going deeper.

It was when he realized he'd backed her up against the wall, he abruptly ended the kiss. Burying his face in her shoulder, a small smile touched his lips as he listened to the pounding of their hearts between them.

This was when he knew he'd never be able to get enough of her, hold her close enough. But this didn't mean he wasn't going to try.

"Come..." Smiling down at her dazed expression, he took her hand to lead her down the hall to her bedroom. His gaze never leaving hers, he swiftly removed his coat, throwing it on the chair. After pulling off his boots, he emptied his pockets.

To put your mind at ease, Hannah wasn't frightened by Sean's behavior. She was more curious than anything else.

She knew he would never hurt her, nor would he ask her to do something she wasn't comfortable with. This she'd be willing to swear on whatever was put in front of her.

Be it a bible, or even a stack of bibles… definitely, she'd do this.

Obviously, something momentous had happened, something affecting him deeply. And the knowledge he'd left the bachelor party to seek her out, had her ready to help him in any way she could.

Her arms tightly wrapped around herself, she watched him. "Sean…"

He took her hand and gently pulling her down on the bed with him, his mouth claimed hers in another kiss. But this was gentler, more reassuring . His fingers tracing the outline of her jaw, he smiled down at her. "*Shh…* I hadn't meant to come at you like that. And now, I only want to lay with you, be able to put my arms around you and hold you close. I need to know you're here."

After settling her against him and giving a long, contented sigh, this is exactly what he did.

They lay in silence.

It was when he finally stirred, pressing a kiss in her hair, she cautiously pulled away to gaze up at him. "Sean, what's wrong? What happened?"

He answered this with another kiss. Mostly because he wasn't sure how to answer her, so much running around in his mind. You'd think he would've tried to figure this out during the drive to her condo. But, at the time, all he could think about was how much he needed to be with her, his only goal to get to this moment with her.

He gazed into her eyes, her beautiful eyes.

Eyes that never hid from him what she was thinking.

Eyes you want to gaze into for the rest of your life.

And he was kissing her again, the frenzied beat of her heart against the palm of his hand making it almost impossible for him to pull away. Sifting his fingers through her hair, a move that never failed to soothe him, he finally gave a long sigh, his breath brushing against her cheek. "My brother called me tonight, Ryan. It was while Kevin and I were right in the middle of a game of pool."

A smile hitched the corner of his mouth. "I was winning. At the time, this was the most important thing in the world to me. I wanted that high I always get when I win. But, I feel like this is all I've been thinking about lately... winning."

He shrugged. "I guess it's all part of playing the game, what is expected of me. Winning, being the best... proving to everyone how good I can be at what I do."

She surprised him by pressing a quick kiss to his mouth. "You're all of those things to me."

He smiled down at her, pulling her even closer. "Ah, Hannah Michaels... this is why I want to hang around with you. You make me believe I can be so much better than I think I can."

Of course, he had to kiss her again, this time finding it even harder to pull away.

This has to stop. You're to the point you've almost forgotten the real reason you're here.

He groaned. "If I intend to finish what I want to say, I need to stop kissing you. At least for now, I do."

He gazed down at her, an abstract smile on his face. "So, where was I? Ah, yes... Ryan. When I answered the call, even though I could hear him breathing, he didn't say anything. Then he started to cry."

Briefly closing his eyes, his voice was strained. "In my whole life, I don't think I've ever heard or seen him cry. Yeah, he shed a few tears when he and Tina got married... when they exchanged their vows. The same when Carly was born. But both of those times, it was different. You know, it was a joyful, happy cry."

He pressed another kiss in her hair. "I didn't know what to think... maybe my father had a relapse? Or something happened to my mum, or someone else in the family? But, thank God, it wasn't any of those. He told me Tina left him, taking Carly with her. She refused to give him a reason, only insisting their marriage was over and she was filing for a divorce."

Dragging his hand back through his hair, he gave a long sigh. "I was on the phone with him for about a half-hour while he kept going over what happened, trying to rationalize why she'd want to leave him. And, I couldn't think of a damn thing to say that would help him. But this was because I found it all so unbelievable. Even now it still doesn't make sense. He and Tina have known each other since grade school. It has always been Tina and Ryan. Everyone assumed they'd get married and grow old together. They were always the perfect couple. And now? I feel like I've let him down. Even though I told him he could call me anytime, to talk, or whatever. But being so far away, what can I do?"

Bringing her hand to his mouth, he pressed his lips to her fingers. He couldn't seem to stop touching her, kissing her. He wanted to get lost in the comforting feel of her.

His hope was this would erase the helpless feeling that hadn't left him since Ryan's call.

Hannah wasn't sure what to say, so she did the only thing she thought might make him feel better. She curled in closer to him, wrapping her arms around him before she finally spoke. "I'm sorry. I can't even imagine what he's going through right now. But I'm sure talking to you, helped. And I remember you telling me how close he is to Carly. Maybe this will help bring them back together again."

"Yeah… you're right, we can only hope."

He sighed. "After we ended the call, I found I didn't care about the game with Kevin… or about winning. The only thing I could think about was you, how much I wanted to be with you. So, here I am…"

He suddenly moved to his side and propping himself up on his elbow, he gazed down at her for the longest time.

"Hannah…"

This coming from him in a sigh, she wasn't at all prepared for the next words to come out of his mouth.

"Marry me…"

Did she hear wrong? Surely, he couldn't have said what she thought he did. Her eyes wide, she searched his face.

Marry me?

Then she opened her mouth, but for the life of her, she was only able to repeat what he said.

She swallowed, her voice coming out in barely a whisper.

"Marry you?"

From the time he'd left the bar and up until he arrived at Hannah's condo, Sean hadn't been able to stop thinking about Ryan's call. He didn't even want to even imagine this happening to him and Hannah.

And if it did? It would just about kill him. He'd swear it would.

How had he arrived at this point? Never did he think he'd be one of these love-struck- head-over-heels-about-a-woman kind of guy.

But with Hannah? The attraction had been instantaneous. He'd liken it to a bolt of lightning, coming down from the sky, hitting him right on.

Even though you knew nothing about her. Nor shared a single word. You just knew...

This was when he realized there was some truth about this love at first sight thing. Proof was in the breathless, heart stopping and mind racing symptoms that had hit him, head on.

So, for him, there hadn't been the least bit of hesitation in asking her to marry him. Nope, not at all. But, by the look of bewilderment on Hannah's face, he could see she was struggling to find an answer.

Yeah, this certainly wasn't the reaction he'd hoped to get from her. In his mind, he had her diving into his arms, crying yes over and over before they sealed the proposal with a kiss.

But, at the same time, he wasn't too concerned. Because, if he wasn't mistaken, there was a hint of something else in her eyes.

Trust... she trusts you.

And after the phone call from his brother, he now knew what an important role this played in a relationship with the one you loved.

So, no... he wasn't worried at all.

To say Hannah was in shock, would be an understatement.

She couldn't even begin to tell you what she was thinking.

But there was one thing she knew for sure.

She couldn't marry Sean.

At least right now she couldn't.

She needed to get back more of the before-the-accident-Hannah, the real Hannah, before she made any kind of commitment.

And Sean?

That she couldn't remember she had been in love with him, was so mind boggling to her.

How could you forget something as momentous as being in love with someone? And not only just someone, but a man like Sean?

Nope, she didn't see how this could be possible.

And this is what was holding her back, this uncertainty. Even though she knew she was falling in love with him all over again.

Maybe Sean was right... with a little patience, this really could turn out to be a January to remember.

A second chance at love.

She gazed up at him. "I'm so sorry... I wish..."

Pressing his fingers to her lips, his expression was tender, while at the same time, his words so serious. "Ah, Hannah, *shh*... it's okay. I understand. I can't even imagine how frustrated you must be, not knowing what is going to happen, when your life will all make sense to you again."

He shook his head. "And then I come along, making things even more complicated, throwing all of these demands at you. Darlin' I believe I should be the one apologizing to you."

She reached up to give him a kiss. "No, no... it's okay. But, I think... well, give me time."

He smiled. "You can have all the time you want... My offer will always stand, you only need to say the word."

She reached up to press a kiss to his cheek. "Thank you."

"You are more than welcome." A big grin lit up his face. "But, right now? Please don't send me back out into the snow. It's so damn cold out there. And here? With you in my arms, well... it just wouldn't be fair."

Her attempt to press another kiss to his cheek turned into so much more when he turned his head to capture her mouth instead.

So, of course there was no way she was going to let him leave.

After he'd asked her to marry him?

Absolutely not.

Like he said… it just wouldn't be fair.

CHAPTER 21

$\mathcal{I}$t was morning and Sean had been awake for quite some time. Even before he'd opened his eyes, a slow smile had begun to travel across his face.

And it was still there. Because, this wasn't a dream. No, this was as real as it could get. Hannah was real. And in his arms.

He glanced over at the clock on the nightstand. It was a little past seven.

Good... it's still early, so you can hold her for a little longer.

He pulled her closer, pressing a kiss in her hair. She stirred and, snuggling against him, she mumbled something he couldn't quite understand. Then she gave a soft little sigh.

He lifted his head to gaze down at her. She had gone right back to sleep.

There was one little problem. She was pressed against his arm, which had now gone almost completely numb. As he slowly began to ease it out from under her, her lashes fluttered open, a brief look of surprise flickering in her eyes.

Then she smiled.

Just as he was about say something, she beat him to it. "Hey, cowboy..."

After a sharp intake of breath, his gaze locked with hers. His heart pounding in his chest, the sound was magnified in his head. Almost to the point he couldn't think.

"Hannah?" This came out in a hoarse whisper.

Her lips parted in confusion, she slowly shook her head. She was having a hard time. Suddenly, everything felt different, a momentous change about to take place. Unable to keep this from happening, she could only hang on, hoping everything would eventually right itself.

When Sean saw the struggle in her eyes, it all clicked in his mind. He knew what he had to do. Something he should have done from the very beginning.

He dove off the bed. Dragging his hand through his hair, he glanced down at her. There was a sense of urgency in his voice. "I'll be right back. Don't move." These words hadn't even left his mouth before he grabbed his keys off the nightstand and went running out of the room.

It was when he was sprinting down the front steps of Hannah's condo and headed for his truck, he realized he hadn't stopped to put on his boots. Or his jacket.

Not one of his better moves, since it was still snowing… or more like a mini blizzard. And it was cold, close to single digits, he'd be willing to bet.

But he didn't care.

What mattered was he didn't let this moment escape them. Because it had the potential to change everything.

After he grabbed his hat from the back seat of his truck, he turned to see Hannah was standing at the front door, the quilt from the bed wrapped around her.

A bewildered look on her face, she watched as he made his way back to her. As he started up the steps, she glanced up at the sky, to then look over at him. She shook her head. "Look how hard it's snowing and you're without your jacket." Then she glanced down to see his socks were the only barrier between his feet and the snow. "*Oh, Sean… you didn't even put on your boots…*"

He didn't answer, a grin on his face as he came to stand in front of her. Vigorously shaking the snow from his hair, his grin grew even bigger as he lifted his hat and placed it on his head.

He adjusted it, slowly he did this. It was important he get this exactly right. The whole time, his eyes never left her face, the intensity of his gaze making her shiver even more than she had from the cold.

Finally, he let out a slow, deep breath. "Your one and only, darlin'…"

Her breath catching in her throat, she became completely still.

Except in her mind… there everything had begun to spin like crazy, making her dizzy. Closing her eyes, she could only wait, willing the missing part of her memory to finally fall back into place.

Like the final pieces of a puzzle. Remember? Just like the doctor said.

When she finally opened her eyes, it was to the love shining in his.

She was back.

She was home.

A strangled cry coming from her, she threw herself into his arms.

"Oh my God… Sean…"

And then she began to cry.

His arms wrapped around her, he held on tight.

He had his Hannah back.

Sean didn't want to let her go… but then, it was more like, he *wasn't* going to let her go. He was afraid if he did, she'd somehow slip right back to where she'd been since her accident.

So, even after her tears had stopped and she stirred against him, he kept his arms wrapped around her, holding her close.

He buried his face in her hair, giving a long, contented sigh.

Silk… as always.

It was only when she pulled back to gaze up at him, he finally eased his hold on her. Gazing up at him with a look of wonder on her face, she reached up to stroke his cheek before she went on to trace the line of his jaw with her fingertips. Searching the face that was now so familiar to her, she couldn't get enough. She'd gaze at him forever if he'd let her.

Waiting patiently for her to look her fill, Sean could only imagine how overwhelming this had to be for her. Finally, brushing the hair from her face, he pressed a kiss to her forehead. "Are you okay?"

She nodded, her answer coming in a sigh. *"I missed you, cowboy..."*

His heart hitching in his chest at her words, he smiled. *"I missed you, too, darlin'..."*

He gazed up at the sky, a huge groan coming from him. "I can't believe it all came down to my hat. And here all this time, I've been carrying it around in my truck."

Her fingers going to his lips, she shook her head. "It doesn't matter now. It's okay... *we're okay.*"

He cleared his throat. "You're right... we are. But, out of curiosity... does everything match up to what you remember? Am I still as handsome as I was when we first met?" He couldn't hide the teasing tone in his voice, the thought briefly entering his mind this was probably a moment that should be taken more seriously.

But come on... he was just so damn happy.

He was happy about everything.

Her gaze slowly traveling over him again, she sighed. "Yes, you are. Maybe even more so. You look wonderful. So wonderful."

She rested her forehead against his chest. "Oh, Sean... I goofed everything up terribly, didn't I?"

He pulled her closer. "Sweetheart, to tell you the truth, that you remember me is all I care about right now." He brushed his lips lightly over hers. "Ah, Hannah Michaels... do you know how badly I want to kiss you? Yes, I know we've had our share of kisses in the past few days, but this is different."

His voice sank to a whisper. "I want to kiss the Hannah I left behind... the Hannah I was so afraid I'd lost. The Hannah I'd come to love."

She wound her arms around his neck, her eyes shining into his. "I wouldn't mind if you did, cowboy."

Cowboy... how is it this simple word is now like the sweetest music to your ears?

So, of course, he kissed her.

It was a kiss they both fell right into. As though no time had passed since the magical summer night they shared back in June.

A kiss so familiar, yet at the same time different, so wonderfully different.

The knowledge they'd been given another chance, one not to be taken for granted, they poured everything they had into the kiss.

And if you stop to think of all they'd gone through?

You'd have to agree, it was as close to a miracle you could get.

He was the first to move, his deep chuckle tickling her ear. "I don't mean to spoil the moment, but even as tough as I seem… and as happy as I am right now, I'm beginning to lose any feeling in my feet."

They both gazed down at his feet, buried in the snow drifted over the steps. Hannah began to laugh. "Oh, Sean… I can't believe this. Come on, we need to get you inside and out of those socks."

Once they were inside, she started for her bedroom, smiling at him over her shoulder. "I'm going to get you some socks."

But he grabbed her hand and pulling her back and right into his arms, he grinned down at her. "I don't need socks. The only thing I need right now is you."

She was shaking her head as she untangled herself from his hold. "No, I insist. I don't want you to get sick."

So, with him following right behind, only because he didn't want to let her out of his sight, she continued on into her bedroom and began rummaging through one of her dresser drawers.

She finally held out a pair of heavy wool socks. "Here… these are my brother's. They'll warm you up. He let me borrow them when he got this notion in his head I needed to know how to ski and he was going to be the one to teach me."

She shrugged, her face scrunched up at the memory. "It didn't go so well. I wish I could say I learned to ski, but let's just say I spent more time on the ground than I did on skis."

He shook his head.

He couldn't stop grinning.

Let's face it, you love everything about her... every one of her expressions, her laugh, everything.

She moved closer. "Sean?"

He took the socks from her and after tossing them on the dresser, he surprised her by taking her into his arms and tumbling them both onto the bed. Gazing down at her astonished expression, he buried his face in the hollow of her neck, pressing a leisurely kiss to the pulse beating there.

He lifted his head, his gaze slowly roaming over her face. "Darlin', stop worrying, I'll be fine. I promise. Right now, I want you to talk to me, tell me everything you remember... about us, you, me... what sticks with you the most." He trailed his fingers along her jaw, his voice dipping to a husky drawl. "*My God, Hannah...* I want to hear you say you missed me as much as I missed you."

The burning intensity in his eyes stalled her breath, and for a moment, she was at a loss for words. She finally swallowed, her voice as hushed as his.

"I did. I missed you so much."

She reached up to wrap her arms around his neck. Her fingers sifting through his hair, loving the way it curled over his collar, she tried to gather her thoughts.

But *wow...* this wasn't easy. There was so much going on in her mind right now. All of these memories were coming in a rush, fighting for her attention, each too important not to be shared. Never before had she felt so vulnerable, ready to open her heart and share her most private thoughts.

Her fingers slipped under the collar of his shirt and coming in contact with the intoxicating heat of his skin, she almost lost her train of thought. It was his mouth swooping down to capture hers in a gentle, yet insistent kiss that was a subtle reminder he was waiting for more.

She sighed. "After you left, everything felt so different. Sort of how it feels the day after Christmas... or your birthday."

At his low chuckle, her words became more earnest. "You know what I mean. Everything is so perfect and exciting... there's that feeling of anticipation about what's going to happen next. Then just like that, it's the next day and the celebration is over. The excitement is gone. Your life is now back to ordinary and you're left with the feeling something is missing. This is how I felt after you left."

He pressed a kiss to the top of her head. "*Ah...* this is what Ellie told me."

She was confused. "Ellie? Who is Ellie?"

He was smiling. "Ellie... Ellie Cook. She works at Café Latté. When I stopped in to pick up your banana muffins, she recognized me from when you and I met there. She said you went to school together. She also told me the last time you'd stopped in the café, you seemed down and this was when you told her something was missing in your life. At the time, I hoped the something might be me."

She pressed a kiss to his cheek. "Yes, yes... it was. I missed you so much. But I told myself this was crazy. We hadn't known each other long enough, certainly not for me to have developed such strong feelings for you. Like you said, we hadn't even gone on a real date. And even with all of the promises we made to each other while you were away, I was so afraid when you came back, it wouldn't be the same. We'd feel differently. You'd feel differently. Or you had changed your mind about us."

Her eyes suddenly lit up. "The brownies in my refrigerator? I ordered those from Abby, special for you. I remembered how much you liked them when we were at Sophie and Chester's barbecue. So, I wanted to surprise you."

She laughed. "If I remember, you ate three of them... in almost the same amount of bites."

She had to stop and take a deep breath. With everything coming at her so fast and all at once, it was to the point she almost couldn't think at all.

Sean was watching her. The excitement shining in her eyes was the Hannah he remembered, the Hannah he'd loved from day one. That she would even think he would change his mind was unfathomable to him.

So, it was up to him to convince her this would never happen. And he knew exactly how to go about this. He only had to make a few phone calls and get Hannah on board.

He grinned. "Speaking of brownies, I'm starving. I think it's time we made a trip back to Café Latte, this time for breakfast. I know everyone will be happy to see you, since they've asked about you every time I stopped in for the muffins and coffee. What do you think?"

She smiled. "I think that sounds wonderful."

"Good, because there is someplace else I'd like to take you. I need your opinion on something. We may be outside part of the time, so you'll need to dress warmly."

He left the bed and reaching for her hand, he pulled her up and into his arms. Leaning in to give her another kiss, he abruptly pulled back. "Nope, I'm not going to do it. It's just too damn tempting. The next thing I know, I'll be tumbling you back on the bed and having my way with you."

His thumb lifting her chin, he gazed into her eyes. His voice was deep with longing. "That will come later. And I know it's going to be nothing short of amazing. This, I promise you."

This had her blushing like crazy. The things he hinted at, well… it was enough to drive her insane. Now she was the one who wanted to tumble him back on to the bed.

Yeah, she could do this. Then have her way with him? Of course… she could do that, too.

And if she didn't get it quite right? She was pretty sure he'd be willing to help her out with that, too.

When she emerged from her bedroom twenty minutes later, she found Sean standing by the window, gazing out at the snow still coming down pretty hard.

Hands in his pockets, he appeared deep in thought.

As she made her way over to him, she stopped to pick up his hat from where he had tossed it on the sofa.

He turned. A slow smile coming over his face, he held out his hand, his voice a husky whisper.

"Hey, come here…"

As she walked into his embrace, she was filled with such an incredible feeling. You know the one… where any uncertainty clouding your mind had finally disappeared, leaving everything so clear and absolutely right.

The old saying, a lightbulb went off? This could definitely apply to this moment.

Because, God help her… this was when she realized what she'd told Sophie… that she thought she was falling in love with Sean?

This was no longer true.

She had gone past falling. Yep, she had made the plunge and was now completely in love with him, as deeply in love one could be.

Overcome by this sudden revelation, she tried to hide the shakiness in her voice as she held out his hat. "Here, cowboy… you don't want to forget your hat. I'm beginning to think there might be some magic there when you put it on."

She smiled.

"Magic of the best kind."

CHAPTER 22

S ean pushed open the door of Café Latte, gesturing for Hannah to go ahead of him.

After stomping the snow off his boots, he took in a deep breath, the aroma of freshly perked coffee and baked goods enough to make his stomach give a loud growl in anticipation.

He smiled down at Hannah. "Ah… smells good in here doesn't it? Reminds me of home. And of how hungry I am."

Her answer was interrupted by the sound of someone calling her name. They both turned to see it was Ellie. She was waving from behind the counter, a big grin on her face.

She came over to give Hannah a hug. "Hannah… you're back. Oh, my goodness… I've been so worried about you." She waved around at the interior of the little shop. "In fact, almost everyone here has been worried about you. We've all been pulling for you."

Her hand suddenly going to her mouth, she frowned. "Oh dear, I'm so sorry. Maybe you don't quite remember me yet? That's okay, I'll be more than happy to introduce myself. I'm Ellie, Ellie Cook. We went to grade school together. When Sean stopped by to pick up banana muffins and coffee, he told us what happened and how you were having trouble remembering parts of your past."

When Ellie finally paused to take a breath, Hannah laughed. "No, it's okay. I know who you are. And I think I'm going to be okay now. At least my memory has returned."

She glanced up at Sean. "Thanks to Sean."

His answer was to drop a kiss to the top of her head before he reached over to pull out a chair at one of the empty tables. "Here, you get comfortable, darlin'. I'll go put in our order."

After he left, Ellie shook her head. "How did you get so lucky to meet someone like him? Oh my Gosh, he's absolutely perfect… the hat and everything. The first time he stopped for coffee and muffins on his way to visit you in the hospital, he looked so sad. I think every woman in here wanted to be the one to make him feel better."

At the worried look on Hannah's face, she burst out laughing. "Oh, Hannah…you have nothing to worry about. He's definitely *so* into you. This is obvious by the way he looks at you."

Before Hannah could comment, Sean was back, coffee and muffins in hand. At the same time, Ellie suddenly began to back away from the table. She was staring at the entrance, a look of panic on her face.

Her voice fell to a whisper. "Oh no, he's here again." She nodded towards the door. "The guy that just came in."

Wringing her hands, she nervously glanced at Hannah. "His name is Michael. Over the past week, he has come in every day and I keep catching him sending glances over at me." She sighed. "He seems so nice."

Hannah and Sean glanced curiously over at the entrance.

Hannah smiled. "I know him. It's Michael Stewart."

She turned to Sean. "The Michael I ran into his motorcycle."

At the same time, Michael glanced over in their direction and saw Hannah. A smile lighting up his face, he swiftly made his way over to them. "Hannah… you're looking fantastic. Gosh, seeing you like this has made my day."

He paused, smiling over at Ellie before he turned to Sean, holding out his hand. "Hi, I'm Michael Stewart. It was my motorcycle that did all the damage to Hannah. Fortunately, it now looks like she is so much better? Thank God for that."

Hannah had told Sean about Michael's visit to the hospital, that he had asked for her number, suggesting they keep in touch. Wondering if this meant Michael was interested in Hannah, he now saw he had no reason to worry. It was obvious by the glances he and Ellie kept shooting at each other, there was some serious chemistry brewing between them.

Hannah was watching Ellie, who was nervously backing away from their table, her cheeks a bright shade of pink.

It was when Michael sent Hannah a questioning smile, she quickly jumped in to say something. "Michael, have you met Ellie? She and I go all the way back to grade school. She works here part time while studying for a degree in medical research."

She glanced over at Ellie. "You're graduating in the spring, right?"

Ellie nodded. This was the best she could do.

Michael took Ellie's hand in a firm grasp as he gave her a big smile. "The only thing I know so far is your name… Ellie. And that you have a beautiful smile. But, wow… that's great about your degree. What an interesting field to be in. I'm sure you have some great stories to share."

He shook his head. "I'm sort of boring, accounting."

All he knew so far? What did this mean? Did he want to know more?

Now even more flustered and since it appeared she had now also completely lost her voice, she nodded again. All the while wondering… was it just her imagination, or was he refusing to let go of her hand?

Gently easing her hand from his, she took a deep breath. "I'm sure accounting isn't boring. Everyone needs to know about numbers. Or how to count money."

Oh… my… gosh… could you have even made a more stupid remark? Everyone likes to count money? What must he be thinking?

She needed to get away from him before she said something even more ridiculous. Backing away, she sent a smile around the table. "I better get back to work. It was nice meeting you, Michael. And Hannah, I'm so glad you're okay. Sean, keep taking good care of her."

After she almost fell over the chair behind her, this resulting in enough noise to make everyone turn around to see what was happening, she almost ran back to her place behind the counter.

If she could, she would've crawled right under it.

Hannah was watching Michael, who was watching Ellie. She glanced over at Sean. He was smiling.

Shaking his head, he loudly cleared his throat.

Michael turned to them, a bemused smile on his face. "She's cute, isn't she? I noticed her when I first started coming here a week ago. But, for some reason, I don't think she likes me. I tried to talk to her, but you saw what happened. She runs off."

Sean chuckled. "Man, if you ask me, I think it's the opposite. You need to stop thinking so much and go for it… ask her out. What have you got to lose?"

Michael glanced over at Hannah.

Busy buttering her muffin, she nodded. "I agree with Sean." It wasn't that she didn't care, or wasn't paying attention… she was just so hungry.

Michael appeared to think this over before he finally smiled. "You're right. In fact, I'm going to do it right now."

He sent them both a nod. "Nice meeting you, Sean. And Hannah? Again, I'm so glad to see everything worked out for you."

He grinned. "Wish me luck."

His shoulders thrown back and a determined look on his face, Michael made his way over to where Ellie was clearing a table. After a short conversation, the huge smile on his face before he left to place his order, was a sign all went well. Holding a tray in her hands and still standing where he had left her, Ellie's smile was almost as big.

Sean glanced over at Hannah. He was grinning as he reached for his coffee cup. "Well, look at us… playing at matchmaking. I think we did good, really good."

He held his cup to hers in a toast. "Cheers to us, darlin'."

After he set his cup back on the table, he gave her one of those smiles she loved so much, his eyes crinkling at the corners. This had her leaning towards him in anticipation, waiting for what he was about to say.

She wasn't disappointed.

He reached over to wrap one of her curls around his finger. *"Ah... but, do you think they'll ever be as happy as we are?"*

She pressed a kiss to his cheek. "I don't think that's possible."

Sean and Hannah had been driving for almost an hour, the slippery and snow covered roads slowing their progress. But now the flurries had begun to taper off, the late afternoon sun breaking through the clouds.

They were now in an area occupied by luxurious homes, rustic outbuildings and picturesque barns. With the fresh snowfall, it was as though they'd driven right into a print from a Currier & Ives Christmas card.

Hannah glanced over at Sean. "Where exactly are we going? I feel like we're in horse country. Or an English countryside."

He chuckled. "That's exactly where we are, darlin'. Horse country. In the rolling hills of suburban Cleveland. Bet you didn't even know this was here, did you? I didn't either until Chris started sending me listings."

He slowed to turn onto a narrow and winding driveway. "Ah... here we go... this is the address Sam gave me, 120 Country Lane Road. He sent me a listing of this property only yesterday. He thought I might want to check it out."

He put the truck in low gear as they made their way down the long driveway leading into a forest of pine trees. "Hmm... very secluded, wouldn't you say? One of the things I told Sam I wanted in a property. Especially with horses."

Hannah was studying him. "You want to buy a horse farm?"

His concentration on navigating the unplowed driveway, he gave a vague nod. "It depends on what I find, I guess." He grinned. "It's not like there's a lot available."

They traveled on through the wooded area to finally come upon a large and rambling rustic styled house. There was a barn situated not far behind, along with a few other small buildings.

Hannah glanced over at Sean. He wanted a property like this? To her, it seemed so large, so overwhelming. "How would you be able to take care of such a large property with your schedule and all?"

He shrugged. "I guess I'd have to hire someone to help me out. This shouldn't be too much of a problem. I wouldn't be surprised if there was already someone doing that job now." He smiled over at her. "My guess is they would be more than happy to stay on."

He waved his hand at the forest of pine trees around them. "Look how beautiful this is. Imagine it in the summer, when everything is green and growing."

She nodded, getting caught up in his excitement. "It would be so much fun to do a separate drawing for each season. I'm sure the autumn foliage is absolutely breathtaking. And now, with everything covered in snow, it's so beautiful and peaceful."

She sighed. "This would be such an inspirational place to work."

Sean glanced over at her, catching the wistful expression on her face. This had him almost steering the truck right off the driveway before he snapped back to attention, swerving them back to where they should be.

He nodded, guiltily clearing his throat. "Sorry about that. It would be, wouldn't it? I'd love to see what you'd come up with."

After he pulled up next to the house, they trudged their way through the deep snow to the front door. With Sean muttering the whole time he needed to get her a good pair of cowboy boots.

Custom made boots, he said. Not the cheap, imitation leather brands you could buy almost anywhere.

He put in the code for the lock box and opening the front door, this took them right into a large and open great room. Rustic in design, the walls, ceiling and floors were all paneled in a warm oak, the highlight of the room a huge stone fireplace reaching all the way up to the high beamed ceiling.

There was also an absolutely fantastic view from the huge windows showcasing the barn and wooded backyard.

Hannah watched as Sean casually strolled around the room, stopping every so often to inspect something, before he finally turned to her. There was a smile on his face. "Reminds me of my parent's place."

She walked over to stand next to him. "Do you miss being home?"

He looked down at her, and *damn* if he didn't fall right into her eyes. And, just like that, he had his answer.

"No, not anymore. I did at first. But now I've learned you can live almost anywhere as long as you have what means the most to you within your reach."

He tucked one of her curls around his finger, his voice turning enduringly deep. "Are you within my reach?"

Yes... yes. For always....

She reached up to give him a kiss. "Yes, for as long as you want me there."

"Then I have no reason to miss home, do I?" This said, he reached for her hand. "Come on, let's tour the rest of the house. Then we'll go check out the barn."

Hannah could feel the excitement emanating from Sean when they reached the barn. After giving her a big grin, he slid open the door and gestured for her to go in front of him.

She held back, sending him a worried look. "Are you sure it's safe?"

She peered inside. "Something isn't going to come charging right at us, will they?"

The look he gave her was incredulous. Then he began to laugh. "You really think, if there are horses in here, or any other farm animal, they're going to come at us in a stampede if we try to come into the barn?"

She shrugged, her smile tentative. "One can't be too careful, can one?"

He was shaking his head. "You mean, one can't be more trusting, don't you?" He chuckled. "You really don't have much experience with horses, do you? Let me assure you, they will be in their stalls and completely safe to be around. If anything, they'll probably be excited to see they have visitors."

They were no sooner inside, when two cats came sprinting out of nowhere. Hannah grabbed on to Sean's arm, letting out a little cry.

He looked down at her, shaking his head. "Well, I stand corrected. Something did come charging at us... and from the looks of them, they're pretty darn ferocious. Don't tell me you're afraid of cats, too?"

She dropped her hand from his arm. An offended look on her face, she gave a huffy sigh. "No, I am not afraid of cats. They surprised me, that's all."

Meowing in unison, the cats wove in and around their legs. But once they sensed there was no food to be had, they took off, disappearing in a streak of fur.

Sean sent Hannah a teasing glance. "Probably off to spread the word there are visitors in the barn. You better stick close to me. Because, where there are cats, you're apt to find a mouse here and there. Ready to come charging right at us."

Even though she knew he was teasing, at least she was pretty sure this was what he was doing, she moved closer to him, casting a nervous glance around the floor.

Hannah wasn't really a big animal person. Puppies and kittens were her limit. But when it came to farm animals? She really had no experience with them at all.

There was also one additional fact she hadn't shared with Sean and this was horses had always scared her to death.

It's just that when it comes to a horse? Well... they're so big.

Maybe if she were to ride on one with Sean holding her in his arms, she'd be okay?

Definitely... she'd make sure of that.

This more than explained her reaction when a horse poked his head out and almost right into her face as they passed by his stall.

She gave a horrified shriek, bringing a startled neigh from the horse as it reared back, bumping against the stall and making a lot of noise. Convinced the horse was going to kick open the stall door and come right at them, she completely forgot Sean's assurance this would never happen, ducking behind him for protection.

And what did Sean do?

He burst out laughing before he reached over the stall door, his voice soft and soothing as he stroked the horse's nose.

Hannah watched this from a safe distance until he motioned for her to come next to him. At this point, completely embarrassed about her dramatic reaction, she did as he asked.

He smiled down at her, shaking his head. "It looks like I definitely have my work cut out when it comes to you and horses." He took her hand and, placing it on the horse's nose, guided it in a gentle stroking motion. "See? She likes this. We want her to know she didn't scare you."

He gave her a pointed look. "And that you're no longer afraid of her."

Hannah looked up at him, momentarily confused. "How do you know it's a she?"

She knew she had made a mistake as soon as this came out of her mouth and she saw the startled expression on his face. Then he slowly began to smile. In fact, she was pretty sure he was trying not to laugh.

He cleared his throat. "Well, darlin', if I have to explain this to you, I guess I really do have my work cut out for me."

Casually leaning against the door to the stall and adjusting his hat, he nodded towards the horse. "It's pretty simple. If you take a good look at the back of the horse, you'll notice she's missing a very important part of anatomy known only to the male species and…"

She was laughing as she clamped her hand over his mouth. "Stop… I am completely aware of the difference between the female and male species. After the shock of coming so close to an actual horse, I guess I wasn't thinking properly."

He pulled her into his arms. "Thank God for that. I was beginning to wonder if I should be worried."

He pressed a soft kiss to her forehead, his whisper brushing against her skin. "You make me happy, Hannah Michaels. I'm so glad you're back." Just as he was thinking this would be a perfect time to kiss her, his hat was lifted off his head and went sailing through the air.

Sean put his hand on his head. "What the hell?"

"Sugar, cut it out. You know you're not supposed to do that. One of these days you're going to do it to the wrong person and you'll be in big trouble."

Hannah and Sean turned to see this was coming from a middle-aged man striding in their direction. A big smile on his face, he held his hand out to Sean. "Hi, I'm Peter O'Conner. You must be Sean Young. Though I'd recognize you anywhere."

He grinned. "I'm a loyal Cleveland baseball fan and I've really enjoyed watching you pitch. Missed you at the end of the last season. But I understand your reason for leaving. Family should always come first."

After introducing himself to Hannah, he sent a nod over at the horse, who was trying to nose closer to her. "There's no need to be afraid of her, Hannah. Her name is Sugar, so that should give you an idea how sweet of a horse she is. She also got her name because of a fondness for sugar cubes. I'd have to say she only has one problem... she likes people too much and is always trying to get their attention. Be it for a sugar cube or a carrot. Or better yet, someone willing to take the time to talk to her."

As he spoke, he reached in his pocket and pulled out a sugar cube. He handed it to Hannah. "Here... hold it out in the palm of your hand and she'll gladly take it. I guarantee after that, she'll be your friend forever."

He had picked up Sean's hat. Handing it to him, he laughed. "This is one of her favorite tricks. One time she actually sent the hat up into the rafters."

He shook his head. "She's a real character, this one."

Hannah gingerly held out the sugar cube, with Sugar taking it out of her hand almost as cautiously. Both men watched this before Peter turned to Sean. "I'm what you'd call the all-around maintenance-slash-caretaker-guy here on the property. I'm responsible for basically everything needed to keep this property running smoothly... the house, the barn, the horses, the people... you name it. Right now, I have a new litter of puppies to add to my list."

Sean watched Hannah's eyes light up. "Puppies?"

Peter laughed. "Yes, the owner's dog Mazie had six puppies about a month ago, three females and three males. Come on, I'll show them to you."

They made their way to the last stall, now being used as temporary housing for the puppies. An adorable mix of white and black balls of fur, they were all curled into each other, sound asleep. The mother dog watched intently as Peter picked up a puppy and handed it to Hannah.

He chuckled. "This little one is the runt of the litter and the feistiest of the bunch. She is the only one that hasn't been claimed."

He winked at Hannah. "Now, doesn't that make you want to take her home with you?"

When the puppy settled in her arms and went right back to sleep, Hannah gazed over at Sean.

He knew that look, her eyes going bright, her bottom lip starting to quiver. It was a warning she was about to have another attack of uncontrollable tears.

In an attempt to lighten the moment, he smiled over at Peter. "I have a feeling you may have found a home for your last puppy. It's either that or a horse. But I think for Hannah, it would be best to start out small. We can work on the horse later."

He sent Hannah a wink. "That is, after she learns more about the breed… both male and female."

This had her half laughing, half crying, a stray tear rolling down her face. Wiping it away with the back of her hand, she smiled at Peter. "Yes, if this puppy really is available, I'd love to have her."

Even though Peter was slightly confused by Hannah's emotional response, he wasn't going to try to figure it out. He didn't understand women and was resigned to the fact he never would. Heck, he'd been married for over forty years, had four daughters, and they still managed to confuse him ninety-nine present of the time.

So instead, he merely nodded. "Great, after I double-check the pup hasn't already been claimed, the only thing you'll need to do is come up with the perfect name. I won't have this information until the middle of next week, when the owners return."

He smiled reassuringly. "But, right now? I don't foresee any problems."

This all settled, he was ready to get down to business. After all he had work to do. He turned to Sean. "I take it you've already checked everything out? Any questions you want to ask?"

When Sean told Peter there were a few things he wanted to ask him about in the main house, Hannah told them to go ahead, she'd be happy to stay in the barn with the puppy.

"Well, well… look at you. Suddenly so brave… willing to stay here with only a handful of fur to protect you." He grinned at the face she made at him before he reached over to gently run his hand through the puppy's fur. "We shouldn't be long. Then we'll leave, decide what to do for dinner. I'm getting sort of hungry."

Hannah laughed, shaking her head. "Why am I not surprised?"

Sean shrugged. "What can I say? It's a fact I'm always hungry. Even more so when I'm happy." With a wink, he and Peter left.

When Sean returned to the barn, he found Hannah seated on a bale of straw. Leaning back against the boards of the stall, her eyes were closed, the puppy asleep on her lap.

His steps slowed and for a few moments, the overwhelming rush of love that flowed through him had him frozen in place.

This was when he felt it… there was magic in the air… this barn, the house, the land. And he and Hannah were destined to be a part of this. They only had to make the move.

At the sound of Sean's boots hitting the worn brick floors, Hannah opened her eyes to look right into his. His hands jammed in his pockets, and a bemused smile on his face, he slowly walked over to her. He reached out to stroke her cheek, his fingertips trailing down over her jaw.

He was searching for words, but he couldn't seem to find any. But when she closed her eyes at his touch, her whole body reacting in a long, contented sigh, he realized it didn't matter.

There was no need to say anything.

He cleared his throat, nodding down at the puppy in her lap. "It looks like the two of you have bonded pretty well." Gently taking the puppy from her, he carefully placed it back with the other puppies.

He pulled Hannah to her feet and framing her face in his hands, he brushed his lips over hers, the huskiness of his voice sending a shiver through her. "There's magic in the air, darlin'. Can you feel it?"

Her eyes drifting shut, the parting of her lips was her only answer. He was smiling as he took her up on her invitation, capturing her mouth in a sweet, unhurried kiss.

Giving a long sigh, he rested his forehead against hers. "You're mine, Hannah Michaels. I don't want you to ever forget this."

After one last kiss and linking her fingers with his, they left the barn to find the sky was in the dusky stage of early evening, only seconds away from sinking into darkness.

It had also started to snow again. After the comforting warmth of the barn, the winter air felt so much colder than it was, bringing them to hurry over to Sean's truck. Even so, before he unlocked the doors, he paused to take a long look around them.

He nodded. "I like this place. It has good vibes."

He smiled at Hannah.

"Sometimes, you get lucky. And I have a feeling this is definitely one of those times."

CHAPTER 23

Sean pulled into a parking space in front of a fairly new townhouse.

It was one of the many identical townhouses in the complex. Down to the red color of the brick, the color of the shutters and the front doors, all of these a very boring black.

He switched off the ignition before he smiled over at her.

"I thought maybe you'd like to see where I live." He waved his hand at the row of buildings. "And... here we have it. Not my first choice, but it's worked out okay so far."

Hannah studied the building in front of them before she glanced over at him, shaking her head. "Wow, it's quite a change from where we just came from, isn't it?"

He nodded. "I know. And now having seen what I've been missing, I can't help but wonder what the hell I'm doing here."

He was laughing as he opened his door. "I guess I'm just a country boy at heart. You stay where you are, I'll be around in a jiffy to help you out."

He paused halfway out of the truck to grin back at her. "Just one of the perks of driving this monster. I get another chance to hold you in my arms every time I help you get your feet back on solid ground. So, like I said, stay put. Don't deprive me of this."

She watched as he hurried around the truck to open her door. A big smile on his face, he tipped his hat. "At your service, ma'am."

And you just fell in love with him a little bit more.

He swung her to the ground, but this time, he didn't let go. Right there in the parking lot, he lowered his head, his mouth searching for hers. The kiss he gave her was thorough and long enough to make her weak at the knees.

Only when she was left clinging to him, her face pressed in his chest, he nuzzled his cheek in her hair, a long sigh coming from him. "Ah... this is what you do to me. You've put a spell over me. Why else would I be kissing you in the middle of a parking lot and in full view of everyone?"

"Come on..." He grabbed her hand and began running towards his townhouse, pulling her along with him. Both laughing when they arrived at his front door, he reached for her again, this kiss almost as passionate as the one he'd given her in the parking lot. It was only when there was the sound of a car door slamming, followed by a loud whistle, he looked up.

It was his neighbor, a big grin on his face as he waved. "Hey, don't mind me. Enjoy."

"Hey..." Tipping his hat, Sean watched the man hurry to his condo, still whistling. He chuckled as he gazed down at Hannah. "Ah... looks like you were saved by a whistle." His fingers tracing her lips, his eyes held hers. "That is, if you want to be saved. I'm beginning to think, for me, this isn't an option anymore."

Her gaze unfaltering, she shook her head.

And now you're falling even deeper...

He unlocked the door and once they were inside, he began moving around the room, switching on the lights.

After casting a curious glance around her, Hannah slowly began to remove her coat. She hoped he wasn't going to ask her what she thought of the décor. Because she really didn't know what she could possibly say.

Maybe that it would be perfect for a hotel lobby? Or the reception area of a modern office building?

Yeah, it was that bland. Definitely basic and not what she'd expect from him.

Nope, not after you saw how happy he was today in a setting so familiar to him.

Sean was suddenly next to her, taking her coat. "*Geeez...* where are my manners. I should be helping you with this."

When she smiled, about to tell him it was no big deal, he gave her a quick kiss, shaking his head. "No, I've already put my claim on you and I need to treat you right. "

A big grin settled on his face before he reached out to stroke her cheek. "After all, you are my woman. And I want to take care of you."

She gazed up at him, incredulous. "Your woman?" She began to laugh. "Is this cowboy talk?"

He took a bottle of wine out of the refrigerator before he sent her a leering grin. "Absolutely. We cowboys don't mess around. Once we find the woman we want, we treat her like the lady she is. This is our guarantee she'll stick around."

He raised an eyebrow. "So, what do you say? Are you in? Will you be mine?"

Even though he was smiling as he said this, he'd never been more serious. She *was* his woman... had been, ever since he saw her. And he was determined she always would be.

Hannah was smiling. How could she not?

His woman? He doesn't even have to ask. You've been his since the very first time you saw him on that hospital elevator.

The bottle still in his hand, Sean stilled... waiting.

She nodded. "You're mine and I'm yours. Cowboy hat and all."

The smile on her face was so big, he found he was smiling back at her. "Good, that's settled then. And no going back."

"I promise. I'll be more than happy to be your woman."

Her comment made him want to leap right over the island, an

impossible feat he knew, so he could kiss the living daylights out of her.

Or at least kiss her until she begged for more.

He glanced down at the wine bottle in his hand.

Then why are you even opening this bottle? This isn't what you want.

Shaking his head, he got back to work on removing the cork. Their time would come.

He cleared his throat. "So, tell me... what do you think of my humble abode? Sort of blah, huh? Don't worry, I won't be insulted if you agree."

After removing two wine glasses from the cupboard, he hesitated, his gaze on her for a few moments. "I think I've been biding my time, knowing I wasn't going to stay here permanently. Then with my trip home, the possibility of moving, along with everything else, got put on the back burner."

He didn't feel the need to tell her Amanda had a big part in the decor of the townhouse. Horrified when she first saw this was where he expected her to live, she'd immediately reached out to one of her pretentious interior design friends from college.

But this 'so called friend' had definitely failed at the job. He had the suspicious feeling this was because Amanda had made it so clear she didn't want to move to Cleveland. Nor did she want to live in this townhouse. She'd had higher expectations for him... New York... Boston... or even Los Angeles.

So, maybe it was out of stubbornness he'd left the décor as it was.

But now that Hannah was here, it all seemed so wrong.

A cookie cutter design... this is what your description would be.

He frowned.

Don't get the wrong idea. He wasn't up on interior design terms. This was coming from a segment of House Hunters he'd watched out of boredom one night on TV.

The frown creasing his forehead had Hannah worried. Joining him in the kitchen, she smiled. "It's fine. And if you had no intentions of staying, why go through all the stress of remodeling? I know when I decided to re-do my kitchen, I thought it would never be finished."

She made one of those little faces he liked so much. "I spent a lot of time working at Café Latte, just to stay out of the mess."

She glanced around the room once more. "But if you ever do need help with decorating, you should talk to Chester's sister, Carrie. She's really good at matching people with what they really want in their own personal space."

In a rather intense battle with the corkscrew, he paused just long enough to give her a nod before he went back at it, tugging at the cork. Finally giving it one strong pull, this sent the cork shooting right out of the bottle. Unfortunately, this was followed by an explosion of wine, headed right at Hannah.

Before she had time to duck, there was wine in her hair, dripping down her face and spattered all over the front of her light blue sweater.

She looked like part of a crime scene.

For a moment, they didn't move. Hannah was in shock. While Sean, besides being completely horrified by what happened, was also feeling like a complete idiot.

Damn... can't you do anything right?

He grabbed for the paper towels and in his haste, he lost his grip on the roll. This sent it to the floor where it went rolling across the room, leaving a long trail of paper almost all the way to the front door.

Damn, damn, damn...

Tearing off a big section of the roll, he began to, not so gently, dab at Hannah's face, "I'm sorry, I'm so, so sorry. What the hell is wrong with me? I shouldn't have yanked on the damn corkscrew so hard."

Hannah took the towel from him. At the same time, she started to laugh and after a short hesitation, he did, too.

Then she was suddenly in his arms and he was kissing her. Everywhere... her mouth, her eyes, along her jaw. His lips traveling down her throat, he finally ended back at her mouth.

His lips turned up in a smile. "*Ummm... so good.* You, Hannah Michaels, are like a fine wine. A man could get drunk just being with you."

Her eyebrow raised, she started to laugh again. "Seriously?"

He pressed another kiss to her mouth. "I know, I know… corny, huh? But you need to give me a break here, darlin'. Because right now, you have me so I can't think straight."

Puling her closer, his voice dipped to a seductive whisper. "The only thing I know, the only thing I want, is you. I want you in my bed, so I can make slow, passionate love to you. I want this more than I've ever wanted anything in my life."

And now laughter was the last thing on Hannah's mind as his hands slipped under her sweater, his fingers gently caressing her skin, leaving her holding her breath in anticipation. Knotting her fists in his shirt, she pulled him hard against her until he answered by claiming her mouth in a deep kiss.

Urged on by this sudden eagerness coming from her, he slid his hand under the waistband of her jeans to press her even more intimately against him. Heat jolting through him at the contact, he let out a low groan, burying his face in her hair.

The helpless moan that rose from her throat in response had him lifting his head. His heart pounding in his chest, he searched her face.

He didn't even have to ask.

The desire was there, it was shining in her eyes. It was also in the kiss she reached up to give him. And in the one single word she whispered.

"Yes…"

The passion between them now risen to a whole new level

Sean picked up the wine bottle and handed her the glasses. After capturing her mouth in another kiss, his whisper brushed against her cheek. "We need to get you out of this sweater, don't you think?"

He nodded at the glasses and wine bottle. "We'll take these with us… just in case."

Hannah wouldn't be able to tell you how many times he stopped to kiss her as they made their way down the hall to his bedroom. She only knew she hadn't wanted him to stop.

She also didn't remember what the room looked like, only that it had a bed.

Nor did she remember him removing the wine glasses from her hands.

But once she found herself in his arms?

She knew it would be a night she'd never forget.

Sean pressed a leisurely trail of kisses over Hannah's face. Then his lips slowed, hovering over hers, teasing, taunting. At the same time, he slipped his hands back under her sweater, leaving a tingling sensation wherever he touched.

Slowly moving them across the room, he fell back on the bed taking her with him. Then he was kissing her again, his mouth even more demanding, his hands never leaving her body,

A slow heat had begun to spread through her. Almost as if she was on fire, a fire only he could extinguish. Wrapping her arms around his neck, she pulled him closer. Everything he wanted, she wanted and more. Starting with being able to experience the feeling of him under hands.

Her intention to remove his shirt, she reached up to undo the top button. But this proved to be harder than she thought, the fabric of the shirt slipping through her trembling fingers. She tried the next button, but again, her efforts were to no avail.

Remember, this was a whole new experience for Hannah. That she was having a hard time trying to keep up with all of these new sensations, coming at her and all at once? This was to be expected.

She groaned, closing her eyes.

"It's okay, darlin', we'll get there." Watching her struggle, Sean reached for her hands, and after pressing a kiss to each finger, he raised his eyes to her face. A shudder ripping through her at the heat of his gaze, the simple task of undoing the buttons was completely forgotten. Instead, she kissed him.

Sean slowly, *so slowly*, traced her lips with his finger. "We're getting into dangerous territory, darlin . And I want nothing more than to take that leap because I know it's going to be nothing short of amazing. But what happens next is all up to you. You will always be the one to call the shots when you're with me."

She was having a hard time getting past those two words...

Dangerous territory?

She shivered. What was happening between them was beyond dangerous. Inexperienced, she might be, but she wasn't naïve. Again, give her some credit.

Any promises they made right now didn't guarantee these same promises would hold up tomorrow. But she didn't care. She was already in too deep, her heart signed on for good.

But, there was one little thing she needed to do, something he needed to know. And she wasn't quite sure how to tell him. Again, this was all so new, this place she was in. A place, even in her wildest dreams, she'd never dared to imagine.

Dangerous territory, indeed...

Sean could tell Hannah was worried about something. Nudging her chin up with his thumb, he held her gaze. "*Hey...* what is it? Tell me. Whatever it is, together, we can work it out."

She swallowed, but when she opened her mouth, the words wouldn't come. So, she tried again. "There's something I have to tell you. I... well..."

She closed her eyes and took a deep breath. "I've never been with anyone before. Not like this." Her lashes flying open, she searched his face. "But I want this. I want to be with you. More than anything, I want this."

"*Ah, Hannah...*" Her vulnerability so obvious, the tenderness that flooded him almost put a halt to his desire right there on the spot.

Well, not quite. You have to remember, he'd been waiting a long time for this.

But with what she just confided in him, he was now the one at a loss for words. It had never even entered his mind she would be telling him this.

He would be her first?

This was a hell of a lot of pressure.

What if he didn't live up to her expectations?

Or, God forbid, you botch it all up? Look at all the dumb things you've done so far.

Even though Sean would be the first to tell you he'd always thought of himself as a confident kind of guy, he was far from perfect. Yeah, believe it or not, he had his faults and problems like everyone else. And with the way things had been going lately, maybe even more than before.

When it came to baseball and working the ranch, there wasn't a problem. He could pull it off. Hadn't he earned the reputation back home as one of the top rodeo contenders? And rightly so... his skills on a horse were unsurpassed.

This wasn't bragging, only simply the truth.

That he played professional baseball was also a big plus. A man needed a lot of confidence to make it in the pro's. The pressure was enormous, everyone always quick to put the blame on the pitcher when things started to spiral out of control in a game.

He should know. Been there, done that. A few more times than he'd like to admit.

He'd also be more than happy to show you the room his mum had set up back home filled with all his trophies. If this impressive collection wasn't proof of how much he'd accomplished so far in his life, he didn't know what would be.

But reading into what a woman wanted and the intimacy that was such an important part of a relationship? His brain was always quick to desert him when it came to this.

The fact he was thinking he could use a little advice certainly didn't mean he was inexperienced in situations like this. After all, he'd been engaged. Made it almost all the way to the altar.

But with Hannah it was different. For them, at least on his end, the connection had been there from the very first.

And passion?

Oh, it was there, all right.

Just waiting for the right moment.

And when this happens, you want it to be perfect.

Sean didn't seem to have anything to say.

So, you can imagine the relief Hannah felt when he finally propped himself up on his elbow to down at her.

His gaze holding hers, he wrapped one of her curls around his finger. "Darlin', it's gonna be okay. I believe when two people are meant for each other, the rest comes easy. Which means, you and I? We'll knock this out of the park."

As soon as these words left his mouth, he groaned.

Seriously? This is the best you could come up with? You're not pitching sports here...

Briefly closing his eyes, he dragged his hand down over his jaw. "*Damn...* that certainly wasn't what you'd consider romantic, was it? I, well, you've got to give me a little time to work on this, find the right words. What we have is all pretty new to me, too."

She began to smile.

This was encouraging. Maybe he was better at this than he thought. After he pressed a soft kiss to her mouth, he smiled. "Yeah... we've got this."

Ready to give it another try, she slipped her fingers under the open collar of his shirt, fingering the button. "I like the sound of what you said... *dangerous territory.* There's no one I'd trust more in the presence of danger than you."

"*Mmm...*" This was about all he could manage, every nerve in his body on high alert. As her fingers traveled down his shirt, he remained completely still, almost holding his breath each time she stopped to undo each button. She had barely freed the last button before he shook off the shirt and sent it flying.

He closed his eyes as her hands drifted over his bare skin, her fingers exploring everywhere she could reach. Her touch was electric, her curiosity now making it even harder for him to remain still. He didn't dare look into her eyes, knowing if he did, he'd lose any control he still possessed.

But it was when she placed a slow, open mouthed kiss to the hollow at the base of his neck, he lost it, any chance of restraint no longer in his control. A low groan rumbling from deep inside of him, he claimed her mouth in a demanding kiss.

After she kissed him back, just as passionately, he began to pull away, his intention to go about removing what remained of their clothing. But she pulled him back. "Don't stop… please…"

This had a smile tweaking the corner of his mouth. "Darlin', there's no hurry. Believe me, we're not going to rush this. But first, we need to get rid of the rest of these clothes." Then pulling her closer, his voice dipped even lower. "Only then, do I plan to get lost in you."

Capturing her soft moan with his kiss, at the same time, he pulled her sweater up and over her head. He tossed it through the air, watching it land on the floor right next to his shirt. Then he became all serious again, his mouth coming down on hers, his hands never leaving her body. And in the blur that followed, along with Hannah's help, the rest of their clothing was sent flying.

Now it was his turn to do the exploring. Lost in the intoxicating feeling of her under his hands, his mouth… her scent filled his lungs. And like he'd promised, he made every attempt to take his time.

But she wasn't making this easy for him, her eagerness urging him on. Nor could slow down he passion building between them, each kiss coming faster, more urgent.

He lifted himself over her. Closing his eyes in an effort to take it all in, he marveled at how perfectly her body fit to his, the pounding of her heart almost in unison with his.

But he wanted more. He wanted to be one with her.

And Hannah… what about Hannah?

Hannah could feel all of him, everywhere. The hard length of him pressed against her, the heat of his body surrounding her. But like Sean, for her this wasn't enough.

She was desperate for more. Desperate for him.

Wrapping her arms around him, she whispered his name.

"Sean, please..."

Desire fogging his mind, he slowly lifted his head. Her cheeks were flushed, her eyes closed. Framing her face in his hands, he brushed his thumbs over her eyelids. "Darlin', look at me."

Her lashes fluttering open, she gazed up at him. Pressing the softest of kisses to her mouth, the message in his eyes one of such tenderness. "You, Hannah Michaels, are my dream come true. You will always be my everything."

Then he was inside of her, stealing her breath, swallowing her cry with a crushing kiss.

For Sean, this feeling of being connected with Hannah was almost surreal. His heart hammering in his chest, he rested his forehead against hers. "Okay?"

She reached up to pull him closer, her answer barely a whisper in his ear. But for him, the words were so clear... coming from her, he would've heard them anywhere. This was the one thing he'd dared to hope for, waiting so patiently to hear.

"I love you, Sean Young. I will always love you." And before he could respond, she kissed him.

They were one... the love that followed was more than enough proof of this.

One body, one heart, one soul...

What Sean had dared to believe all along, was finally a reality.

He'd finally found his place to call home.

CHAPTER 24

The sheets in a tangle around them, and tucked against Sean, Hannah's eyes half closed, her hand resting on his chest. She'd placed it over his heart, the slow beat against her palm, so calming... so mesmerizing.

But she didn't understand... how could this be? When her heart was still galloping a mile a minute, as though it was out to beat some kind of new world record?

So, she took a deep breath, hoping this might slow things down a little.

Thinking this was a sign she wanted to say something, the slow circles Sean was lazily tracing on her arm came to a halt. He glanced down at her.

Nope, her eyes were closed and he could see she even had a smile on her face.

Good.

He didn't want to let go of this lazy aftermath they'd fallen into together. Nor was he ready for the magic to end. And yes, as dramatic as this might sound, coming from him, this was exactly what it was. There was no other way he could think to describe this time he'd shared with Hannah, loving her.

Yep, it was pure magic...their magic....

Sean would've been very happy to know, in the euphoric state she was in, Hannah had no intentions of going anywhere. Sated from their love, she wanted to savor all of these new sensations that had found a place in both her heart and memory.

Even though she was a little worried about what she'd blurted out right in the middle of things.

"I love you, Sean Young."

Of course, she hadn't meant for this to come out. But, somehow it had. Maybe, because at the time, it had seemed like the right thing to do?

The right thing to do?

She wasn't sure, was there any right or wrong when you were in the midst of making love to someone?

Dangerous territory...

Sean was right with what he said. They had definitely ventured into dangerous territory.

She closed her eyes and rubbing her cheek against his chest, she breathed in the scent she'd come to know as his.

She smiled when he pressed another kiss in her hair.

Dangerous, indeed...

Nope... she wasn't going anywhere.

After pressing a kiss to the top of Hannah's head, Sean settled more comfortably against the pillows. He couldn't seem to wipe the lazy smile off his face.

Never had he imagined he'd find a woman like Hannah. She was everything he wanted, matching the image he'd been carrying around in his mind for what seemed like forever. It was to the point, when he first saw her, he was like, hey... so where've you been? What took you so long?

Her passionate response was one he had never before experienced before. Together, their love had risen to a level he was sure most people wouldn't reach in a lifetime. She met him, kiss for kiss, touch for touch…with an eagerness beyond his wildest dreams.

She was made for love… and now that he'd finally shared this life-changing moment with her—at least this is what it had been for him—he wanted to keep her with him for always.

There was also the one brief, but ever so important moment, that stood out above all others.

"I love you, Sean Young."

And yes, these were her exact words. He'd swear on this.

He wondered, had this come out only in the heat of the moment?

You'd like to think the answer to this would be a no.

Maybe she felt this was expected of her?

If so, you really botched it up, since you didn't respond. What a surprise…

Or… was it now that she was back to the Hannah he'd first fallen in love with, and ready to commit to him?

Remember, she did tell Sophie she was falling in love with you.

Well, he wasn't going to push it. He could wait.

After all, as far as he was concerned, they had a lifetime to figure it out.

"Hey, you're not falling asleep on me, are you?"

Sean's husky whisper coming in her ear, Hannah opened her eyes to fall right into his.

A smile slowly spreading across his face, he reached over to wrap one of her curls around his finger.

He cleared his throat. "Silk… it's like silk."

She scrunched up her face. "Silk?"

Her expression made him smile even more. "The first time we actually shared a conversation with each other, the whole time, I couldn't stop thinking about how I wanted to run my fingers through your hair, that it would feel like silk." He leaned in to press a soft kiss to her mouth. "I was right."

He watched the curl slowly slip from his finger, his voice casual. "So… you're okay?"

She nodded. "Yes, I'm fine." Her mouth curved into a smile. "I am, really. More than fine."

"Good, that's good…" He bowed his head. But not before she saw his obvious relief.

Wondering how he would even think she'd feel otherwise, she reached up to stroke his cheek. The roughness of his five o'clock shadow made her feel almost sinful, as if she'd entered a forbidden territory. It also made him look so unbelievably sexy.

You need to tell him this.

Her fingers, tracing the line of his jaw, she smiled. "Have I told you how sexy you are? Because you are. You make me want…" Her voice trailed off, her cheeks slowly coloring.

He lifted his head, the corner of his mouth quirked up in a smile. Aimed right at her, along with the teasing glint in his eyes, and there you have it… two of the traits that made up such a big part of that sexiness she was referring to.

He almost looked embarrassed. "Sexy, you say? *Aww…* coming from you, I'll take this as a compliment any day."

She nodded, her blush deepening. "You are… so much so. You're my sexy cowboy. I think every woman has this dream of a handsome stranger coming into her life, or in my case, a dark haired, brown-eyed and sexy cowboy." Here she paused to smile up at him. "He'd come galloping over to her, swing her up in front of him on his horse, and they'd go riding off into the sunset, or sunrise. Whatever is happing at the moment. We'll take either one."

She sighed. "And they'd live happily ever after."

Running his fingers through her curls, something he couldn't seem to stop doing for the life of him, he looked thoughtful. "*Hmm…* is this something you dream of, too?"

She nodded. "Of course. Even though, I'm a little leery about the horse part. You've witnessed that. But this is because my only memory involving a horse was when I was about eight years old and on a school field trip to a farm. A horse charged right at us and even though I was on the other side of the fence, it scared me to death. So, I'm not sure how well I'd do with one that's galloping."

She gazed up at him, her eyes wide. "You have to agree, they are awfully big."

He chuckled at her seriousness. "Yeah, I guess you could say that. But they're such amazing animals, and after you're with them for a while, you don't even notice how big they are. And while I'm around, you'll have no reason to worry. Of course, this all depends on if I'm the cowboy of your dreams."

She smiled. "Always."

He pressed a kiss in her hair. "Good, because I'm planning to take the role seriously. But right now, I'd like to ask you about something you said… what exactly is it I make you want?"

Oh geez… you should've known he'd pick up on that. So, what are you going to tell him?

One look into his eyes and she had her answer. "You… only you."

His gaze traveled over her in a leisurely manner, all the way down to her toes, before finally coming back to rest on her face. The huskiness of his voice betrayed the state he was in. "Remember what I said? You and me? That we'd be perfect together? *My God, Hannah…* you have me already thinking how I want to love you all over again…" He gave her a kiss. "And again…"

After another kiss, his voice dropped to a whisper. "I want that feeling again… the thrill of when you come apart in my arms. I want to be the one to make your every fantasy come true."

She closed her eyes, a blush slowly spreading across her cheeks.

He drew her closer. "Darlin', it wasn't my intention to embarrass you… never. But I want us to always be open with each other, share what we're feeling."

Speaking of sharing…

Damn if he didn't come out and do the one thing he'd decided he wasn't going to do. Let's just say the words shot out of his mouth before he had a chance to hold them in.

After all, he was known to do this.

A lot…

He cleared his throat. "There's something you said. Maybe it was something you hadn't meant to say? But, I'm sort of hoping you…"

She stopped him, her fingers pressed to his mouth. That she was smiling, he hesitantly smiled back at her.

Gently removing her fingers, she pressed a kiss to where her fingers had been. "But I did mean it. I meant it more than anything."

In mere seconds, his hands were framing her face, his eyes burning into hers. "Then say it… say it again."

His gaze was so intense, so hopeful, she had to close her eyes.

She took a deep breath. "I love you, Sean Young. I believe I've loved you from the moment you walked into that hospital elevator and I looked into your eyes. And I'll say it again and again… I love—"

She never got to finish.

He swallowed her words with his kiss.

Hannah woke with a start.

Someone was talking. Very loudly, they were doing this.

Coming to a sitting position on the bed, she peered into the darkness, confused. This was when she realized where she was. She was in Sean's bed.

And he was talking in his sleep.

She glanced over at him. His arm flung over his face, he was agitatedly shaking his head. Just as she was about to wake him, he spoke again.

His voice was loud, and so clear in the darkness. "Amanda, listen to me. We need to talk about this, straighten it all out." Then he grew even more agitated, throwing his arm down on the bed, a loud groan coming from him. "Come on, you loved me at one time. So, you have to know how I feel."

Hannah had become frozen in place. She almost couldn't breathe. Then she did the one thing she shouldn't have.

She leaned in close to whisper. "Do you still love her?"

Even in his sleep, he smiled. "I will always love her."

Slowly lowering herself back down on the bed, she pulled the quilt up to her chin. Her eyes closed, she listened to the sound of her heart beat. Echoing in her head it was so loud, she was afraid it was going to wake Sean.

When he started to speak again, she squeezed her eyes shut, everything in her, hinging on what he was going to say.

"I have to tell Hannah." And then he was quiet.

But for her it was enough.

She had to leave.

She didn't want to, but she needed to put some distance between them, so she could think about what happened. Something she wouldn't be able to do if she stayed.

Slowly easing herself off the bed, she began searching the floor for her clothes.

"Hannah? What are you doing?"

She stilled. The next thing she knew he was next to her. He wrapped his arms around her, nuzzling his face in her hair. "Hey, what's going on?"

The feel of him, all warm bare skin pressed against her, was almost enough to make her forget everything.

Closing her eyes, she took a deep breath.

"I thought maybe I should leave. I..."

He pulled away to look down at her. "Hannah, baby... it's the middle of the night. Come on... come back to bed."

She let him lead her back to the bed, to then tuck her against him. After he placed a kiss to the top of her head, he gave a long sigh.

She gazed up at him to see he was looking down at her. A smile on his lips, he pressed another kiss in her hair

She just blurted it out. "Make love to me."

Lord help her, she wanted him. Even though she wished she didn't. But she needed something to hang onto when she found herself alone again.

He began pressing a trail of kisses over her face, ending with a murmur against her mouth. "Magic... this is what you do." His mouth coming down on hers in one long passionate kiss, he proceeded to make slow, sweet love to her.

This was when she realized, even if she had the memory to keep, it would never be enough.

Hannah listened to the sound of Sean's steady breathing.

Wrapped in his arms, her body still humming from the love they'd made, she could almost forget what he'd said in his sleep.

Almost... but not quite.

She should've left. This would've been the smart thing to do. The logical thing.

And now she didn't know what to do.

Burrowing closer to him, she squeezed her eyes shut, willing herself not to cry.

He stirred, pressing a kiss in her hair, his voice a sleepy murmur. "This is the best, isn't it? You and me, together... safe and warm, nothing between us."

The tears flowed.

Because he was wrong.

There *was* something between them.

And it had changed everything.

CHAPTER 25

Sophie scooped up the clothes from the floor and threw them into the washer. As she added the detergent, she listened to the conversation Trevor and Hudson were carrying on with Hannah.

This was if you could actually call it a conversation. It consisted mostly of the twins, picking up every toy they could find and after handing it to Hannah, explaining their actions with their own unique style of baby babble, along with a lot of waving their little hands for emphasis.

Chester blamed this gesturing of sorts on her. He claimed she always did this when she was excited or angry about something. Fortunately, he was smart enough not to comment about where the twins constant chatter may have originated. Or baby babbling, as they liked to call it. This probably had a lot to do with the warning look she gave him when he'd brought this up.

You don't babble. Granted, you tend to talk a lot. But, if you remember correctly, didn't he tell you this was one of the things he loved most about you?

She smiled. Yes, he did. More than once, in fact.

Still smiling, she glanced over at Hannah, who had scooped Trevor into her arms and was tickling him. The sound of his giggles was so contagious, she started to laugh, while at the same time, she began shaking her head. "Oh boy, Aunt Hannah, now you've started something. They love to be tickled. Until one of them begins to cry for no reason, setting them both off."

Hannah grinned as she switched over to tickling Hudson, this sending him into a fit of giggles, too. "Well, that's not going to happen. There will be no crying when Aunt Hannah is around."

As she watched this, Sophie was almost the one who wanted to cry. But this would be happy tears. She couldn't believe how thankful she was Hannah was back to the Hannah they all knew, her memory finally back with her.

She waited until the twin's giggling had died down to tell her this. "I can't believe how relieved I am everything is back to normal for you."

Then she grinned. "But I know for a fact, I'm not anywhere as happy as Sean is about this."

She began pulling the towels out of the dryer, waiting for Hannah's response.

There was only silence.

She sent her a curious glance. Flat on her back on the floor, Hannah was holding a twin on each side of her, tucked in her arms. Thumbs in their mouths, Hudson and Trevor were in a struggle to keep their eyes open, while Hannah's were closed. There was a wistful smile on her lips, which Sophie was pretty sure had been brought on by the comment she'd made about Sean.

At least she hoped it was. The fact that Hannah hadn't responded, was a little worrisome.

She decided to dig for more information. "So...I take it the two of you are still planning to attend Livy and Sam's wedding, together?"

Hannah slowly turned her head to gaze over at her. She nodded just as slowly before she blurted it out. "I have fallen completely and without a doubt, madly in love with him. And I am scared to death about what's going to happen next. Because I'm pretty sure I did something really stupid."

Sophie studied her for a long moment. Then she glanced down at the pile of towels, giving a resigned sigh. It looked like folding them would have to wait until later. She made her way over to scoop up a now sleeping Trevor before motioning to Hannah. "Come on, you're in charge of Hudson. Let's put them down for their naps and then we can talk."

She grinned. "We'll open a bottle of wine. I have a feeling this is definitely going to be a glass of wine, or maybe two, kind of discussion."

Sophie pushed a glass of wine across the counter to Hannah. After she settled on the stool across from her, she picked up her glass and held it up in a toast. "Here's to us and the good times."

Then she grinned. "And to love. Crazy, unpredictable and we-just-can't-live-without-it-love."

After she set her glass back on the counter, she propped her chin on her hand and gazed over at Hannah. "Okay, spill… I want to hear everything. Beginning with what you did that's so stupid, it's got you scared. Because it's obvious Sean likes you. Or, come on… let's be serious here… the guy is head over heels in love with you. My gosh, Hannah, he about drove himself crazy when you were in the hospital… coming to visit you every day, bringing you gifts, or just being there for you. And if that wasn't enough, he insisted on being the one to stay with you once you were released from the hospital."

She gave a huge sigh. "So, tell me… because I don't understand. What happened? Is it too much? Too fast? Do you feel like he's pressuring you?"

Hannah shook her head. "No, it's none of those. I know this sounds crazy, but it all feels too perfect." She hesitated, fingering her napkin before she spoke. "Yesterday, he asked me to go with him to look at this horse farm he's interested in and…"

Sophie interrupted her, her eyebrows raised in surprise. "Horse farm? Here?"

"Yeah, I know. My reaction exactly. But when we drove east of here, it was as though we'd ventured into a whole different country with these large, rambling estates with barns, tables, or whatever. The property Sean wanted to check out was absolutely beautiful. He told me it reminded him of home."

A faraway look came over her face. "He seemed so happy while we were there." Then she smiled. "There was a litter of puppies in the barn. They were all spoken for except this cute little black and white sweetheart of a pup. When Peter told us she was the runt of the litter, and the last one available, I told him I'd take her. I'll find out if she's mine when the owners return from a trip next week."

She smiled over at Sophie. "You know I've always wanted a puppy."

"Yeah, I remember how insistent you were about getting a condo that was pet friendly." Sophie was nodding, but she was also more interested in what else Hannah had said. "Who is Peter?"

"He's the caretaker of the estate. He told Sean he's been there for over forty years and he hoping to stay. Sean was happy about that."

Popping a cracker loaded with brie into her mouth, Sophie appeared to be deep in thought. Then, after a sip of wine, she shook her head. "So, I still don't get it. Is this the problem? You don't want to live on a horse farm?"

Hannah laughed. "No, no… that's not it. Anyone would be thrilled to live there. It's beautiful… the house, the barn and all the land. But it just seems so big, and so much for him to take care of."

Sophie frowned. "*Oh geeez…* don't tell me Sean doesn't want to get married."

Hannah took a sip of wine and set her glass slowly back on the counter. She didn't know if she should tell Sophie about what happened the night of the bachelor party. When Sean surprised her by showing up at her condo. But you know how that goes… it came spilling right out of her.

"He's already asked me to marry him. The night of Sam's bachelor party, he came to see me. But that's a whole other story. Because he asked me before everything had come together in my mind, before I remembered who he was."

In the midst of putting another brie topped cracker in her mouth,

Sophie almost spit it across the counter. "What? Are you serious? Why didn't you tell me?"

She looked so comical, her face all screwed up in disbelief, Hannah began to giggle. But Sophie's threatening expression had her shrugging instead. "It just happened. And to tell you the truth, I'm still trying to make sense of it all."

Sophie was shaking her head. "I can't believe you've kept this to yourself. And what did you tell him? Start from the beginning and tell me everything."

So, this is what Hannah did. She began with Sean's visit the night of the bachelor party, and ended with their trip to the property Sean wanted to check out.

Sophie poured more wine into their glasses and after setting the bottle on the counter, she shook her head. "Hannah, I don't know what to say, except… what the heck is your problem? Again, the guy is obviously in love with you and you're in love with him. It also sounds like he definitely sees you as a big part in his future. He knows what he wants… and this is you."

Hannah watched Sophie spread more brie on crackers, hesitant to tell her what she was most worried about. Only because she was afraid Sophie's answer would be, yes, she had every reason to be concerned. At the same time, she needed her help to erase the doubt clouding her mind.

She took a deep breath. "Unfortunately, there's more. Did you know Sean was once engaged?" At Sophie's surprised look, she nodded. "He was, and her name is Amanda. But on their wedding day, she left him standing at the altar. To make things even worse, she disappeared without a trace, giving him no reason for backing out at the last minute."

She took a sip of her wine, slowly setting her glass on the counter before she continued. "We ran into her at the restaurant the night we went out to dinner. Since she lives in Boston, it was the first time Sean had seen her since that day." She frowned. "I don't know why she was in Cleveland."

She rested her chin in her hands. "Oh, Sophie… she is one of those perfect model types. And as much as I hate to admit it, you were right about the dress you picked out for me. It really is more conservative than most." Her smile was resigned. "Next to her, I felt like the small-town girl up against the big city socialite."

Sophie gave a short laugh. "Your exaggerating. You look great in that dress. "

Hannah sighed, "Thanks, but next to her? Hmm... I don't know about that."

"So, what happened?" Sophie really didn't care about this Amanda, what she was wearing or where she was from. She was more interested in Sean's reaction to all this.

"While we were still at the restaurant, he told me about her... their sudden engagement, how she became caught up in the dream of a big wedding, and the perks of marrying a professional baseball player, blah, blah, blah. He also told me he had already shared this information with me before my accident. But of course, I had no recollection of any of this."

Fingering the stem of her wine glass, she briefly closed her eyes. "He seemed so upset when he saw her again, so I asked him if he'd loved her. He said he didn't think so."

She paused, staring down at the wine in her glass. "He didn't think so, he said. And this is what scares me. He didn't think so? The word *think*, along with his strong reaction to her, leads me to believe he still has feelings for her."

She gazed over at Sophie. "Now that she's had time to think about him, and realizes what a big mistake she made by running away, maybe she's decided she wants to win him back?"

Sophie was frowning. "Oh, Hannah... I think you're imagining the worst. Do you really think Sean is the type of guy to go running back to a woman who dumped him?"

She shook her head. "I'm sorry, but I just can't see this happening. Not with Sean."

Again Hannah stared down at her wine again before she responded."There's something else. And this isn't something I imagined. After we went to look at the property, instead of coming back to my condo, he suggested we go to his. He said he wanted to show me where he lived. Then, since it was so cold and snowy outside, the plan was we'd stay in and order out."

She glanced down at the cracker she was crumbling with her fingers before she finally gazed over at Sophie. "We, well we... let's just say we didn't have dinner until later." A faint smile touched her lips at the memory. "A lot later. One thing led to another and well... before we knew it, we..."

Her words trailing off, she took a big gulp of her wine.

Anticipating Hannah was about to share something momentous, Sophie had moved forward, almost slipping off the stool. Eagerly waiting, she was holding her breath.

But Hannah only shook her head. This hesitation on her part was completely normal. She had never been one to share her feelings. And when it came to something like this? Something so personal?

God, no...

Where Sophie was the complete opposite. She was more than happy to share every little detail. And never shy when it came to letting someone know what she was thinking. So, it stands to reason, she expected the same of everyone else.

But right now? This wasn't happening.

She groaned. "Hannah, just spit it out... what happened?"

Hannah was looking everywhere except at Sophie. Finally closing her eyes, a big sigh escaped her. "I had no idea how it would be with Sean. I was afraid I wouldn't know what to do... or I'd goof it up... not do it right. Though, I'm not sure, is there such a thing as the wrong way when you are loved by someone?"

For Sophie, this is when it all sank in. Hannah and Sean had made love. An experience she knew was all so new to her.

You know how she feels. Remember what it was like with Chester? Even thinking about how wonderful he was after you told him he was your first, makes you wish he was here right now. So, you could tell him how much you love him.

She cleared her throat. "No, I, *ah...* no, of course there is no wrong way. Not as long as you are both in complete agreement and have decided to make the ultimate commitment to each other."

She burst out laughing. "Oh *geeez...* I'm not laughing about what you told me. I'm laughing because I sound like Aunt Louise when she gets started in on one of her lectures."

She put her hand to her mouth, still laughing. "Did she give you the sex talk when you turned thirteen, too? I remember thinking I was going to die of embarrassment. All her quotes about love, along with all the little nicknames she had for everything, had me even more confused. I couldn't look a boy in the face for months. Maybe even years."

Hannah was laughing. "Yes, it was an experience I tried to forget as soon as it was over. I think I learned more at a pajama party I went to in junior high." She shook her head. "Poor Aunt Louise... I think she was overwhelmed by the three of us."

Relieved to see Hannah was also laughing, Sophie spread another cracker with brie and handed it her before preparing one for herself. She was chattering all the while. "But getting back to you and Sean. Wow... I can certainly understand how you're feeling right now. Because I had the same experience with Chester. But at the time, deep in my heart, I knew it was so right."

About to put a cracker in her mouth, Hannah set it on her napkin instead. Then she took a deep breath, her words coming out all shaky. "But, after you both finally fell asleep, did Chester wake you up because he was talking in his sleep about another woman? Because this is what Sean did and his words were so clear. He said he needed to find Amanda. It was very important he talk to her."

Her words were barely audible. "Then I did something I wish I hadn't... I asked him if he still loved her. And he said, yes, he would always love her. These were his exact words."

She gave Sophie an anguished look. "I tried to leave, but he heard me and persuaded me to stay. So, I waited until morning to ask him to take me home. I needed to be alone, think about what happened. And now I can't shake the feeling I'm going to lose him."

She put her head down in her hands. "Everything had finally fallen into place, everything was going so good…" Her words fading off, she waited. She wanted Sophie to say she was being silly. It was only a dream and probably meant nothing.

But the silence between them seemed to drag on forever.

Sophie finally gave a huge sigh. "I'm so sorry. I don't know what to tell you, only that you need to talk to Sean. You need to tell him everything… how you felt about his reaction when he saw Amanda, along with what he said about her in his sleep. If you don't, you'll go crazy. And eventually some little, insignificant thing will set you off and you'll come out and say something you don't mean."

She shook her head. "Trust me, this is what will happen. I should know. Chester and I almost broke up over something like this. But instead of talking to him, I kept my fears to myself. Then it all snowballed into a major misunderstanding."

Hannah sighed. "He's probably wondering what's going on as we speak. This morning, I told him I wanted to leave because I had a lot of things to do. When I refused to tell him more, he finally took me home. Then, just a while ago, I sent him a text I was going to be busy tonight, but we could meet after my author meeting tomorrow morning. It took him forever, but he finally sent a reply… okay. This was all he wrote… okay."

Resting her elbows on the table, she dragged her hands through her hair. "I know I should've called instead of sending a text. But I was afraid when I heard his voice, I'd start crying and make a mess out of everything as soon as I opened my mouth. This is when I decided to come see you."

Sophie smiled. "I'm glad you called me. But again, he is the person you need to talk to. You can't keep avoiding the elephant in the room."

This time it was Hannah who burst out laughing. *"Oh my Gosh…* you are full of these quotes today, aren't you? I remember that's what Uncle Paul used to say all the time when we were little. For the longest time, I was afraid this would actually happen, constantly searching for that elusive elephant."

"They both certainly knew how to make their point, didn't they?" Laughing as she began gathering the food and glasses off the island,

Sophie glanced over at the clock on the stove. "In about ten minutes, I have a babysitter coming. I promised Aunt Louise I would fill in for her at the boutique for the rest of the day. She and Uncle Paul are on a committee for some gala the Cleveland Orchestra is having and there's a meeting they have to attend. Why don't you come with me and we'll find you a dress for the wedding?"

Hannah re-corked the wine before she looked over at Sophie. *"Oh geeez…* can't I just wear the dress I wore to dinner with Sean? "She frowned. "And who knows? Maybe now we won't even go together."

Sophie shook her head. "That's not going to happen. And now you have even more of a reason for a new dress… one that will erase any thoughts of Amanda right out of Sean's mind for good."

She started to laugh. "The poor guy. I bet this very minute, he's trying to figure out what happened, what he did wrong. Trust me, he doesn't have a clue. But even if he thought he did, he'd still be confused. Men are like that. They just don't get it."

After Hannah put the wine bottle in the refrigerator and shut the door, she shrugged. "You're probably right."

"Trust me, we'll get this fixed." Sophie grinned as she handed Hannah her coat. "The babysitter is here. So, let go do some serious dress shopping."

Sean didn't have a chance…

CHAPTER 26

"*Stop it... just leave me alone already.*"

Sean was jerked awake by the sound of someone yelling.

Turns out it was him.

He slowly came to a sitting position on the sofa and, dragging his hands down over his face, glanced down at his watch.

It was almost noon.

After he'd driven Hannah home and was back in his place, he'd plopped down on the sofa, his intent to figure out what the hell happened.

But that hadn't worked out all that well, so he turned on the TV. And this was when he must have fallen asleep.

He hauled himself off the sofa and gave a long stretch. Thinking he should probably eat something, he went into the kitchen and opened the refrigerator door. Almost in a stupor, he stared at the meager assortment.

His mind was still caught up this latest dream.

It was the same damn dream.

It always started out with Amanda, and ended with her coming after him. And no matter how hard he tried to get away, or at least reason with her, practically begging her to leave him alone, she just wouldn't let up. So, this is when he'd start yelling and wake himself up.

He'd been having this same dream ever since he saw her at the restaurant the other night.

And you want it to stop.

Talking in his sleep was something he'd been known to do since he was a kid. It usually started up when there were changes in his life.

When he'd first come to the states, an overwhelming experience to say the least, he couldn't even count the number of times he'd woken himself out of a sound sleep. Yelling like a crazy man all because of some dream he was having.

But he couldn't be worrying about this right now. He had more important things to think about.

Like... what the hell happened?

Or more to the point...

What the hell did you do?

This was the common thread running through his mind. It just wouldn't leave him.

He slammed the refrigerator door. Well, maybe slammed was a bit of an exaggeration. He wasn't one to take out his anger in such a way. Slamming doors, punching walls, or throwing fits? No, he was more of a silent anger kind of guy.

So, let's just say he shut the door hard and leave it at that.

Massaging the back of his neck, he gazed around the combined kitchen-living room area. Or what he suddenly thought of as a very pathetic and lonely space.

Especially now without Hannah to make it feel more like home.

This brought on his long and overly dramatic sigh.

Yeah, he knew he was being dramatic, but he couldn't seem to snap out of it.

After another sigh, this one echoing his frustration, he glanced down at the pair of earrings on the counter in front of him. He'd found the simple gold hoops on the nightstand next to the bed where Hannah had left them.

He picked up one of the earrings and held it in his hand, caught up in the memory of how this had come about. Afraid his fingers would get caught up in the hoops when he'd buried his hands in her hair to bring her closer for a kiss, she'd removed them.

He groaned…

Damn… don't even go there.

Already he'd seriously considered jumping in his truck and driving over to her place so he could give them to her.

He thought this would be a nice gesture of sorts. After all, they could be her favorite earrings. Then once she thanked him for being so thoughtful, maybe he could persuade her to tell him what was really going on, why she had been in such a hurry to leave him this morning.

Like this even has a chance of happening. She probably wouldn't even answer her door.

Nothing was making sense.

When he'd first opened his eyes this morning, he found her dressed and sitting on the edge of the bed. Before he even had a chance to ask her what was wrong, she'd asked if he could take her home.

Her reason when he asked?

There were some things she had to do, she told him.

Things she had to do? So early in the morning? What kind of things?

After that, he must have asked her at least a half-dozen times, maybe even more, if something was wrong. Or, was it she didn't feel well? Did she have a headache? Or maybe she was having dizzy spells? These last two were symptoms the doctor warned could be possible side effects from her accident.

It might not be serious, but it would be best if she contacted them, so they could check it out.

She'd kept shaking her head, no.

So, even though he was extremely unhappy about what was happening, he threw on the first clothes he could find. This turned out to be his favorite old and worn black tee shirt, and the red and black striped flannel pajama pants his mum had given him. Not the wisest choice, but hey, give him a break. Not a morning person, at least not until he had his first cup of coffee, he was still half asleep. This, along with Hannah strange behavior, had him almost to a point he couldn't think straight.

But, he did as she asked.

He drove her home.

The whole situation became even more confusing when he pulled up in front of her condo. After almost jumping out of the truck before he'd even come to a stop, without uttering a single word, she ran to her front door. There she turned to blow him a kiss before she disappeared inside.

In a state of shock, he'd stared blindly at her condo. It was only after another car pulled up next to him, he finally came to life. Backing his truck out of the parking space, he headed for home.

Again, he didn't understand.

Was it something you did? Something you said? Something you didn't do? Didn't say?

Maybe he'd hogged the bed... or started to snore?

Strange as this may seem, he could only pray it had been one of these, because he didn't want to even think about the other possibility.

And this would be that he didn't measure up to Hannah's expectations.

You know... as a lover.

Damn...

He groaned, closing his eyes. This had to be the absolute worst thing for a guy to contemplate after he spent the night making love to a woman. Talk about a direct hit to one's ego.

What ego... you really don't have one at this point, do you?

He set the earring back on the counter and glanced over at the clock. It was now almost half past noon. A good workout is what he needed. This would take his mind off his problems and work off some steam at the same time.

He also wanted to check on the offer he put in for the property he and Hannah had viewed yesterday. The text he'd received earlier from Chris had hinted the outcome looked very promising. And since the seller had only until noon to respond, he should have an answer by now.

He was about to change into something more presentable, when he heard his phone buzzing, a sign he had a text message. Almost diving over to where he'd left the phone on the sofa, he snatched it up from the cushions.

He let out a big sigh of relief.

It was from Hannah.

Hi, I'm going to be busy tonight.
I want to spend time with Sophie and
the twins. I have an appointment with
one of my authors tomorrow morning.
Maybe we can meet at Café Latte
around noon? I need to talk to you.

He stared down at his phone, that uneasy feeling taking over again. *She needs to talk to you?*

He should be happy she'd even sent him a text. But this last sentence? It certainly wasn't very promising. Not after her actions of this morning.

He began writing a message, only to delete it. He had to be sure of what he wrote. Otherwise there was the chance he might say something that could make things worse.

After a few minutes of deep thinking, he typed out a long message. He re-read it, only to shake his head and again delete what he'd written. This was followed by more serious thinking before he typed out his final message and hit send.

It wasn't what he wanted to say, but for now it was all he had.

Okay. Yep, that was it. Just okay.

He wasn't going to take any chances. Short and simple, that's what he was going for. He was basically agreeing to everything and anything.

He certainly couldn't get in trouble for that, could he? And right now, this was his goal. At least until he got more of a clue as to what was going on in Hannah's mind.

Throwing on his jacket, he grabbed his keys and headed for the door. His hand on the doorknob, he looked down.

He was still wearing the flannel pajama pants. He was also minus his gym bag.

He groaned, and returning to his bedroom, changed into his sweats and grabbed his bag.

In his truck and after starting up the engine, he turned on his favorite country music station. He pulled his hat more firmly down on his head.

Things would work themselves out. So, he wasn't going to worry.

Easier said than done…

Little did Sean know, when he later passed the Chic Boutique on his way home from the gym, Hannah was standing in front of the full view mirror in the little shop.

After critically examining her reflection, she glanced over at Sophie again.

Sophie gave her a big smile and a thumbs up.

Hannah sighed. "Oh, Sophie… I don't know. I do like it. After all, it's red and you know red is my favorite color. But, why should I even bother? A dress certainly isn't going to fix things, is it?"

A voice came from behind them.

"I disagree completely. The right dress can change everything. It can make a man take one look and… *Bam!* He suddenly realizes, after all this time, how much in love he is with the woman who is standing in front of him. And he's hooked."

Hannah and Sophie both turned to watch their Aunt Louise come bustling into the room.

She glanced over at Sophie. "Sophie, do you remember the fashion show you and Chester modeled for us? I can still see the expression on Chester's face when he saw you in the dress you had on. He looked like he was seeing you for the very first time. He almost tripped and fell on the steps in his haste to get to you."

She smiled, nodding at the memory. "It was definitely an *ahhh...* moment for him. A falling in love moment. And I guarantee everyone who was there saw this happening."

She nodded over at Hannah. "So, yes... a dress can bring magic into your life. It can change everything."

Sophie and Hannah grinned at each other. This was the Aunt Louise they knew, a true believer in the power of love. This was also why her shop was such a success. She always made sure that every woman who walked out of the boutique with one of her dresses had been made to feel beautiful.

Sophie sent her an inquiring glance. "I thought you were at a meeting?"

Louise had already moved over to Hannah, her glasses on and her pincushion in hand. She began adjusting the dress, tucking and pinning it to fit.

"Yeah, it's still going on. But I told them I had to leave. Paul can handle this one. The man who heads the committee likes to hear himself talk, and at the rate he was going, the meeting could go on for another couple of hours."

She stepped back, nodding at Hannah in the mirror. "So, now tell me... what do you think of the dress now? A few adjustments and now it fits like a glove. Very flattering on you."

She winked. "Sexy, too."

She tilted her head, deep in thought. Then she smiled. "If I remember correctly, we received a catalog in the mail featuring these bronze heels that would be a perfect match. They'll pick up the gold metallic highlights in the fabric of the dress."

Studying her reflection in the mirror, Hannah nodded. "I do like it. But..."

In a flash, Sophie was next to her, unzipping the dress. "Too late, you already admitted you like it, so it's yours. Now go get changed and we'll go shopping for jewelry. I am a free woman tonight. Chester volunteered to take care of the boys."

She grinned over at their aunt. "Since, it's almost time to close up shop, you should go with us, auntie. We'll make it a girl's night out, dinner and shopping."

She hurried over to lock the door to the boutique before she turned to Sophie and Hannah with a smile.

"Perfect… I'm so glad we came back home from Paris earlier than expected. I can use a night out with my favorite girls. Let me send Paul a text and I'm ready to go."

CHAPTER 27

*S*ean had fallen into an exhausted sleep, completely oblivious to the sound of the basketball game he had intended to watch on TV.

He had spent almost the whole afternoon at the gym working out. Then he had worked for a while with both the pitching coach and the new rookie pitcher. Once he had returned home and made himself a quick dinner, he practically collapsed on the sofa, immediately falling asleep

But evidently this wasn't meant to last. Instead, he was jerked awake at the sound of someone knocking on his front door. Pounding, would be a better way to describe the noise. Whoever it was, they sure sounded like their intention was to break down the door.

My God, is someone in trouble and looking for a place to hide?

He lifted his head, groggily rubbing his eyes.

Then he was suddenly wide awake.

Maybe it was Hannah?

This had him diving off the sofa, hope building in him as he sprinted to the door. He opened it just in time to see a taxi pull away from the curb.

Unfortunately, the person the taxi had left behind wasn't Hannah.

Instead, Amanda was gazing up at him, a look of complete agony on her face. Before he could even say a single word, she put her hand over her mouth and pushing him aside, she stumbled past him to head towards the bathroom.

He could hear the sound of her desperate retching. Over and over, she did this. While he remained by the open door, trying to take in what just happened. It was the bitter cold that finally shocked him out of his fuzzy state and into action.

Closing the door, he dragged his hands through his hair.

No... please say it isn't so. You can't deal with this right now.

Slowly making his way to the bathroom, grateful for the silence now coming from inside, he cautiously peeked inside.

Amanda was sitting on the floor, leaning against the wall. Her eyes closed, she was a mess. The wet streaks down the front of her coat told him she hadn't quite made it to the bathroom before she became sick.

There was also a huge rip in the one knee of her leggings, as though she had fallen. On closer inspection, he could see the exposed knee was scratched and bleeding.

He sighed.

What the hell happened?

Did someone attack her?

Sensing his presence, she slowly angled her head to gaze up at him. There were mascara streaks down her cheeks, brought on by the tears still sliding down her face.

Her voice came out in a hoarse whisper. "Please, don't say anything. just give me a few minutes, okay?"

He left to get some towels from the linen closet and returning to bathroom, he set them on the vanity.

He cleared his throat. "Here... why don't you take a shower. There's toothpaste and an extra toothbrush in the top drawer. Then after we check out your knee to make sure there's no chance of infection, you can tell me what happened."

He closed the door and headed for the kitchen. For a moment, he stared blindly at his surroundings, unsure of what to do next.

Coffee... you need to make coffee.

It was obvious Amanda had been drinking. So, he needed to get her sobered up, out of his townhouse and back to wherever she was staying, as soon as possible.

You don't want her here.

He wanted nothing to do with her, period. And most of all, he didn't want Hannah to find out she was here.

He wasn't quite sure why, but he had a feeling she didn't believe him when he told her Amanda was a part of his past he wanted to forget, that she meant nothing to him. Even though he thought he had made this perfectly clear.

There was only one woman he wanted in his life. And this was Hannah.

His laugh was harsh. Because it now appeared she was questioning whether she wanted him in hers.

About a half-hour later, Amanda emerged from the bathroom. She was weaving unsteadily as she made her way over to the kitchen. Deathly pale, there were huge dark circles under her eyes.

She looked pathetic.

Sean frowned when he saw she was wearing his red and black striped pajama pants.

Damn... why did she have to choose those? Of all things?

At the flash of annoyance in his features, Amanda ran her hands over the fabric of the pants, avoiding his gaze. "I'm sorry, they were there... so I thought you wouldn't mind. My leggings are just about shot. I fell when I was getting out of the taxi."

At his raised eyebrow, she scowled. "It was the taxi driver's fault. He started moving before I even got out."

He made a move towards her. "Let me see your knee."

She vigorously shook her head. This had her closing her eyes, a soft moan coming from her. "Oh God, I feel so sick. And my knee is fine. It's just a little bruised. Don't worry about it."

Almost relieved at this, he nodded before he poured out a cup of coffee, setting it in front of her. "You're welcome to the pajama pants. In fact, consider them yours. But for now, we need to get some coffee in you so we can get you sobered up and back to wherever you're staying."

Irritated, she glared at him. "I'm not drunk. I may have had one drink too many, but I am in complete possession of my mind. I... I... it's just that... what am I going to do?" This coming out in an agonized cry, her head went down on her arms as she began to sob.

Now, as much as Sean wished she was anywhere but with him, he couldn't help but feel sorry for her. It was obvious something traumatic had happened for her to get to this point. Pouring a cup of coffee for himself, he sat across from her, waiting until her tears finally came to a stop.

His voice was gentle. "Hey, what happened? You're not the type to go out and start drinking when things aren't going right." A smile twitched at the corner of his lips. "Nope, you tend to be more vocal, letting it all out for everyone to hear. Trust me, I should know."

He'd swear she smiled as she lifted her head.

Good... if she's going to be here, you want her in a good mood. An angry Amanda is not what you want. God, no...

He shoved the cup of coffee closer to her. "Come on, drink up. It will make you feel better."

After she did as he asked, chin in hand, she studied him. "You always made me laugh. I have to give you credit for that." Her expression saddened. "I want you to know I'm really sorry for what I did with the wedding, running off on you. I should've put a stop to everything way before that. But it was so crazy with all of the planning in high gear and you moving. And then..." Her words died into silence.

He waited. But she seemed to be lost in thought. He finally spoke. "And then? Are you going to give me more?"

Her eyes began to tear up again. "I'm such a fool. Why didn't I see it's always been Joel? I've been in love with him forever, since I was a kid." She gave a sad smile. "I'd hoped with you, I'd be able to put him out of my mind. But when I saw him only a couple of days before the wedding, I realized what a mistake I was making. So, that's why I bolted."

Sean frowned. He didn't know how he felt about her using him as a replacement for the guy she really wanted. He wished she would've figured that all out from the beginning.

On the other hand, who was he to judge? He hadn't been honest about his feelings either. He cleared his throat. "The guy you were with when we saw you in the restaurant… was that Joel? And why are you in Cleveland? Does he live here?"

She nodded, a disgusted look on her face. " No, he has always lived in Boston. We're here for his cousin's wedding. I swear he's got about a hundred of them, and he thinks I need to meet them all."

She sighed. "But, now I don't know if this is going to happen, because the subject of you and I once being engaged seems to have become an issue. I thought he was okay with it, but he's insisting my reaction to you at the restaurant was proof I still have feelings for you. I tried to tell him this wasn't true, but he just wouldn't let it go."

She wrapped her hands tightly around her coffee cup. "Tonight, I finally had enough. I told him if he couldn't believe me, then we're through. And he did what I thought he never would… he turned and walked away." Her head suddenly dropping down on her arms, her next words came out in a loud wail. "So now, I've probably lost him for good."

Again, Sean waited.

She finally lifted her head. "I've been trying to reach him, but he's ignoring my calls. I left all these messages telling him how much I love him, but he still hasn't responded. I don't know what to do." Her face was a study of defeat, made even more desperate in her hung over condition.

He slowly shook his head. "I guess if you really love him, you'll need to keep fighting for him. I have a sneaky feeling he might be in the same condition you are right now. This is, if he loves you, too."

She stared at him before she abruptly came to her feet. Gripping the edge of the counter, she turned and lurched her way over to the sofa, her voice shaky. "I may not have told you the truth. I drank far more than I should have. And now I don't feel very well. I need to lie down."

After he watched her curl up into the cushions, closing her eyes, he left to get a blanket.

By the time he returned, she had passed out completely. It was obvious she wouldn't be going anywhere for a long time.

Holding the blanket, he stared down at her in dismay.

Great... just great. Now what are you going to do?

Since the answer to this was a big nothing, he covered her with the blanket and turned out the lights. Tomorrow morning, before he left to meet Hannah, he would make sure he got her back to where she belonged.

But now?

He was going to bed.

Hopefully, there would be no more late-night visitors.

And, please... no more dreams.

Hannah was sitting in her car in the parking lot of Café Latte.

The author she was supposed to meet had just called to say she had to cancel because her daughter became sick during the night. This meant she now had about two hours before she was to meet Sean.

Putting her head back against the head rest, she closed her eyes. She was exhausted. She hadn't slept well last night. After many glances over at the clock on her nightstand, the hours creeping closer and closer to morning, she finally hauled herself out of bed. After taking a long hot shower, hoping this might revive her and making sure her finished illustrations were all in order , she left for Cafe Latte.

She couldn't stop thinking about Sean.

The advice she received from both Sophie and her aunt during dinner last night had her wondering if she may have over-reacted to what happened. She was also feeling guilty about the abrupt way she ended what had been such an amazing time they had shared.

You acted exactly like Amanda had, leaving him with no explanation, no warning... nothing...

And now? There was nothing she wanted more than to see him. She wanted to apologize, tell him exactly why she left. How she was wrong to even think there was any truth in what was only his silly dream.

He would wrap her in his arms, assure her there was nothing for her to worry about and everything would be back to where it was before.

Problem solved...

She was smiling as she got out of her car, a plan in place. She was going to march into Café Latte and place an order for two coffees and two banana muffins. Then she would drive to Sean's townhouse and surprise him.

Yes, this is exactly what she was going to do.

She couldn't wait to see the look on his face.

Sean glanced down at his watch. Only one minute had passed since he last checked the time, but to him it felt like fifty.

Where the hell was the taxi? The driver had promised he would arrive in fifteen minutes. This meant he was already five minutes late.

Trying not to pace, but doing it anyway, Sean sent a vague smile over at Amanda. Even though she'd managed to choke down the toast he'd made for her, she was still looking pretty ragged.

She gave him a tentative smile in return. "Thanks for putting up with me." She glanced down at the red and black striped pajama pants she was still wearing. "Are you sure you don't mind I'm still wearing these? If you want, I can send them to you. I was planning to wear my leggings, but they're shot."

He shook his head. "No, like I said before, keep them, they're yours."

Finally, there was the sound of a vehicle pulling up in front of his townhouse. Letting out a sigh of relief, he quickly ushered Amanda to the door.

Before she started down the steps, she turned to him and wrapping her arms around his neck, she gave him a big kiss. "Sean, thanks again. I wish you the best, always."

Extricating himself from her hold, he gave her a big smile, if only because he was so relieved she was finally leaving. "Yeah, sure. I hope things work out with Joel. Take care."

She gave him another kiss , this one on the cheek, before she ran down the steps. There she stopped to blow him one final kiss before she got into the taxi.

After watching the taxi drive away, he was about to go back inside, when for some odd reason, he felt this need to turn around and scan the parking lot.

A woman, standing on the sidewalk, caught his eye.

He blinked.

Please, please... don't let it be who you think it is.

But it was…

His heart dropping to his stomach, he closed his eyes.

Damn... damn... damn...

Hannah had pulled into the parking lot of Sean's townhouse only a few minutes before.

Carefully retrieving the coffee and muffins from the passenger seat, she began making her way to his townhouse.

A taxi came from behind her, screeching to a halt in front of Sean's townhouse. This sent his front door flying open.

Hannah's mouth slowly curved into a smile as she watched Sean come out onto the steps. But her smile swiftly disappeared when Amanda appeared beside him.

She was wearing Sean's pajama pants.

In total shock, she watched Amanda throw her arms around Sean and they shared a kiss. She followed this with what appeared to be another kiss before she ran down the steps, a smile on her face. There she turned to wave and after blowing him one final kiss, she got into the waiting taxi.

To Hannah, the smile on her face said it all.

It was only when Hannah realized Sean had turned to see she had witnessed this, she came to life. After she looked down at the tray she was holding, she glanced over at him. She slowly shook her head.

No, no, no... you can't do this. You can't. You need to leave before you lose any dignity you have left.

Sean took off after her. "Hannah, wait... let me explain. Come on, Hannah. *Please...*"

Calmly setting the tray on the sidewalk, she turned and began walking back to her car, ignoring his pleas.

It was when he was right behind her, she whirled around to face him. She was trying not to cry, but having failed miserably at this, her voice was choked with tears. "No... nothing you can say will be good enough. I saw all I needed to know, what I thought all along was true. You still love her."

The vague thought popped into Sean's mind he had been right on about her thinking this. But this certainly wasn't making him feel any better.

Damn... you've got your work cut out trying to explain this.

He groaned. "Darlin', come on. You have to know that's not true. You're the..."

She cut him off, her breath coming hard , every word a struggle to get out. "Don't call me darlin'. Is this what you call Amanda, too?"

Sarcasm laced her words. "*Ah...* now I get it. You lure a woman in by calling her darlin', wait until she falls in love with you and then move right on to the next one."

She closed her eyes, shaking her head. "*Oh my God,* I've been such a fool..."

Now this made Sean mad. Because what she was insinuating was so far from the truth.

Hell, it wasn't even close.

You've already made it obvious you can barely handle one woman. So why the hell would you want to start up something with another one?

He moved closer, crossing his arms over his chest. "Now hold on, that's not true. You are the only woman I've ever called darlin', and up until now, the only woman I thought I always would."

For a long moment, their breaths coming hard in the frigid air, they remained silent, glaring at each other.

It was Sean who finally broke the silence. "Hannah, you've got to believe me. I would never—"

Again, she cut him off. "You were talking in your sleep to Amanda. You were telling—no it was more like you were begging her—that you needed to talk." She swallowed. "I asked you if you still loved her and you said yes, you would always love her. I don't think you could make your feelings any more clear than that."

He only closed his eyes, shaking his head.

So, she kept on talking.

When she thought about this later, she realized it was definitely not one of her better moves. She should have shut her mouth, turned around and left.

What was it Aunt Louise always said? Always think first about what you say in a moment of anger. Because once the words leave your mouth, true or not, the damage is done.

Well, that didn't apply here, did it? She knew what she was talking about… she had proof, didn't she?

Dragging her hand across her face to wipe away the tears, she dug right back in. "When we ran into Amanda at the restaurant, I saw how much it upset you to see her again. It was so obvious, even after what she did, you still have feelings for her."

He groaned. "Hannah…"

Her eyes flashing with anger, she vehemently shook her head. "No, please don't deny you were upset. Because you were."

A sudden weariness consuming her, she shook her head. "I can't do this, Sean. I can't. I'm beginning to think we're not meant to be. Look at everything that's happened… the chance meetings, to then not see each other again for months, my accident and now this? It certainly doesn't seem as though fate is on our side. If anything, it looks like it's determined to keep us apart."

He shook his head.

There was a reason he was silent.

Along with the confidence he was so proud of, even though it certainly wasn't making an appearance at this moment, he hated any kind of confrontation.

This was when he either backed off or attempted to introduce some humor into the situation.

This would definitely not be the time, or place, for any kind of humor, this you know for damn sure.

He also had absolutely no idea of what to say, as it appeared Hannah had already made up her mind. And the more he thought about what she said, that she even believed this of him, had him a little angry.

No, he'd have to say this would be more than a little. But again, he was smart enough to know it would be best if he didn't tell her this.

He wasn't stupid.

But it's understandable his silence was enough to convince Hannah he agreed with everything she had said.

You just want him to say something... anything...

But this didn't happen. Leaving her with no option but to leave. After giving him one last look, she nodded towards the tray she had set on the sidewalk. "Those are for you. Enjoy."

She turned and began walking away.

When Sean realized Hannah was leaving, and there was the possibility she might be walking out of his life for good? All that anger inside of him? It completely disappeared.

You are not going to let this happen. Not without a fight.

Her name coming from him in a long groan, he took off after her. *"Hannah, come on...* You need to listen to me, give us another chance. You can't just walk away. Not from what we have."

She came to a stop. And for what felt like forever, she didn't move. Nor did she say anything. But any hope that she might be about to change her mind was dashed when, without even turning around, she shook her head. "I can't. I don't want to compete with your past. Don't worry, I'm sure you'll get over me in no time."

He watched as she got into her car. To then go out of her way to avoid him as she drove out of the parking lot.

Slowly dragging his hand down over his jaw, he continued to watch until her car disappeared from view. Her last words to him, running over and over in his mind.

You'll get over me in no time...

He shook his head.

How could she even think this?

It was never going to happen. Never in a million years.

He was in too deep.

A woman's voice cut through the stupor he was in. "My goodness, Sean, where are your shoes?"

He turned to see it was his neighbor, two doors down.

He glanced down and sure enough, once again he had neglected to put on his boots. The beginning of a hysterical laugh rising in his throat, he quickly pressed his lips together.

Concerned at his wild appearance… shoeless, hair sticking straight up and in every direction, along with the distraught expression on his face, his neighbor peered more closely at him. " Are you okay? I don't want to sound bossy, but you need to put some shoes on. And a coat. According to the weather forecast, it's only supposed to reach into the lower teens today. It is January, you know."

She pointed to the tray Hannah had left on the sidewalk. "Your coffee is also going to turn into iced coffee if you leave it there." She gave the tray a closer inspection. "I see it's from Café Latte, huh? I've never been there, but I've heard they have great coffee."

He picked up the tray and held it out to her. "Here, you can test it out for yourself. There are banana muffins in the bag, too. They're amazing."

He grimaced. "Unfortunately, they turned out to be a wrong order."

He didn't even wait for her answer. Turning to run up the steps to his townhouse, he gave a vague wave at her loud thank you.

Inside, the door closed and still reeling from what happened, what he just said was enough to haunt him.

A wrong order...

He hoped to God this didn't apply to him and Hannah.

It was surprising Hannah even made it home. Her hands gripping the steering wheel, she could hardly see through her tears.

She couldn't stop thinking about what happened.

You're done. No more falling in love for you.

Nope, it was too risky. Look where it got her. Nowhere... absolutely nowhere.

But first, she needed this overwhelming pain inside of her to go away .

Why are you surprised? Your heart has been ripped right out of your chest. The heart you so foolishly gave to Sean.

At the same time, she was so, so angry.

How could he do this to you... lead you on to believe he loved you?

But most of all? She was feeling so stupid... so, so stupid.

Yes, this is what happens to other people, not you. Women who had you shaking your head, wondering why they hadn't been more careful to guard their heart. Well, it looks like you're now one of them.

If she could, she wouldn't even go back to her condo. She would keep driving, until she was where no one could find her. Where she could close her eyes and block out everything that happened.

Maybe losing your memory had been a good thing? Because, it would certainly be better than this.

Checking her rearview mirror to change lanes, she caught sight of the shopping bags on the back seat from her outing last night with her Aunt Louise and Sophie. This was a reminder she needed to call her aunt to let her know adjustments to the dress were no longer needed. She certainly wasn't going to the wedding alone.

This sent the tears flowing once again.

CHAPTER 28

Sean didn't even look up when Chester entered the gym. Sweat rolling down his body, he absentmindedly shook it out of his eyes. He was focused only on one thing and this was the screen in front of him. A quarter mile and he will have surpassed his best time ever on the bike.

He geared up, increasing the resistance. He was determined to do this, even if it killed him. And he wasn't going to make it easy.

Remember? Sean liked to win. And now that it appeared he was a loser in life, most notably when it came to women, he decided he could at least shine here in the gym.

"Come on, you can do it. You can do it. You're not a loser. You, Sean Young are a winner. A big time, all out champion." He didn't realize he was repeating this over and over as he put everything he had into reaching his goal.

Slowly removing his coat, Chester watched this drama play out in front of him. He had come to the gym because he had a feeling Sean would be here trying to work off some steam.

Yep, he already knew what happened.

This was because Hannah had already told Sophie the whole story. At least this would be Hannah's side of the story.

He sighed… another one of his friends was screwing up the most important thing of his life. Not that he had been immune to this kind of behavior. No, if you remember, he goofed up big time when he first met Sophie.

But now, with almost three years of marriage and two kids under his belt? He considered himself pretty much of a pro on the subject of love and marriage.

Well, sort of… Sophie might beg to differ with this.

He shook his head. He didn't know how women did it, but they always knew when something was about to happen. He'd swear they could smell trouble. At least Sophie could. Hadn't she told him, only last night, she had this bad feeling about Hannah and Sean? Somehow, they were going to mess up their relationship?

How could she have known this? This could only have been brought on by that women's intuition she was always talking about.

It was damn scary.

He had become resigned to the fact he couldn't get away with anything when it came to her. He was seriously looking forward to when Trevor and Hudson got a little older so he'd have a little male support around the house.

He shook his head, a wry smile on his face. The last time he was here, it had been to find Kevin on the verge of passing out from a gash to his head. But all had ended well, with Kevin and Abby now the parents of their new little baby girl.

And now you have Sean to deal with…

He glanced over at him, still pedaling like a maniac, his voice becoming louder and louder. "Yes… *you did it.* You, Sean Young, are damn hot." He followed by raising his fist into the air before he practically collapsed on the bike.

After he slowly slid off the seat, he grabbed the towel from where he had thrown it on the floor. Wiping off his face, he turned to see Chester sitting on the bench.

Chester grinned. "Hey…"

Sean slowly made his way over to him. "Hey to you, too." Then he groaned. "I didn't know you were here."

Chester was still grinning. "I'd say that's pretty obvious."

He cleared his throat. "So, Mr. Damn Hot… what the hell are you trying to accomplish? Are you in some kind of fight with yourself? Or trying to see if you can kill yourself off with exercise? If Joe knew you were working out so hard, he'd probably have a heart attack. You know how he is with you pitchers. Especially with both Goober and Murph out of the picture, not slated to pitch until June at the earliest."

Plopping down on the bench, Sean slowly dragged the towel through his hair. He let out a big sigh. "Yeah, I know. I needed to blow off some steam, had a lot to think about."

He gave a short laugh. "More like, I have a lot I don't *want* to think about. Working out always makes me feel better. At least, it usually does."

He glanced slowly around the room before shaking his head. "Not so much today, though."

Chester sent him a sideways glance. "I heard what happened with you and Hannah." He quickly put his hand up. "Let me re-phrase that… Hannah told Sophie what happened and then Sophie told me. So, who knows what the real story is at this point. Why don't you fill me in?"

Sean leaned back against the lockers and closed his eyes. After a short silence, his eyes still closed, he began to talk.

He gave Chester a rundown of what happened, including a brief history of his relationship with Amanda. Their plans to get married and how that sure as hell didn't work out.

As he went on to explain, everyone knows two people are needed to perform a marriage ceremony. If one runs off, your plans are pretty much at a standstill, right?

And as much as it killed him to come out and share this with anyone—*anyone*, mind you—he told Chester how everything had started to go downhill after Hannah spent the night. How he woke in the morning to find her sitting on the bed, all dressed and requesting he take her home.

Chester grimaced. "Ouch…"

Sean groaned and barely opening his eyes, his gaze shifted over to

Chester. "Yeah, not a good thing to have happen, is it? As you can imagine, I've been driving myself crazy trying to figure out what it was I did. Or more like, what it was I didn't do. And this was after she told me that she… well, never mind. I'm not going to share that with you. It's personal."

This brought on another silence before he groaned again, raking his hand through his hair. "But it was only this morning everything escalated into a full-grown mess. She sent me a text asking me to meet her at Café Latte after her meeting with one of her authors. This was to be at noon today. Instead, she showed up at my condo almost two hours before that and at the exact same time Amanda was leaving. It didn't help matters Amanda was wearing my pajama pants."

Chester raised an eyebrow. He was beginning to think it certainly wasn't looking good for Sean at this point. "I'm confused… your pajama pants? Why the hell was Amanda wearing your pajama pants? Even more importantly, why was she even at your place?"

Shaking his head, Sean closed his eyes again. "Trust me, it's nothing like it sounds. She showed up last night, drunk. When I opened the door, she shot past me, barely making it to the bathroom before she got sick. She was a mess. One knee of her pants was ripped, she was bleeding… all of this happening when she fell out of the taxi. Or so she said…"

"*Oh geez…*" This came from Chester.

Sean nodded. "Yeah… like I said, she was in bad shape. She took a shower and when she came out of the bathroom, she was wearing my pajama pants. So, I told her she could just keep them. Hell, at the time, that was the least of my concerns. I only wanted her out of my condo. This was when she told me she was in love with the guy she was with the night we met up in the restaurant. Evidently, he is now having a hard time with the fact Amanda and I were once engaged. Long story short, he took off and she got drunk. I tried to get some coffee in her, hoping to sober her up, but she wound up passing out on my sofa. And I mean, she was out cold. So, I left her there and went to bed."

He scrubbed his hand over his jaw, a frustrated sigh coming from him. "If I had known what was going to happen this morning, I sure as hell wouldn't have let her leave, wearing the pants. Not that it would have made any difference. I have a feeling Hannah had already made up her mind before this. So, it didn't help my case when she saw Amanda."

He sighed. "She was so angry, throwing out all of these accusations at me. This was also when she told me the reason she asked me to take her home was because I had talked in my sleep. Supposedly, while in this state, I told her I was still in love with Amanda. This, along with how I reacted to Amanda at the restaurant, was all the proof Hannah needed, I guess."

His look was one of bewilderment. "Of course, I reacted… I was upset. I was mad, everything suddenly coming back to remind me of that time. Amanda was the last person I ever wanted to see again."

He shrugged. "And there you have it… my version of the story."

Chester let out a long breath. "*Ah…* according to Sophie, from what Hannah told her, your first bad move was at the restaurant when you told her you didn't *think* you loved Amanda anymore. The word *think* is the main culprit here. I guess, for Hannah, this was proof you still weren't over her."

Sean stared at him, his jaw dropping. "What? You've got to be kidding. After I told her the whole story again, I told her I doubted I even loved Amanda in the first place. Or that she loved me. We got so caught up in the extravagant wedding plans, we weren't together enough to see this. When I look back now, I wish we had talked. Instead we let everything turn into a huge, unfortunate mess."

Shaking his head, he gave a short laugh. "As you can see, women and I don't hit it off. I thought with Hannah it was going to be different. From the first moment I saw her, I knew she was the one. I didn't even need to talk to her to know this. You probably think I'm crazy, but there was something about her that drew me like a magnet."

Chester shook his head. "You don't have to convince me. Been there, done that." He grinned. "But now that I've heard your side of the story, your best bet is to come up with a plan to get the two of you back together. According to Sophie, Hannah is miserable. And you don't seem to be doing much better."

"Whoa… I think I've got a call." Digging into his pocket, Sean pulled out his phone. After he checked the number, he began walking away, glancing back at Chester. "Sorry, I've got to answer this. It's Chris. I made an offer on a property and this could be why he's calling."

After a few minutes, he returned. His hand slowly going to his head, he had a big smile on his face. "They accepted my offer. The place is mine, providing there are no issues with the inspection."

Chester reached up to give him a high five, his grin just as big. "That's great, congratulations. I know how you were waiting for something to come up."

Sean let out a long breath. "Yeah, I can't wait until everything goes through and I'm holding the key. Hannah was with me when I checked it out yesterday. I'm pretty sure she thinks I'm crazy, but I need land and horses in my life. Along with all the trimmings. It's in my blood, I guess."

He frowned. "But I need her to be a part of this. This is what my plan has been all along. Without her, all the land and horses in the world won't mean a thing to me."

He groaned, dragging his hand down over his jaw. "*Damn*… everything was going so good. I thought… well, I guess I thought I finally got this one right."

Chester came to his feet, giving him a pat on the shoulder. "We'll come up with something. What are your plans for tonight? I know the girls are going over to Abby's to help her finish decorating the wedding cake. With the new baby, she can definitely use the help. Kevin and I are meeting Sam at the party center to set up some kind of mood lighting Livy dreamed up."

He shook his head. "Definitely not my line of expertise, but I told Sam I'd help however I can." He grinned. "If only to boss everyone around. And provide the beer."

He smiled. "Have you seen the baby? Madeline Rose… she's a cute little thing." He laughed. "I have a feeling my boys will be fighting over her with that red hair of hers."

Sean stood, and pulling his shirt up over his head, he began to head for the showers. "Yeah, I'll help. As it stands now, I have nothing else to do. And no, I haven't seen the baby yet. Hannah and I had plans to go see her today since both she and Abby are home now. But..."

He shrugged. "You know how that went." He nodded to Chester. "Text me the time and everything."

Chester watched him leave. He glanced down at his phone. He should call Sophie to tell her what he learned from Sean, but this would be risky. The next thing he knew, she'd have him dropping by to talk to Hannah... or setting up some kind of rendezvous for the two of them.

Massaging the back of his neck, he smiled. He'd swear, he felt like he was living in a sitcom sometimes. Every time he turned around, there was someone else Sophie was trying to save.

Your own little Wonder Woman... that's what she is. And you love her for this.

Since his mind had already moved on to the routine he was going to tackle, he decided he was going to get in his workout before he called her.

It would be a lot safer this way.

CHAPTER 29

Hannah watched as Sophie carefully lifted a fondant rose off the tray, to then just as carefully position it on the top layer of the cake.

After letting out a sigh of relief when this was accomplished with no mishap, she gazed down at the bundle of pink she was gently rocking in her arms.

She'd been holding Madeline Rose for over a half hour and she still wasn't ready to give her up. But why should she? Perfectly content and sound asleep, it would be silly to move her, taking the chance of waking her.

Abby came to stand beside her. "I can put her in her baby seat if you're getting tired of holding her."

"Oh, Abby, how can you stand it... she's so precious. I certainly don't mind holding her, unless you're afraid she'll get spoiled."

Laughing, Abby shook her head. "Are you kidding? I fear that's already happened. I almost have to bribe Kevin to put her down. But, going by the time, I think she'll probably be looking for her bottle shortly."

As though Madeline recognized Abby's voice, she opened her eyes. Stretching and scrunching up her face, she began crying in earnest.

Hannah handed her back to Abby. "Let me know if you want me to do anything else. In the meantime, I'll help Sophie."

Returning to Sophie, she was just in time to hand her another rose to put on the cake.

Sophie smiled over at her. "Have you picked up your dress from the boutique yet? Aunt Louise told me it was all finished and ready to go."

After sending a furtive glance around to see everyone else was involved in their own conversations and not the least bit interested in what she and Sophie were talking about, Hannah shook her head. "Sophie, I can't go. I can't show up by myself. Sean will be there. It would be so awkward."

Sophie was shaking her head. "You're crazy. You need to talk to the poor guy. Chester saw him at the gym this afternoon and said he looked pathetic. He said he looked like a man who had just been condemned to death."

Hannah sighed. "I'm sure Chester was exaggerating. But I just can't see him yet. I still can't get over what happened, that he would do such a thing. I don't know, maybe everything between us is moving too fast, we need to take a little break."

She was trying to sound as casual as she could. Even though this was far from how she was feeling.

She was more miserable than she'd ever been in her life.

If Sophie hadn't roped her into helping Abby out with the cake, she'd be hiding away in her condo right now, trying not to think about the constant ache where her heart was.

Or, should you instead say... where your heart used to be? Since you had already given it to him...

Even though it had just about killed her, she had ignored all of Sean's calls. And now that the calls had stopped, she would give anything to have him start calling again. He had taken over her mind to the point she was unable to think of anything else.

This scared her, because she knew this wasn't going to change, not for a long, long time.

She missed him.

You miss him a lot. More than you thought possible.

Watching the play of emotions on Hannah's face, Sophie nodded. "I know, I know. But sometimes, you have to jump in, take a chance. Before it's too late. You don't want to look back and wonder what would have happened had you not let your pride take over."

She picked up a fondant leaf, to suddenly tilt her head. "Is that my phone ringing? It's in my purse, right behind you. Can you get it?"

Retrieving the phone, Hannah glanced down at it before she held it out to Sophie. "It's a text from Chester. It says…"

We've hatched up a plan. Call me.

She laughed. "*Hmm…* sounds serious."

Sophie abruptly came to her feet and grabbing the phone out of her hand, she began walking away. "I need to answer this. It might be about the boys. I'll be right back." She nodded towards the cake. "In the meantime, you keep adding the flowers. Since they will be covering the whole cake, Abby said there's no real pattern to follow… whatever looks good"

Hannah had just placed the last fondant leaf on the cake when Sophie returned, a worried look on her face. "Chester has a message for you from Sean. He got a call from Peter about the puppy. If you still want it, the owners want to meet you, something they do with every puppy they place. But it has to be tonight, since they're off to Italy tomorrow for a wedding or something."

A dreamy smile on her face, she stared off into space. "Italy… I love Italy. That was the best surprise ever, Chester setting up the trip there and to Paris for our honeymoon. Wait… let me take that back… it was the second-best surprise. The first would have to be how he surprised me with the wedding. Why, I never would've thought…"

She was interrupted by Hannah, who was still trying to take in the news about the puppy. "Sophie... yes, those were both amazing surprises and Chester's even more wonderful, but about the puppy..."

At Sophie's hurt look, she quickly went on to add, "I'm sorry. I couldn't ask for a better brother-in-law. Seriously, I mean this. But, again... the puppy. You said if I don't go right now to meet the owners, it might not be mine?"

Sophie nodded. "Yep, according to Chester this is what you have to do. Maybe there's someone else who's also interested in the puppy? Which means you should go, right?" She waited for Hannah's response, almost holding her breath.

Finally, Hannah smiled. "I want the puppy. So, I have really don't have a choice. I only hope I can remember where the place is."

Sophie nearly fell over her own feet in her haste to get her coat and keys from the table. "I'll go with you. In fact, I'll drive."

Bewildered, Hannah stared at her. "But what about Abby? Haven't you promised to help her out tonight?"

Already heading for the door, pulling her coat on as she went, Sophie responded over her shoulder. "I'm not letting you go alone. You're not supposed to be driving yet, remember? There are more than enough people to help out and I already told Abby we're leaving, so come on... let's go."

So, what was Hannah to do, but grab her coat and follow her.

Because she really did want the puppy.

Even though she'd give all the puppies in the world in exchange for even just a few seconds with Sean.

In a heartbeat, she would do this.

"Hold on tight, because here we go..."

In order to make the turn before the light turned red, Sophie stepped on the gas, sending them careening around the corner.

She glanced over at Hannah, who was clinging to the armrest, a horrified look on her face.

She laughed, reaching over to pat her arm. "I'm sorry, I wanted to beat the light, since it's always such a long one. Chester complains about it all the time."

But it was when she got irritated, rambling on about drivers who didn't understand the reason for turn signals, Hannah sent her a wary glance. "What the heck is wrong with you? Why are you acting so crazy?"

She suddenly groaned. "Oh my God… what have you done? What are you planning?"

"No, no, no… I've done nothing, no plans. Just trying to do a good deed… make my sister happy."

Sophie was being completely honest with this answer. She did not help with the planning, she was only following orders. All the credit would go to Chester and Sean for this one. This was fine with her. If anything were to go wrong, she'd be able to claim complete ignorance.

And she really did want Hannah to be happy… even more so with Sean.

She quickly changed the subject. "So, tell me… what kind of puppy are you getting and when will you finally be able to bring it home? You'll have to bring it over to meet our dogs."

She laughed. "The boys will go crazy over a puppy. I think our dogs are getting too old for them. They can't keep up and usually wind up running off somewhere to hide."

In typical Sophie fashion, she chattered on for the rest of the drive, giving Hannah no chance to get a word in, except maybe a yes or no, here and there.

Finally, she was guiding her SUV down the long winding drive-way. She glanced over at Hannah. "Now, you're sure this is the place, right?"

Hannah only nodded. For some reason she was suddenly extremely nervous, her stomach tied up in knots. She had this funny feeling something momentous was about to happen. And this would be taking place very soon. Gazing out of the window, she intently searched their surroundings. But even in the darkness, everything seemed as before, with nothing unusual to see.

What exactly are you looking for? Possibly a brand new black pick-up truck? Coincidently, belonging to Sean? And why would you even think he might be here? Wishful thinking, no?

Sophie pulled up in front of the house and picking up her phone, she turned to Hannah. "You go on ahead. I was told you're supposed to meet them in the barn where the puppies are. I promised Chester I'd let him know when we got here. He always worries about me, since I'm not all that great with directions. Once I call him, I'll join you."

When Hannah didn't move, she grinned. "Go on, go get him... or uh... I mean her... or whatever."

Hannah got out of the SUV and after one last hesitant glance back at Sophie, who was already talking on her phone, she began making her way towards the barn. This turned out to be quite a challenge since the wind had begun to kick up and it was starting to snow. Pulling up her hood, she put her head down against the swirling flakes.

It was when she finally looked up, she came to an abrupt halt.

Her breath catching in her throat, her hand went to her mouth. While her heart began to beat so fiercely, she could actually hear it pounding in the hushed silence of the winter night.

She didn't move, slowly taking in the amazing scene in front of her. The path to the barn was lit on both sides with, what looked like, a hundred luminaries. They glowed softly, the snow swirling around them, sparkling like glitter.

It was absolutely magical.

A huge gust of wind, whipping up the snow around her, brought her to life. Wrapping her arms around herself , she slowly made her way up the path, stopping twice to twirl around so she could take in the beauty of the flickering candles again.

She couldn't stop smiling.

It was a smile that couldn't get any bigger. Because even though she was trying not to get her hopes up, she'd be willing to bet the owners hadn't arranged this display.

Now even more eager to see what else could be waiting for her, she pulled open the barn door and slipped inside.

For a few moments, she stayed where she was, soaking up the

warmth and peacefulness of the dimly lit space, the only sound coming from the horses stirring in their stalls. This was in response to the wave of frigid air that swept through the barn when she entered.

Besides that, there was only silence.

The same cats who'd greeted her and Sean the first time they came into the barn, came bounding over to meet her again. But this time, they didn't leave. After she bent down to pet them, she stood and called out, her voice sounding so loud in the hushed stillness.

"Hello?"

This was greeted by only more silence. Moving further into the barn, she smiled when she saw Sugar had poked her head out over the door to the stall and was watching her. Nodding her head, she snorted a greeting.

Moving closer, Hannah cautiously reaching out to stroke her nose. "Hi, Sugar. Remember me? Tell me, do you know where everyone is?"

A sudden commotion came from behind her, sending the cats scattering. When she turned to see the puppy racing towards her, she scooped up the wiggling bundle of fur, laughing as her face was showered with wet kisses.

She waited until the puppy had settled more comfortably in her arms before she spoke in a whisper. "I have a feeling you and I are going to be the best of friends. But tell me, who let you out of your pen? And are they still here?"

Someone cleared their throat. Her head jerking up, she saw it was Sean. Standing about ten feet away, he was holding his hat, his fingers nervously twisting the brim.

His smile was tentative.

"Hey..."

Try as she could, Hannah couldn't answer, almost overwhelmed by the fact he was really standing in front of her. Her eyes searching his face, she slowly drank in the sight of him, wanting nothing more than to run straight into his arms.

Let's face it, there was nothing that was going to change the way she felt about him. No matter what he did. Or what he said. She'd already given herself to him in every way.

He was her other half. He was in her heart, in her mind and would always be the only man she would ever love.

She swallowed and opening her mouth, she managed to just barely croak out her response.

"Hey, cowboy..."

Her greeting bringing an expression of such relief to his face, she had to bow her head. Hiding her face in the puppy's fur, she tried not to cry. Or, worse yet, start babbling like a baby.

He'd moved closer, his voice husky with longing. "*God...I've missed you.*"

She lifted her head. Met with a look so tender and filled with so much love, any restraint she'd been trying so hard to hold onto? Well, it was gone... just like that. Bringing her to do exactly what she'd hoped she wouldn't.

She started to cry. "I missed you, too. I did...so, so much. I didn't want to be mad at you. I can't be mad at you. I only want everything to be back to the way it was. I couldn't..."

And then she was in his arms, the familiar scent of leather and spice surrounding her, calming her.

Everything was as it should be.

Yes, the world has righted itself again.

For the longest time they stayed in this embrace, the kisses Sean pressed in Hannah's hair coming between his soothing whispers.

It was the puppy, wiggling up between them and covering Sean's face with a barrage of wet, sloppy kisses, that finally had them breaking apart. And once the puppy was settled back in the pen with the other puppies, Sean grabbed Hannah's hand and pulled her down next to him on a bale of straw.

He put his arm around her, giving a long, contented sigh. "This is where I'm meant to be. With you."

She smiled up at him. "Are you responsible for the luminaries? If so, I love them."

Wrapping one of her curls around his finger, he nodded. "I was told women love things like that. Adds a little bit of magic to the moment."

"It was a beautiful surprise. Thank you" She gazed around them, a long trembling sigh coming from her. "This place really does feel like magic, doesn't it?"

He smiled, and putting his finger under her chin, he tipped her face up to his. "Darlin', magic is everywhere you are. But right now, I want to put a hold on that magic. We need to talk. You need to let me explain."

When she began to protest, he shook his head, pressing his fingers to her mouth. "No, let me do this. I want you to know exactly what happened. Once and for all, you need to see you have nothing to worry about. You will always be able to trust me."

She nodded, settling back against him.

He began by explaining his reaction to Amanda the night they ran into her at the restaurant, claiming this was only due to the shock of seeing her again. And his talking in his sleep? When he'd claimed he would always love her? She was the woman he was referring to, the woman he would always love. Not Amanda.

He then gave a rundown of what happened when Amanda showed up at his condo. He was about to explain how she'd passed out on his sofa, but Hannah shook her head, reaching up to wind her arms around his neck.

"Stop… I don't need to hear anything more. I believe you. I love you." She followed this with a kiss that convinced him she meant this with all her heart.

A huge gust of wind whipped past the barn, sending the door shaking and rattling in protest. Abruptly pulling away from his arms, Hannah glanced over at the door, then at Sean. "*Oh, no…* Sophie… she must still be outside, waiting in her SUV."

He grinned. "Nope, she's gone, has been for a while. She left as soon as I sent her a text letting her know it was okay to head back home."

Comprehension began to show on Hannah's face. "You and Chester... you set this all up, didn't you? Do I even have to see the owners about the puppy?"

The guilty shake of his head confirmed this wouldn't be necessary. "Well, part of it is true. They did call me to say the puppy is yours, due to the glowing recommendation Peter gave you. And they would still like to meet you before the puppies are finally cleared to leave."

He tucked a curl behind her ear. "I was determined to see you, to talk to you, to explain. I love you too much to even think of losing you. So, Chester and I came up with the idea to use the puppy to lure you here."

He shook his head. "I don't know, it seems like I've had to work so damn hard and for such a long time, to win you over." A grin spread across his face "But I believe I've also already told you how much l like to win. Especially when the stakes are so high."

He stood. "And now, I want to take you home." Offering his hand, he pulled her up and right into his arms. "Tell me you'll stay with me tonight. I want to make up for the time we lost."

His mouth searching for hers, his intention was to give her a kiss that was a preview of what he was promising. But this was interrupted by the sound of the barn door abruptly sliding open, sending a blast of icy air right at them.

A man entered, all bundled up in a bulky winter coat, hat and gloves. Setting a large carry all bag on the floor, it was only after he struggled to close the door against the wind and yanked off his hat, they realized it was Peter.

He stomped his feet, sending a shower of snow across the floor before he grinned over at them. "I thought you might still be here. I hope you aren't planning to go out in this, because it's turning into more than the few flurries they'd previously predicted. Now the forecast has changed and we could be looking at up to a foot of snow. I think the temperature is also supposed to dip down to near zero tonight. They're blaming it all on an arctic blast coming down from Canada."

Proof of the worsening conditions, the lights in the barn suddenly dimmed, flickering off and on a few times before returning to normal.

Peter smiled at the worried expression on Hannah's face. "No worries, Hannah. We have a generator for situations like this. You couldn't be in a better place right now. Here you'll be safe and warm. Of course, if you want to stay in one of the guest bedrooms in the house, you're more than welcome to do that."

Sean grinned. "You know what? I think we are going to stay right here in the barn. I think it's about time I showed Hannah how to embrace life on a horse farm."

Hannah sent him a startled glance. "We're going to stay here? In the barn?"

Peter and Sean both laughed before Peter shoved his hat back on his head and pulled on his gloves. "Hannah, everything you need is here in this barn. A bathroom, blankets and pillows in the cupboards. Even a refrigerator. Believe me, we've spent many a night in this barn, coaching a birth or nursing an ailment of some kind. So, we've learned to be prepared."

His hand on the barn door, he turned to them, nodding down at the carry all bag still on the floor. "Oh… this is dinner my wife packed up for the two of you. It's probably still warm. I added a bottle of wine."

He winked. "I thought you might have some celebrating to do. I'll leave the side door unlocked in case you decide to come up to the house. I hope you have a good night."

He slipped out into the blur of white, closing the door behind him.

Sean picked up the carry-all bag.

He peered down into it, inhaling a deep breath. "*Ah...* smells wonderful. I'm starving."

Glancing over at Hannah, there was an almost embarrassed expression on his face. "I know, what a surprise. But, believe it or not, I haven't had much to eat over the past twenty-four hours or so. I sort of lost my appetite."

"I know. Me, too."

The love shining in her eyes had him leaning in to give her a kiss. "Ah, Hannah Michaels… this goes to show we're a perfect match. Let me find some blankets and we'll spread them out, have a picnic. A winter barn picnic. What do you think?"

She leaned in to kiss him back.

"I think that sounds wonderful."

Sean poured the last of the wine into their glasses.

After settling back more comfortably against the bales of straw he'd covered with almost every blanket he found in the cupboard, he pressed a kiss in Hannah's hair.

He was smiling.

For him, this was the best of adventures, in a surrounding he found so familiar. That he was with the woman he loved… the woman he'd been so afraid he'd lost, made this even sweeter.

He listened as another gust of wind rattled the barn doors and sent the rafters creaking. Pulling Hannah closer, he gave a contented sigh. "So, pretty nice, huh?"

Hannah gazed up into his face. "I'm so happy to be with you, I don't think it would matter where we were. But, you're right, it's wonderful."

Sean had already become lost in her eyes, even before she spoke. Like stars, they drew him in. Stars, he'd swear, he'd follow anywhere.

Taking her wine glass from her, he moved them down onto the blanket. The familiar softness of her curves beneath his hands was enough to bring back the memory of the last time they were together.

He wanted this again. He wanted proof everything between them was back to where it should be.

"Hannah…" Her name coming from him in a groan, he pulled her down with him deeper into the blankets. His kiss starting out as a here-I-am-remember-me kiss, swiftly escalated to one of passion.

His promises came at her in a husky whisper. Between the kisses he pressed with agonizing slowness down her throat and along the vneckline of her sweater, he pushed every button, striking every nerve. When he lifted her sweater up and over her head, his lips then going on to leave a trail of heat across her exposed skin, the sigh she gave was almost one of relief.

"Oh, Sean… I was so afraid we…"

He stopped her in mid-sentence, his fingers sifting through her hair, smoothing it back from her face. "I know, darlin', I know. Me, too. But we didn't and we won't. We're together and my plan is to keep it this way. Starting now, and right here where we belong."

His gaze holding hers, the burning intensity in his eyes had her now even more eager for his touch. Wrapping her arms around him, she pulled him closer until he was kissing her again.

The storm raging outside was completely forgotten. While in the barn, the heat between them was more than enough to keep them warm.

True love has a way of doing this.

Sean tucked the blanket more securely around them before he pressed a kiss to the top of Hannah's head.

"I love you."

His whisper making her smile, she lifted her head to gaze up at him. "I love you, too."

He chuckled, shaking his head.

She scrunched up her face. "What?"

This, of course, had him giving her another kiss.

"I never thought I'd be making love to you here… in a barn. Dreamt about it, for sure. But to have it actually happen?" He slowly shook his head, pulling her closer. "Very enjoyable and memorable, something I know I'll never, ever forget."

He grinned. "Even sort of risky, wouldn't you say?"

Worry immediately flooded Hannah's face. She sat up, pulling the blanket with her as she sent a furtive glance around at their surroundings. "Maybe we should get dressed. Someone could come in at any minute and since we don't even belong here, it…"

He pulled her back against him, planting another kiss in her hair. "Darlin', I believe we belong here more than anyone right now. I also doubt someone is going to brave the weather just to walk in on us. At least not until morning. Trust me on this."

Hannah knew this made sense, what he said was completely reasonable. No one would be out in the storm. Certainly not only to check on them.

Right?

And to be honest? She was perfectly happy to stay right where they were. She'd go as far to say she'd even be willing to live here, if it came to this. As long as she was with Sean.

He suddenly threw aside the blanket, sitting on the edge of their makeshift bed. He smiled at her. "I don't know about you, but I'm ready for one of those big pierces of chocolate cake."

He leaned down to give her a big kiss. "Like I've told you, when I'm happy, I'm hungry. And right now, I'm very, *very* happy…"

CHAPTER 30

Marry that one person who's settled in your heart.
You know... that one person you can't live without.
~ Anonymously Yours

The day of Sam and Livy's wedding arrived with clear blue skies and a new dusting of snow over everything, turning the city into a bright and sparkling winter wonderland. All the worries of the night before, with the surprise of the sudden blizzard-like conditions, were now gone.

The long driveway leading to Sam and Livy's house had been cleared and the guests were already beginning to arrive.

The cake and the flowers had been delivered and it was now less than a half-hour until the ceremony.

In the master bedroom of her and Sam's house, Livy was absent-mindedly studying her reflection in the mirror as Sophie adjusted her veil.

Sophie stepped back to view her handiwork before she gave a huge sigh. "There, you're all set. And you look absolutely stunning."

Livy merely nodded.

Now, if you're wondering why Livy wasn't saying anything, this was because she was afraid if she even opened her mouth, she would start to cry. These would be happy tears, but definitely not advisable after all the time spent on her make-up.

She reached for her lipstick, appropriately named *Kiss Me Now*. As she applied it, she smiled, thinking about the part this simple little tube of lipstick had played in her first real date with Sam.

Such a rocky beginning it had been for the two of them before that night. And to think, in less than an hour, he would be her husband.

She still couldn't believe she was going to marry Sam. If there was ever a time to believe in fairy tales, this would be it. In fact, she sometimes wondered if this could all possibly be a dream.

She took a deep breath and finally gave Sophie a tremulous smile. "I'm sorry. It's just that… Thank you… yes, I want to thank you for everything. I… I…"

And shaking her head, the tears flowed…

Quickly handing her the box of tissues, Sophie grinned. "Here, you don't want to ruin your make-up. You can cry as much as you want after you and Sam are married."

She glanced over at Livy's phone, setting on the vanity counter. "It looks like you have a message. Oh boy, I'll bet you anything, it's from Sam. Hold on to that box of tissues."

Livy picked up her phone.

And Sophie was right… it was from Sam.

Bringing on more tears.

> *Hi baby,*
> *You know how I hate texting, but this*
> *text is a special one. I can't believe*
> *after today, I will be able to call you*
> *my wife.*
> *And I know when I see you coming*
> *down those stairs, I will be looking*
> *into the eyes of the most beautiful*
> *bride ever and the woman of my*
> *dreams.*

*So, imagine I'm raising my glass in a
toast. Here's to one of the first and
many amazing days to come of our
married life.
I love you baby. Always have and
always, always will.
Sam*

A knock on the door put a halt to Livy's tears.

Sophie's Aunt Louise, who was bustling around, making sure everything was going smoothly, sent Livy a smile. "It seems you have a visitor, Livy."

It was Gracie.

A tentative smile on her face, she slowly made her way over to Livy. She was holding a small white jewelry box, tied with a white satin ribbon.

They had met two days ago when Gracie made a surprise visit to Sam's office to let him know she was back in town, this time for good. It had been an emotional reunion between brother and sister, with Sam insisting both Gracie and Jack attend the rehearsal dinner and the wedding.

Livy gave her a big hug. "I'm so glad you're here. And I know Sam is happy, too."

Gracie smiled. "So am I. But, my gosh, Livy… you look absolutely gorgeous. How are you holding up?"

Livy laughed. "I'm doing fine. But a little emotional, I guess." This was confirmed by Sophie, who rolled her eyes as she nodded, bringing a laugh from everyone.

Livy's voice a little shaky, she shrugged. "Right now, I only want to see Sam. Have you seen him yet?"

Gracie grinned. "I just left him and he was extremely jealous I was coming to see you. He's pacing the floor, he said he'd give anything to be with you right now."

She handed the box to Livy. "He sent me here to give this to you. He wanted to give it to you himself, but everyone talked him out of it."

She laughed. "Honestly, you should have been there. The guys were all so serious, warning him about the superstition of seeing the bride before the ceremony. I think they had him scared to death. So, here I am, the unofficial delivery girl."

Livy opened the box to find a pair of exquisite diamond drop earrings.

The accompanying note was simple, yet right to the point.

Livy, I love you with all my heart.
You will always be my dance partner,
no matter what. Because, baby?
I love all your moves. Sam

Livy laughed at the last line, to only follow with more tears.

Sophie gasped. "Oh, Livy… those are gorgeous. They're going to look amazing with your dress. Did you know he was going to give you these? If so, now I see where you were going with your choice of dress."

Livy was smiling. "No, I never told him anything about the dress. But, they're perfect. I love them."

There had been an ongoing argument between her and Sophie about the dress. Sophie thought she was being too conservative. It was her wedding, she'd reminded her. A once in a lifetime chance to pull out all the stops and wear a knockout dress.

Livy had held firm and picked out a very sleek and simple, fitted dress with a shawl collar that dipped down in the back, the skirt flowing into a long train. The fabric was a luminous cream satin, the style screamed sophistication. She had loved it from the moment she put it on.

But now the dress didn't really matter.

She only wanted to be with Sam.

Livy was definitely grateful for Chester's support as she made her way shakily down the stairs to where Sam was waiting for her. But once her gaze locked with his, filled with so much love, she'd seriously felt as though she could've floated down the rest of the steps.

It was just as she'd envisioned when she and Sam first saw the house, exactly how she had imagined a wedding would be.

But never had she dared to dream it would be their wedding.... with her eyes searching only for him.

CHAPTER 31

*H*annah pulled the brush through her hair one last time. After she slipped her lipstick in her jeans pocket, she turned out the bathroom light and wandered into the living room.

She was waiting for Sean. He had returned to his townhouse just a short time ago to shower and change. He told her there was also something else he had to do before he came back to pick her up.

They were planning to drive out to Sean's new home. The inspection was taking place this very minute and he wanted to be there before they finished, in case there were any problems.

Had she been surprised when Sean told her he'd purchased the property? She'd have to admit she was. But, at the same time, she'd suspected from the beginning, this was what he planned to do. The short time she had known him, she'd learned once he made up his mind, it was a done deal. His confidence stepped in and, committed to making it work, he never looked back.

Like you... you're still amazed at how he never gave up on you. But thank goodness he didn't.

As she waited, she thought about how the past few days had passed in pretty much of a blur, starting with the night she and Sean had spent in the barn.

It was a night she would never forget. She had almost been disappointed when the snow ended almost as quickly as it had begun, making it possible for them to leave in the morning. Sean had dropped her off at her condo, with the promise he'd come back to pick her up for lunch. Then their plan was to stop by Abby and Kevin's, so Sean could meet Madeline Rose.

For lunch, they had gone to Café Latte. Where they weren't surprised to see Michael seated at one of the tables and working on his computer. This, along with Ellie's blush when she saw them, was enough to let them know things were going well with her and Michael.

It was when they stopped to buy a baby gift, Hannah realized just how popular Sean was with the Cleveland baseball fans. She watched as the women blushed, becoming flustered when he even as much as smiled at them. But she knew exactly how they felt. She still felt a flutter start up inside of her when he aimed one of his smiles at her.

She wrapped her arms around herself in a hug, thinking about the one little incident that took place, one she would always remember.

Someone in the crowd had yelled out to ask if she was his girlfriend. He'd gazed over at her and in the expectant hush that followed, his smile spread all the way up to his eyes, the corners creasing in agreement. And even though it had been a teasing smile, she'd swear what he said came straight from his heart.

He reached over to brush his fingers down the side of her face, the husky tone of his voice like a vow. "She is more than my girlfriend. She's my everything."

After following this with a tip of his hat and a wink, he went right back to signing autographs.

Honestly? If the two of you hadn't been surrounded by so many people, you would've thrown yourself right into his arms.

From there, they had gone on to spend time with Kevin, Abby and Madeline Rose before returning to her condo and ordering a pizza.

The next day was Sam and Livy's wedding.

She had worn the dress Sophie had picked out for her from Chic Boutique.

She definitely owed Sophie and their Aunt Louise a huge thank you, because she absolutely loved the dress and how it fit so perfectly. Maybe it was because it was red, but she felt so fun and flirty when she had it on.

It turned out Sean liked it, too. More than liked it. When he'd arrived at her condo to pick her up and she opened the door, for the longest time he didn't say a word, his gaze leisurely traveling over her. Then, a smile working its way across his face, he took her into his arms and gave her a kiss that rivaled, or maybe even surpassed any he had given her in the past.

He told her she wasn't playing fair. The dress and the way it made her look, had him wishing they could skip the wedding so he could take her straight to bed.

Now that she thought back to his kiss, she was surprised they even made it to the wedding. Throughout the reception, he had been attentive to the point he never left her side. And with each touch and every glance they shared, their awareness of each other, their desire to be alone, only grew stronger.

So, by the time they left the reception, she was just as eager to be with him as he was with her.

Let's just say he wasted no time at all helping her out of the dress .

When the doorbell rang, still caught up in these memories, she was smiling when she opened the door. Swept up in Sean's arms, there was a smile in his voice. "Hey, Darlin', did you miss me?"

Grinning down at her, he gave her no time to answer. "Get your coat. I called and the inspection is moving along faster than anticipated. I don't want them to leave before we get there."

Once Sean merged onto the freeway, he reached over to take her hand. "So, now that we're on our way, tell me... what are you thinking?"

She studied him, her mouth curving into a smile.

Go ahead, tell him what you really want to say.

She brought his hand to her mouth, dropping a soft kiss to his fingers. "How much I love you."

His smile matched hers. "I love you, too. More than you could possibly imagine."

For the rest of the drive they talked of ordinary things… yes, they even discussed the weather, happy for once it wasn't snowing, the sky a bright and cloudless blue.

Life couldn't get any better.

Sean pulled his truck up next to the house. After he swung Hannah to the ground, he gave her a kiss. This was because he wanted to… and just because he could. Then, while Hannah went to the barn to check on the puppy, he went off to find the inspector.

When Sean finally came out to the barn, he was surprised to find Hannah carrying on a conversation with the horse she had once found so intimidating. Silently sauntering over to her, he smiled as he listened.

Hannah sighed, gently stroking the horse's nose. "I'm sorry I don't have any sugar cubes or carrots on me. But I promise, I'll definitely bring these with me in the future. Hopefully I'll get a chance to visit you often and we'll become friends. Maybe I'll even become brave enough to let you take me for a ride. This, of course, all depends on what Sean has to say."

When Sean cleared his throat, Hannah whirled around to give him a guilty smile.

"Hi, Sugar and I were getting to know each other." She tilted her head, a concerned look on her face. "So, did everything work out all right?"

Nodding, he smiled at the seriousness of her expression. "Yeah, everything is fine. Once all the final papers are drawn up and signed, the property will be all ours."

Ours?

She searched his face, not quite sure if she'd heard right. Deciding it was only a slip on his part, she smiled back at him

The whole time she had been waiting, she knew there was something she needed to say to him. But now that he was actually here, and even though she had practiced, over and over in her mind what she was going to say, she wasn't sure if this was the best time. Or even the right place.

She jammed her hands in her pockets, sending him a tentative smile.

He raised an eyebrow. "What's up?" He glanced over at the puppies. "Have you changed your mind about the puppy? Because it can very easily make its home here now."

Do it. Just do it. You know you want to.

She shook her head. "No, no… it's not about the puppy." She swallowed. "There's something I want to ask you."

He leaned against the stall door, his arms crossed over his chest. He was intrigued by her behavior, wondering what she was so nervous about. Whatever it was, it must be important.

He tilted his head, sending her a reassuring smile "You know you can ask me anything."

She took a deep breath. "I know. It's just that… well, this is about something you said."

Hmm... could it possibly be what you think it is?

He nodded, prompting her to continue. "Do you remember the night you came to my condo? The night of Sam's bachelor party?"

Ah… He nodded again, filled with a sudden anticipation.

Now refusing to meet his eyes, her voice now so soft, he took a step closer to hear her words. "You asked me something."

He smiled. It was the smile of a man who was confident about what was coming next. And even though he knew he should help her out, he wanted her do this on her own.

He needed this.

God... how you need this.

So, he tried to look as serious as he could. Which wasn't easy, not by a long shot.

His head tilted, he studied her. "I did? *Hmm...* I sort of remember, but then again, that was a crazy night and I said a lot of things. So, why don't you refresh my memory and tell me again what it was."

She briefly closed her eyes.

What? Is he teasing you?

Finally meeting his gaze, she saw that no, he looked completely serious. She swallowed again. "You... well, you asked me to marry you."

When he had nothing to say in answer to this, she hesitated slightly before her words came out in a rush. "I want you to know, if you still want this, my answer is a yes. But then, it's always been a yes. When you asked, I think I was so confused, not sure of what I wanted or even who I was. Now I know. I love you and I want to marry you. I want this more than anything."

A tentative smile on her face, she waited.

Again, there was only silence.

Sean knew he should put her out of her misery, but he wanted to savor this moment. He wanted to be able to save every word, every second in his memory so he'd always know how much she loved him. Jamming his hands in his jacket pockets, he fingered the small box there.

When the silence continued, Hannah wanted to just die. So many different thoughts began galloping through her mind.

What were you thinking?

Why isn't he answering you?

Has he changed his mind?

How are going to get home if he tells you no?

Or, please don't let him think you brought this up only because he's now the owner of this property?

She waved her hand around at the interior of the barn. "It's not because of all..." This was when she noticed he was smiling. He was also holding what looked like a small jeweler's box in his hand.

Her breath catching in her throat and her heart drumming loudly in her ears, she watched as he slowly sauntered over to her before going down on one knee.

Then she watched, barely able to breathe, as he removed his hat, setting it gently and so, *so* slowly on the floor. Only then did he gaze up at her, his mouth turned up in a small smile.

He cleared his throat. "Hannah Michaels, my answer to that is a definite yes. If I could, I'd marry you in a heartbeat. In fact, my plan all along had been to ask you the very same thing. Right here and right now. Never did I think you'd beat me to it. But it really doesn't matter because I now have the answer I was praying for."

Her request came in a strangled sob. "Will you ask me again? Please?"

He took the ring out of the box and as he put it on her shaking finger, his gaze never left hers. "Hannah Michaels, will you marry me?"

"Oh, Sean... *yes*. Yes, I'll marry you. *Yes, yes, yes...* for always."

She was half crying, half laughing before he was finally able to capture her mouth with his, the kiss they shared, sealing this promise they made.

Sean and Hannah had no idea how long they had been sitting on the floor of the barn.

Sometimes talking, sometimes silent, or simply taking the time to share a kiss, they were in no hurry to leave. They wanted to soak up everything that happened, treasure this time together.

Leaning back against a bale of straw, Sean pressed a kiss to the top of her head. He watched as she held up her hand to study the ring, the diamond sparkling in the warm lighting of the barn.

He gave a low chuckle. "I take it you like what I picked out?"

She reached up to give him a kiss. "I love it. I love it to pieces and plan to never take it off. But, I would love whatever you gave me."

She suddenly sat up, a serious expression on her face. "About the wedding..."

He burst out laughing. "Already you're planning the wedding?"

He glanced down at his watch. "Let's see, we've only been engaged for not even close to an hour. But, those wheels have already started turning in your head, moving right on to planning the wedding. What kind of extravaganza are you dreaming up?"

When he saw he'd embarrassed her, he hugged her close. "Darlin' I'm only kidding. Whatever you want, it's yours. Now tell me, what about the wedding?"'

She shook her head. "I never know when you're serious."

He smiled. "I'm always serious about you. That's a given."

She settled back against him. "What I was going to say is, I don't want a big wedding. Or a bridal shower. Or any of the other stuff that makes up a wedding. Maybe a cake… yes, a cake for sure. And a dress… Not a fancy dress, but a dress that's special."

He was shaking his head. "Just as long as you don't wear the dress you wore to Sam and Livy's wedding. I want my mind on the vows we'll be exchanging, not on what I want with you after it's all over."

The memory of that night prompting another kiss, she smiled up at him. "I'll save that dress for special occasions, okay?"

He nodded. "It's a deal. But, help me understand… you're telling me you don't want a wedding?"

"I want it to be more like a big party. Arrange it so no one even suspects it's our wedding day until we're ready to exchange our vows. It will be a big surprise. We could tell everyone it's a party to celebrate your new home."

She gazed up at him, her face scrunched up. "And maybe… *maybe* somehow we could have it here?"

"*Our home…* it's *our* new home, darlin'. Remember? We're in this together. "He smiled, pressing a kiss in her hair. "When would you like to have this happen?"

"If we could, tomorrow. But, since I know that's not possible, as soon as we can pull it off." She sighed. "I just want to be married to you."

She suddenly grinned. "I want to ride off with you on that horse, no matter how far up from the ground I'll be. And we'll live happily ever after."

He was smiling, his mind storing away this information. If this is what she wanted, he was going to make it happen.

He smiled. "Then this is what we'll do."

About to give her another kiss, they both looked up as the barn door came sliding open and Peter walked in.

Scrambling to his feet and pulling Hannah up with him, Sean grinned. "You are the first to know we're now engaged." He grinned down at Hannah. "In fact, we both said yes."

Peter came over to shake Sean's hand before giving Hannah a quick hug. "Congratulations to both of you." He grinned. "Wow… a new home and getting engaged, all at the same time. Have you set a date?"

Sean and Hannah glanced at each other before they smiled at Peter. Sean was the one to answer.

"It's funny you should bring that up. Because there's something we'd like to talk to you about."

CHAPTER 32

If you have to leave, then go. But know I will always stay right here.
For as long as it takes, I will wait for you
~Anonymously Yours

Since Hannah and Sean could use some time to get everything all set up for the 'surprise un-wedding' they were planning, let's take a quick jaunt across the country. Newport Beach, California, to be exact.

It was already pushing mid-morning when Darcey unlocked the door to her office, her name etched in gold on the heavy glass door.

Darcey Hollister, VP/Director of Marketing

Walking across the luxuriously thick and padded shag carpeting, she tossed her purse on her desk.

When she realized she'd left the door open, she hurried over to close it, resisting the urge to slam it as hard as she could.

She wondered… if she did slam the door?

Would the glass shatter?

Nah... you seriously doubt this.

As the headquarters of Hollister Investments, no expense had been spared in the construction of this building. Built over seventy-five years ago, inside and out, it was still as solid as the rocky terrain it was situated on, overlooking the panoramic and sun baked view of Southern California.

As her father always liked to remind everyone, even though the business had been around for as long as it had, nothing about what it represented had changed. It was still a symbol of stability and growth. And honesty. This was a trait he demanded from all his employees, from the maintenance crew, all the way to the top executives.

There were no exceptions.

If only this was true... the honesty thing, that is. Instead, it looks like, in fact, a lot has changed... and not necessarily for the better.

David would be proof of this.

Angrily plopping down in her desk chair, she removed her sunglasses. The covert glances she'd received from everyone in the office when she walked by told her the glasses had fooled no one.

Muttering to herself this didn't matter, nor did she care, she flipped opened her computer. She had more than enough work to keep her occupied. Hopefully this would help her forget about everything else.

Starting with David.

David Hanson, the lawyer her father had hired almost a year ago. The same David she had been dating for almost half that amount of time.

She gave a frustrated sigh. What a fool she had been, thinking she'd finally found a man she could trust.

Abruptly pushing away from the desk, she went to gaze out the window. Wrapping her arms around herself, she stared out at what was usually a magnificent view of the distant mountains. Unfortunately, today they were barely visible, shrouded by the mid morning haze. This meant they were in for another hot day.

Hit by another wave of such overwhelming sadness, she took in a deep, gulping breath. This is something she had been doing on a regular basis for the past thirty-six hours or so. She'd found this was the only thing that seemed to help her from bursting into another bout of hysterical tears.

Leaning her forehead against the window, she closed her eyes.

She was tired of it all... the constant sun, the stifling heat, the twenty-four-seven rush of traffic.

Add in the constant meetings, where she was expected to be at her best and most accommodating, always reaching for that elusive deal. Completely at the mercy of the company, her life was no longer her own.

She'd even become weary of the people... every single one of them.

Yes, living in California had its' perks, but at the same time, it was draining the life out of her, aging her with each passing second. Even this morning, she'd noticed new wrinkles forming at the corners of her eyes.

What's next? Your hair will start turning gray?

She sighed...

So, what is it you really want?

Given that David would no longer be part of her life, what she needed was a chance to start over. Where the Hollister name would no longer define who she was.

What is wrong with you? Most people would envy you. They'd say you're acting like a spoiled brat.

She'd thought her life had taken off in a whole new direction when she met David. He was handsome, smart and his expectations for the future were, she had so foolishly believed, on goal with hers. She had even dared to dream he would give her a ring for Christmas.

But, here it was, almost to the end of January and there was no ring on her finger.

As her father would say, evidently David hadn't got the memo.

Nope... and now? It looked like there would be no more memos for David in the future. Not after what happened.

How was she to know, only two days ago, her whole world would come crashing down on her?

She closed her eyes.

And once again she was re-living the whole miserable experience. If only to somehow make sense of it all.

She had been working late, caught up in the logistics of an outdoor mall project. Reading over the tenant regulations, she'd become confused with the wording. Since David was probably somewhere in the building, the dedicated employee that he was, she decided to ask for his help.

She had hoped, not only would he help her decipher the text of the document, she would also be able to persuade him to take her out for a late dinner at their favorite restaurant.

Lately, their time together had been limited and she missed his company. She realized he was swamped with work, but this hadn't stopped him from finding time for her in the past. So, maybe it was about time to fire up a new spark in their relationship?

If you had only known...

Just as she thought, she found him in his office. Unfortunately, he wasn't alone.

Nor was he working.

Let's just say he was taking a break. One that didn't involve coffee and from the looks of it, one he was very familiar with.

He had Melanie Myers in his arms and they were both so deep into a passionate kiss, they hadn't even noticed she had walked into the room. That Melanie was one of her closest friends in the company had made this situation even more difficult to bear.

Had been, you mean. And to think you had considered Melanie as a possible bridesmaid in your, now never to be, wedding with David.

For a few moments, she hadn't moved, almost fascinated by the kiss.

It was only when David's hand had drifted down Melanie's thigh to slide underneath her outrageously short skirt, definitely falling short of the company dress code, she'd come to life. Shaking her head, she began backing her way out of his office, not even aware the low, keening moan was coming from her.

This is what had finally captured David's attention. Lifting his head, he looked up and right into her eyes, just as she reached the door.

"Damn..." This coming from him in a long groan, he pushed away from Melanie, shoving her hard enough into the desk to bring on her shocked scream.

Melanie's scream echoing in her head, Darcey had taken off down the hall, slipping into the first place she could find. This had turned out to be the women's restroom. Locking the door, she'd leaned against it, trying to catch her breath. Tears spilling down her face, she couldn't stop the sobs rising in her throat.

Ignoring David's repeated knocks and requests they needed to talk, she'd waited until there was only silence coming from his side. Opening the door to find no sign of him, she took off in a sprint to her office. Her plan had been to grab her purse and leave.

Instead, she came face to face with him. Sitting at her desk, his expression was calm, confident... as though he hadn't a care in the word.

Ah... why hadn't you thought something like this might happen?

He'd given her one of his movie star smiles. The same smile that won her over the first time they met.

"Ah, Darcey..."

Her hands clenched at her sides, she'd glared at him. "I want you out of my office. Now."

When he didn't move, only continued to smile at her, she'd grabbed her purse from the desk and turned to leave. "Fine, stay here. But you better not be here in the morning."

The confidence in his expression now a thing of the past, David jumped to his feet, almost knocking over the chair. Running his hand through his hair, a nervous laugh escaped him. "Darcey, please... let's not be unreasonable about this. What you saw was nothing, and for me, a complete surprise. Melanie initiated the kiss, refusing to let me go. I went along with it because I didn't want to hurt her feelings."

He didn't want to hurt her feelings? What about your feelings?

Afraid she would start crying again—an out of control and hysterical kind of crying, she began walking towards the door.

His words stopped her. "*Aw... come on*, Darcey. Think of it as a harmless kiss between co-workers."

Whirling around, she'd stared at him in disbelief. First, he accused her of being unreasonable? And now he expected her to believe what he did was... what was the word he used?

Harmless?

Ah, yes... harmless.

And he thought you'd be so stupid to believe this?

Again, she'd turned away, her response coming over her shoulder. "I don't believe you. And after this, I know I'll never be able to trust you again. From this point on, we may work together, but beyond that, you mean nothing to me. We're done, David."

This hadn't stopped him from calling out after her. "Wait... you're not planning to go running to your father to tell him about this, are you?"

For a few seconds she had been filled with so much anger, she didn't think she'd be able to respond.

Running to your father? This was the only thing that concerned him?

She had slowly turned back to him, her words coming out very, *very* slowly. "No, I'm not going to go running, as you just insinuated, to my father. And do you know why? Because I know he will say he tried to warn me about you. In case you haven't figured it out yet, he has never really liked you."

At David's horrified expression, she'd laughed. Yes, actually laughed. Granted it had been a hysterical laugh. But it was enough to have David step back, an even more alarmed expression on his face.

She shook her head. "Don't worry. What's important, he thinks you're good at your job. Though I do remember him saying there was something about you that didn't set right with him. I guess I should have taken note, as he's always been a good judge of character. This certainly would've saved me a lot of grief."

With this, she'd turned and stormed out of her office, leaving him staring after her, speechless.

While she had been waiting for the elevator, one of the interns came running over to her, holding out a small package. "Darcey, this just came for you, priority mail."

Then she'd peered more closely at her. "Are you okay? Don't you feel well?"

No, as a matter of fact, you had felt awful. Your life had come to a complete standstill. Everything you thought was so perfect was now gone, leaving you broken.

But, somehow managing a smile, she took the package and stuffed it in her purse. "Thank you. I'll be fine."

Her next words had come out much wobblier than she'd intended. "I think I just need a break from all of this. Do me a favor and take all my calls. If something urgent pops up, I'm sure you'll find someone here who can figure it out."

Afraid if she said anything more, this would only bring on a flood of tears, she'd practically sprinted into the elevator, thankful it was empty.

She had cried her entire drive home... and on into most of the night. To then call the office yesterday morning to let them know she wouldn't be coming in.

She'd thought of making up some kind of excuse. But the probability of what happened between her and David already making the rounds through the office, well... this would've made her look even more of a fool.

And this is exactly what you were... a fool.

So, now that Darcey was back at work, and in the sanctuary of her office, it was understandable the mood she was in.

Work... you need to immerse yourself in your work. The one thing it appears you're good at.

She dug through her purse, searching for her phone. Instead, she pulled out the package the intern had given her.

She had forgotten all about it

She glanced at the return address. It was postmarked Cleveland, Ohio.

Cleveland? Who would be sending you something from Cleveland?

She was familiar with the city, having lived there for a short time. But this was years ago. When she was about eight or nine years old and in the second grade.

But she hadn't been back there since.

This isn't true, and you know it.

Wearily running her hand through her hair, she sighed. Yes, there was one other time, but she didn't want to start thinking about that… not now…

Yes, why bring up another failure in your life?

Instead, she thought back to when she'd lived in Cleveland. A time that could've been a very stressful year for both her, and her younger brother Niles. Instead it had turned out to be one of the best years of their childhood. All because of their grandmother, who had gone out of her way to make sure their life was as normal as possible while their parents battled their way through a messy and drawn out divorce.

She'd loved her grandmother.

And she'd loved her grandparent's house.

The large and traditional two-story brick house gave off the impression it was fit for royalty, or a famous celebrity. And in a way, this was exactly what it was. Her grandmother had been a famous actor and dancer on Broadway and her grandfather came from an upstanding and prestigious family in upstate New York. So, a big part of their time was spent in the company of the rich and famous.

There was always something going on. Early afternoon garden parties, or formal dinners going into the late evening hours. In the summertime, it was nothing to see large tents set up in the backyard for barbecues or even impromptu picnics.

In her pajamas and hidden in the corner of the landing, Darcey loved watching as the guests arrived for the latest get together. Sometimes she got lucky and was invited to join the festivities, if only for a little while.

But once the divorce had been finalized, her father had whisked her brother and her off to start a whole new life in California. Since then, she had only returned to Cleveland once.

And her grandmother's house? About six months ago, her father had put it up for sale. It had become a white elephant, he claimed, and the cost to restore it would be astronomical.

Though she'd tried to convince him otherwise he stood firm on his decision. Unless she had plans of moving to Cleveland and living in the house herself, he saw no reason to keep hanging on to it.

But at the time, she'd just met David.

She frowned.

If only you had known what you do now...

She picked up the package and tore it open. Inside was a small box tied with a narrow pink ribbon. There was also an envelope with her name on it.

She opened the envelope to find a hand-written note.

Dear Darcey,

I don't know if you remember me, but we were both in Mrs. Robinson's class at Lakeside Elementary.

We weren't really friends, but I will always remember your amazing birthday party when you were living at your grandmother's house. Shortly after that, you moved away.

My fiancé, Sam Bridges, recently purchased the house. It was while I was there with him, I found this ring on the floor in the foyer. When I saw the initials on the inside of the band, I thought it might be yours. Sam was able to get your address through the real estate transfer so I could send it to you.

I think you might be happy to know that Sam, who specializes in restoring century and older homes for a living, is slowly bringing the house back to how it used to be.

If you ever happen to be in Cleveland, please stop by to see what he has accomplished so far. I think you will be pleased with the results.

Feel free to keep in touch.

Sincerely yours,

Livy Michaels

P.S. I hope I did the right thing by sending you the ring. Or that it's even yours.

Darcy stared down at the box. Her heart had jumped into high gear, and was now beating almost out of control.

The ring... you thought you'd never see it again.

Unable to get up enough nerve to open the box just yet, she closed her eyes, trying to picture the girls who were at the birthday party. She didn't remember Livy. But to be honest, she couldn't remember most of the girls.

But this wasn't surprising. After her parents had decided to divorce, upset and embarrassed about what was happening, she'd kept to herself. It was better that way. Why take the chance of becoming close to someone, only to lose them?

She read the note again. So Livy and her soon-to-be-husband were the owners of her grandparent's house.

This should make you happy. This means the house has fallen into good hands.

She put the note back in the envelope. After she put it in her purse, she made a mental note to write Livvy to thank her. Then she picked. up the box, turning it around in her hands.

She wasn't sure how she felt about this. It was a nice gesture on Livy's part to send it to her. But at the same time, she knew if she opened it, she'd be opening up a part of her past she didn't want to revisit.

No, that time was over.

Wasn't this the message she'd received? From the one person, who at the time, had mattered the most?

She was about to put the box into her purse, when she changed her mind, carefully setting it on her desk. Then she leaned back in her chair and closed her eyes.

It was only when someone passed by her office, talking on their phone, she opened her eyes.

Hoping the box might have disappeared, she glanced over to see that, no, it was still there.

Come on... this is crazy. Just do it...open the box.

Before she could change her mind, she grabbed the box, untied the ribbon, and lifted the lid.

She stared down at the ring inside.

Overcome by the flood of memories it brought, she had to close her eyes.

The last time she saw this ring, it had been on her finger. This had been on a cold and snowy January day, almost exactly three years ago. At the time, she'd foolishly thought it was the start of a whole new adventure with the man she had so deeply fallen in love with.

But she had been wrong.

Wrong, wrong, wrong... so wrong.

She took the ring out of the box and clutching it tightly in her hand, she was overcome with grief.

At the same time, she was also filled with such anger. So much anger, that for a brief moment, she wanted to throw the ring across the room, or right into the trash. So she wouldn't have to ever see it again.

But even as she was thinking this, she slipped it on her finger.

It still fit...

She pulled at the ring, her intent to put it back in the box. But it appeared to be stuck. But this really didn't matter. Whether she kept it on her finger, or put it back in the box, she'd never forget what it stood for when it was given to her.

The promise of a lifetime.

You have no reason to believe this ring still holds the same promise.

But wait... what about the email her father sent this morning about a property in Cleveland he wanted her to check out?

Her father's email, and the note and ring from Livy, had all come on the same day.

If this isn't some kind of sign, you don't know what it is.

She shook her head. That she was even thinking this was insane.

Against her better judgement, she signed into her account to find the email from her father. When she saw it earlier, she hadn't even given it a second glance. She didn't need any reminders of the last time she was in Cleveland. It hurt too much.

But now?

She glanced down at the ring on her finger.

Was it just her? Or did everything now feel different?

Now impatiently scrolling down through her emails, she finally found what she was looking for. Her fingers tapping impatiently on the desk, she waited for the listing to load.

It finally popped up.

NEW LISTING! #36199062

Commercial Property -
The Regency Party Center
650 Lakeside Avenue Cleveland, Ohio
Description: Venue for Special Events:

Ideal for weddings, conventions, reunions, etc. Located on the shore of Lake Erie, this is a well-known and popular landmark in the Cleveland area.

Description: With a few updates, this property could become an even more promising and profitable venue.

Managed by the same owner for the last fifty years, they've made the decision to turn the reigns over to a buyer who will commit to keeping the party center in the city.

Everything, inside and out, has been well kept up, all codes are up to date.

There are four party rooms, ranging in size to accommodate events for parties of twenty to five hundred people.

There is a more than adequate restaurant sized and well-equipped kitchen. Most of the appliances have been updated within the past five years.

Besides the large parking area, a sizable and partly wooded area is located in the rear of the building. This could house an addition, such as a chapel for wedding ceremonies. Or it could be turned into an outdoor reception area.

With the magnificent view of Lake Erie and the right planning and attention to detail, the sky is the limit for this property.

Only serious buyers need contact our office.

Viewing by appointment only.

Darcy leaned back in her chair, staring down at the ring on her finger.

The Regency Party Center... the memories this evoked. Such a wonderful beginning, If only the ending could've been the same.

She frowned.

No, this was impossible. Too much time had passed.

Or had it?

And just like that, her mind was made up.

She printed out a copy of the listing and headed for her father's office.

As she passed David's office, a brief glance showed the door was closed, the room dark. Blinking furiously, she found she had to take another one of those big gulping breaths.

She gave a frustrated sigh. She had a feeling it was going to take her a long time to get over what happened. Spending six months with someone you were beginning to think might be a big part of your future, certainly wasn't something easily forgotten.

But maybe this Cleveland project was a sign? A way to fix what had gone so terribly wrong in her past?

She abruptly came to a stop and pulling the ring off her finger, she dropped it in her pocket.

Later, when she got home, she would put it on a chain. This way she could wear it around her neck.

Tucked right next to your heart.

She could dream, couldn't she?

CHAPTER 33

Sophie and Chester

Almost in a run and trying to button her shirt at the same time, Sophie came flying out of the bathroom.

She ran right into Chester.

"Whoa..." He steadied the both of them, shaking his head. "What's going on with you? You've been like a tornado all day, running all over the place. It's just a party, not the Presidential Ball or something."

"I know. For some reason, and I don't know why, I feel like it's going to be a fun night... a special night." She grinned. "But then every night out, with the chance to have an actual adult conversation, is exciting."

He laughed. "Yeah, you're right about that."

As she was putting on her earrings, she saw he was watching her, the intensity of his gaze bringing her to begin chattering non-stop. "I got a text from Livy just a few minutes ago. Their flight landed and once they go home to drop off their luggage, they will head for out Hannah and Sean's place."

Chester thought about this. "Why don't you send a text we'll pick them up so they don't have to drive? I'm sure they're exhausted after their long flight."

Sophie was on her phone in seconds, sending the text. Once she was finished, she looked over to see Chester was still watching her.

He began making his way over to her, a faint smile on his face.

She sent him a puzzled look. "What did I do now?"

Taking her into his arms, he slowly shook his head. "Nothing. I'm thinking about how lucky we all are. Especially me."

He lowered his head, capturing her mouth in a leisurely kiss before he gazed down at her. "You did say the babysitter was planning to stay the night to take care of the boys, didn't you?"

She nodded, a shiver going through her at the gleam in his eyes.

He pressed a kiss in her hair. "Good… I need a night alone with you. In fact…"

In one swift move, he locked their bedroom door and swept her up in his arms. After gently dropping her on the bed, he stretched out beside her. His mouth teasing hers, at the same time he began unbuttoning those buttons she had just worked so hard at fastening.

He pressed a slow, hot kiss to her throat. "It appears I need some alone time with you right now."

"Sam and Livy's party…" this came from Sophie in a long surrendering sigh.

"Don't worry, we'll get there in plenty of time." His hand moving down to the waistband of her jeans, his whisper settled just below her ear. "I'll never get tired of getting lost in you, angel. Let me love you."

So, of course, this is what she did.

Livy and Sam

Livy moved closer to Sam in the backseat of the taxi, muffling a huge yawn against his shoulder. It had been a long flight.

Then she smiled. The last week had been wonderful… the

wedding, honeymoon, everything. Caught up in her thoughts, she didn't even realize her phone was buzzing.

But Sam did. After reading the message and slipping her phone back in her pocket, he pressed a kiss in her hair. "Sophie just answered your text. They're going to pick us up. It's going to be tight, with the babysitter and the boys, but at least we won't have to drive."

Livy sighed. "That sounds wonderful, kids and all."

"Yeah, it's been a long day, hasn't it? And I don't know about you, but I could eat a horse. Don't worry, I'll make sure not to say that when we get there." He chuckled. "But knowing Sean, the spread will be amazing. Right now, this is what keeps me going."

She smiled. "I know, me, too. Though I'm really eager see the property. And the house. Sophie said it's beautiful."

He glanced down to see she was studying the rings on her fingers. All three of them... the engagement ring, the wedding ring and the promise ring.

He pulled her closer. "Having second thoughts?"

Resting her head back against the seat, she gazed up at him. "Never. Never in a billion years."

He smiled. "A billion, huh? I like the sound of that." Cupping her chin in his hand, he gave her a gentle kiss. "I love you, baby."

"I love you, too."

For the remainder of the drive they were silent, content in each other's company.

Abby and Kevin

Kevin glanced down at the pile of baby equipment on the sofa. Scratching his head, he looked over at Abby. "Be honest with me, here. Do we really need all of this stuff?"

He nodded over at Madeline Rose, who was sound asleep in her carrier. "Look at how tiny she is... and look at this big pile. It just doesn't make sense."

Abby laughed. "I know. But you're the one who insisted we take her to this party. And there's all kinds of things that could happen.

She needs to eat. And what if she makes a mess in her diaper? So, we need a change of clothes." She sighed. "The list goes on and on…"

An anxious look appeared on her face. "I hope she'll be good."

He was shaking his head. "Since she seems to thrive on being held and I'm willing to bet there will be plenty of volunteers to do this, she'll be just fine."

At that exact moment, Madeline Rose let out a huge wail, her feet and hands moving wildly in unison. Picking her up, Abby immediately wrinkled up her nose. "Uh, oh… it looks like that diaper change needs to happen right now. Hopefully this will be it for her this evening." She sighed, sending a hopeful glance over at Kevin. "I still have to get dressed, too."

He chuckled. "Here, give her to me. I'll change her so you can finish getting ready. Take your time, sugar. This little peanut and I are in no hurry."

"Umm… it's probably about time for her bottle, too." With this reminder, she handed him the baby and made a hasty retreat to their bedroom before Kevin could even respond. Since Madeline Rose had come into their life, she had learned to take advantage of any break she could get.

She could hear Kevin talking to Madeline Rose as he began changing her diaper. It was when he started to sing to her, she began to move at a faster pace.

She couldn't wait to get back to the two people she loved most in the world.

Gracie and Jake

Gracie was sitting at the bathroom vanity, finishing up the final touches of her make-up. In the mirror, she could see Jake had come to lean against the doorframe, where he was watching her.

She sent him a smile. "I'm almost done. Did you get Bella all settled?"

Bella was spending the night with their next door neighbor,

Elaine. A widow and childless, she had become like a grandmother to Bella in the short time they had come to know each other.

Jake nodded before he slowly sauntered over to put his arms around her. Placing a slow kiss right below her ear, he smiled at the tremor racing through her at his touch. His voice came at her, low and husky. "Can I ask you something?"

She smiled at his reflection in the mirror, her hand going up to stroke his cheek. "Anything… you can ask me anything." She grinned. "Though I can't guarantee you'll like my answer…"

His mouth catching hers, the kiss he gave her was slow enough to send her heart beating even faster. Again his voice was low, even more dangerously seductive. "When are you going to marry me?"

Her mouth dropping open, she stared at him in the mirror. For a long moment, she didn't move, the tears pooling in her eyes making them seem so big, brighter than all the stars in the sky.

He smiled, his gaze searching. "Well?"

She swallowed, her voice coming out in a whisper. "You really want to marry me?"

He nodded. His fingers trailing over the same spot he'd kissed, his voice became even huskier. "I've wanted to marry you ever since you planted that kiss on my mouth when we were at the beach, watching the Fourth of July fireworks. I think I'd just turned twenty-one."

"I remember… I was sixteen and madly in love with you." A wistful smile on her face, she nodded. "I wanted you to notice me, to see how was sophisticated I was. So, I put on all this make-up. When I gave you that kiss, and it left a lipstick print on your face, I was thrilled, hoping it sent out the message you belonged to me."

He pulled her up out of the chair and framing her face in his hands, the intensity of his gaze was enough to have her clinging to him for support. He brushed his lips over hers. "I am yours. I've always been yours. And I always will be. But I want to do this right. I want to marry you."

He could feel she had started to shake as she continued to stare at him, trying to take it all in. A faint smile on his face, he shook his head. "I know I'm going about this all wrong. I have no ring to give you yet. Nor did I plan a fancy dinner or set up something special. Like fireworks… or my proposal written out in the sky. I only know I don't want to wait anymore. I want to get a real start on spending the rest of my life with you."

He pulled her closer. "So, Gracie Bridges… will you marry me?"

She threw her arms around him, capturing his mouth in a kiss like they had never shared before.

He finally lifted his head, his voice coming at her so deliciously deep. "Is that a yes?"

She nodded, her tears brimming over.

Letting out a long sigh of relief, he rested his forehead against hers. "You've made me the happiest man on earth, peaches. First thing tomorrow, we're going shopping for a ring. Any ring you want."

When she started to protest, he pressed his fingers to her lips. "No, we're going to do this right. After all you've been through, I want the best for you. No exceptions. Okay?"

Her hands going to her face, she began nodding like crazy, "*Oh my God*, this is really going to happen. We're going to get married. I love you. I do. So, *so* much."

And then he was kissing her again. She didn't realize what he was planning until he toppled her over on the bed. His hands roaming over her, his mouth covered hers in a deep, passionate kiss.

She tried to tell him. "The party… we're going to be late for Hannah and Sean's party."

He dipped his head, his mouth brushing over hers. "*Hmm*… so we are. Correct me if I'm wrong, but isn't it considered acceptable to arrive fashionably late to an event? Because this is exactly what we're going to do."

He was smiling.

"Right now, this time belongs to us."

Ellie and Michael

Michael was seated at one of the tables in Café Latte, watching Ellie go through the process of closing up for the night.

Now before you start wondering why he wasn't helping her, rest assured, he had offered his assistance. More than once, he had done this. But she had been so adamant she could do it herself, almost to the point of becoming angry, he had backed off.

Obviously, something was bothering her. He would be a fool not to know this. But in the past and even though his experience with women was somewhat limited, he knew she'd eventually break down and tell him what was going on.

Hopefully, it isn't because of something you did. Or maybe didn't do. Or said... or didn't say. Geeeez... you don't know.

He glanced down at his watch.

They should've left ten minutes ago for Hannah and Sean's party. Even with the roads in good condition, it would still take them about forty minutes to get there.

A loud crash had him nearly diving right out of his chair. Glancing around the room, he almost went into a panic when he saw no sign of Ellie. Then he heard her muttering from behind the counter.

He sprinted over to find her sitting on the floor, her eyes closed and pieces of broken coffee cups scattered around her.

"Honey, what happened?"

For some reason, this simple question had her bursting into tears. "I don't know..."

Now he was totally confused.

He helped her up off the floor and leading her over to one of the tables, he pulled out a chair. Once she was seated, he grabbed a couple of napkins from the counter and handed them to her.

He waited.

She finally looked up at him. She was a mess. There was mascara streaked down her cheeks and her nose was all red. But, honestly? He saw none of this. Instead he could only think how adorable she looked.

Man, she has really found a way into your heart, hasn't she?

This thought made him smile.

She sent him a suspicious look. Then, comprehension dawning on her face, she put her fingers to her cheeks. When she saw the mascara smeared on them, she began crying again. "*Oh noooo...* look at me... I'm such a mess. And now I'll never be your honey. Once I'm gone, you'll find someone else to call honey and forget all about me."

He pulled his chair closer to her, taking her hands in his. "Ellie, you could never be a mess. You always look beautiful. And, tell me, exactly where is it you're going, to have me forgetting all about you? Is there something you're not telling me? Have you signed up for some kind of meditation retreat? Or have plans to set off on a quest to save an endangered species somewhere across the world?"

A faint smile flickering across her face at his comment, she took a deep, gulping breath. "No, no... nothing like that. I got a letter today from Ohio State..."

She paused, bringing him to nod. "And?"

She took a deep breath. "I was accepted into their medical research internship. It starts in June and lasts for one year, two if I do well the first year."

A big smile on his face and his eyes never leaving hers, he nodded. "But this is wonderful news. I can imagine the program isn't easy to get into. I'm so proud of you."

She was shaking her head. "But this means I have to leave here and move to Columbus." She gazed up at him, her next words a whisper. "I want to stay here... be with you."

And now he couldn't stop smiling. Ever since their first date, he had wondered if she was beginning to like him as much as he liked her.

This was more than enough to let him know she did.

Why don't you just come out and admit it... you've already started to fall in love with her. Hell, you've already fallen...

He cleared his throat. "Honey... and you'll always be my honey, my baby, my sweetheart, my love, whichever you prefer... we'll find a way to make this work. Columbus is only two hours away and I can work from just about anywhere most of the time. Give me my computer and I'm all set."

This had her closing her eyes, her whole body slumping in one long sigh of relief.

Now, Michael hadn't kissed her yet. At least not the mind blowing, passionate kind of kiss he'd stayed awake at night, envisioning he'd give her. He'd kissed her on the cheek, but that was about it. From the very beginning, he had made the decision he was going to wait for that special moment to present itself.

Simply said, she had become what he wanted. So, he certainly wasn't going to take the chance of messing things up.

He was also pretty sure this 'special moment' had arrived.

He reached over to cup her chin in his hand. And before he could change his mind, he leaned in, capturing her mouth with his. He did this slowly, giving her every chance to pull away.

Instead, she encouraged the kiss, her hands sliding up his arms to pull him even closer.

But it was her soft sigh of surrender that did him in.

And just like that… he was all hers.

Hooked...

He had fallen into a whole new world. And he'd be the first to tell you, this was the best feeling ever.

As he buried his hands in her hair, drawing her even closer to deepen the kiss, a brief thought flashed through his mind.

They were definitely going to be late for Sean and Hannah's party.

But this was okay… more than okay.

Chris and Carrie

And where were Chris and Carrie?

Stranded in Denver.

This was because their three day stay for a national real estate conference had now been extended.

With no warning what-so-ever, a huge snowstorm had swept in, bringing the entire city to a halt. Including the airport.

Had they known what a special night this was going to be for Hannah and Sean, well… you can imagine how upset they would be.

Gazing out their hotel window at the blizzard-like conditions,

Carrie smiled up at Chris when he came to stand behind her, wrapping his arms around her.

His voice was a low rumble in her ear. "Our dinner should be here around eight."

She gazed up at him, a surprised look on her face. "Eight? Why such a long wait?" She sighed. "Not that it matters, I guess."

He turned her to face him, pressing a soft kiss to her mouth.

He knew how disappointed she was they weren't going to make it home in time for Sean and Hannah's party. But now? Why not take advantage of this time they had? To him, it felt like they had been running non-stop the past few months, working twenty-four-seven.

You need this.

You both need this.

He pulled her closer, his whisper brushing over her mouth. "I told them we wouldn't be available until then, there was something I needed to do."

Gazing up at him, a smile began to curve her lips. "And what might this be?" At the same time, she let him lead her over to the bed, gently pulling her down with him.

His hands framing her face, he claimed her mouth in a deep, passionate kiss before he gazed down at her. "This... kissing you, loving you. God, I've missed you, princess."

She sighed. "I've missed you, too."

It was after he gave her another kiss, he smiled. "I'm beginning to think we might need more time than I thought."

He was right.

They did.

But this was a good thing.

Lisa and Alex

Remember Lisa and Alex? And their daughter Chloe?

They had arrived back in Cleveland only a few days ago.

After tearing the cartilage in his right knee during the last game of the season and the surgery and rehabilitation that followed, they had decided to spend a few weeks in Florida, do the whole Disney experience.

After all, Chloe was now nine… even though she'd be quick to tell you she was really closer to ten… and involved in a lot of school activities and sports. This could be their last time to get away as a family before their schedules became even more hectic.

Alex had picked up Chloe from her gymnastic class and they had just walked into the house. He could hear Lisa talking on her phone, but he didn't think too much of this. No doubt it was either Sophie or Abby, calling about something to do with Sean and Hannah's party.

He shook his head, watching as Chloe went tearing down the hall. He smiled when he heard the shower go on. He had told her she had twenty minutes, max, to get ready. He figured this way, they might be lucky enough to be on the road in about a half hour or so.

Get real… you'll be lucky if it's an hour.

This also hinged on Lisa and if she had finally decided what she was going to wear. Earlier, he had watched her rummaging through her closet, wailing about her lack of wardrobe. His assurance she would look beautiful, no matter what she wore, didn't seem to help. These emotional outbursts had been happening a lot over the past few days, but he attributed this to his departure for spring training in a couple of weeks.

He strolled into the kitchen and grabbed a bottle of water out of the refrigerator. As he was opening it, he called out to Lisa.

"Hey, babe… we're back. Chloe said she only needs about fifteen minutes to take a shower and get ready. So, I hope you solved your wardrobe dilemma."

"Alex…"

He whirled around to see Lisa had come into the kitchen. She was holding her phone, a stunned look on her face.

Immediately setting the bottle on the counter, he went to her side. "Sweetheart, what's wrong?"

She gazed up into his face and this was when he saw the tears brimming. Taking her phone and tossing it on the table, he grabbed her hands.

They were trembling.

Her words came out all shaky. "Something… I can't… but…"

His heart dropped to his stomach.

What happened? Why was she so upset?

Gently taking her into his arms, he held her close. "I'm sort of confused… but whatever happened, I'm here for you. It's nothing we can't handle together, okay?"

This was when she started to giggle.

Now he was really concerned. Was she becoming hysterical? He leaned back to look at her, completely surprised at the brilliant smile on her face.

And this is when he knew… what they had been trying for, the miracle they had been hoping and praying for so long, had finally happened.

He could barely speak, his question a hoarse whisper "You're pregnant?"

She nodded.

And she kept on nodding, this sending her tears spilling over.

He buried his face in her hair, disbelief, elation and every other imaginable emotion hitting him all at once. But most of all, he was so damn relieved. Since Chloe had been a result of Lisa's first marriage, he'd feared he was the cause of her not being able to become pregnant. He knew how desperately she wanted another child.

So do you.

Her words were coming out so fast, he almost didn't catch all of them. "I took the pregnancy test this morning and it showed I was pregnant, but I wanted to make sure. When I dropped the urine sample off at the lab, they were backed up, so they told me they would call when they got the results. I didn't tell you this, because I didn't want to get your hopes up. And now they called to tell me, yes… I'm definitely pregnant."

He grinned. It was a huge grin. "We did it… we made a baby." He picked her up and after spinning her around with him, he gave her what could possibly be the longest kiss on record.

At least for them, it was.

For a few long moments, they remained in each other's arms. Then he abruptly pulled back, a worried look on his face. "Maybe we shouldn't go to this party tonight, instead stay home, take it easy."

She reached up to straighten his collar, her expression becoming serious. "*Oh Alex...*you can't start worrying like this, Because I'm going to be fine. I may become impossible to live with at times, but I'm counting on you to be the strong one here."

He pressed a kiss to her forehead. "You can be as impossible as you'd like. And as far as not worrying?" He shook his head. "There's no way I'll be able to stop that from happening. I'll try, but..."

"Hey, I did it. In less than twenty minutes, too."

At the sound of Chloe's voice, they turned to see she was standing behind them. She rolled her eyes. "Oh boy, I hope you two are ready to go."

She grinned. "I can't wait to see Hudson and Trevor. I bet they're talking like crazy now. And Madeline Rose. I hope Abby lets me hold her. " She glanced down at her hand. "*Ooops...* I forgot my bracelet. Be right back."

They watched her go flying out of the kitchen before they looked at each other, both speaking at the same time.

"Let's not tell anyone yet..."

"When are we going to..."

Laughing, Lisa put her finger to his lips. "I want to keep this to ourselves for a while. Please? This means we'll have to wait to tell Chloe, too. You know she would never be able to keep this to herself."

Wow... he didn't know if he would be able to keep it to himself either.

But, hell... he'd do whatever she wanted.

Seriously, you mean anything.

She smiled up at him. "I love you."

His kiss was said it all and more. "I love you, too."

A baby...

He was over the moon.

CHAPTER 34

$\mathcal{H}$is hand on the door to the kitchen, Sean gave one long, last look at the main room of the house now belonging to him and Hannah.

Even though it wasn't official yet.

The rustic décor of the room had now taken on a whole new look. Candles flickered everywhere, along side of the huge vases of white carnations, red roses and evergreen. A magnificent spread of hors d'oeuvres were laid out on a long table, so conveniently located next to the well-stocked bar. A huge fire roared in the fireplace.

The room was filled with most of Sean and Hannah's family and friends. The sound of laughter and shared conversations, along with the clink of glassware as the bartenders worked non-stop to fill drink requests, was a sign everyone was having a good time.

Satisfied everything appeared to be running smoothly, Sean slipped out of the room.

He had someplace he needed to be.

Sophie had wandered over to where Sean's brother Ryan was telling a story to the crowd gathered around him.

She gazed slowly around the room. If she hadn't known this was a welcome-to-our new-home party, she'd swear the set-up was suited for a more elaborate or special event.

Like a wedding, maybe?

Nah... that's a crazy thought.

Since her arrival, she had been searching for Hannah. But she hadn't been able to find her. In fact, no one seemed to know where Hannah was.

She also hadn't seen any sign of Sean, her Aunt Louise, her Uncle Paul, or her brother Brian.

"Sophie…" Her aunt had come up behind her. Taking hold of her arm, she whispered loudly in her ear. "You need to come with me."

An air of excitement about her, she gaily made her excuses to everyone as she pushed her way through the crowded room, dragging Sophie along with her.

She opened the door to what was a study or library and once they were inside, she quickly shoved the door shut behind them.

Hannah was standing by the window. Wearing a long, white lacy dress, stunningly beautiful in its simplicity, she turned to smile at Hannah. "So, are you ready to be my maid-of-honor?"

For a long moment, Sophie stood where she was, her mouth open and her eyes wide with disbelief. Then with a small cry, she went flying across the room to wrap Hannah in a big hug.

She was crying and laughing all at once. "Oh my gosh, are you serious? This is your wedding? You and Sean? Right now? Tonight?"

She abruptly stepped back, frowning. "Why didn't you tell me?" Then clasping her hands together, she laughed. "It doesn't matter. This is so exciting. Now I see why you were so insistent we bring the boys."

Hannah was laughing. "Yes, this is our wedding day. You are the one who convinced me this is the best way to get married. Our family and friends are all we need to celebrate our love. And of course, my two favorite nephews, Hudson and Trevor."

She reached out to hug Sophie again. "And don't feel bad. The only people we told were Aunt Louise, because of the dress… Uncle Paul, because Sean wanted to get his blessing… and Sean's brother, Ryan, because Sean wanted Ryan to be his best man."

She waved her hand around the room. "How could we pass up a beautiful setting like this?"

She grinned. "Even though, this isn't where the ceremony is going to take place. We're going to exchange our vows in the barn. Then we'll bring the party back here."

Sophie's hands went to her mouth. "The barn?"

"The barn is very special to us." Hannah laughed. "I don't think Sean is ever going to let me forget this is where I asked him to marry me. Even though I was only giving him my answer to his first proposal."

She shook her head, smiling. "I should've known better, and said yes the first time."

Aunt Louise came bustling over to them, holding a light-blue and lacy dress on a hanger. It was a short version of the dress Hannah was wearing. All business-like as usual, she handed it to Sophie. "Let's get you into this. We don't have much time. Sean and his brother are already out in the barn and your Uncle Paul and Brian are starting to usher all the guests there as well."

She shook her head, a worried look on her face. "I don't even want to think about what kind of story Paul is using to get them out there."

With Sophie chattering a mile a minute while she changed into the dress, Hannah didn't have the chance to check her phone until they were about to leave for the barn. There was a text from Sean.

It was only three words.

I love you.

An onslaught of emotions had her closing her eyes. She had to be living in a dream, right? She could see him so clearly in her mind, his mouth quirked up in a smile as he wrote this.

She quickly typed her reply.

I will always love you.
You're my forever cowboy, you're my life.

Sophie came to stand next to her, reaching for her hands. "In case I don't get the chance to say this later, because I know with all these people, it's probably going to get crazy, I want you to know I wish you and Sean the best. I love you both to pieces."

Hannah nodded as she struggled to hold back the tears, but with her emotional state so unpredictable since the accident, she knew there wasn't much she could do to stop them.

Brian joined them, holding out his arm to Hannah. As her twin, he was quick to sense her emotional state. He searched her face, his voice coming out more than a little shaky. "I'm going to ask you the same thing I asked Sophie before I walked her down the aisle. Are you sure this is what you want? It seems to have happened so fast."

He began to chuckle, shaking his head. "I don't know what's with these baseball guys. They certainly don't waste any time when they find what they want."

Hannah pressed a kiss to his cheek. "Do you want me to find out if any of them have sisters who are available?"

A look of mock horror on his face, he laughed. "*Whoa...* no way. I'm not ready for marriage yet. Don't know when I will be either."

Hannah nodded... slowly. "Ah... we'll see. I'll have to remember you said that."

"You do that. But for right now?"

He chuckled.

"It's time to get you married."

CHAPTER 35

Nobody wanted the night to end. That Sean and Hannah had been able to pull off this surprise wedding, without anyone suspecting a thing, was the talk of the evening.

Everything had worked out as they'd planned. The ceremony was both beautiful and moving. The reception that followed, the relaxed and fun party Hannah had hoped it would be.

It had all begun with the luminaries lighting the walkway from the house to the barn, where white and red rose petals were scattered across the floor. A garland of white roses and glowing lanterns lined each side of an aisle leading up to a rustic ivy and rose covered altar.

Hannah cried the whole time she was walking down the aisle. This wasn't what she wanted, but as had been the case over the past few weeks, she couldn't stop for the life of her. This had everyone crying right along with her.

It was only when she reached Sean and he leaned down to whisper something in her ear, the tears stopped. Then she laughed, a brilliant smile appearing on her face. Where it didn't leave her face for the rest of the ceremony.

And what did he say to her? They both refused to divulge this information, no matter how many times they were asked.

So, I guess we'll never know… maybe it had something to do with a red dress? *Hmm…*

When they were finally pronounced husband and wife, Sean had responded by lifting Hannah completely off the ground, spinning them around until they were both dizzy.

He followed this by removing his hat and holding it up to hide the kiss he gave her. It was a kiss leaving no doubt as to how much in love with her he really was.

When both Hudson and Trevor somehow escaped the hold of both their babysitter and Chester and ran up to join Hannah and Sean after their kiss, this only added to the celebration.

Sophie had a sneaking suspicion Chester had encouraged this, something he denied. But even he knew it wasn't really enough to sound convincing.

The food was fantastic, the band spectacular. Sugar, the other horses and the puppies were also a big hit with the guests. The two cats even made an appearance, but were quick to scamper off when Hudson and Trevor came at them, screaming with excitement.

And now, even after the popular country western band Sean hired had packed up and said their goodbyes, a few guests were still milling about, reluctant to leave.

Sean was looking for Hannah.

Wandering into the kitchen, where the caterers were doing a final cleaning, he gave them a thumbs up. "You guys did a fantastic job. Everyone was raving about the food."

He was surprised to see Hannah's brother Brian come from the walk-in pantry. He was with the woman who owned the catering company.

Julie was her name.

In the midst of laughing at something she said, Brian glanced over to see Sean. An almost embarrassed look coming over his face, he came to a halt.

At Sean's raised eyebrow, he cleared his throat. "Hey… I'm trying to be the nice guy here, lending a hand with the packing up." He smiled down at Julie. "Julie and I went to high school together, but lost touch. So, we've been trying to catch up."

Sean nodded, a knowing glance on his face when he saw the beginning of a blush on Julie's face. "Small world, huh?" He smiled at her. "I was telling everyone here what a great job you did. A lot of people were asking about you. I hope you've been handing out your business cards."

Julie grinned. "We had quite a few promising requests. I can't thank you enough. Abby and I also talked about the possibility of collaborating on jobs in the future, which is very exciting."

She laughed. "She told me this was the first time she made a wedding cake that looked like a barn. With horses, of all things. The brownie and caramel cake, was also something new for her and a big hit with all of the guests."

She shook her head. "She couldn't believe she never once caught on to what you and Hannah were planning."

Sean grinned. "I assure you, I had a much harder time than Hannah, keeping everything a secret. I almost slipped up a couple of times."

He glanced around the room again. "Speaking of Hannah… have you seen her?"

After getting a negative response , he laughed, heading for the door. "*Geeesh…* I just married the woman and already I've lost her. If you do see her, tell her I'm looking for her."

He was about to check the library, when he heard his name called. It was Sophie. He waited as she hurried over to him. "Sean, we're all leaving. Since the babysitter took off a while ago with the kids, my aunt and uncle are driving me and Chester home, along with Sam and Livy. But I didn't want to leave without telling you how wonderful everything was."

She gave him a big hug. "I'm so happy for you and Hannah."

He gave her a big grin, returning her hug. "Thanks. I couldn't ask for a better sister-in-law. Or as I now like to think of you, my partner in crime. Speaking of Hannah, do you happen to know where she might be? I can't seem to find her anywhere."

"The last time I saw her, she told me she was going out to the barn."

Sean gave a slow nod. "*Ah*... thanks."

After he walked her to the door to say his good byes to everyone, he took off in a sprint, stopping briefly to let Brian know where he was going.

Brian winked. "Gotcha. I"ll make sure you're not disturbed."

Sean was smiling when he finally entered the barn. There he found Hannah in the midst of a conversation with Sugar.

She glanced over at him. Her hand dropping from Sugar's nose, she smiled. "We're getting along pretty good now."

A feeling like non-other came over him. The vision of her standing in the soft lighting of the barn, so beautiful in her wedding dress, he'd swear his heart was about to burst. He wanted to take her into his arms and hold her forever. That she was now his wife was over-whelming to him, yet at the same time, the most wonderful feeling in the world.

Slowly making his way over to her, he wrapped one of her curls slowly around his finger, his voice coming out low and devastatingly husky. "I can see that. But right now, I'm looking for my wife. Have you seen her?"

Automatically going into his arms, she rested her head against his shoulder, closing her eyes. "She's right here, right where she wants to be." She gazed up at him, searching his face. "Are you happy? The evening was perfect, wasn't it?"

He was smiling as he began pressing a trail of feathery kisses across her face. "I've never been happier. And yes, the evening was wonderful. But now, here with you, I have all I need." Stepping back, he reached for her hand. "Come..."

He took her to the back of the barn, to where there was a makeshift bed, similar to how he had arranged the blankets over the straw bales the night of the snow storm. But this bedding was fit for royalty, the white embroidered comforter and pillows made from the most luxurious of fabrics.

He took her in his arms, gazing down at her. "Hannah Young, will you stay here with me tonight? Where we can celebrate our first night as husband and wife? It will be the perfect beginning of the rest of our life together."

Wrapping her arms around his neck, she nodded, her eyes shining into his.

"As long as you promise me it will be forever. I love you."

His mouth hovered over hers. "Forever, Darlin'… you have my promise. I love you, too."

Closing her eyes, she became lost in his kiss.

CHAPTER 36

Sean woke before dawn. Slowly gazing around at his surroundings, he soaked up the early morning stillness, the simple familiarity of barn life that was always so peaceful, so calming to him.

His heart was full… this barn, this house, this land… he had finally found a place to call home.

This was all due to the woman curled up beside him, her arm flung across his chest.

Hannah… the woman of his dreams.

Pressing a kiss in her hair, he smiled when she gave a soft little sigh, moving even closer.

Carefully slipping out from under the blankets, he got dressed and pulled on his boots. When Hannah began to stir, he leaned down to give her a kiss. "Go back to your dreams, darlin'… I'll be right back."

Once he was satisfied she'd fallen back to sleep, he left.

A short time later, he returned to settle next to her. Smoothing the hair back from her face and pressing his mouth to hers, his tongue traced her lips until she began to respond, falling into his kiss.

She opened her eyes at his husky whisper. "Hey, Mrs. Young… come on. I want you to get up. I have a surprise for you."

After the faintest of smiles, her lashes fluttered shut.

So, he kissed her again.

Much longer this time.

This had her responding with a passion that had him groaning out loud. "Hannah… *come on*… Don't tempt me Darlin'. I need you to get dressed because there's something I want to show you. Here, I brought you a pair of your jeans and a sweater."

She threw back the covers, and after she gave a big yawn, she leisurely began pulling on the jeans. Barely awake, she was blind to the fact he was watching, captivated by how she managed to make even the most ordinary routine of getting dressed seem so damn sexy.

It was only after another yawn escaped her, she glanced over at him, the burning intensity in his gaze making her aware of what she was doing.

And what he was thinking.

Now suddenly more awake, she was blushing as she fumbled with the sweater, struggling to pull it over her head.

He chuckled, reaching over to help her before he gave her a kiss. "Please don't ever feel the need to hide from me, because I'll never tire of seeing you like this… never. You're beautiful."

He handed her a pair of boots.

Cowboy boots.

Brand new cowboy boots.

She gazed up at him, a big grin on her face. "For me?"

He grinned right back. "Yep, if you're going to be living here, you need the real thing. These were the best I could find until we can get you a custom-made pair. Now hurry up and put them on. Before I throw you back down in this bed and take advantage of you."

When a blush began to fill her cheeks again, he chuckled. "Darlin', you have no idea, do you? Watching you get dressed and the memory of sharing this bed with you is about driving me crazy. But like I said, there's something we need to do."

He kissed her once more before he reluctantly came to his feet, pulling her up with him. The whole time, he told himself to be strong. Loving her would have to wait.

He had a promise to keep.

He grabbed hold of her hand and snatching up one of the extra blankets, he began pulling her with him though the barn.

The whole time she was mumbling about how she certainly hoped he wasn't thinking of taking her outside. She couldn't even begin to imagine how cold it was out there.

Why were they even up at such an early hour? Wasn't it still dark outside?

And wasn't this supposed to be their honeymoon? So they should be allowed to sleep in, right?

All day if they wanted.

At least this is what she'd thought.

He kept shaking his head, refusing to comment. It was only when they reached the door and after he pressed a kiss to her mouth to silence her, he finally spoke.

"Ready?"

She nodded.

After giving her a smile that had her heart giving a little leap, he slowly slid open the door.

A horse was waiting outside, all saddled and ready to go.

It was Sugar.

Almost as though she was letting them know it was about time they showed up, she gave a soft neigh, jerking her head in their direction. This sent the bells, attached to her harness, jingling in the frigid morning air.

Her hands going to her face... you guessed it... Hannah began to cry. "*Oh my God,* Sean... you... " Turning, she threw her arms around him. "I love you. I love you so much. You're definitely my favorite cowboy."

He grinned down at her. "I love you, too. And it's good to hear I'm your favorite. Because like I've already told you, you'll always be my woman and I aim to keep you happy."

He nodded towards Sugar, who had reached over to butt her head against Sean's shoulder. "Look how excited she is to help out with this, she can't wait. So, let's get you up and in the saddle so I can take you for that ride you've been dreaming of for so long."

Hannah leaned back against Sean with a long, contented sigh.

Yes, she was a long way up from the ground. And on a horse, of all things. A breathing, living and moving horse. But with Sean's arms around her, and the blanket shielding them from the cold, she wasn't worried.

It had snowed again during the night, the fresh coating of white bringing a sacred stillness over the land. As Sean guided the horse over the snow-covered trail, the bells jingling on Sugar's harness and the soft clip clop of her slow trot rang out in perfect harmony.

It was magical place and time... and now? It was all theirs.

Exactly like Hannah had envisioned?

No, it was better.

So much better.

She gazed up at Sean to have him aim that smiley-crinkly-eyed grin of his right at her. His voice, so deep, so wonderfully familiar, flowed through her like a caress.

"Happy?"

She reached up to stroke his cheek. "With you? Yes, always. This is amazing. I'll always remember this…"

He held her more securely against him as he guided Sugar over a rough patch in the trail. "Good, I think we should make this a tradition for every anniversary. Spend the night in the barn, have a romantic dinner and then go for a ride… just like this."

She smiled up at him. "I'd like that. I hope this will be for the next hundred years. Or even more."

He chuckled. "Sounds good to me. Though at that point, we may need help getting up on the horse."

She laughed. "I can't do that now, at least not without your help."

"You'll learn, darlin'. I'm not worried. And even if you don't, I'll still keep you." He pressed another kiss in her hair.

She sighed. "I love you. So much."

"And I love you, too. So much."

Sean adjusted his hold on Hannah before winding the reins around his hand. "So, does this mean you're ready to give Sugar the okay to take off in a gallop? I can feel how eager she is, waiting for this command."

Take off in a gallop? With Sean holding you in his arms, yes, you're ready for anything.

She grinned. "Yes… yes I am."

He positioned his hat more securely on his head. "Okay, whenever you're ready, go for it."

She leaned forward, and giving Sugar a hesitant pat, her voice was timid, falling nowhere near a command.

"Giddy up?"

Sean chuckled. "You'll need to be a lot more forceful than that. A horse needs to know who's the boss. Otherwise, they'll stop listening to anything you tell them. Press your knees into her when you give the order."

A determined expression on her face, Hannah pressed her knees into Sugar as Sean suggested, giving her an even harder pat. And this time, she almost, but not quite, yelled out the order.

"Giddy up…"

With a little unbeknownst help from Sean, they set off in a gallop down the trail. Just as the sun began to rise, turning their world into a glittering winter wonderland.

You might say it was the perfect beginning of their own extraordinary fairy tale.

I'm sure you may have already figured out the featured recipe for this book could either be for Café Latte's Banana Nut Muffins or Abby's Salted Caramel Brownies.

Hannah didn't feel she was quite ready to tackle Abby's recipe for her salted caramel brownies. And since Sean now claimed he'd grown to love banana muffins as much as she did, she decided to work on her own version of the muffin recipe from Café Latte.

After quite a bit of experimenting and a lot of trial and error, she was finally satisfied with the results. The muffins turned out so well, she had to hide the last batch from Sean after he ate three in one sitting. His claim was they made him happy.

Hannah's Banana Nut Muffins:

Muffin Ingredients:
   2 cups all-purpose flour
   1-1/2 teaspoons baking soda
   1/2 teaspoon salt
   4 ripe bananas
   1 cup brown sugar, packed
   3/4 cup unsalted butter, melted and cooled
   1 egg
   1 teaspoon pure vanilla extract
   1/2 cup pecans, toasted and chopped

Topping Ingredients:
   1/3 cup brown sugar, packed
   2 tablespoons flour
   2 tablespoons butter, cut in small
   pieces
   2 tablespoons oats
   1/3 cup chopped pecans

Instructions:

Preheat oven to 375°F. Coat 12 standard muffin cups with butter.
Evenly sprinkle each cup with about 1 teaspoon brown sugar.

For the Muffins:

In a large bowl, combine the 2 cups flour,
baking soda and salt; set aside.
Chop 1 of the bananas into small chunks; set aside.
With the mixer on high, whisk together the
remaining 3 ripe bananas and 1 cup brown
sugar for 3 to 4 minutes.
Add in the melted butter, eggs, and vanilla;
beat well, scraping down the sides of the
bowl if necessary.
Mix in the combined dry ingredients just
until incorporated.
Fold in the 1/2 cup toasted pecans and the
reserved banana chunks. Divide batter
evenly into muffin tins.

For the Topping;

In a small bowl, combine the 1/3 cup brown
sugar, 2 tablespoons each of the flour and
butter pieces; mix with a fork until crumbly.
Stir in oats and 1/3 cup pecans. Sprinkle
evenly over muffins.
Bake until a toothpick in the center of the
muffins comes out clean, about 18-20 minutes.
Let cool for a few minutes before removing
muffins from tin. Serve warm or at room
temperature.

Yield: 12 muffins

ABOUT THE AUTHOR

L. B. Joyce lives in Chagrin Falls, Ohio. A freelance artist by day, with designing Christmas ornaments her specialty, she's also a writer by night. She loves getting lost in a good book, has redecorated almost every room in her house more times than she'd like to admit, loves baking up a storm in her kitchen, hates housework with a passion and will drive just about anywhere because of her fear of flying.

To keep up with news of the first eight books of the Twelve Months, Twelve Love Stories series - *A Million Decembers, For the Love of July, February's Angel, Promise Me November, An Unexpected June, A January to Remember, September's Moonlight Serenade and Goodbye Heartbreak, Hello May* - along with the first book of the new Holidays in White Oaks Valley series, *A Grand Slam Kind of Christmas, make sure you check out the* website/blog at: lbjoyceauthor.com

Or visit on facebook: https://www.facebook.com/AuthorLBJoyce

She would love to hear from you: lbjoyce12@gmail.com

And if you have a minute, check out the latest L. B. Bear Christmas Ornament designs and just about everything you ever wanted to know about Christmas at: www.facebook.com/LBGlitterGirl

Credit due:

Cinderella - So This is Love

Lyrics and Music by Mack David, Al Hoffman and Jerry Livingston

Cover by Soxsational Cover Art